G. Allen Wilbanks

ASSASSIN'S SPELL

BOOKS BY G. ALLEN WILBANKS

DEAD TOWN SERIES

Dead Town

Assassin's Spell

Coven Wars

ON DANGEROUS GROUNDS SERIES

Testing Grounds

Proving Grounds

Hunting Grounds

NOVELS

A Life of Adventure

When Darkness Comes

Deadly Seven

SHORT STORY COLLECTIONS

Thirteen Rooms

Not for Bedtime Stories

Deep Dark Thoughts Publications LLC

Assassin's Spell

Copyright © 2025 by G. Allen Wilbanks

Visit my website at www.gallenwilbanks.com

Paperback: ISBN 978-1-952630-14-9

E-book: ISBN 978-1-952630-15-6

Cover design: MoorBooks Design

G. Allen Wilbanks

ASSASSIN'S SPELL

DEAD TOWN

Book II

Deep Dark Thoughts Publications LLC

For Jen, Allison, and Samantha

PROLOGUE

Lieutenant Tim Delaney sat behind his desk shuffling through the latest pile of citizen patrol requests, complaints, and demands for disciplinary investigations. The stack in front of him this morning appeared higher than ever despite his herculean efforts yesterday to clean out his cluttered inbox. It seemed like no matter how many of these things he processed each day, a never-ending supply of angry letters was waiting for him when he arrived at work. If there was one thing the citizens in this county never seemed to run out of, it was reasons to complain about his deputies and plenty of free time to sit down and put it on paper.

He sighed as he dragged another envelope out of the pile.

Picking up the silver letter opener that had been a joke gift from his wife when he promoted to lieutenant, he sliced through the top of the envelope and removed the next tri-folded sheet of paper from its confines.

Unconsciously, Tim ran the tip of his tongue along the edge of his mustache where it bristled over his upper lip. The affectation was an old habit that went all the way back to his teens when he first grew the thing in an effort to look old enough to buy booze without getting carded. It had never worked, but he liked the look of the wispy growth enough to keep it anyway. Thirty-some years later, it remained with him. Tim realized he would need to trim the mustache soon, before the thick brush of gray hair fell out of uniform policy.

Grunting with mounting frustration, he read paragraph after paragraph from a woman who could not sleep at night because fire trucks drove past her house at all hours with their sirens and horns blaring at full volume.

"I have no fucking control over the fire department," he muttered, scratching down a few notes to address the assorted points laid out in the woman's complaint. "Might as well ask me to stick a magic feather in your dog's ass and make it fly."

Tim slapped his pen onto the green paper blotter covering his desk. He almost pushed the entire stack of correspondence aside to move on to something more interesting, but one glance at the financial documents waiting for him in a neat little bundle on the corner of his desk changed his mind.

He dreaded having to explain to the division captain why South Station was once again going to go over their quarterly budget. It was not even his fault. Ever since they opened the damned building last year it had been running over budget due to the nonstop laundry list of uniforms, equipment, and new vehicles necessary for the deputies assigned here. All of those items should have been factored into the original costs of opening the station, but somehow nobody seemed to notice their omission. Now, it was suddenly his problem they did not have enough cars for the patrol deputies on the street?

To make matters worse, the captain acted like every penny spent in this entire division was stolen out of his personal bank account.

Maybe reading another letter from a concerned citizen about making the sirens on the emergency vehicles quieter at night wasn't so bad after all. He grunted again, lifting his black-framed reading glasses with one hand so he could massage the bridge of his nose with the other.

Lieutenant Delaney jotted down his final response on the back of the letter expressing how much he appreciated the suggestion, but due to traffic safety requirements and for the protection of the officers trying to do their jobs… blah, blah, blah. When he finished, he tossed the paper into the "completed" stack to be passed along to his secretary. She would type his hastily scribbled lines into something slightly more professional to be mailed out later.

The scanner on his desk growled and clicked to life as one of the deputies on his team was dispatched to a report of a stolen vehicle. The deputy acknowledged the call and announced he was enroute to meet the victim. Tim listened to the radio almost enviously, recalling his own days driving a prowl car, taking crime reports, and chasing down the bad guys. It was much more exciting and glamorous than the desk-warming, paper pushing assignments he had received since promoting to lieutenant.

He glanced at the letter opener where he had set it down beside the unconquered pile of correspondence. That little gag gift had proven far too prophetic for his liking.

The scanner hissed and crackled again, this time announcing a possible domestic violence incident reported by a neighbor who heard yelling coming from the home next door. Another deputy's voice responded, advising he and his beat partner would contact the neighbor for more information.

"Enough," announced the lieutenant to the empty office. "I need a break."

Tim removed his reading glasses and tossed them into the wire basket that served as his currently mostly empty outbox. There remained a lot of work for him to do today, but what was the point of being the boss if you couldn't say fuck it and walk away from your responsibilities for a few minutes?

He stood up, arching his back until several vertebrae cracked and popped, then he collected his leather equipment belt from a hook on the back of his office door. He fastened the belt around his waist and did a quick manual check of his pistol to make sure the Beretta 92F he carried was loaded and the safety was on. Tim hated the thing. He did not trust that the semiautomatic weapon wouldn't jam at a crucial moment in the field. What was wrong with his original Smith and Wesson revolver? That old wheel gun was always reliable, and the forty-five caliber rounds had plenty of knockdown power. The Sheriff had not given him a choice, however, insisting that all command staff serve as role models during the conversion to the newer weapons. He was stuck with the silly 9mm pea shooter. All he could do was accept that fact and try to make the best of it.

A quick pat check assured him he also had spare magazines, handcuffs, and a portable radio holstered and ready.

Before exiting the office, Tim ran a hand through the unruly curls of gray and black hair on his head then grabbed his campaign hat from a second hook on his office door. On the way out, he made a point of walking past his secretary's desk. The young brunette was busily tapping a staccato tune on the keys of an electric typewriter, but she paused as Tim approached.

"I need some fresh air, Meagan. I'm gonna run out to the stop-and-rob and grab something to eat. Would you like anything?"

"No, thank you," Meagan said, flashing him a smile. She reached beneath her desk and raised a brown paper bag packed full of items she had brought from home. "I'm good."

The stop-and-rob, as he liked to refer to the nearest gas station convenience store, was the closest business to the new

South Station building that offered anything resembling food. Why the Sheriff had decided to build a new substation in the middle of nowhere, Tim would never understand. The deputies working the street could grab meals anywhere, but the poor slobs like him that were stuck in the building had to rely on vending machines or, like Meagan, cold sandwiches in a sack.

"I won't be gone long. If anyone asks for me, I'll be back in a few minutes. If the captain comes by, tell him I'll have the new budget numbers for him by the end of the week. He is really not going to like them."

Tim's secretary wrinkled her nose as if assaulted by an unpleasant odor. "Do I have to tell him that last part?" she asked.

"No. I'm sure he already knows."

Tim settled the campaign hat on his head, tapped two fingers along the brim in a brief salute to Meagan, then headed out to the parking lot to find his assigned vehicle.

One advantage to being stuck in the middle of nowhere was there were not a lot of traffic lights or stop signs between the station and the surrounding locales. It took Tim only a few minutes to reach his destination. He pulled the black, Ford Crown Victoria into a marked parking spot in front of the only gas station within two miles of South Station. The big sedan did not have a light bar on top or bear any markings or stickers that would announce it as property of the local Sheriff's Office, regardless, Tim did not fool himself into believing nobody could tell it was a law enforcement vehicle. The color and shape of it alone absolutely screamed "cop" to anyone with an ounce of common sense. It had a spotlight mounted on the driver's side door, for God's sake. For that reason alone, he never drove it without wearing his uniform and carrying a gun.

He climbed from the car, resettling the campaign hat on his head as he closed the door behind him. He had removed it for the short drive because it kept rubbing against the roof of the car and threatening to fall off. As much as he hated the ungainly thing, department policy dictated that anytime a Sheriff's Office employee was in public wearing the uniform, they must also wear the hat. Rules were rules.

So, he wore the hat.

He strolled into the convenience store and nodded at the sleepy-looking clerk standing behind the register. The teenager nodded back suspiciously, clearly not a fan of law enforcement. Tim veered right and strode through an aisle bracketed by a pair of stocked, five foot tall shelves, directly to the back wall where he knew he would find an assortment of sodas. He felt only slightly more awake than the dozing kid at the front counter, and he wanted something with enough sugar and caffeine to jolt him back to alertness and get him through the next grueling couple of hours of the morning.

As he peered at the available selection of beverages, a chime echoed through the store, announcing another customer entering through the front doors. Tim continued to concentrate on his choices, unconcerned with the new arrival.

A harsh crunching noise startled him, the rough sound of metal working against metal. Tim's heart skipped in his chest, and he felt the rush of adrenaline filling his veins. Only one thing in the world made that kind of noise. Every cop that ever walked a beat knew the sound instantly. Someone had racked a round into the chamber of a shotgun.

"Empty the safe. Do it now!"

The voice was urgent, low, and slightly muffled. Tim ducked to bring his head below the level of the store shelving, hoping he had not already been seen. He drew his service pistol. Thumbing the safety off, he worked his way forward toward the front doors, trying to get a better view of the situation.

"What safe?" asked the frightened clerk. "Take everything in the register. It's yours."

"Don't fuck with me," warned the muffled voice. "And don't treat me like an idiot. The safe is right behind you in the hidden cabinet."

Tim risked peeking out between the aisles to get a better look at the suspect. As the front desk came into sight, he realized there was more than one person involved in this robbery. The man doing the talking was at the counter, holding a large-caliber, silver revolver pointed at the now not so sleepy clerk. The man had a dark blue, knitted cap pulled over his head, concealing his face.

A second suspect, wearing a green ski mask that covered everything but his eyes, was glancing out the front doors nervously, keeping lookout for any potential witnesses that might wander in. It was the lookout that held the shotgun Tim had heard.

The shotgun was the more dangerous of the two weapons, so Tim's attention stayed mainly on the lookout. He needed a moment when the clerk was safely out of harm's way before confronting the two, armed men, but that was going to be difficult given the first robber's lethal focus on the teenager.

Tim debated remaining hidden and letting the robbery proceed uninterrupted. He could let the cashier hand over any money the store had, then follow the suspects outside and confront them in the parking lot, perhaps even after they had climbed into their car where they would be confined and restricted in their movements. That seemed much safer than starting a shootout with civilians so close by and available as potential hostages … or victims.

With this plan in mind, he pulled back, crouching again behind the store's shelving units.

"Come on, man. Hurry up. I don't want to shoot you, but I'll do it if I have to."

The clerk held his hands out defensively. "No. Don't. I'll open the safe. We're cool."

With no imminent violence apparent, Tim settled in to wait for the robbery to conclude.

Then, disaster struck.

Tim's portable radio hissed to life as a deputy in District 6 announced she was initiating a traffic stop on a speeding pickup truck. Lieutenant Delaney's hand flashed to his radio, snapping the volume dial to off, but it was too late. The damage was done.

"What...? Who's there?" shouted the lookout, turning away from the door to scan the store for the source of the sudden noise.

Tim stood to his full height of six feet two inches, raising his weapon over the top of the shelving units and leveling it toward the lookout.

"Sheriff's Department. Don't move," he shouted at the suspects.

The lookout raised the shotgun in his hands and Tim fired his Berretta, three rapid rounds, one after the other. To his surprise and relief, the pistol did not jam or misfire. It cycled each new cartridge smoothly and effortlessly as it ejected the spent casings. The suspect screamed as one or more of the rounds struck him, and he jerked at the trigger of his own gun. A flash of light exploded from the barrel of the shotgun, and a roar deafened Tim. Canned goods exploded on the shelf around him as he ran to the end of the aisle trying to get a better angle on the lookout. Out of the corner of his eye, he saw the first suspect dive behind the front counter with the clerk. He could not worry about that threat yet, not until he was sure he had neutralized the shotgun.

The lookout was on the ground. The man was clutching at the thigh of his right leg, crying out in pain, but he still held the shotgun in one hand. Tim tried to order the second suspect to drop his weapon, but no sound came out when he spoke. He choked on something in the back of his throat. He swallowed, trying to clear the blockage.

Attempting again to speak, he gagged and coughed. Something was interfering with his airway.

Liquid filled Tim's mouth, and he spat to empty it. Bright red blood spattered the tiles of the floor at his feet. Something was badly wrong with him. His neck burned, and he could not properly draw a breath. Tim's heart raced even faster in his chest as motes of silver and black danced in the corners of his vision. He felt like he was drowning.

Tim touched his left hand to his neck and the fingers came away wet and red. One of the pellets from the shotgun had found its mark in the hollow of his throat. He was in trouble. Fumbling at his belt, Tim tried to turn his radio back on and call for help. His blood-slicked fingers slipped ineffectually on the knob. It didn't matter, he realized, at last giving up on the stubborn power switch. Even if he managed to turn the radio on, he could not speak.

Tim stumbled forward into the main space of the store; his pistol raised in front of him ready to confront the armed suspects. Surprisingly, the lookout tossed the shotgun away from himself and raised his hands in surrender. The first robber remained barricaded behind the register with the clerk. Tim attempted to approach the counter, but stumbled, falling to the ground in a sprawling heap. His rapidly numbing fingers lost their grip on his pistol, and the weapon skidded across the tiled floor.

Rolling to his back, Tim struggled to draw in air. It refused to come. As he inhaled against the resistance blocking his airway, he could feel the blood in his throat being pulled into his lungs. He tried to cough it free, but he was too weak to even accomplish that much.

Tim stared upward toward the ceiling of the store. The man in the dark blue ski mask appeared in his vision, eyes opened wide in fear as he inspected the damage his partner had caused.

"Is he okay?" asked the lookout from several feet away.

Tim found himself mildly surprised at the concern he heard in the shooter's voice. Perhaps he could still survive this catastrophe if one of them decided to call for help. Unfortunately, the first suspect shook his head with resigned finality.

"Shit. No, man. He's done. You killed him."

Tim wasn't dead yet, but he was lucid enough to realize the truth in that statement. Even if someone called for an ambulance now, it would arrive too late. He was not going to survive this injury.

The world grew dark around him as his brain shut down the rest of his body in an attempt to conserve the small reserves of oxygen it possessed.

"I'm hurt," said the lookout. "I can't walk. You have to help me. We need to get out of here."

The suspect standing over Tim moved away, presumably to help his partner, although Tim could not be sure. He did not have enough strength left to turn his head and look. A florescent light flickered directly above Tim, and he wondered if the light was really going out or if it was merely his brain losing its last connections to the outside world.

The front door chimed as the robbers fled the store, or perhaps someone new had come inside. Tim didn't know which. Nor did he care. He closed his eyes and slipped into oblivion.

Light and shadows swam in a sickening maelstrom around Tim as consciousness returned. Automatically, his hand reached for his throat, searching for the wound he had been so certain was going to kill him. He felt only smooth, intact skin under his fingers. When he removed the hand, he checked his fingertips closely. They were free of blood.

I'm alive? he wondered in amazement, running both hands over his neck this time, searching for any hint of the injury.

Where the hell am I? was his next conscious thought, as he realized with a start that he was no longer in the dingy gas station convenience store.

He stood in one corner of a brightly lit room. Multiple florescent lights in the ceiling illuminated the bare walls and mirror-polished laminate floor. There were no windows, and only one way out that Tim could see. The sole exit was a wide, silvery steel door with a push bar across the entire width to allow individuals to open the barrier without using their hands.

Three empty, wheeled gurneys lined the wall next to the door.

"I'm in a hospital," said Tim. He cleared his throat, surprised that he could talk without difficulty or pain. He felt fine, surprisingly good, in fact.

"They must have fixed me up," he mused.

His initial excitement at finding himself alive and no longer injured soon dampened as he became aware of other, more disturbing, elements in the room. One wall was covered by two stacked, linear rows of square, steel doors. Each door had a single handle and no hinges, suggesting they did not swing open, but rather would slide out like a massive filing cabinet drawer. In his time with the Sheriff's Office, Tim had visited a room like this on a few occasions. None of those prior occasions had been positive experiences, and this time did not seem likely to be any different.

11

He was in a morgue.

Tim had no recollection of coming to the hospital or entering this room. Had he been in a coma? Perhaps. He knew he had been badly injured. Maybe he had climbed out of his hospital bed while still unconscious and done some sleepwalking. He glanced down at himself, checking to see if he was wearing a hospital gown, but he saw the same green and gold uniform he had been wearing at the convenience store.

His right hand settled onto the butt of his gun. He felt the slick, wooden grip of a Smith and Wesson revolver under his palm and glanced at it, frowning with confusion. He should not be carrying a revolver. He had been wearing the Berretta earlier. He looked again, and this time he found the familiar, black plastic grip of the semiautomatic pistol in his holster.

"What the...?"

He jerked his hand away from the weapon as if he had touched a venomous snake. Was he losing his mind? And where was everyone? Shouldn't someone have noticed him walking through the hospital in his uniform and attempted to wake him up, or ... interrupt whatever it was that he had been doing? He needed to find somebody and figure out what was going on.

Tim jogged toward the door, reaching out to depress the push bar. His hand passed through the door without resistance and his momentum carried him the rest of the way out into the hallway on the other side. He froze as he realized what had happened.

"No, no, no. That's impossible," he told himself. "That can't happen. This isn't real. I'm dreaming, or I'm in a coma. Maybe I'm still lying on the floor bleeding to death."

Tim placed his hands on his face, covering his eyes. "I need to wake up. All I need to do is focus and I'll get out of this nightmare. One. Two..."

"…Three."

Tim opened his eyes and lowered his hands. The hospital morgue was gone. In its place was an auditorium filled with people. Tim stood on the stairs in an aisle that led through two sections of padded, folding bleacher seats and down to a main floor with a raised central stage. All around him, men, women, and children sat staring solemnly toward that stage. The spectators wore suits and dresses that would fit nicely in any formal affair, like a wedding, or a graduation ceremony, or a…

Tim glanced around the enormous space and realized many of the people in the surrounding seats appeared to be crying. He turned toward the stage and took a long moment to process what he saw there. A podium had been erected to one side, and a slender man in a "Class-A" Sheriff's Office uniform stood behind the lectern speaking into a microphone. Tim did not recognize him, nor could he hear what the man was saying. In fact, he realized that the entire auditorium was unnaturally silent.

Next to the speaker at the podium was a mahogany casket, polished to a high gloss and draped with an American flag. A wreath of white flowers had also been laid over the coffin. The casket was closed, which was good. Tim had no desire to see what, or more precisely who, lay within. He already had a pretty good idea what he might find if he peeked inside.

Behind the coffin, a projection screen had been erected, and on the screen was a four-foot-tall picture of Tim's face.

It was a terrible picture, he thought. It was the photo taken for his identification badge when he promoted to lieutenant. He had a cold that day, and his eyes and nose were red and puffy.

Couldn't they have at least found a decent photograph for the occasion?

Tim wandered down the steps until he reached the main floor. The podium, the speaker, and the casket all towered over him from atop the raised stage. His eyes wandered to the front row of seats and the people seated closest to the platform. He found his wife, Joyce, wiping at her eyes with a wad of wet tissues as she listened to the eulogy Tim still could not hear. Beside Joyce were his two daughters, also weeping quietly and dabbing handkerchiefs to their faces. Next to his oldest daughter, Alicia, was his soon-to-be son-in-law, Brian. The rest of the front row was filled with close friends and family.

Oddly, Tim's first emotion at seeing everyone seated along the edge of the stage was irritation. He wondered why no one had bothered to save him a seat. After all, his picture on the stage suggested this entire event was for his benefit.

He pushed the thought aside, realizing how silly it was. He had his own place to sit already. Well, not really sit. He was lying down to be more precise. It was only at this moment that Tim truly began to accept the truth of his situation. He was not still on the floor of the convenience store. He was not dreaming, and he was not in a coma.

He was dead.

Tim turned to face the stage again. He sighed at the unflattering picture on the projection screen. Who picked that godawful image? It was probably his captain, getting back at him for not finishing the financial reports on his desk. That guy could really be a spiteful prick at times.

Tim's attention turned to the far end of the platform. Six deputies in full dress uniforms, including gold aiguilettes on the shoulders and white gloves, ascended the stairs to enter the stage.

They positioned themselves in a row behind the casket. Two of the deputies stepped out of line and approached the coffin.

Standing on the floor and staring up toward the stage with an uncomfortable sense of disorientation, Tim watched the deputies remove the flag from his coffin, fold it with precise, careful motions, then present it to his family. He felt ashamed as he observed the ritual, as though he were a voyeur who had no business being here.

And perhaps he didn't. This was something private that did not concern him. Yes, he was the entire reason this event was happening, the guest of honor you might say, but damn it, he was not supposed to be here. He should be … somewhere else. But where?

Elsewhere, Tim supposed. Wherever that was.

When the deputies returned to the stage, the six men in full dress positioned themselves in two rows of three, each row along one side of the casket. The uniformed pallbearers grasped gold-colored handles along the edge of the mahogany box and lifted it from its stand. They solemnly marched Tim's remains off the stage and out of the auditorium.

His family exited after the pallbearers, followed by everyone seated in the first row of chairs. When they were gone, the remainder of the crowd was left to wander out at their own pace. The casket and Tim's family would go to Dasan's Terrace Cemetery next. Tim already knew that. He had been the one to request his remains go there. At the cemetery, he would be interred in a plot beside his grandparents and his father. There was also additional room reserved at the site for Tim's mother and his wife at some hopefully far off date.

Tim decided not to follow. He already felt out of place witnessing the ending of the memorial gathering; he did not want to be present for the burial.

Unfortunately, despite his determination to remain behind, he did not actually have a say in the matter. After the auditorium cleared out, Tim experienced an uncomfortable tug deep within himself. It felt as if someone had punched a hand through his chest, grabbed him by the spine and was now forcibly dragging him along.

The pain quickly went from unpleasant to excruciating. He opened his mouth to scream, but before he could cry out, blackness enveloped him.

"What the fuck?" Tim shouted as light rushed back.

The auditorium had vanished. Around him now was only manicured lawn, asphalt pathways, and stone markers of various shapes and sizes. He was in a cemetery; the very place he had decided he did not wish to be.

Tim stared upward at a blazing yellow sun and blue sky overhead. The daylight left him momentarily puzzled. He did not think ghosts could go out during the day. But then, what did he actually know about ghosts? He had never before believed in them so had not paid much attention to others who did. He wished he had listened a little closer to those nutjob friends of his with their crystals and astrological charts. Maybe they weren't so crazy after all, and maybe if he had paid more attention, he might understand better what was happening to him.

He believed in ghosts now. How could he not? He was one.

Tim did not catch fire or feel like the sun was burning him, so he decided not to be overly concerned about the hour. He was not a vampire after all.

Were they real, too?

One question at a time, he cautioned himself. Tim had more important details to fill in at the moment. First, he needed to figure out where he was.

Fortunately, that question turned out to have an easy answer. One glance between his feet gave him all the information he needed to solve the riddle. A square, black marble headstone rested in the grass in front of him. It read, "Timothy Merrimont Delaney II." Beneath the name was the legend, "Beloved husband and father, January 4, 1942 – August 17, 1994." There was additional room on the headstone that would one day be used for Joyce when she joined him in the ground.

Speaking of ground, Tim realized the grave beneath the marker was closed with a healthy green carpet of grass covering it. He had missed the actual burial, which was a relief, but it brought to mind the question of how long he had been in the dark limbo of nothing before arriving here in the cemetery. Was it moments? Or years?

Tim knelt and examined the grass more closely. It was new. He could see the lines where the sod had been cut and placed over the grave, which meant the burial had occurred only hours ago, or perhaps a few days at most. He was not sure if he was happy or disappointed that more time had not elapsed. There was a small part of him that hoped enough time had passed that the man who shot him had been identified and arrested. He very much wanted that to happen.

The light around Tim dimmed from the golden haze of a late summer day to an unnatural reddish color. The surrounding lawn seemed to shimmer and flow with life and energy that grass should not have. Tim felt a tug from deep within him again, although this time it was not the insistent pull of a hand grasping his spine. The sensation was a gentle nudge, an encouragement that there was somewhere he needed to go.

The feeling was not painful or frightening and, though he had never experienced anything like it previously, Tim believed the force behind it was benign. The emotional sensation reminded him of being a child playing in the street in front of his house when the streetlights would flicker on in the growing gloom of evening, urging him and his friends to cease their activities and head for the security of a warm, lighted home. The draw he felt was encouraging, comforting, like the embrace of a loved one.

Tim almost yielded to the pull. He wanted to. He wanted to see what waited for him at the end of the offered path, but he also was not ready to leave this world behind. A thief had stolen his life from him, taken him away from his family, and before he could fully be at peace, he had to know the man responsible was punished.

He turned away from the gentle urging, purposefully walking in the opposite direction. He walked until the sensation fully passed before halting again. His short journey took him to the parking lot of the cemetery grounds. To his left he saw a building with wide glass doors and a welcoming, porch-styled exterior facade. This was the entrance to the cemetery's main offices and small chapel. He had visited this building once before while making arrangements for his father.

To his right stood another unremarkable, unmarked building. Curious, he moved closer. On the plain double doors at the front, bold block letters had been painted on the glass announcing this was the "Dasan's Terrace Police Department."

"Police Department? I didn't know this place had their own police department."

Tim decided he wanted to go inside and take a little look around. What could it hurt? He would be in and out in a couple of minutes, tops.

CHAPTER

Mitch Loman raced through the dark cemetery grounds, cutting left then right to avoid becoming an easy target. He dodged between the massive trunks of ancient trees, sprinting through the oldest, mostly untended regions of Dasan's Terrace and trying not to lose his balance in the uneven dirt and brush underfoot. He panted, gasping for breath. His lungs burned and begged him to slow his barely controlled flight, but slowing was not an option. Not yet.

He ran on.

A flash of yellow glinted in his peripheral vision as a bolt of magical force sped past, barely missing his head. Mitch flinched from the light. The reaction came too late. If the attack had been three inches to the left it would have struck the back of his neck, and no amount of dodging would have prevented the fatal strike from landing. The logic of that thought however, did nothing to stop his body from the instinctive desire to shy away from danger, and the brief wince, coupled with a tree root catching at the tip of his boot, caused him to stumble.

Mitch could not move his feet fast enough to match the forward momentum of his upper body and, completely unbalanced, he pitched forward. Flailing his hands for balance, he crashed to the ground in an ungainly tumble of arms and legs.

Sliding through the dirt and grass, he narrowly avoided colliding headfirst into a tree. With no time to contemplate his lucky escape from a nasty concussion, he rolled onto his back anticipating the next attack. That last blast had come much too close for his liking, and he knew another could not be far behind.

Ambient magic swirled around him, and Mitch used the unformed power to shape a concave disk in the palm of his left hand. Responding to his will, the disk extended outward, forming a pale blue shield of light that covered most of his upper body. Mitch pointed the magic barrier in the direction he had last seen his attacker, raising the protective field barely in time to fend off another yellow bolt of light. The offensive magic crackled and dispersed along his defenses in a series of glittering flashes. To Mitch's relief, the shield held against the battering onslaught.

Emerging from the shadows of several nearby trees, a figure dressed in all black appeared. The witch pursuing Mitch strode forward. Her bright red lips, pressed into a tight line of disappointment, provided the only color in that pale face. The woman appeared grim and fully determined to finish the gruesome task she had begun. With long black hair framing the white oval of her face, and dark circles of kohl drawn around her icy blue eyes, the woman's head appeared to float toward him, a disembodied skull foretelling only destruction and doom.

Violet Rose, second in command of the most powerful coven in northern California, paused as she contemplated her quarry sprawled on the ground before her. Mitch held the shield in place, hoping it could withstand whatever she might throw at him next.

Violet flicked the fingers of one hand, sending one more yellow streak of power toward him. The attack did not penetrate through his barrier, but it contained sufficient force to cause his defenses to sputter and break apart. The witch smiled, her blood red lipstick emphasizing her moment of triumph.

Mitch did not have time to gather power and form a new shield. His only option was to attempt something Violet would not suspect. He lunged forward, rushing toward the smirking woman, arms spread wide to grasp her and tackle her to the ground.

Violet clearly had not expected a physical attack; her widening eyes were testament to her surprise. Though startled, the witch was not so easily caught. She sidestepped as Mitch moved close enough to pose an actual threat.

He missed.

Violet danced gracefully out of harm's way, mere inches away from his grasping hands. That was alright with him, though. He had expected she would avoid his clumsy attempt, and the rush forward was only part of his strategy. As Violet moved aside from his awkward, bullish charge, Mitch continued running at full speed, using her momentary distraction to put some distance between the two of them. He dashed through the unlighted recesses of Dasan's Terrace, hoping the terrain and darkness would conceal him long enough to formulate a better defensive plan.

Golden streaks of magical energy cut the air to either side of Mitch as he ran. Zigzagging randomly left and right to make himself a more unpredictable target, he did not slow his pace. At one point, he risked a glance over his shoulder, but he could not see Violet in the gloom behind him. Another flash of yellow lightning sizzled past, causing the hair on the back of his neck to stand on end.

"That girl must have eyes like a damned cat," Mitch muttered, throwing himself to the ground and rolling behind the temporary protection of a white marble headstone.

He heard her light laughter echoing through the cemetery grounds.

"Oh, my," she called out. "I almost got you with that one, didn't I?"

"Not even close," he shouted back. "You're going to have to do better than that."

"So brave. So sure of yourself. I'm going to enjoy seeing the look on your face when I end this little game."

Mitch took several deep breaths, trying to ease the pounding of his heart in his chest and to get oxygen circulating to his fatigued muscles. He felt tired, sore, and almost ready to give up. He couldn't let Violet know that, however. She would show him no mercy when she caught him again.

Holding out both hands, he drew on the surrounding energies, pulling magic from the air as well as up from the ground beneath him. He reformed his shield in his left hand, while creating a swirling red vortex of power in his right.

"Do you think it will be that easy?" he asked.

More laughter. "Oh, I know what you're doing," she said. "Keep the witch talking so you can gauge where she is. Neat tactic. If it works."

Violet's voice came from his left. Sprawled on his back, Mitch shifted so he had a clear view in that direction, attempting to find her black-clad form in the shadows.

"Unfortunately, it doesn't always work the way you hope."

This time her words came from his right, and he whipped his head a hundred and eighty degrees, orienting on the sound.

"In fact, it can be quite confusing at times when echoes don't behave themselves."

Violet's voice rushed toward him from every direction at once. Disoriented by the seemingly undirected noise, Mitch pushed himself to his knees, risking exposure long enough to get a peek in the direction he believed Violet should be coming from. He peered over the edge of the headstone and found only blackness. The blackness of a form-fitting, ankle length dress, to be precise.

His eyes trailed higher until he found the sparkling blue eyes and smiling visage of his pursuer. The witch stood on the opposite side of the headstone, staring down at Mitch's crouching form.

Mitch reeled backward, tripping over his own feet but somehow managing not to fall. He held the new shield in front of him while cocking his right arm in preparation of throwing the unshaped red maelstrom. Violet placed her hands to her hips, cocking one eyebrow doubtfully.

The twisting funnel of power broke apart in Mitch's hand. He tried to hold onto the magic, to force it to reform, but it collapsed into a shower of red sparks that drifted aimlessly for a few seconds before winking out entirely. Mitch's shield met the same fate, dissipating into blue sparks a moment later.

Violet stepped around the grave marker separating them, her hands still gracefully perched on her slender hips. She fairly glided as she walked, shifting her body with each step in a vampish victory stroll. The dress she wore alternately clung and slipped along her body like flowing black paint.

Mitch pulled at the nascent magic around him, attempting to form another shield, but Violet tutted, then waved one hand through the air. A scattering of spinning yellow lights formed between the two combatants, twirling like tiny, bladed shuriken.

24

They split, doubling their number, then doubling again until there were dozens of the wicked little weapons.

On some unspoken cue, they flung themselves forward, impacting Mitch's chest in a flurry and embedding themselves into his black uniform shirt. The shirt glowed bright yellow, forcing Mitch to squint as the glare burned away his night vision.

Violet surprised him then by jumping forward and physically tackling him to the ground. She landed on top of him, pinning him beneath her and grasping his face between her palms.

"Bang. You're dead," she told him, her eyes sparkling with a fierce glee. She leaned her head forward and kissed him deeply on the mouth.

Mitch returned the kiss with mixed feelings. He was angry with himself that he had been bested yet again, but he also realized that his current punishment was not really so bad. The kiss lasted several long, luxurious seconds before Violet pulled away. She shifted on top of him, and Mitch winced.

Violet rolled off of Mitch and extended a hand to help him to his feet. "Are you okay?" she asked. "I keep forgetting about your ribs."

Mitch smiled to reassure her. His recent run in with a golem had left him with two broken ribs and a punctured lung, but despite the seriousness of his injuries, he had rebounded quickly. The doctor had cleared him to return to work almost two weeks ago.

"I'm fine. The doctor said the bones are healed, but they might still give me some pain for a while. Nothing to worry about, though."

Mitch brushed at the dirt and grass on the knees of his uniform pants. He wondered idly if he would be able to wash out the stain.

"What was that attack, by the way? I've never seen you do anything like that before."

Violet moved closer and ran her thumb across his lips. After that kiss, he was probably wearing as much of her red lipstick as she was. She dabbed at his mouth, then cocked her head to examine her efforts at removing the worst of the incriminating smear.

"Doesn't matter if you've seen it or not," she chastised him while still studying his face. "You should have stopped it. Every magical attack comes down to the same thing: if it touches you, it's probably going to kill you."

"There were so many, and you already shut down my shield. What was I supposed to do?"

"Not die," she said simply, giving him another peck on the lips as she stepped away. "Your choices are always the same. You can avoid the attack, deflect it, or disrupt it. Maybe there were too many to avoid, and your shield was down, but you had time to break the assault apart before it started moving. I gave you plenty of time."

"I'm still not very good at that," Mitch admitted. "I can barely manipulate my own magic, much less interfere with someone else's."

"Then keep working on it. I won't have Alyssandra accusing me of being a poor teacher."

Alyssandra was the leader of Violet's coven, and she was the person who had tasked Violet with teaching Mitch how to use magic. The witch priestess made an agreement with the Dasan's Terrace police chief, and she would not be pleased if she felt Violet was failing to keep up the coven's end of the bargain.

"I think you're a wonderful teacher," said Mitch, slipping a hand around Violet's waist and pulling her against him. "But I do wonder how the hell you manage to keep beating me while wearing this dress."

"Maybe if you weren't so easy to beat, I would need to wear something more practical. As it is, I could probably wear a straitjacket and kick your ass."

"That's cold blooded."

"Maybe. But it's true."

Mitch couldn't argue. Violet had been studying magic for over a decade, while Mitch had only discovered magic was real a few months ago. There was so much that she took for granted that he was only now realizing was even possible. She could probably beat him while wearing a straitjacket, gagged and blindfolded, and with her ankles and wrists tied together for good measure.

"That reminds me, I've been meaning to ask you something."

"Shoot," she told him.

"You told me you've been using magic since you were a teenager, but I didn't start until I was thirty. Why did it take so long for me? Is it normal for some people to develop abilities later in life?"

Violet shook her head. "Nope. I don't think you developed any slower than I did. You could probably use magic when you were a kid, but you never had an opportunity to try. You had no idea magic existed until recently, so I'm guessing you didn't have access to it while growing up. Magic users are rare, but what's even rarer are places where raw magic exists in quantities large enough to manipulate it. I'll bet you went your whole life never realizing you could see and use magic."

Mitch nodded, considering the possible explanation.

"Think of it like riding a horse," Violet continued. "Everybody has the basic skills necessary to figure out how to ride a horse. But just because you might physically be able to do it when given the opportunity, what if you didn't know what a horse was because you had never seen one? When would you have had the chance to learn?"

"Do you think it's the same with seeing ghosts? With being an exorcist?"

"Exactly. You've always had the ability, but you didn't know it. You never realized you could see ghosts until your son died and came back to visit you. You might have never run into a ghost before, or – and I think this is more likely – you probably did, but either thought it was a real person or dismissed it as a figment of your imagination. The only difference now is that you know better. You've accepted ghosts and magic are real, so you can begin learning how to identify and work with both of them."

The unexpected mention of Mitch's son sent a jolt of pain through him sharper than the recent impact to his injured ribs. He did not want to discuss Denny at the moment, so he quickly changed the topic. Mitch shaped another shield, holding the blue disk between him and Violet.

"Are you ready for another round?" he asked.

"Actually, no," said Violet. "I think it's time we move on to a different lesson. Alyssandra asked me to begin your training in soul viewing. Magic is much more useful than soul sight in normal situations, so we'll keep working on improving your skills in that area another time, but she and I were talking about you the other day and we realized that it's dangerous for you to continue interacting with ghosts without fully understanding your gifts. There are risks to remaining ignorant, and I don't want you to accidentally get hurt."

Mitch let the shield blink away. "When I found out what I was, Alyssandra mentioned that exorcists sometimes went crazy. Is that what you mean?"

Violet nodded. "That's exactly what I mean. Exorcists can touch human souls, ghosts, and spirits. We do this by using our own souls as a contact point. This gives us a lot of power, but at the same time it puts us at risk. The human soul is normally protected by the physical body it inhabits. It does not leave that protection until the moment of death, at which time it disconnects and goes free. Do you follow me so far?"

Mitch nodded. "Sure. So far."

"You and I have the ability to move small portions of our soul outside of our body at any time. By extending this piece of our life force, we can move past the physical barrier of someone else's body and touch their soul. That makes exorcists very dangerous to other people. However, when your soul is extended outside of your body, others can harm you as well. If you are not very careful, and your soul sustains enough damage, your sanity could be at risk. I have heard of untrained exorcists that have lost their minds. They're like rabid animals, without fear, conscience, or morality. And like a rabid animal, there is only one way to deal with them."

"What if I choose not to use my power? Won't that protect me?" asked Mitch.

"You can't choose not to use it," Violet explained. "It's instinctual. You already used it when you exorcised Harold from the cemetery."

Mitch recalled the hapless ghost he had encountered during his first week working for the Dasan's Terrace Police Department. He had not meant to harm the fragile specter, but when he reached out and touched Harold, he had unknowingly destroyed him. Fortunately, Harold had only been an echo, an unconscious remnant of a person who had died, and not a lost human soul.

"What you need to do is learn how to harness your ability. When you have sufficient control over it, then you can prevent yourself from accidentally harming someone else or allowing yourself to be hurt."

"I've lasted this long without getting hurt. Maybe I already have more control over it than you think."

Violet pressed her lips together in a tight line. She arched one eyebrow mockingly. "I don't think so. I'm sorry, Mitch, but I've already seen you take risks you didn't even know you were taking. When you met Lieutenant Delaney, you shook his hand, right?"

"Um, yeah. So what?"

"In order to make physical contact with a spirit, you were exercising your powers without realizing it. If Delaney had been a hostile ghost, he could have injured you when you took his hand. He's not the only example, either."

Mitch's chest began to ache, but this time it was not from his broken ribs.

"When I hold Denny...?"

Violet nodded, not needing him to finish the thought. She touched his arm lightly, offering what comfort she could.

"When you hold your son, your soul is interacting with his. Denny loves you, and I know he would never purposefully hurt you, but..."

"He could," Mitch finished her sentence.

"Yeah. He could."

Mitch sighed loudly, bringing his emotions under control. "Okay. So, I have been taking risks that could make me lose my mind. I need to figure out how to stop doing that. What do I need to know?"

"A lot," Violet told him. "I will try to teach you everything you need to know to stay safe, but first, we need to get you up and running on some basics. You need to learn how to see a human soul."

"I can already do that," said Mitch, surprised. "I've seen several ghosts. What more do I have to learn?"

"You've seen ghosts separated from their human shells. That's true. I'm talking about seeing human souls still anchored in this life. It isn't like seeing magic. With magic, you either have the ability to see it, or you don't. Even the ambient, unshaped magic around us is still visible if you know it's there and focus on it a bit. That's how I kept finding you in the dark, by the way."

"What?" Mitch took a beat to follow the sudden change in topic. "That's how…? You were cheating?"

"How is using magic cheating when I'm teaching you how to use magic?" Violet laughed. "Moron. I was simply using a trick you don't know how to do, yet. That's all. If you concentrate on the ambient magic in the air and in the ground, you can feel anything that temporarily disrupts it. Every time you drew on it to shape a spell, I could feel exactly where you were."

"Hmm. You're going to have to teach me how to do that."

"It's not really something you can teach. You have to practice by examining how the magic behaves normally and then watching it when someone nearby is using it."

"Can you show me?" asked Mitch, hopefully.

"Mitch! You're like a kid with a new toy. A dangerous new toy at that. Stop going off topic and stay focused on what I'm telling you. I'll teach you anything you want to know about magical tracking later. We're talking about souls right now."

Chastised, Mitch remained silent.

"Like I said, with magic, you either possess the ability to see it, or you don't. With souls you have to have the innate ability, but you also have to learn how to look properly to find them. You need to know *what* you're looking for as well as how to look for it."

"Can you see my soul?" Mitch asked.

"I can. Your spirit sits right at the surface of your skin. It's why you can physically interact with ghosts, but it's also a problem. Holding your soul so close to the surface makes you vulnerable. You need to learn how to draw it more deeply within you. That's a lesson for another day, though. For now, I want you to concentrate on me. I want you to try to see my soul."

"How do I do that?"

"Honestly, it's less about seeing with your eyes, and more about sensing with your mind and feelings. You look at someone and try to understand what kind of person they are. Let your eyes go slightly out of focus, like you're trying to catch something with your peripheral vision, then imagine you're burrowing past a person's clothing and skin and seeking the core of who they are."

"Like I'm digging a hole into their chest?"

"Don't be so literal. You aren't digging into anything. You are simply trying to see past the decoy of the physical shell. Try imagining peeling a mask away to see a person's face."

"Okay. And what should I see? What am I looking for?"

Violet paused as she considered how to answer his question. She took several long, slow breaths while she thought through her next response.

"Every soul looks a little different. They change based on the person and their life histories. Basically though, a soul is a collection of personal experiences. If you look at the soul of a newborn, it will be clear, unblemished, and almost translucent. Each new event in the child's life will appear as a streak or mark of bright silver. Every new experience leaves its reflection on the soul. If the event is minor, the silver will eventually fade and disappear. If the event has lasting permanence, it will darken and leave a scar. That scar then breaks apart and spreads, filtering through the entire soul and adding a little more gray to its appearance."

"What does the gray mean?"

"It means the event in that child's life was important enough that it has in some way shaped the way he or she views the world. A soul is a sum total of a person's life. Experiences can be positive or negative, it doesn't matter. They all affect the soul the same. Remember that. If you see a very dark soul inside someone, that doesn't mean they are good or evil, it merely means they have led an eventful existence."

"What do you see when you look at me?" asked Mitch.

Violet lowered her gaze to the ground. She glanced at Mitch's feet, then scanned him slowly upward until she met his eyes again. "Do you really want to know?"

"I do."

"Your soul is neither dark nor light. I don't think your life in general has been much harder or easier than most. I do see several dark scars, however, that are only now beginning to break apart. I also see three streaks of silver. They're quite bright, so are obviously new."

"What do they represent?"

Violet wagged a finger in front of his nose. "Nope. I'm not going to dig that deep. Not yet. Not until you understand fully what you are asking. For now, I will tell you there are three new things in your life that appear to be affecting you quite deeply. What those three things are, you will have to figure out for yourself."

"If you wanted to go deeper, could you?"

Violet's expression turned serious, and Mitch could see her carefully phrasing her response in her mind before answering.

"When you learn to see a human soul, to really see it, there is nothing about that person that they can hide from you. You will know them better than they could ever possibly know themselves. Your soul is who you are. I hope you understand what I'm telling you, and I hope you understand why I won't look any deeper into your soul without your permission and your *full* knowledge of what that request means."

She patted Mitch's chest gently, her expression still serious. "And I hope you will give me the same courtesy in the future. Right now, you are learning, and I am the only guinea pig around here for you to practice on. I trust you will respect my privacy as much as you are able."

"Of course, I will. But so you know, I'm not trying to hide anything from you. You have my permission to look as deeply into me as you want. I want you to know who I am, and I hope you don't see anything that scares you away."

"Stop!" Violet told him. Her brow furrowed in frustration. "You have no idea what you're offering, so I'm going to pretend you didn't say anything quite so stupid. One day, you'll get it. We can have this conversation again then."

She stepped back two paces and spread her arms out to her sides. "Let your eyes go out of focus, and peel away the shell. What do you see?"

Mitch stared at Violet, completely lost as to how to start. He looked at her chest trying to peer through the layers of clothing, skin and muscle, into her heart. After a moment, he realized he was simply admiring her breasts in the snug confines of her dress. Embarrassed, he lowered his gaze slightly and stared at her stomach, trying again to sense deeper than the external trappings.

"What do you see?" Violet asked him after a full minute had passed.

"A knockout in a black dress," he responded.

34

"Stop screwing around. This is serious." But Mitch could see the grin she was trying to suppress. "Don't force it. It should come fairly naturally, but you will have to discover what works for you. The man who taught me told me to search for an internal light in the person you're looking at. That method never did me any good. I never saw any light, though maybe that image will help you."

Mitch tried again. He stared at Violet, letting his examination move from the top of her head down to her feet, then back up again. He let his vision go slightly out of focus, causing Violet's form to blur. The black dress she wore fuzzed and almost disappeared into the backdrop of night behind her. Still, he did not see anything that might remotely be considered a soul as Violet had described it.

Next, he tried looking for a light as Violet had suggested. Mitch imagined a pale illumination glowing outward from deep within, shining brighter and brighter until it revealed itself to him. That image failed as well. He still saw nothing except the lovely young woman who had been kicking his ass all night long.

"Maybe you're trying too hard," Violet told him. "Seeing souls should come easily to someone with the gift. If you find yourself straining to see something, then you're doing it wrong."

Relaxed or straining, Mitch saw nothing. Maybe he did not actually have the gift, he thought. Maybe he wasn't the exorcist everyone believed him to be. No, that couldn't be right. How else could he explain what he had done to Harold? And how had he been able to touch Lieutenant Delaney, and Denny?

He had the ability. Violet had assured him of that fact, and he believed her. He simply needed to figure out what he was doing wrong. He thought about the lieutenant. Delaney was a human soul trapped and wandering the Earth after the death of his body. He was a soul, and Mitch could see him clearly. He did not appear to be a gray mass with silver streaks as Violet described a soul should be. Instead, he looked like a real person. What was the difference between the ghost and a still living soul?

Delaney's spirit was completely separated from the body, but so what? Why should that make any difference? Then Mitch remembered Violet's comment, "a soul is who you are."

Delaney was a trapped ghost, pretending to still be human. That was who he was. Violet was a still living woman. The soul inside her did not have to pretend to be anything other than what it truly was: a collection of all her hopes, desires, and experiences.

Mitch looked toward Violet and let his vision once again slip out of focus. This time he did not force his eyes to blur the images in front of him, he simply relaxed and let his mind see what it wanted to see.

"Who are you?" he muttered under his breath, letting his emotions direct the search this time. He wanted to know this woman. He cared about her, perhaps even loved her if he was being completely honest with himself, and he wanted to understand her to the very core of her being.

"Who are you?" he asked again.

For a moment, Violet shimmered out of existence, leaving a glistening gray ghost in her place. The ghost was roughly human shaped, with a head and torso, but it had no distinctive features. As soon as Mitch attempted to focus his attention on the image it blinked away, and only Violet's quiet form remained in its place, her back straight, and her arms still outstretched.

"Shit!" Mitch swore.

"What?" Violet asked, dropping her arms and taking a concerned step toward him. "Are you okay?"

"Yeah. I'm fine," he assured her. "I think I almost had it, but it got away from me."

Violet smiled. "Great. Whatever you did, try to do it again. This time, when you see it, don't try to hold onto it so hard. This will get easier, I promise. Once you've done it a few times, you're going to start wondering why you had so much trouble in the beginning."

Mitch took a deep breath and blew it out. He shook his hands as if preparing for some difficult physical task, then waved Violet back to her original position. She complied, but this time she kept her hands by her side.

Letting his vision relax, Mitch again stared at the woman in front of him. He told himself how badly he wanted to know who she was, opening himself emotionally and mentally to experience her very essence. He reminded himself of the time they had spent together, getting to know each other, laughing, exchanging tales of their lives, and the intimate moments they shared in each other's arms.

As he stared at Violet, seeing her through his eyes, his mind, and his heart, the gray shimmer returned. Violet did not completely disappear this time, instead the woman and the shimmer that was her true self remained together, juxtaposed over one another. Mitch saw the gray soul clearly now. He could not tell if it was a dark or light gray. He did not have anything else in his personal experiences to which he could compare it. Still, he recognized her soul for what it was. The feeling was too deep, too intimate, for him to be seeing anything else.

He now had the barest understanding, even from such a tentative glimpse, of what Violet had meant when she refused to peer any further into Mitch's own soul. He felt a bit like a voyeur, peeking through a keyhole into someone's private world as they acted freely within, unaware of the intrusion.

Mitch almost pulled away in embarrassment, breaking the connection, but something caught his attention. In the gray void that was Violet Blue Rose, he saw a single streak of bright silver. It was so clear and stark in contrast to the gray around it that it appeared to be a lightning bolt trapped in mid flash in the midst of a roiling cloud filled sky.

Mitch felt drawn toward the light. He instinctually knew that if he examined it closely enough, he could tell precisely what it was. It was that very knowledge of how deeply he could go that caused him to at last back away.

"Oh, shit," he said again. He realized he was panting slightly.

"Yes?" asked Violet. "What happened? Did it get away from you again?"

"No," he said, shaking his head. "I-I got it. I saw it. I saw *you.*"

"How much did you see?" she asked. Violet tried to sound nonchalant, but Mitch could hear the hint of trepidation in the question.

"I saw a beautiful streak of silver. Just one, but it lit up your entire soul. I wanted to touch it, to see what it was, but … I stopped myself. I felt like I was intruding on something I wasn't supposed to see. Do you know what it was?"

Violet laughed. "You really are a dumbass, aren't you?"

Mitch was taken aback by the question. "What? What did I do?"

"Oh, I don't know. Let's see. What brand new experience has entered my life recently that might have had an impact deep enough to leave a mark on my soul?"

Violet grabbed Mitch by his shirt and pulled him toward her. Rising on her tiptoes she pressed her lips to his.

Mitch returned the kiss enthusiastically. Lipstick be damned.

CHAPTER

2

Mitch sat silently at the briefing table in the squad meeting room, waiting for the evening shift to begin. Beside him, on his left, Adam "Tink" Zapien rocked backward in his chair, legs stretched out under the table for balance and to prevent him from toppling completely over. With his hands linked behind his head and his elbows akimbo, the short sleeves of Tink's uniform shirt had pulled up far enough for Mitch to see a partially exposed tattoo on his right bicep. The green-slippered feet of the man's namesake, Tinkerbell, were visible to just above the knee before the bare legs disappeared under the black material of his shirt.

Tink's left arm had been broken during the same fight with the golem that had left Mitch with broken ribs. However, after several weeks in a cast, he had healed with no permanent damage and been pronounced fit to return to full duty by his doctors. Tink's return to the shift had preceded Mitch's own by a couple weeks. Since Mitch had also suffered a punctured lung along with his broken bones, the doctors had been slightly more cautious before allowing him back to work.

Sergeant Jorge Smythe sat at the head of the briefing table, running a finger down the daily activity log as he updated himself on any dayshift calls that might be relevant to his own team. From the brief perusal, Mitch guessed there was not much worth mentioning.

Nothing too surprising there. Like most cemeteries, very little happened at Dasan's Terrace. It was mostly months of sheer boredom, followed by rare moments of life-threatening excitement. Of the two choices, Mitch found he actually preferred the boredom. Having nothing more interesting to do than watch the cemetery lawn grow was infinitely better than a massive dirt creature trying to cave your head in or crush the air from your lungs.

Mitch let his gaze drift around the room, scanning the mostly bare, beige walls. Behind the sergeant's head, hanging on the wall, were the only two real items of decoration in the entire briefing room. To the left of Jorge, hung a picture of the Sacramento County Sheriff, wearing his Class-A dress uniform. The man in the photo was clearly attempting to appear commanding and distinguished as he gazed off into the distance at nothing in particular. Mitch, however, felt the narrowed eyes and pursed lips of the Sheriff's face looked more constipated than commanding.

To the sergeant's right was a glass covered shadow box holding an assortment of uniform patches. Ten uniform shoulder patches lined the case in two rows of five, showing the various iterations worn over the years by Sacramento deputies since the department's founding in 1850. The box including a muted SWAT patch and a sesquicentennial celebratory patch only authorized to be worn for one year in 2000. In addition, there were three patches in the display for the cities that had contracted with the Sheriff's Office for law enforcement services when they did not have the resources to fund their own police departments: Citrus Heights, Rancho Cordova, and Elk Grove.

Mitch stared at the glass case and wondered idly why Dasan's Terrace didn't have their own patch. Maybe he should have a chat with the police chief later about designing something unique to their agency. They had their own badges after all, why not patches to go with them?

At one minute before seven o'clock, Officer Brad Kodama strolled into the briefing room and dropped into a chair across the table from Tink and Mitch. The man was like clockwork. He never showed up early for briefing, yet somehow managed to never show up late either. Brad smiled at Mitch, then tapped two fingers to his forehead in a brief salute to Jorge. Above Brad's right shoulder jutted the slender black handle of the katana he always wore on duty.

Brad shifted slightly in the chair, moving the Japanese sword to a more comfortable position before settling in his seat. Mitch had long ago stopped wondering why the department allowed him to carry the ostentatious weapon, especially after witnessing the man wield the katana in the field. Dasan's Terrace was … not a typical department, and sometimes the weapons and tactics necessary to deal with its more unique aspects also needed to be on the atypical side.

"Movie night!" said Brad, slapping one hand on the table to emphasize the announcement. "Are you joining us tonight, Mitch, or do you have plans to roll around in the mud with your girlfriend again?"

Thursday nights at the DTPD had evolved into a regular gathering for the officers to view a selection of movies and enjoy snacks in the command staff break room. The weekly tradition was thanks to Jorge, who had gotten the idea authorized by the chief, and also was the main supplier of the films they watched. The sergeant, in an attempt to build rapport among the officers on his team, and to relieve some of the rampant tedium of the job,

41

began bringing DVDs of popular movies in over a year ago. Thursdays soon became the most anticipated night of the work week. It did not hurt that the officers also got to slack off a bit on their normal schedule of foot patrols in the cemetery.

"The rolling in the mud stuff is only on Wednesdays. I'm free tonight," said Mitch.

"I hope you're doing more than rolling in the mud," said Jorge, setting the activity log aside. "You're supposed to be learning from Violet, not chasing her around the graveyard like a horny teenager."

"I can do both," Mitch responded, defensively.

Pulling in a small amount of magic from his surroundings, Mitch allowed a trickle of power to trail from his fingertips to the clipboard in front of Jorge. When the magic touched the activity log, he retracted it, dragging the clipboard across the table along with it.

Jorge shook his head. "Please don't do that. It's creepy."

"It's cool as fuck!" insisted Tink, grabbing the clipboard and sliding it back to the sergeant. "Do it again, Mitch."

Jorge slapped a hand over the board, firmly pinning it to the table. "Nope. No need. I believe you when you say you've been practicing. You don't have to prove it to me."

Despite Jorge's assurances, Mitch reached for the clipboard once again with his magic. The moment the board began to move, Jorge snatched his hand back as though he had suddenly discovered he was touching something angry and in possession of multiple rows of large, sharp teeth. The board skated across the tabletop to Mitch, and Tink howled in appreciation at the display.

"That's not cool to prank the sergeant like that," Brad admonished, scowling at Mitch. "I think you owe him an apology."

"Are you serious right now?" asked Tink with a scoff. "This is coming from the same guy that glued my boots to the bottom of my locker last week."

Brad attempted to keep his expression serious, but the right corner of his lip quirked up slightly. "Technically, whoever glued your boots was never identified. It could have been anyone."

"They're still fucking there!" blurted Tink. "I don't know what you used, but I couldn't get them loose. I had to buy new ones."

"You needed new boots, anyway. Your old ones were falling apart. I did you a favor.... I mean, whoever glued them to your locker, did you a favor." Brad was laughing openly now.

"Okay, I think that's enough," interrupted Jorge. The sergeant held out a hand toward Mitch, and Mitch slid the clipboard back toward him.

Pulling a pen from his shirt pocket, Jorge flipped the pages to the current duty roster. "There isn't anything to pass on from dayshift today. Brad, what beat do you want tonight?"

Brad was the senior officer on the shift, so automatically had the first pick of assignments each night. Tink had been assigned to Dasan's Terrace a couple years later, and Mitch had only begun working at the cemetery a few months ago, leaving him low man on the seniority totem pole.

"I'll take Front Half," Brad told the sergeant, referring to the newer section of the cemetery grounds closest to the administrative buildings.

Brad usually took Front Half. It was well lighted and had several paved paths meandering through it that made foot patrol much easier than the mostly untended acres of Back Half, but Mitch knew that wasn't why Brad selected it. Mitch's four-year-old son, Denny, had passed away several years ago, and he had been buried in Dasan's Terrace. Denny's grave was in Front Half, and the other officers on the shift had quietly decided that Mitch shouldn't have to patrol the area where his son was buried. On the rare occasions that Brad didn't ask for Front Half, Tink always selected it.

Mitch did not feel the gesture was necessary, and believed he would have no problems working in Front Half, but he appreciated the sentiment behind it, so said nothing to either Brad or Tink about their choices of assignments.

"I'll take Back Half and North-West," said Tink.

Jorge nodded. "All right. Mitch, that leaves you with perimeter."

"Yup," Mitch acknowledged.

Perimeter meant Mitch would be responsible for patrolling the full length of the fencing and walls surrounding the cemetery. It was his job to make sure everything was properly secured and intact, reporting on any tampering or graffiti he might find along the way. It was the most physically taxing of the three beats since the borders of the cemetery stretched to a little over five miles in total distance. Walking the full length would take Mitch about two hours to complete at a comfortable pace.

He did not mind. He enjoyed the exercise, and at this time of year, the sun would still be up for most of that time. He would not need his flashlight until the last half hour or so of his circuit.

"Hit the bricks," Jorge told the team. "Go to work and try not to get eaten. I'll see you all in the breakroom at ten."

Mitch completed his nightly rounds at 9:30. He had taken his time checking the perimeter tonight as the late Spring evening was unseasonably warm and he did not want to start sweating under his uniform and ballistic vest. The fence was intact and secure, and he did not find any damage or vandalism that had occurred over the last twenty-four hours. Nor had he expected to find any. Most people had a healthy respect for cemeteries, and even the most prolific vandals in the surrounding areas generally left Dead Town alone. It was rare that Mitch found anything amiss on his evening patrols.

He returned to the police department building and used his key to let himself inside. It was past normal hours of operation and the main lobby doors had been closed to the public and locked by the daytime employees. Mitch took the stairs to the second floor, where Jorge would soon be in the administration break room hooking up his DVD player to the television. For now, he had almost a half hour before the first movie would begin.

With time to kill, Mitch wandered past the administrative assistant's desk in the entry area of the second floor. The desk took up most of the space here and was the first thing anyone coming out of the stairwell or exiting the elevator encountered when they reached the second story. On the other side were the department chief's office, and the assistant chief's office. Both doors were currently closed.

Mitch crossed to the assistant chief's office and turned his head, not quite touching his ear to the polished wood door. He listened for a moment outside the room but heard nothing. Grasping the doorknob, Mitch turned it and found it unlocked.

"Yes?" he heard someone say from inside the office.

Mitch pushed the door open and entered. He found Lieutenant Timothy Delaney inside, seated at his desk. Delaney was in his fifties, with curly gray hair still sprinkled with patches of dark black. His face was lean, and mostly covered by the burly, gray mustache covering his upper lip and growing out over his cheeks. The lieutenant wore an old-fashioned, green and gold Class-A uniform, with patches announcing he was a member of the Sacramento County Sheriff's Office.

"Did I say you could come in?" Delaney asked petulantly as Mitch eased the office door closed behind him.

"No, sir. You didn't," Mitch admitted.

"Then get the hell out," huffed the lieutenant.

Mitch remained where he was. Even though the man outranked Mitch, Lieutenant Delaney did not have any actual authority over him. Partly because the lieutenant had never been formally assigned to the Dasan's Terrace Police Department, but mostly because Timothy Delaney had been dead for more than thirty years.

The lieutenant was a ghost.

Recalling the lesson Violet had given him on viewing souls, Mitch let his vision blur slightly as he peered into the depths of Delaney's spectral form. Since the lieutenant was a ghost, there was no physical body to hinder Mitch's examination. The man was already a manifestation of his soul, so it required little effort to look deeper into the fragile, projected image seated at the desk.

Delaney's soul was a uniform, deep gray. Though he searched, Mitch could find no evidence of variation to the ghost's deepest self. There were no streaks of silver or scars of black. It was as if, after his death, Delaney's spirit stopped growing or experiencing new things. He was locked into whatever he had been at the moment he died.

There was one oddity, though, now that Mitch was looking more closely. Tendrils of dark gray streamed from the lieutenant's ghost, like the indistinct streaks you might find on a blurred photograph of an object moving too quickly to be captured. A dozen or so of the tendrils trailed from his spirit, drifting toward the north until they disappeared through the wall of his office.

Mitch recalled what Violet had told him about ghosts being tethered to objects or places, and he wondered if these were visible evidence of the tethers that held Delaney in Dasan's Terrace.

"Last warning," said Lieutenant Delaney, breaking Mitch from his reverie. "Leave now or I will have you fired and removed from this department for insubordination."

"I have some questions for you, sir. I hope you'll be able to answer them for me. And I'm pretty sure you can't have me fired. You don't actually work here, after all, since you're ... well, dead, sir. You do know that, right? You don't think you're still alive, do you?"

The lieutenant's form flickered, blinking in and out of existence rapidly. The ghost solidified again, and Delaney glared at him. The lieutenant leaped forward, too fast for Mitch to follow with his eyes. Delaney seemed to disappear, then appear out of nowhere right beside Mitch, the ghost's face inches from his own.

"Out!" Lieutenant Delaney howled.

Startled, Mitch threw up his hands to push the lieutenant away. Even as he tried, he realized the gesture was futile. Delaney had no body, which meant no mass to push against. Still, surprisingly, Mitch did make physical contact with Delaney's chest. His fingers began to tingle as he felt the material of the ghost's uniform against his skin. The cloth was rough and warm under his palms.

The expression on Delaney's face went from anger to abject horror in the span of a heartbeat. The lieutenant flickered again, this time reappearing at the far corner of the room, his own hands now extended before him in terrified surrender.

"Please," the ghost whimpered. "Don't. I'm sorry. Please don't do that."

Do what? Mitch wondered. Why was the lieutenant suddenly frightened of him? He held his hands in front of his face, feeling the odd tingling slowly fading.

Then, Mitch remembered Harold, the poor spirit echo that had at one time haunted the cemetery. He had accidentally exorcised Harold from existence with only a touch. Mitch had not done it on purpose, he wasn't even sure what he had done to make it happen, but Harold was still gone forever because of him.

Had he been about to do the same thing to Lieutenant Delaney? Was he capable of that?

Mitch lowered his hands. "I'm sorry, Lieutenant. I'm not going to hurt you. I promise. I really only came in here to ask you some questions."

"Wh-what? What do you want?" Delaney asked. He stood a bit straighter and dropped his arms to his sides, but he still looked tense and uneasy.

"Why are you still here?" Mitch asked.

"Why...? I work here," the lieutenant stammered. "I mean, I used to work.... I live here, I suppose is what I mean. I can't go anywhere else."

"No. I don't want to know why you ended up in the cemetery. Your family buried you here. You're probably tethered to your grave, just like my son. What I wanted to know is why haven't you moved on to ... wherever you're supposed to go when you die? Why did you stick around?"

"I was murdered. I don't know who did it."

Mitch nodded, expecting some such response. "Lots of people are murdered. They don't stick around. Why is it so important for you to figure out who killed you?"

48

Delaney peered at Mitch with narrowed eyes, as if searching for the punchline of a bad joke. "Of course it's important. I spent my entire adult life catching criminals and making sure they paid for the crimes they committed. Do you think I could walk away before finding the person that did this to me? It's not who I am. Frankly, I'm surprised you needed to ask such an ignorant question. How about you? Could you leave if it had happened to you? If you were the one murdered while trying to buy a bag of chips, could you drift off to whatever comes next without so much as a backward glance?"

Mitch thought about it for a moment. He believed he could do exactly that. Dead was dead, and it did not really matter much to him what, or who, killed him. Justice, or vengeance, was for the living. However, he did understand Delaney's point, and he did not fault the poor ghost for his decision to stay.

"Can you still leave?" Mitch asked. "Can you change your mind and give up if you wanted to?"

Delaney shook his head sadly. "I don't think so. I've been here too long. A few times in the past, I've tried to move on, but I don't really know how to do it. I think I missed my opportunity to leave thirty years ago. I'm stuck here until I accomplish what I originally started."

"And if you never find the man that shot you?"

"Then I will be here, answering these same stupid questions from nosey officers hundreds of years from now."

The admission left Mitch slightly depressed. He could not imagine being doomed to wander the same dreary hallways for eternity, and it made him think of Denny, his son. Would the boy also be forever trapped in a repetitive purgatory of his own making? He prayed the answer was no.

"I'm sorry I bothered you. I'll leave you alone, now."

"Wait," said the lieutenant, taking one step forward before halting. He still seemed afraid to get too close to Mitch. "I'm sorry I tried to make you leave. Truth is, except for Dot and the chief, no one ever tries to talk to me. If you wanted to come back again sometime and see me, I would be okay with that."

"Yeah. Sure," Mitch told him. "I can do that. I'll see you later, sir."

Mitch let himself out of the office, closing the door as he stepped into the hallway. With his thoughts circling around the lieutenant's plight, and with nowhere in particular to go, he wandered into the administrative break room. He expected to be the first one in as he still had twenty minutes before ten o'clock. Instead, he found the entire shift already waiting. Jorge, Tink, and Brad were seated around the table looking pensive and agitated.

"Am I holding you guys up?" Mitch asked. "I thought I was early, but if you're all waiting for me, go ahead and start the movie."

"It's not the movie," said Jorge. "We have a problem. On his rounds, Brad found a gravesite that had collapsed and sunk into the ground."

"That's not a problem, is it?" asked Mitch, somewhat confused by the somber tone with which the sergeant had announced the news. "Tink and I found a collapsed grave a couple months ago. We let the groundskeepers know, and they repaired it."

"I remember," said Jorge. "That's the problem. One grave caving in every few years is expected. But two in a few months is a bad trend, especially in Front Half where they use concrete for the grave vaults."

"Trend? A trend for what?"

"We have uninvited guests," said Brad. When Mitch turned toward him, eyebrows raised in query, Kodama elaborated. "Ghouls."

Mitch laughed, but when no one else joined in on the joke, his mirth died away. He looked around the room incredulously at the somber faces of his teammates.

"Ghouls? What? Seriously?"

He received no response to his question, but the others' silence was answer enough.

Yeah. Seriously.

CHAPTER

 3

Chief Simon Jefferson stood a few feet back from the open grave, overseeing the excavation. The backhoe had done most of the early work but had since been removed to allow two groundskeepers to finish the job with shovels. This way, he could be sure that any damage to the casket or grave vault was already there, rather than caused by an errant swing of the tractor's massive scoop.

Simon wore a dark gray suit with barely visible pinstriping running vertically along the coat and pants. A cream colored, button-up shirt under the jacket completed the look. The outfit had been tailored to fit him perfectly, though today, as he watched the groundskeepers working their way deeper into the soil, the collar of his shirt felt a bit tight and constricting about his neck.

Only a few minutes after ten o'clock in the morning, the temperature had already climbed to eighty-five degrees, and it grew hotter by the moment on this sunny day in May. Simon wiped a hand across his face, finding a light sheen of sweat had appeared along his upper lip. Unfortunately, the perspiration was only partly due to the heat. The chief of Dasan's Terrace Police

Department really did not want to find what he was pretty sure he was going to find at the bottom of this grave.

Sergeant Smythe had called him on Friday morning to report the damaged gravesite, along with his suspicions that the cemetery had adopted a stray ghoul. Ghouls could be bad news for a cemetery and for anyone on the property at night, especially if their unwanted visitor started getting bold and began foraging above ground. The vicious things were extremely dangerous to anyone they might catch unawares. For now, this creature – if this was indeed a ghoul – had remained underground and hidden, but that could change at any time.

Chief Jefferson spent most of his day on Friday trying to push through a court order to allow Dasan's Terrace to excavate the grave and examine the damage. Judges were notoriously hesitant to put their name on any documentation allowing exhumations of human remains. Angry family members could raise serious hell over such things. It had taken until the following Monday to find a judge sympathetic to Simon's plight and who knew enough about what he was dealing with to agree to allow the grave to be opened. Still, over three days had passed. That was a very long time to wait with an unpredictable monster prowling through the cemetery.

The moment Simon had a signed warrant to exhume, he had notified the dayshift sergeant to remove any visitors from the cemetery and close the front gates. He did not want witnesses beyond the workers and officers under his command. Closing the cemetery for a day could cause some negative publicity if the wrong people were discomfited by the move, but it was still the better option when the alternative was risking someone seeing, or photographing, whatever the groundskeepers might unearth six feet below their feet.

Beside Simon stood the department's administrative secretary, Dorothy Kristiansen. Everyone on the department knew her as "Dot." She was small, only five feet tall, and barely one hundred pounds, with skin as pale as Simon's was dark. Today, she wore a wide-brimmed, straw hat on her head to protect her face from the bright overhead sun. It wasn't exactly professional attire, but it was understandable given the current situation.

A few shouts could be heard from the open hole as the workers found the concrete grave liner. The crew continued digging, moving to the sides of the vault and excavating to open space on all sides of the heavy, rectangular container.

"Do you think they'll find anything?" asked Dot, leaning forward and trying to peer into the hole without getting close enough to risk falling in or getting struck with a shovel-full of flying dirt.

"I hope not," Simon responded. "I'm really hoping to discover the vault cracked and fell apart because it was badly made. It's much easier to deal with a company selling us a faulty product than catching what Jorge thinks might be down there."

Dot nodded and the two went silent again as the digging continued. Another half hour passed before the groundskeepers climbed out of the hole and indicated the vault and casket were available for the chief's inspection.

The grounds crew erected a small ladder to make entry and exit from the grave easier, and Simon used it to lower himself into the exposed excavation. As he stepped from the bottom rung onto the cement slab that served as the vault cover, he could see immediately that one side of the concrete box had broken and collapsed, causing the dirt around the new opening to crumble and spill into the previously protected space.

The groundskeepers had removed the dirt and the larger pieces of concrete to allow visual inspection of the interior of the vault. Simon knelt and lowered his head to peer into the grave liner's damaged side. It was dark inside, making it impossible to see anything beyond the first few inches of space.

Simon called up to the workers gathered above and asked if anyone had a flashlight. A pocket-sized light was found and dropped into the grave. Simon caught it and clicked the button at the base of the small cylinder, bringing it to life. Again, he kneeled and peered into the hole. This time he could see the condition of the casket inside.

The side of the coffin was broken away, exactly like the side of the concrete vault. The wooden casket, where it remained intact around the missing portion, was scored with several long, narrow grooves. The lines reminded Simon of the gouges he had found on trees while hiking through Yosemite Park; gouges made by the massive claws of a bear marking its territory.

Only the damage to the casket had not been done by any bear. Bears did not burrow underground and break into concrete burial vaults. These claw marks were made by something much more dangerous. Something that was not simply marking its territory.

Angling the light so he could see more easily into the damaged coffin, Simon discovered only strips of pink satin lining inside. The container was empty. The body inside had been removed.

"Aces," he muttered to himself. "Simply aces."

Simon turned off the flashlight and climbed out of the hole. As he brushed dirt from the legs of his suit pants, he gazed around, searching for the head groundskeeper. He waved the man over.

"Fill it in, Martin. Make it nice and neat. By tomorrow, I don't want anyone to be able to tell we were ever here. I'll notify the family of the court order, but if they come to visit, I don't want them to see any reminders that we had to go in."

The groundskeeper nodded his understanding and began barking orders to his people to repair the site.

"Simon?" asked Dot. "What did you see?"

"Nothing," he told her. When he saw the relieved look on her face, he shook his head. "No. I mean there wasn't anything there. The body was removed."

"Then it's...,"

"Yeah. It looks like Jorge was right. I'm heading back to my office. Can you please call Alyssandra and have her come talk to me as soon as she can? We need her help, and it can't wait."

Alyssandra Freid, leader of one of the three local witch covens, sat in a guest chair in front of Simon's desk. Her legs were crossed at the knees, and one raised foot bounced in agitation. She did not appear at all pleased to be in the chief's office.

Alyssandra was a dark-skinned, slender woman, all angles and lean muscle. She appeared to be somewhere in her seventies, though she moved with the speed and agility of someone much younger. Her hair was a mix of black and streaks of gray, and it had been recently straightened to fall in a severe line to her shoulders. The sharp edges of her cheekbones and jaw outlined intense brown eyes and a wide mouth that currently dipped at the corners into an unhappy frown.

Behind Alyssandra's chair, Violet stood quietly, her arms crossed over her chest as she allowed the coven leader to take the lead in any conversation with the station chief. Violet wore her long black wig and had circled her eyes with thick bands of kohl, giving her already pale complexion an alabaster appearance in comparison. The only color in her face was the blood-red lipstick she used when assuming her most witchy persona.

"I do not appreciate being summoned like a lacky or pet, Lost Child," Alyssandra said petulantly. Her eyes sparkled with suppressed menace. "If it was not for the nature of your concerns, I would have refused to come at all. I do not work for you, nor have I ever been at your disposal."

"I understand your feelings, and I assure you, I did not intend this to be a summons. I was merely trying to impress upon you the urgency of what we are facing."

"Ghouls," stated Alyssandra, plainly.

"Ghouls," agreed Simon. "I have confirmation that a ghoul has raided at least one, and possibly two, graves at Dasan's Terrace. I believe we need to find it and remove it from the cemetery before it decides to make this a permanent home and attract others of its kind."

"Yes. You do seem to have a problem. What you have not established clearly, however, is how this is also *my* problem. Dasan's Terrace is your responsibility. Therefore, the ghoul is your issue to deal with. Unless of course, you are proposing to offer me something in return for my assistance."

"I am, actually. I am willing to forgive your debt in exchange for your help locating the ghoul's den."

"My debt?" Alyssandra's voice lowered dangerously. "I fail to recall a debt to you or Dead Town."

Simon frowned but did not otherwise address the unpleasant colloquialism others sometimes used to refer to the cemetery.

"We eliminated the golem that was disrupting the magic in Dasan's Terrace. Officer Mitch Loman in particular suffered great bodily injury dispatching the monster. I am willing to forgo the debt you incurred when we removed the golem for you."

"Lost Child, I believe you have overstepped. The golem was your problem to eliminate from the beginning. Your purpose is to stop crimes that are occurring in your jurisdiction, and the golem's creator was committing crimes. You were required to address that problem regardless of any impact it may have had on me or my kind. In addition, neither I nor my coven requested your assistance and therefore we cannot incur debt. Nothing was asked, so nothing is owed."

The chief leaned forward, resting his elbows on his desk and clasping his hands in front of his chin.

"How did Officer Loman discover the golem the first time? Do you remember? I'm referring to when he was knocked unconscious and hospitalized with a concussion," he said. "We didn't know the golem existed until he stumbled across it. Can you refresh my memory on exactly how he found it?"

"Alyssandra led him to it," said Violet. "She found Mitch in the cemetery and sent him after it."

Alyssandra spun in her chair and glared at Violet. Violet did not step away, although from her posture and the tension around her shoulders, she obviously wanted to. The coven leader's gaze could be as cold and dangerous as a fragmenting glacier, and instead of meeting that frigid stare, Violet looked toward Chief Jefferson. She pressed her lips tightly together, knowing it was best if she went back to playing the silent observer in the room.

After a moment, Alyssandra straightened in her seat, returning her attention to Simon. She smiled, visibly changing tactics.

"Perhaps, I should reconsider the role I may, or may not, have played in your elimination of the golem. But even so, if – and I stress the word *if* – our interference could be misconstrued as a request for aid, the debt we would have incurred would be to Officer Loman, not to you, or the department as a whole."

Simon nodded in agreement. "I agree. That seems fair. Then let me instead propose this trade. If you and your coven assist in locating the ghoul so that we can remove it from Dasan's Terrace, I will assume your debt to Officer Loman. I will discharge that debt as I see fit, and you will be under no further obligation to either Mitch or anyone else employed by the police department. Would that suit you?"

Alyssandra gave one more unhappy glance toward Violet, who did not react to the silent rebuke. Then with a terse nod in Simon's direction, she assented to the offer.

"I accept those terms. Tomorrow morning, Violet and I will return to the cemetery and begin our search…"

"Tomorrow?" interrupted Simon. "Why not tonight? Why not right now? The sooner we locate the ghoul, the sooner we can start making plans to get rid of it."

"Ghouls sleep during the morning hours," said Alyssandra in explanation. "They return to their dens and go dormant for only a few hours at a time. In the afternoon and evening, the creature will be moving throughout the grounds, burrowing and creating new tunnels. As I was saying, we will return tomorrow morning. This way when we locate the ghoul, we will also have ascertained its lair."

Simon pursed his lips, still unhappy with the timing, but he grudgingly recognized the logic in the plan. "Tomorrow morning, then."

Alyssandra rose and gestured briefly toward Violet before exiting the chief's office. Simon stood with her and followed the two women into the receiving room outside. He paused beside Dot's desk and watched as the coven priestess and her second in command disappeared through the exit doors on their way toward the stairway. When the door closed behind them, Simon turned to Dot.

"I'm going to have the B-Nights team handle this on Wednesday. Reach out to them and let them know to be ready for a hunt when they come in for their next shift. Let Martin know he will need to bring the backhoe out onto the grounds again. We'll need him to excavate Wednesday night and then come back to fill the hole in before the gates open again Thursday morning."

Dot jotted a few notes to herself on a pad of paper on her desk. "I'll arrange for lights and equipment for the hunt. Do you want the usual bait?"

"Yes. And one more thing. When you talk to Mitch, tell him to come in a few minutes early and come see me. I have some things I'd like to discuss with him."

CHAPTER

4

"Is this the correct grave?"

Alyssandra held her arms folded across her chest, huddled against the chill in the air. The days had been uncomfortably warm recently and neither she nor Violet had expected they would be underdressed even at this early hour. They were both garbed for more temperate surroundings and the sudden dip in temperature was an unwelcome surprise.

Neither complained about the conditions, however. They would probably be out wandering the cemetery for a while, and before long, any discomfort from the cold would be a fond memory. Of the choices available, they were better off braving the early frost than having to sweat through heavier, uncomfortable clothing later in the day.

Violet followed Alyssandra's pointing finger to the name on the nearby headstone. Shading her eyes from the sun where it hovered low on the horizon in the eastern sky, she bent over to read the engraved name. As she did, she retrieved a slip of paper from the pocket of her jeans. The names on the paper and the stone matched. The brand-new sod covering the grave was further evidence that this was the location of a recently excavated and repaired burial site.

"I believe so," Violet told Alyssandra, tucking the note back into her pocket. "This should be where the ghoul stole its last body.

The two women positioned themselves on either side of the grave and closed their eyes. Violet let her awareness drift down into the soil below her to search for the flow of magic underground. Sensing the unformed power's movement as it passed through rock, dirt, and pockets of air, she viewed the hidden terrain through her mind's eye as clearly as if she were searching with modern sonar equipment.

Seven feet down into the earth, a narrow tunnel connected to the disturbed gravesite. The burrow trailed away from their location to the north.

"I feel it," said Violet, and pointed along the path of the tunnel.

Alyssandra nodded her agreement. "I have it, as well. Let us see where this goes."

The women paced calmly north, letting the magic guide them along the correct path. They moved slowly enough that they would notice any branches or changes in direction to the tunnel without having to backtrack and relocate the trail. In this manner, their progress remained measured and steady. Anyone watching the process from a distance would assume it was merely two visitors to the cemetery taking a leisurely morning stroll through the grounds.

With little idea how long their search might take, they chatted as they worked to pass the time.

"Did you check on the new girl in Missy's coven as I asked?" said Alyssandra.

Michelle Eaton, or Missy as she preferred to be known, was the leader of one of two rival covens in Sacramento County. Missy and the members of her group had no real power and were seen by most of the paranormal community in the area as pretenders and wannabes. No one worried too much about them as their lack of magical ability kept them from becoming any kind of threat. Until now, she and her entire bunch were largely ignored and left alone. Unfortunately, a young woman by the name of Tanya Kushing had recently joined the ranks of Missy's coven, and rumors suggested the new member did have real talent.

"I visited with her this weekend."

"Who? Missy, or the girl?"

"The girl," Violet clarified. "Tanya. I did a few simple tests on her and discovered she has promise. Even though she has no formal training, she can see and manipulate magic on an instinctual level. She's strong. Not as strong as Willa or Gabby, but perhaps a bit more ability than Rachelle," said Violet, comparing the new witch to members of their own coven.

"Did you manage to recruit her, then?"

"No. I didn't offer. I only wanted to talk to her, get a feel for how much power she has. I can go back and speak more seriously with her later."

"Do that," said Alyssandra. "If Missy complains, I'll offer to trade her one of ours for this Tanya girl. We don't need fourteen members in our group. It's an unlucky number."

"Trade?" asked Violet. "Who are we going to trade?"

"Any of the bottom five will do. They can't see magic, and barely have enough force of will to contribute to a circle. It will be a good trade up for us."

Violet strolled a few more paces in silence as she digested Alyssandra's statement. It did not feel right to her to discard one of their own so easily, but she also knew she needed to be careful about challenging Alyssandra. The coven leader was already upset that Violet had supported Chief Jefferson's claim that the witches owed Mitch a debt for defeating the golem, she did not need to get any deeper into the woman's bad graces.

Still, she felt she should say something on behalf of the lower ranked witches.

"Don't you think it's a bit callous to kick someone out of the coven? I mean, couldn't we keep all fourteen members, but only use thirteen for ceremonies? Like sports teams, we could have someone in reserve for times of emergency."

Alyssandra snorted derisively. "Thirteen is a power number. We stay at thirteen."

"We teach our witches a lot of things the other covens don't. Even the women who can barely manipulate magic have a great deal of advanced training."

"And?" asked Alyssandra, failing to see Violet's concern.

"If the person we trade to Missy is angry about being kicked out, she could teach Missy's coven a lot more real magic than they have now. She might even give the others enough skill to become a problem later. Maybe it would be better to let Missy keep Tanya. At least for now."

"No." Alyssandra stopped walking and Violet paused beside her. The coven leader turned a speculative eye on her second in command. "If Tanya has real ability, as you believe she does, we need to get her on our side. Chang'e is probably also aware of her and will be making plans to recruit her as well. If Tanya is not one of us, she will soon be a threat. Certainly more so than some powerless witch with a grudge against me because she wasn't strong enough to keep her position in the coven. Approach Tanya. Show her what we can offer if she comes to us."

Alyssandra began moving once more, following the path of the underground tunnel. "Chang'e is a problem. She will only become a greater problem if she manages to claim Tanya before we do."

"I agree, but–"

"Stop. No more." Alyssandra slashed her hand through the air in emphasis. "Speak with Tanya. Convince her to join us. Let me worry about how we will make room to fit her into this coven. Am I clear?"

"Of course. I understand."

Violet did not like the idea of losing a coven member, especially since she considered them to be more than merely acquaintances or friends. To Violet, the coven was closer to a family than a group or gathering that could casually cast away its own people. In fact, they were the only family she had known for many years. The only family she had had since...

She shook the dark thoughts away. Alyssandra had made up her mind, and if Violet had learned one thing about the older woman since joining her so long ago, it was that no amount of discussion or argument would change her plans once she had made a decision.

"Left," said Alyssandra, with a gesture of her left hand.

"What? Oh, yes."

Violet felt the tunnel veer to the left and adjusted her direction to follow it.

"How is your Officer Loman progressing?" asked Alyssandra, changing the topic of the conversation.

"He is getting much better. He learns fast and doesn't mind that I push him. Last week, as we discussed, I began expanding his training from strictly magic to teaching him how to see souls. It's time he learned to control his exorcism abilities."

"You think he's ready?"

"I think if I don't start teaching him to control his gifts, he's going to practice them without me and get himself hurt or killed. I started by teaching him how to see souls. We haven't gotten much further than that so far."

Alyssandra stroked a finger across her lips as she considered the information. "Has he looked into your soul?" she asked, speculatively.

"Not deeply. He is only learning how to see them at the moment, not how to read them."

"But he will discover that little trick rather quickly, don't you think? Once he knows how to find the soul, peering more deeply will come naturally, whether you instruct him or not."

"Yes."

"So, what happens when he gets a look at you? I mean a truly deep, considered look."

Violet shrugged, trying to appear less concerned than she actually felt. "It will be fine. He will see what he sees. He'll know I have been honest with him."

"Honest?" Alyssandra laughed at the word. "There is nothing honest about you. All I want to know is whether you believe you can continue to control him, or if you think he might try to break away from us."

"It will be fine," Violet promised a second time, still hiding her discomfort at the idea of Mitch seeing her for who she truly was. "I won't lose him."

"See that you don't," Alyssandra ordered. The harshness in her voice made it clear she expected to be obeyed. "One uncontrolled witch in our midst is bad enough. We do not need another."

Violet, unhappy with where her own thoughts were going, pushed the conversation in a new direction. "I was thinking it might be time to show him how to do an exorcism. On purpose, this time. He needs to know how to control the ability, to keep himself safe from the spirits he comes into contact with."

"I have no objection to that. How will you do it?"

The two women stopped walking. They had both noticed the tunnel they followed had ended, dumping into a new burrow that ran perpendicular to the one they had been tracking. The new path ran left and right, and Violet's senses could not detect an ending in either direction.

"Left, or right?" asked Violet. "Or do we split up?"

"No. Go left. If we find nothing, we return and try the right."

They turned left and continued their trek through the cemetery. After a few moments of silent tracking, Alyssandra spoke again.

"How will you do it?"

"Do what? Oh, yes. Train Mitch," Violet said, remembering the earlier conversation. "I know two families who are in possession of haunted items. One lives in San Jose and reached out to me because they have a ghost connected to something in their living room. They aren't sure what object is causing the haunting, but from what they tell me, I believe it's only an echo they're dealing with. Easy enough to remove."

"And the other?"

"The other family runs a small bookstore in Carmel. They picked up a poltergeist when they purchased a rare book recently. Both have asked me to come do exorcisms. I think these would be good opportunities to teach Mitch."

"I agree," said Alyssandra. "But, out of curiosity, why doesn't the family with the bookstore simply get rid of the possessed book?"

Violet smiled. "I suggested the same thing. Apparently, the poltergeist is smarter than most. It stole the book and hid it somewhere. They can't find it, much less get rid of it."

"That does sound like a problem," Alyssandra agreed. "May I ask, how did these people know to reach out to you? The more people that know about your abilities, the more danger exists that the wrong ears will hear your name."

"I know. Both families talked to someone I helped a few years ago. Do you remember Eugene?"

"The boy whose mother died, but she wouldn't leave the house because she was afraid he wouldn't take care of it? I remember him. I also remember I told you not to get involved with that one."

"You did, and you were right, as usual. The mother was a real bitch to get rid of. Anyway, since then, Eugene developed a new hobby to keep himself occupied. He decided to become a ghost hunter."

Alyssandra laughed, an unpleasant cackle deep in the back of her throat.

"Yes," Violet continued after the interruption. "He likes to investigate ghosts and reports of paranormal activity. He found these two hauntings, and surprisingly they turned out to be legitimate. He didn't tell the people my name, or even where I am. He reached out to me himself and asked if I would be interested in contacting them. Until now, I've told him no. With Mitch to train, though, I'm thinking I will say yes this time."

"Do what you think best. Minimize witnesses, of course. Perhaps you should wear your wig. Use a false name, or ... wait. The tunnel."

The burrow came to an abrupt end. At ground level, where Violet and Alyssandra stood, they found themselves beside another grave. The headstone announced the man buried in that location had died only a few months ago.

Violet knelt and placed her hands in the grass, pressing her fingers against the soil in an attempt to "see" the terrain beneath her more clearly. She let the magic guide her senses as she searched the grave vault and coffin buried a half dozen feet down.

"The vault is damaged," she said to Alyssandra as she watched the magic flow through the unexpected gap in the concrete. "And the coffin ... is broken. It's empty."

Violet stood, wiping the grass and dew from her hands onto the legs of her jeans.

"The ghoul was here. It fed and left. There's no way to know if this happened before or after the other grave was emptied."

"Nor does it matter," said Alyssandra. "What matters is we still have searching to do. We will go back to where we found this tunnel and try following it to the right. Let us see where that direction leads."

CHAPTER

5

Mitch arrived at the police department on Wednesday evening for his first shift back following his long weekend. After changing into his uniform and buckling on his gear belt, he headed for the top floor of the P.D. building to meet with the chief as he had been directed to do by the chief's administrative assistant. Dot had been most insistent on his attendance, and he was curious what Chief Jefferson wanted to tell him. It was an abstract curiosity at best, however, since most of his thoughts, as they had all week, remained fixated on other concerns.

Even the prospect of the job his team would be performing later that night did not completely distract him from the obsessive questions circling in his head. He was about to embark on a ghoul hunt – an actual fucking ghoul hunt – something he had not even believed could be real only five months ago, and still Mitch could only peripherally focus on that remarkable idea.

Where was Violet, he wondered for the thousandth time. *And why was she avoiding him?* He was stuck like a hormonal teenager fixated on his first crush. He did not like this feeling, but his displeasure did nothing to change the fact that he had spent his entire weekend hanging out at home, eating cold leftovers out of the fridge, and wondering when Violet would call him.

They had not seen each other since their training session last Wednesday, and while they did not typically get together every day, they usually met at least once or twice on his days off. These last several days, however, she suddenly did not seem overly eager to see him.

Violet was not completely avoiding him, he had to admit. She had answered the phone both times Mitch had reached out to her, but when he suggested they meet for dinner, or see a movie, she demurred with vague references to "coven business."

Had he said or done something last week that upset her? Mitch could not think of anything that would account for Violet's current behavior, but that didn't mean it was not in some way still his fault. His ex-wife had frequently been mad at him for things he did not recall doing, or for things he had not done that she felt he should have. Had she been right all along?

Was that it? Had he forgotten something, and now Violet was angry at his forgetfulness?

Mitch took a deep breath and chuffed it out, trying to clear his head. He was getting nowhere by chasing the same circle of destructive thoughts he had pursued all week. As he climbed the stairs of the police building, he forced his mind to focus on more immediate matters.

The chief wanted to talk to him. He did not think he was in any kind of trouble. Mitch could not think of anything he had done that would require disciplinary action from the top of the department food chain, so he was not particularly worried about the meeting. Then again, he also had no idea why Violet would not talk to him, so his judgement could easily be in question here, too.

Dot refused to explain why he was being ordered to the chief's office, but Mitch was pretty sure she would have given him some warning if there was a problem.

Wouldn't she?

Maybe something good was actually happening. The chief might have great news for him today. He hoped that was the case. It would be a nice change of pace given some of the crap that he had been forced to deal with over the past several years. His divorce, almost getting fired, the death of his son, and that wasn't even including almost getting murdered by a rampaging golem last month.

Good or bad, Mitch would know soon enough.

Reaching the top floor of the building, he placed his hand against the door leading into the administrative offices and pushed it open.

As he stepped through the doorway into the administrative lobby, he saw Dot sitting at her desk, typing furiously on her computer keyboard while frowning at her monitor. The chief stood behind her, peering over her right shoulder. Chief Jefferson pointed at the monitor, jabbing his finger at something repeatedly while muttering something Mitch did not catch.

Mitch cleared his throat to announce himself, and Dot glanced up from her task. She smiled happily when she saw him, while the chief continued to glare at her computer.

"Mitchell. Hi. Just give us one second please while we finish a little bit of housekeeping."

"Dot, forget the e-mail," said the chief with a frustrated wave of his hand. "There's too much detail to try to write it all down. Set up a meeting. This will be easier if we have a face-to-face conversation anyway. The Emissary didn't say when he would be back, but I'd like to have an answer for him when he does."

"Meeting. Check."

Dot jotted a note to herself on a pad of paper, then gestured for Mitch to approach.

The chief's expression finally relaxed, and he too smiled at Mitch.

"Sorry about that. I'm juggling a few too many things at the moment, and I don't want to let any balls drop."

"No problem, Chief," assured Mitch. "I can come back another time if…,"

"No, no, no. Now is fine. I have something for you, Mitch. I wanted to hand it to you personally, not simply pass it along through Jorge."

Chief Jefferson reached into an inside pocket of his suit coat. His hand came back out holding a blue, laminated card. Mitch could see it was a Dasan's Terrace Police identification card, and it had his face on the front. The chief set it on Dot's desk and slid it toward him.

This was odd. He did not reach for the card right away as he tried to figure out the significance of the item. Mitch already had an I.D. card. It had been issued to him the day he started his new assignment at DTPD. Confused, but not wanting to offend the chief, he stretched out a hand to pick it up. Mitch paused again, withdrawing his hand when he at last saw the words written beside his photograph. Instead of "Police Officer," as was printed on his current identification, this one said, "Police Detective."

"Sir?" he asked, unsure how to respond.

"I've decided to promote you back to the rank of detective. With the work you did on the golem murder, I think you earned it. Besides, we have never had a detective assigned to this department, and I think it is long overdue."

"Thank you, but ... my disciplinary findings said I couldn't be a detective anymore."

Before being recruited into DTPD, Mitch had been under investigation for dereliction of duty. The charge was largely motivated by his old detective lieutenant's personal dislike of Mitch, but the Internal Investigation's review of the charges could have easily led to him being fired. Mitch had been lucky merely to lose his detective rank.

"The findings required that you be stripped of your position as detective. That was done. There was nothing in the final recommendations that said you could not be reinstated at some future date. I am exercising my prerogative as Chief of Dasan's Terrace and promoting you back to your previous position."

Chief Jefferson smiled again and shrugged his shoulders ruefully. "Of course, you will still have to work night shift, and I expect you to continue to fulfill all of your patrol duties as before. Working any additional cases will need to be supplemental to your current assignment. Oh, and any overtime you work will need to be directly approved through me."

"So, nothing changes except my title."

"You get a five percent raise with the promotion," said the chief.

"I'll take it!" announced Mitch, snatching the I.D. card from the desk and slipping it into his shirt pocket.

"Congratulations, Mitchell," said Dot. "I'm very happy for you."

"Good," said Chief Jefferson. "That's settled then. I will let Alyssandra know that her debt to you has been paid. Dot has already ordered you a new badge with a detective's banner. It should be here in a couple weeks. You can head back down to briefing. You've got a long night ahead of you and Jorge needs to get everyone ready for the hunt."

Mitch almost turned to leave, but the chief's words suddenly penetrated his euphoria over the five percent raise. "Wait … what? What debt are you talking about?"

"It's okay, son. It's not a big deal. Alyssandra sent you after the golem. Although she did not expressly ask you for help, she is directly responsible for putting you in the creature's way. As such, she owes you a debt for removing the golem from the cemetery grounds. I recently needed her help and used that for leverage. In exchange for her assistance locating the ghoul in our cemetery, I advised her that I would discharge her debt to you."

Mitch stood silently for several long seconds, trying to sort through the mixed feelings swimming in his head. Finally, he reached into his shirt pocket and removed the detective's I.D. He placed the card back on Dot's desk.

"I can't accept this, sir," he said reluctantly. "I don't want to be promoted because you feel that you owe me something. I don't want anyone else saying I only got the assignment to pay off a debt. Tell Alyssandra whatever you like. I never thought she owed me anything anyway, so you can let her know that she and the department are square. When I finally do get my detective badge back though, I want it to be because you honestly believe I deserved it, and because you thought it was the best thing to do for this department."

"Pick up the I.D.," the chief said solemnly. "You're right, and I apologize, Mitch. I've handled this whole thing very badly. You deserve to be a detective. You earned it. I honestly feel it should never have been taken from you in the first place, and I *do* believe it is the best thing for me and this department. I was trying to take the easy way out by doing the right thing and at the same time discharging the debt I accepted from Alyssandra."

Chief Jefferson gestured toward the detective's I.D. card. "That belongs to you. No one can dispute your right to it. I will simply have to find another way – a legitimate way – to meet my debt to you."

Mitch retrieved the card and returned it to his pocket. "Thank you, sir. That means a lot to me. And you really don't owe me anything. Like I said, there wasn't any debt."

"There was," the chief said. "And I will make it right. I just need to figure out the proper way to balance our books."

"I told you," Dot said to Chief Jefferson. Her voice was soft, but Mitch heard her, nonetheless.

"You did," the chief replied with a bemused nod. He looked toward Mitch again. "Go on. You need to get to briefing ... detective."

Mitch grinned. He liked the sound of the title. He was a bit surprised, now that he was hearing it again, how much he had missed it when it was taken away.

A new thought occurred to him.

"Sir? If you insist on balancing the books like you said, I think I might have an idea how you can pay your debt to me."

Chief Jefferson's eyebrows raised, and he replied cautiously, "Yes? How might I do that?"

"I'm not sure if I can do anything to help Lieutenant Delaney, but I would like to try. Chief, for my first case as a newly reinstated detective, I would like permission to re-open his homicide investigation. Will you let me pull his file?"

The chief and Dot glanced toward one another. Chief Jefferson merely seemed surprised by the request, while his administrative assistant looked deeply concerned.

"Technically, the case was never closed since no suspect was identified," said the chief, still looking at Dot. He turned to meet Mitch's gaze. "Okay. Contact Homicide and ask them to hand over all files they have on Timothy's murder. Dot will send them an email tonight to let them know you are acting on my authority. I'm not certain I should be allowing this, but if this is what you want, I will consider my debt to you paid in full."

"Thank you, sir. I'll reach out to them tomorrow morning."

Mitch pivoted on his heel and marched out of the lobby, heading downstairs to meet his team for briefing.

As the door closed behind Mitch, Dot shook her head and placed a hand on Simon's arm.

"Do you think that was a good idea? That case hasn't had a new lead in thirty years. You even looked into it yourself right before you were promoted to chief. You told me it would probably never be solved."

"I know what I told you," said Simon. "I still believe that, but maybe Mitch will manage to turn up something no one else has. Maybe we'll get lucky this time."

"Simon. He's going to hit the same brick walls everyone else has. You know that. And when Tim finds out...." Dot did not finish her thought.

"He doesn't need to find out, not right away at least. Don't worry about it, I'll talk to Tim when I think the time is right. A debt is a debt, and this is what Mitch wanted."

Dot sighed. She let her hand drop back into her lap.

"Okay. I understand why you did it, but when Tim goes full-on poltergeist again because another investigation has failed, don't forget...,"

"Yes, I know. You told me so. Again."

Mitch stood at the edge of the open pit, looking down into the shadowy darkness. The groundskeepers finished digging the hole several hours ago, then they had all left to go home and get some sleep. They knew they would be coming back early in the morning to repair the damage the ghoul hunt created and to get the cemetery fit to receive any visitors that might arrive later in the day, so they had wasted no time hanging around when they were given permission to leave.

The ghoul's lair was currently empty, but that was to be expected. Even if the creature had been here when the digging started, the commotion of the tractors ripping the roof off of its earthen home would have driven it scurrying into the surrounding tunnels. That was why the hole had been opened so early. Jorge wanted enough time to pass for the ghoul to calm down. If it was still running away, frightened by the noise, it would not return even when the team deployed the bait.

Under the wan starlight, the hole in the ground appeared as a black patch in the center of lighter gray surroundings. Spotlights had been erected at three locations, all angled toward the open pit, but so far the artificial lighting remained off. When the time came to activate the lights, they could be powered with the push of a button on a handheld remote; a remote that at present hung attached to Jorge's equipment belt. With only a sliver of moon in the sky overhead, the cemetery in this area of the grounds was abnormally dark. Only a pale glare from a few distant path lights reached Mitch and the other officers.

Mitch stroked his left palm over the smooth metal pommel of a machete dangling from his hip. Tink and Jorge carried similar weapons, while Brad had the ever-present katana strapped to his back. Edged weapons were going to be the tool of the day, and the sergeant had made sure everyone was equipped properly before they left the police department. Ghouls were notoriously difficult to kill, and bullets or other projectile weapons were not capable of doing the job effectively.

In addition to the blades on their persons, Jorge and Brad held crossbows in their hands. The crossbows were specially outfitted with cranks and reels, and a heavy-duty nylon line that attached to the bolt loaded into the arrow track of the weapon. The bolt itself had jointed metal blades at the head that would fold against the shaft as they penetrated into a target, then spring outward to prevent the projectile from pulling loose. This allowed the arrow to stay planted in whatever it hit, and the crossbow could then be used like a fishing rod to reel in the user's intended prey.

In this instance, that prey would be the errant ghoul rampaging through the cemetery and desecrating gravesites.

"Does everyone understand their jobs?" asked Jorge. The team was ready and responded in the affirmative. "Good. Brad and I have done this once before, so we'll take lead. Mitch and Tink, you guys are backup if anything goes sideways. Keep on your toes."

"Ready for the bait?" asked Brad.

"Dump it," directed Jorge.

A large plastic bin, the size of a residential bathtub, rested at the edge of the pit. The bin was covered by a flat lid with clasps that snapped down to create an airtight seal. Brad circled around the sides of the container, popping the fasteners loose. They released with loud, echoing snaps of metal on plastic. When the lid came free, he lifted it and tossed it to the side.

A thick, gamey smell filled the air. Mitch threw an arm across his face, trying to shield his sensitive nose from the sharp reek attacking him, while simultaneously attempting not to vomit. He coughed, gagging once before he could bring himself under control.

"Dear God," he moaned. What the hell is in there?"

"Horse guts," Jorge said. The sergeant spat into the grass several times, attempting to remove an unpleasant taste from his mouth. "Several days old, too. We got it from a rendering plant on Keifer Road. They have tons of the stuff, and don't mind giving up a small amount every now and then."

Brad used his foot to shove the bin forward, toppling the container and its noxious contents into the dark recesses of the hole. Mitch did not see the offal hit the bottom of the pit, but he certainly heard it. The wet squelch, followed by a heavier gust of the fetid smell, caused him to gag a second time. Fortunately, he managed to keep his dinner in his unhappy stomach where it belonged.

"Now we wait," said the sergeant. "I don't want to scare it away, so no talking until the ghoul shows up."

"How long is this going to take?"

"What part of no talking are you struggling to understand, Tink?" asked Jorge.

"You know Tink isn't very smart," interjected Brad. "He only knows a couple of words, and most of those are related to food."

Jorge sighed. "I don't know how long. It depends on how far away the ghoul is and if it's hungry. If it doesn't show up in two hours, we'll start taking shifts watching the pit until morning, then fill it back in. Now please, all of you, shut up."

Mitch considered making a stupid comment about how good he was at shutting up but thought better of it and kept his mouth closed. Besides, the smell of offal was bad enough as he breathed the particulates through his nose. He definitely did not want any more of that noxious miasma in his mouth, or going unfiltered directly into his lungs.

Mitch settled himself in a comfortable position on the ground, crossed his legs beneath him, and watched the inky blackness of the hole. He was not sure what might happen next, but he figured if the ghoul emerged tonight, it would have to come at them through the excavated pit.

Tink had the same idea, sitting down on his side of the hole. Mitch saw Tink's face suddenly illuminated with a pale blue light as his partner decided to kill time by doing something on his cellphone. Mitch stayed focused on the opening in front of him. He had never faced a ghoul before, and he had no idea how quickly the creature could come at them from the depths of its damaged lair. He wanted to be ready.

In the darkness nearby, he could see the shadowy silhouettes of Brad and Jorge. Jorge was pacing nervously a few steps back and forth as they all waited for the ghoul to arrive.

The minutes ticked by uneventfully, and after a while, boredom began to set in. Even the possibility of a ghoul popping up in their midst at any moment began to lose its immediacy. Staying alert over long periods of time was difficult, especially with nothing else happening to keep the mind stimulated.

Mitch let his gaze wander from the pit and up to the narrow crescent of the new moon in the sky. He tried to calculate by the moon's positioning exactly how long he had been waiting beside this open hole in the cemetery. It did not seem to have moved much. With a shrug, he slipped his own cellphone out of his pocket and tapped the screen. The time display lit up and Mitch saw they had only been here about forty-five minutes. He had at least another hour and fifteen minutes of sentry duty before Jorge would consider letting anyone take a break. The idea of another hour sitting quietly in the dirt, without being able to even hold a conversation to break up the monotony, felt like an eternity yawning in front of him.

Mitch tapped his phone again. Maybe he had some new emails to read. That would kill two or three minutes while he sat here, and it was better than letting his thoughts wander aimlessly. Particularly since they always seemed to circle back to… Nope! He could deal with Violet and the status of their relationship later.

One monster at a time.

He found two new emails. The first he deleted unread as it was an obvious bit of spam. As he swiped his finger across the screen, sending the unwanted message to the trash file, Mitch heard a soft squishing sound. He held his phone to his right ear, confused as to why the phone had made such an odd noise. The sound repeated, and he realized with a start that the squelch had not come from his phone at all. It had come from somewhere down in the darkness of the pit. Something was moving down there.

Mitch jumped to his feet, stuffing his cellphone back into his pocket to free his hands. He grasped the handle of his machete but did not draw the weapon. His job right now was simply to remain alert and ready to assist if needed. He stared into the darkness at his feet, peering into the nothingness so intently that his mind began to play tricks on him. He imagined shapes forming and dissipating in the murky gloom when in truth he knew he could not see anything at the bottom of that hole.

He closed his eyes, shutting out the false images and focusing instead on trying to hear any activity down below. Another soft squishing noise reached his ears. There was something in the pit, moving slowly, cautiously, through the spill of horse intestines. The noises paused, then were followed by a new series of sounds. It took Mitch a moment to recognize what he was hearing. It was the sound of … chewing.

The ghoul had stumbled onto the offered bait and was now settling in for a midnight meal.

Bile rose to the back of Mitch's throat, and he was forced to swallow the bitter wad of sick. If he spat the nasty taste out now, the noise might startle their target and send it scurrying back into the series of surrounding tunnels. Once it bolted, they would not get another chance tonight to catch it.

There was a soft click from somewhere to Mitch's left and the spotlights around the pit flared into life. The sudden illumination dazzled his dark-adapted eyes. Mitch squinted and blinked as he struggled to see through the harsh glare.

At the bottom of the hole, something human shaped was on its hands and knees, its face buried in a pile of rotting animal guts. The creature was naked, its exposed flesh a pallid gray color in the beams of the spotlights. It was thin, and Mitch could see the bones of its spine and ribcage bulging outward against the thing's bare skin.

It was the ghoul. It had to be. Mitch had never seen one of the creatures before, but there was absolutely nothing else that this could be.

The ghoul reacted to the light, covering its face with its hands and hissing angrily. Mitch thought it might try to run, but it remained in place, peering between protective fingers as it shifted its gaze from light source to light source in startled confusion. It hissed again and rose to its feet.

"Brad, take the shot," ordered Jorge, raising his own crossbow to his shoulder.

Brad did not hesitate. Although his own eyes had to be stinging and watering from the bright lights, he showed no signs of disorientation as he leveled his weapon and carefully aimed for the distraught ghoul below him.

The crossbow fired with an audible *zswip!* as the drawn string sent the seated bolt flying. Mitch watched the released arrow zip through the air with its nylon tether trailing behind, streaking toward the ghoul.

The razor tips of the arrowhead cut through the ghoul, punching into its back and emerging from the emaciated ribcage in its chest. After confirming his shot had found its target, Brad began cranking the reel's handle, pulling the line taut.

The ghoul did not seem to notice the crossbow bolt impaling it. Instead, it continued to hiss and growl at the overhead lights. The creature only realized it had been shot when it felt the cord attached to the arrow begin to pull it toward Brad. Before it could react to this new development, Jorge fired his weapon, this time sending a bolt into the ghoul's chest and out through the back. The sergeant went to work on his own reel, taking all the slack out of his line and leaving the creature pinned between the two tethers.

"Keep reeling!" shouted Jorge.

Brad and the sergeant pulled at their lines and reeled in the competing cables one agonizingly slow inch at a time. They looked like two sports fishermen trying to land an eight-hundred-pound marlin. Worse than that, they stood on opposite sides of the pit and were both trying to reel in the same fish. As they fought, the tethers pulled tighter and tighter until the ghoul was lifted off its feet and held dangling near the top of the pit.

"Tink! Come here," ordered Brad, panting with effort. "Take the bow and keep it tight."

Tink took the proffered weapon. The sudden tension in his hands pulled him an awkward step forward, toward the edge of the pit. He stuck out a booted foot and braced himself, regaining his balance and managing to shuffle one step back. The ghoul rose in the air another few inches.

Brad drew his katana. The razor-edged blade flashed under the glare of the spotlights.

"Okay, I'm ready," he announced. "Sarge, bring the little guy out of the pit so I can start carving."

The ghoul thrashed helplessly in the air. Several times it swiped clawed fingers at the lines holding it, but the sturdy nylon held. The creature screeched, a shrill, childlike cry of distress. Jorge began moving to his left, bringing the suspended ghoul toward Brad, who waited with his sword held at his side.

Another screech pierced the air, but it did not come from the ghoul pinned between Jorge and Tink. Mitch searched for the source of the new noise, and when he found it, he froze, uncertain what to do next. At the bottom of the hole, a second ghoul had emerged from a side tunnel. The new monster, upon seeing its companion hanging in the air above it, rushed to one wall of the pit and buried its claws in the soft earth. It pulled itself upward, climbing toward open air and the men attacking its fellow subterranean dweller.

"Brad! There's another one," shouted Mitch. "It's coming up the side toward you. It's almost to the top."

Jorge stopped moving. He and Tink held the first ghoul in place, allowing Brad to focus on the unexpected arrival. Brad leaped backward, putting some room between himself and the top edge of the pit. He waited with his katana in hand as the second ghoul emerged. The creature pulled itself forward, dragging its body out of the hole and into full view of all four officers.

On its stomach, the ghoul slithered like a snake toward Brad, then pushed to its hands and knees. Brad chose that moment to attack. He lunged forward, raising the katana over his head. As he reached the ghoul struggling to its feet, he slashed the sword downward, striking the creature through the neck. The katana's blade passed through desiccated skin, flesh, and bone in a single sweeping arc, cleaving the monster's head from its body.

The head struck the ground and rolled awkwardly past Brad's feet, but the ghoul's body continued climbing to its feet. Blind and deaf, the headless nightmare continued trying to reach Brad, swiping its taloned hands wildly through the air in an effort to find its attacker. Brad did not shy away. The sword moved again, this time separating the ghoul's right hand from its wrist. Still the creature refused to die or give up its attempts to catch the person who was cutting it to pieces.

These creatures really were resilient, thought Mitch. How was it still alive with no head?

Everyone's attention was on Brad and his duel with the headless ghoul. The first ghoul, still suspended in the air between Jorge and Tink was now largely forgotten. Mitch was so enthralled by the spectacle in front of him that he failed to notice the head of yet another creature poking above the edge of the pit closest to him. His first warning that he was in imminent danger was an angry hiss as the third monster dragged itself to the surface right at his feet.

"Fuck! There's another one. Mitch, watch out!" Tink was the first to see the new threat, but his warning came too late.

Instinctively, from years of emergency drills on the range, Mitch drew his service pistol and fired three quick shots at the approaching ghoul. All three shots found their target, but the gray creature crawling toward him did not so much as flinch as gobbets of gray flesh erupted from its body.

"Watch your crossfire," shouted Jorge. "Mitch, put the gun away."

"Shit!" muttered Mitch, jamming his weapon back into its holster. He had been warned that bullets would not be effective, but he had panicked and simply reacted to the danger with the first thing that came to mind. In doing so, he had also put his partners at risk of being hit with a stray round.

Mitch danced backward two steps to give himself a little more distance and time. He grabbed the machete at his belt. When the blade came free of its sheath, he swung the heavy weapon at the creature. His attack was too slow. The ghoul charged much faster than Mitch anticipated, moving with a speed he did not think should be possible from such a scraggly, wasted figure.

The thing lurched forward, leaping from a low crouch directly into Mitch's chest. His machete swung harmlessly, cutting empty air behind the ghoul's back.

The weight of the creature knocked Mitch off his feet, and the two went crashing to the ground with the furious ghoul landing on top. The impact drove the air from Mitch's lungs. White-hot pain erupted from his injured ribs. He wheezed as he tried ineffectually to draw another breath, but his lungs stubbornly refused to refill. The creature remained on top of him, and Mitch knew he did not have the luxury to wait until his diaphragm stopped spasming before dealing with the threat perched on his chest. The ghoul bared filthy, yellow teeth and leaned forward, preparing to take a bite out of his face.

Mitch grabbed the creature by the throat with his left hand, trying to hold it away from its intended target. The writhing ghoul continued to push closer, snapping its jaws open and closed in a frustrated frenzy.

Damn, but the thing was strong. Its teeth continued to inch closer despite his attempts to keep them at bay. The creature's fetid breath washed over Mitch's face, somehow overpowering even the stench of rotting horse flesh still circulating in the air.

Mitch dropped his right arm to his side and angled the machete so it pointed at the ghoul's torso. He rammed the blade forward, feeling it meet flesh and pierce the tough, leathery skin. The point of the weapon found an opening between two ribs and sank deep. The skeletal monster screeched and twisted, jerking the blade from Mitch's hand as it thrashed.

Reacting to being stabbed, the ghoul turned away from Mitch's face and attacked his right hand. He did not have time to pull away or defend the extended limb, and the rotting teeth of the beast fastened on his forearm. Mitch felt cracked yellow fangs pierce his flesh, and a new pain streaked up his arm, exploding in his head.

"Mitch!" called Jorge when he saw the ghoul biting down on Mitch's arm. "Hang on!"

Jorge dropped his crossbow and ran toward Mitch. The ghoul trapped between Jorge and Tink fell back into the pit, dragging the abandoned weapon with it. Tink held on to the remaining line, too far away to help Mitch, and unwilling to let the snared ghoul escape.

Brad, in the meantime, remained focused on his fight with his own ghoul. He had already removed both of the monster's legs, its head, and one arm, and still the body continued to struggle towards him.

Mitch did not hear Jorge. He had no idea if, or when, help might come his way. All he knew was the pain of the creature biting down on his arm. The ghoul's teeth sank deep and were now putting pressure on the bones of his forearm. At any moment, the monster's relentless bite would break his arm.

He cried out in pain and terror. He could not reach any of his weapons, and he did not have the strength to push the ghoul away. In a last, desperate attempt to break free, he pulled at the ambient magic around him. His panic gave him strength, and the magic came to him faster than it had ever come before. A glowing aura of power grew around his left hand, and he pressed his palm to the ghoul's chest.

With no time to form a proper spell, Mitch released the magic in his palm with a raw percussive force. The ghoul screeched, releasing its hold on his arm as it was launched upward into the air by the ferocity of the magical assault. The creature arced several feet up and away from Mitch before plummeting back into the pit from which it had emerged.

Mitch rolled to his hands and knees and scrambled to the edge of the hole to see where the ghoul had landed. He was in time to see his attacker dive into a tunnel and disappear, the machete still buried in its side. The first ghoul tried to follow its partner, but Tink managed to pull the tether tight and keep it from escaping into the same passage. Tink was struggling to hold the creature, though, and Mitch could see the officer being pulled closer to the hole, inch by stubborn inch.

"You okay?" asked Jorge, reaching Mitch and placing a hand on his shoulder. "Did that thing injure you?"

"I'm fine," said Mitch, ignoring the pain in his arm. "Help Tink. It looks like he's going to get dragged into the pit."

Jorge nodded and raced away. With Jorge assisting Tink, and Brad busy hacking the last of his monster into small squirming chunks, Mitch tucked his injured arm against his chest and curled up on the ground. The world spun crazily around him. He allowed himself a few moments to let the pain die down and to catch his breath, knowing that the others could deal with the remaining situation. He only needed a minute, he told himself. Only a minute, then he would be able to help again.

When he was once more in control of his breathing and he felt that he could stand up without falling over, Mitch pushed to his feet. He saw Jorge and Tink reeling in the line attached to the struggling ghoul, dragging the creature up the side of the pit

89

toward them. Brad had finished with his own opponent, and now stood at the edge of the hole, waiting for the original ghoul to emerge.

Because only one of the two lines attached to the ghoul was still under control, as soon as the monster was out of the pit, it would be free to charge Jorge or Tink. Brad anticipated this problem and as soon as the creature was visible above the lip of the hole, he swung his katana, removing the top of the creature's skull from its head. Tink dragged the rest of the ghoul to the surface. It wriggled on the ground, directionless for the moment.

Before it could reorient itself and attack, Brad began systematically dismantling the ghoul into smaller pieces. First, he took the arms, then the legs, followed by several cuts to separate the torso into four sections. When he was certain there was no longer any threat, he wiped his sword with a cotton cloth he carried in a pocket for precisely this purpose, then sheathed the blade. Next, he picked up the squirming pieces of the dismembered ghoul and carried them to the pile he had made with his last victim.

Jorge, Tink and Mitch helped with the grisly chore of stacking all the ghoul parts into a single mound. One disembodied arm attempted to crawl away, dragging itself along by its clutching, gray fingers. Brad picked it up and tossed the fleeing body part back into the pile.

"I hate ghouls," Brad said, staring down at the wriggling collection of pallid ghoul chunks. "They refuse to die. It's very off-putting."

"What do we do now?" asked Tink, staring at a ghoul finger, twitching and wriggling through the grass like a pale worm. He shuddered and kicked the offending anatomy back toward the rest of the gathered parts.

"We burn it," said Jorge. "All of it. It's the only way to be sure they don't figure out a way to put themselves back together again."

"They can do that?" Mitch asked. A cold shudder ran up his spine at the idea this pile of body parts might be able to reassemble.

"They can do that. Somebody needs to grab my gear bag. I left it next to one of the light stands. I have a couple flares in there that should be able to finish this job."

"Wait," said Mitch. "Let me try something."

Mitch held out his uninjured left hand, fingers spread wide. He concentrated on the magic around him and began pulling the ambient forces into his extended palm. The magic coalesced into a pulsing yellow sphere roughly the size of a softball. Forcing his will on the yellow light, he clenched his hand into a fist and commanded the ball to compress, to shrink and become denser, until it compacted to an orb barely larger than a marble. The focused power turned a bright red.

The others could not see the magic. They only knew Mitch was attempting something based on his hand gestures. Still, they watched him intently, fascinated by his actions and waiting for whatever was about to happen.

Opening his hand again, Mitch tossed the tiny red sphere of power into the wriggling collection of ghoul fragments.

"Fire," he said aloud, using the word to help focus his concentration on what he wanted the magic to do.

He willed the compressed power to change, to convert its energy into heat. In his mind's eye, he visualized the red sphere of magic as the pinpoint of light formed by a magnifying glass; condensing harmless, diffuse sunlight into a devastating source of combustion.

"Fire," he repeated.

In response to his urging, the magic shifted from red to white. Mitch's efforts were rewarded by tendrils of smoke and a small flicker of flame.

"Holy shit," whispered Tink.

Mitch continued to push the magic, willing it to grow hotter, the flame to grow larger. Soon, the entire pile of shifting body parts was alight. When he was certain the fire was large enough that it would continue burning on its own, Mitch released his focus. The remaining magic dissipated, leaving the blaze to grow more naturally as it consumed the available fuel.

Ghouls were apparently highly flammable, and the expanding bonfire quickly reduced the thrashing pieces to ash.

"Very nice," said Jorge with a nod. "Still creepy, but I suppose magic does have its uses."

"What about the one that got away?" asked Tink. "Should we go after it."

"No," said the sergeant. "You don't chase a badger into its hole. We can worry about that one another time. I'll let the chief know what happened and he can decide what to do next."

Mitch held out his injured arm. Blood flowed freely from the bite wound. A great deal of the ichor covered his hand and had begun dripping from his fingertips.

"That thing bit me pretty bad, Sarge. What should I do?"

Brad's eyes grew wide in shock, and he drew his katana. "It bit you? Quick, lie down and stick your arm out. I'll cut it off. There might still be time to save you."

"Fuck! What?!" Mitch blurted. "You need to cut it off?"

"Goddammit, Brad," swore Jorge. "Could you not be a dick for like five minutes, please? Put the sword away. No, Mitch. We don't have to cut it off. It's okay."

"I'm... I'm not going to turn into one of them, am I?"

Mitch's mind conjured horrible images of him turning gray, eating human flesh, and burrowing underground through Dasan's Terrace.

"No. These are ghouls, not zombies. What's going to happen is, you're going to the emergency room tonight, getting that wound cleaned and stitched shut. You're probably going to need a tetanus shot, too. Ghouls are filthy things. That's about it, though. You're going to be fine."

Mitch glared at Brad, but the senior officer only smiled as he sheathed his sword.

"I'll still cut the arm off if you want me to," he suggested.

"I think I'll keep it. Thanks."

"Anybody else hurt?" asked Jorge. Tink and Brad responded in the negative. "Okay. Good. Tink, get Mitch to the hospital and stay with him until the docs release him. Brad, head back to the station and call Martin. Let him know he needs to come in right away to fill in this hole. I don't want to leave it open any longer than necessary in case anything else decides it wants to crawl out into the cemetery tonight."

"He's going to be pissed. He only went home a few hours ago."

"I know," said Jorge "That's why you're making the phone call, not me. Maybe next time you feel like being an asshole, you'll think twice before you open your mouth. I doubt it, but maybe."

CHAPTER

 6

The following night, Mitch was back in briefing, battered and bruised but cleared to return to duty. His bandaged arm throbbed off and on around the bite wound, though the doctor had assured him the injury was not severe.

At the hospital, he received stitches to close the deepest of the cuts, was handed prescriptions for antibiotics and ibuprofen, and then given a tetanus shot before being released. Tink drove them both back to the police station where Jorge then ordered him to call it a night and go home.

Tonight, Jorge sat at his usual spot at the head of the table, but unlike the beginning of most shifts, he had plenty of things he wanted to discuss before releasing the team to go to work. The sergeant was currently debriefing the details of the ghoul hunt, discussing tactics and ways to avoid some of the previous evening's mishaps should they encounter a similar incident in the future. Mitch listened only half-heartedly, staring at the bare tabletop in front of him. While Jorge warned about complacency getting officers killed, Mitch's mind insisted frustratingly on wandering to other matters.

Violet still would not talk to him.

He had texted her twice in the past twenty-four hours. Once when he got home from the hospital, and again this afternoon. She had not responded to either text.

"...maybe Mitch wouldn't have gotten hurt. What do you think?" Jorge's question caught Mitch's attention, but he was unsure how to answer, having missed the first part of the statement.

"Sorry. I, um.... What were you asking?"

Jorge frowned but didn't address Mitch's apparent distraction from the conversation. "I was saying if we had taken a moment to pay closer attention to the hole, we might have seen the last ghoul and you wouldn't have gotten hurt."

"Um, maybe, but I think that was mostly my own fault."

"How so?"

"You and Tink had one ghoul pinned between you. Brad was fighting a second. None of us was expecting a third ghoul to show up, so I was watching Brad. If anyone should have been checking the open lair it should have been me. I was supposed to be watching your backs, not staring at the fight like a spectator. That was a straight-up rookie move."

Mitch slumped in his chair, glancing sheepishly at the other officers seated around the table. "We're all responsible for paying attention to our surroundings and looking out for our own safety, so I can't lay that at anyone's feet but my own. Maybe if we had more people last night, or we were warned that there were going to be multiple ghouls it would have been different. With the people we had, and the information we were given, the third ghoul was my responsibility. My fault."

"I'm not sure I agree with you," said Jorge, "but I appreciate the thought. You're right though about having bad information. We were expecting one ghoul. When the second one showed up, we were all too surprised to even consider there might be more. I suppose we should consider ourselves lucky there weren't four or five."

Mitch's phone chose that moment to vibrate in his pocket. The distinctive double buzzing told him he had received a text. The sergeant was still talking, but he could not resist a quick glance at his cell to see who was trying to reach him. His heart sped up when he saw the screen name. Violet had finally responded to his messages.

God, I really am acting like a teenager, he thought. He tapped the screen to open the text. There were only two words:

Free tonight?

He set his phone face down on the table. He desperately wanted to answer her text, but he did not want to be any more rude or disrespectful to Jorge than he had already been. Besides, Violet had blown him off for the last seven days, she could wait five lousy minutes for him to finish briefing.

"...with at least one ghoul still in the cemetery, this is going to happen again. I'll make sure we're better prepared when it does. For now, I'm waiting on the chief to decide how he wants to follow up. I'm afraid the problem has become bigger than one stray ghoul. With this many, we might be dealing with a lich, a necromancer, or maybe something worse. Regardless of what is creating the ghouls, the responsibility for this problem officially went above our paygrade. I'll let you know when I get new orders. For now, keep your eyes open, report anything out of the ordinary..."

Despite his determination to wait, Mitch snatched his phone from the table and opened his texts. Holding the cell under the table so as not to be too obvious, he typed in:

I can be.

Flipping the phone over, he replaced it on the table. It immediately buzzed again.

Jorge paused and looked toward Mitch. He nodded his head toward the cellphone. "Is something important going on?"

"I... I'm not sure," he admitted. "It's Violet."

"Business or pleasure?" asked Brad. "Or both? Any business with Violet is a pleasure, especially if it's funny business."

"Well, answer it," said Jorge. We're about done here, anyway."

Mitch picked up the phone again.

I'm in North-West, by the gate. Meet me when you can. It's important.

"She didn't say what she wants," admitted Mitch. "But she says it's important."

"Fine. Movie starts at ten. If we don't see you, we won't come looking for you. Brad, what beat do you want?"

Mitch wasted no time after being dismissed from briefing. He exited the police department building and headed directly for North-West. Even without detours, it took him almost a half hour of fast walking to reach the gates that led into the oldest section of the cemetery.

As she had promised, Violet waited outside the locked gate. She wore her black wig and long black dress; her business attire as she had once jokingly called it. Dark circles of kohl surrounded her eyes, and blood red lipstick highlighted her mouth. Mitch's heart sank at the sight.

Ordinarily, when they met outside of work, Violet wore a plain t-shirt and jeans. She used little to no makeup, and she typically tied her naturally blond hair into a neat ponytail. The wig and the dress were a sign. She was here on coven business, not for personal matters.

"You made it," Violet said as he approached. "I'm glad."

"Are you?" he asked, the words coming out harsher than he had intended.

Violet's brows pulled together, and her nose crinkled in distaste.

"That's quite a tone. What happened?"

"Are you avoiding me?"

Mitch had not intended to be this blunt, but he also had no time for juvenile games. He was too old to pass notes around the classroom, asking girls if they liked him. If Violet wanted to end this relationship, she needed to do it to his face, not simply ghost him and hope he got the message.

Violet's face relaxed, and her lips twitched up in a sad smile.

"Yes," she admitted. "I have been. But, Mitch, it's not what you think."

"What do I think?" he asked.

"Probably that I don't want to be around you, or that I've decided we're not a good fit. The opposite is actually the problem. I very much like spending time with you, more than I ever thought I would, but I think that what happens next might be the reason that you leave me."

Violet stood with her spine straight as she answered, her shoulders thrown back, and her chin pushed forward. The posture was not aggressive, however. It was more of a defensive reaction to something unpleasant. Mitch recognized the behavior for what it was. Violet was afraid of something, and she was preparing herself to face whatever that something was. She was bracing for battle.

"What comes next? What are you so worried about?"

Instead of answering, Violet approached Mitch. She placed her hands on his shoulders, stood on her toes and kissed him. Violet held the kiss for a long, intimate moment before at last breaking away. With her thumb, she stroked Mitch's mouth, brushing at the crimson streak she had left on his lips.

"Thank you," she said. "I wanted to do that one more time, in case I can't later."

"Now you have me worried. What the hell is going on, and what are you so afraid of?"

Violet blew out a slow breath. "Okay," she said. "Last week, I taught you how to see souls."

"Yeah. I remember."

"I told you to practice whenever you had a chance, but not to look too deeply. You learn things about people when you soul touch that you can never unlearn. You … see things that people want to keep hidden. Bad things. Dark things."

Mitch nodded his understanding but remained silent.

"Tonight, I will teach you how to read someone at their most fundamental level. Since there are only the two of us here, you will read me."

"And you think I might see something I'm not going to like? That I'm going to learn something that will make me feel differently about you?"

99

"No. I *know* you won't like it. How you react afterwards is what frightens me. Still, I decided last week that the next time we saw each other, I would teach you how to read me. All of me. You need to know how to use your ability, and I'm the only one in a thousand miles that can teach you. That's why I haven't been eager to get together with you lately. I've been … putting this moment off for as long as I could."

It was Mitch's turn to blow out a long breath. It was a sigh of relief, releasing a week's worth of tension.

"So, you aren't simply tired of me."

Violet gave him another sad smile. "Never," she promised. "You're way too much fun to have around."

"Speaking of fun," Mitch said, holding up his bandaged arm. "You missed a great time last night. Do you know any tricks to heal a ghoul bite?"

"I told you when you broke your ribs, magic doesn't work like that. It can close wounds or hold pieces of you together, but your body has to heal on its own." Violet laid a gentle hand on Mitch's wounded arm. "Does it hurt much?"

"Nah. I've had worse. Recently, in fact."

They both laughed, but there was a tension in the sound that Mitch heard clearly. The merriment rang hollow in the still night air. They were putting off what was about to come next, and they both knew it. Violet was terrified Mitch might see something that would cause him to leave her, and now Mitch was afraid that she might be right.

"Should we do this?" Mitch asked after a long, awkward silence settled between them.

"Yes. I've already delayed this longer than I should have."

Violet straightened her shoulders and brushed the black hair of her wig away from her face. "Alright, before you soul touch, there is something you need to learn how to do. You need to know how to contract and expand your soul within your body."

"Are you kidding? How do I do that? I don't even know where my soul is."

"That's what you have to figure out. When you soul touch, you don't need to physically touch another person, but you have to extend a tiny portion of your own soul to make contact with theirs. Your soul fills you, Mitch. The edges of it sit right at the surface of your skin. Expanding to touch someone else will be easy for you. That's why I told you last week to be careful and not look into anyone too deeply. You could probably soul touch by accident."

"Like I could exorcise a ghost by accident?" Mitch asked, recalling the hapless spirit of Harold that he had destroyed a few months back.

Violet nodded. "Exactly. For you, I think the hard part will be learning to pull away and retreat back into yourself."

"Okay. How do I do that?"

"That's why you need me. Give me your hand."

Mitch extended his right hand, and Violet took it in both of her own.

"Don't worry. This won't hurt. When I stroked your soul in the diner, I cut into it. That's why you were sick and in so much pain."

"I remember," said Mitch with a small shudder at the memory. He had vomited into his own lap which made that moment extremely hard to forget. Violet had hurt him at Alyssandra's direction back then. He trusted Violet and knew she would never intentionally harm him now, but the incident had left him with a healthy respect for her abilities.

"I am only going to touch your soul this time. When I do, I want you to focus on what it feels like, and where exactly you are experiencing the touch."

Mitch noticed an odd sensation in his hand. It was not a physical touch so much as a tingling, like the pins and needles feeling of a limb when it loses blood flow and falls asleep.

"I feel something," he said. "I'm not sure what, though.

"Concentrate on where the feeling is originating. Try to pull away from it."

Mitch jerked his hand from Violet's grasp.

"No, dummy," Violet laughed, rolling her eyes. "Not you. Your soul. Pull your soul away from the touch."

"Oh." Mitch replaced his hand in hers.

He felt the gentle tingling again. This time he focused on the feeling and mentally tried to escape it. He imagined trying to shrink himself into his own body, to escape deep inside of himself away from his own skin.

Nothing changed. The tingling sensation continued.

"It's not working. I'm not sure what I'm doing."

"It's different for everyone. You have to figure out how to do it for yourself. I can only provide a source of contact. It's like learning to wiggle your ears or raise one eyebrow. I can't tell you how it's done. You have to discover which muscles move the parts you want to move. Give me your other hand. We'll try giving you another point of reference."

Over the next half hour, Violet touched Mitch in various locations on his body, including a few of his more intimate areas for good measure. At each contact, Mitch attempted to withdraw his soul from Violet's probing. With each effort, he felt he gained a better understanding of how to move his spirit within his body. It still required intense concentration for even the most minimal of successes, but Mitch was confident that, with more practice, he could figure this out.

"I think that's enough for now. We will do more practice with contracting your soul later. It's time to work on expanding outward."

Violet's face was carefully neutral when she announced the shift in training. Mitch was not fooled.

"This should be much easier for you than pulling away. Your soul is pretty open and accessible. Before you start, though, please remember one thing. I care about you very much. You are important to me, and I don't want to lose you. Whatever else you learn, I beg you to remember that much."

"Tell me what to do," he said.

"Find my soul. Look into me and tell me when you see it."

Mitch had been practicing his technique all week and it took him only a few seconds to find the amorphous gray mass of spirit inside Violet. He located her soul contracted deep into her body. It shifted and rippled at the edges, with tiny motes of silver sparkling in its depths, as well as the one bright streak he had seen before. Next to the brightness, Mitch spied a deep slash of black in the gray background that he had not noticed when looking into Violet last week. It was not new; in fact, it appeared to be quite old. He realized he must simply have missed it before since he had pretty much no idea what he was doing at the time.

"I see it," Mitch said.

"Like I said, you don't need physical contact to soul touch, but it can make things easier when you're learning. Give me your hand."

Mitch did. Violet took his extended hand and placed his open palm on her chest, over her heart.

"Now, look deep, not with your eyes, but with your emotions. With your feelings. Let yourself experience what's inside me. Reach in and touch the essence of who I am."

There were tears in Violet's eyes. Before they could fall, Mitch moved his gaze away from her face and peered into the frightened spirit within her. Violet's terror was infectious, and Mitch felt his own heart begin to beat erratically.

The shimmering gray engulfed him, and all at once, he understood. He knew Violet. Not simply with his mind, but with his whole being. Touching her soul was more than comprehending facts and data about her, it was observing her on a deep foundational level. He knew who she was. He knew *what* she was.

He felt her strength, her force of will and character. He also felt the fear that fueled that strength, the fear that everything she fought so hard for might one day be taken away from her if she was not strong enough to hold onto it. He felt her insecurities and doubts. She knew she was not a good enough person for anyone to care about her. Those that came into her life and said that they loved her were only being kind, or else wanted something from her. She believed she had too much evil and darkness inside her to ever truly redeem herself, although she desperately yearned for absolution.

Mitch turned to the brightest streak of silver, entering the light. He found joy, a sense of undeserved security, and … yes, there was love here, too. The joy was fragile, however. It might one day take root in her overall sense of self. It could someday become permanent; if it lasted. It could also be shattered in an instant, left to fragment and fade, and to eventually be swallowed by the surrounding self-loathing in Violet. Mitch also understood that whichever way it went, he was the one who would be responsible for the outcome.

Finally, he turned to the deepest slash of black. This was a scar that would never heal, a foundational piece of who Violet was. Most experiences that left scars, good or bad, eventually dispersed throughout the soul, shaping the person's essence while the incident itself faded. This scar, however, was very old, yet it was as hard and unyielding as the day it had formed. This scar was the murder of Violet's parents and family.

Mitch felt like an intruder as he experienced the horror of her tragedy. He wanted to look away, to pull back, but he was already committed. This piece of Violet was already a part of him.

You learn things about people you can never unlearn.

This scar was where Violet's hate lived. She never found the people responsible for her family's deaths, never had the opportunity to avenge them. Violet wanted to be a good person, but this darkness gave her the desire and the will to do evil. She could hurt people if she felt it was necessary. She could kill.

Mitch did not fault her or shy away from this part of her. He was a police officer. He had accepted a similar darkness within himself long ago. He knew that, with the proper circumstances, he could take a human life. He could kill, and he could justify that outcome to himself later.

Was this what she feared him learning? he wondered. If so, it was foolish. His feelings for her had not changed.

He touched the scar again. He felt the emotional walls she had built around herself since the murders. There was an overriding guilt that she had let their deaths happen. She had not been strong enough to stop it, and she had promised herself at that moment that she would grow stronger. So strong, no one could ever harm her or steal from her again. That promise still drove her today.

Most of all, Mitch experienced her distrust of people, and her pain at having everyone she loved taken from her. She would never let herself experience this devastation again. The grief was never worth the fleeting moments of joy. This was the guiding premise that ruled her existence.

Mitch finally saw it, the one thing Violet did not want him to see. This was why she had avoided him for the entire week. This was why she was so frightened to let him in. It was also why she had given him one last kiss. He knew.

He *knew!*

He did not want to be here anymore. This was too much. He wanted out. Mitch tried to pull back, to reestablish his sense of self, of individuality, but he could not break free. He was stuck. Physically, he stepped away from Violet, a whimper of panic in his throat. Still, his soul remained linked to hers.

"It's okay, Mitch," Violet said softly. Her words were kind and reassuring. "You're okay."

Mitch felt something envelope him. A soft bubble of warmth surrounded the trapped part of his extended spirit. The touch tingled a bit, but the feeling was not unpleasant. It was … familiar. The bubble pushed, gently freeing him and returning him to his own body.

It was Violet. She had rescued him, saved him from causing whatever damage he had been about to do to himself, and possibly to her.

"Mitch? How do you feel?"

"You couldn't…," he said. "I saw it. You never could…. So, why?"

Violet gasped, a sharp intake of breath. She understood his reaction. How could she not? But she waited for Mitch to gather his wits and ask a coherent question, not offering any information until she knew exactly what he was asking.

Mitch shifted left to right, then turned in a tight agitated circle, his inner turmoil translating into impotent physical action.

His mind reeled, trying to translate his experiences while connected to Violet's innermost self, attempting to convert the deep understanding into conscious thoughts. Several long seconds passed before he felt able to speak rationally.

"Did you ever love me?" he asked. "Or was it all a lie?"

"I never thought ... I could love ... anyone," Violet said carefully. "It hurts too much when it gets taken away, and I have already experienced enough of that kind of hurt. I was never going to put myself in that situation again."

"You made me think you cared to keep me close to the coven," Mitch told her.

"Mitch. Please."

"Stop. Just tell me the truth. Alyssandra put you up to this, didn't she?"

Violet wiped at her eyes. The black circles of kohl smudged and streaked across her face as she brushed at the wetness forming there. She pulled the black wig from her head and flung it to the ground in frustration. "Stupid wig," she growled, running her fingers through the sweat matted blond hair underneath.

Violet blew out one hard breath, attempting to calm herself, but her expression remained twisted, displaying obvious pain and remorse. Her left hand clenched into a fist, and she took one step toward Mitch, reaching out toward him with her right.

He stepped away, staying out of her reach. Another tear fell, marking a dark path down Violet's cheek.

"Just tell me," he said.

Nodding, Violet let her extended arm drop back to her side. "When I met you at Carrie's Diner that first time, Alyssandra sent me. She wanted me to find out if you had any magic potential. The next time we met was because I wanted to see you again. I was drawn to you. You have a lot of power, but it was more than that. I was curious about you, too. I won't say I felt anything personally for you, though. That would be a lie. I've spent a lot of years alone, never letting myself get close to people."

Violet paused for a moment, giving Mitch an opportunity to comment. He stayed quiet, so she continued.

"When Alyssandra found out I was still seeing you, she was angry. Later, though, she decided it could be a good thing. If you liked me, she could use that to keep you close to the coven. I played along."

"When you brought me home from the hospital?" Mitch asked, his voice barely above a whisper. "The first time we…?"

Violet shook her head. "I was doing what Alyssandra wanted. I didn't mind, but it was still…,"

"Still an act," Mitch finished.

"Still an act," she admitted. "But something changed after that. I don't know when, but it did. I stopped pretending. I wanted to be with you. I wanted to be in your house, in your bed, close to you. I love you, Mitch. I didn't want to, but it happened anyway. You have no idea how terrified I am to have let myself become this vulnerable."

Mitch did know. He had seen all of it when he and Violet had soul touched. He saw the love was real. Unfortunately, so was the betrayal, and he was not certain he could move past that. Not yet.

"You lied to me," he said. "You played me like I was some kind of mark, and now you want me to give a shit about how *you* feel?" He knew he was being cruel. That was the point. He was angry and hurt, and he wanted to lash out, to share some of that pain.

"I lied to you." Violet dropped to her knees, the strength going out of her legs. "Yes. I lied to you. And then I fell in love with you knowing how dangerous it was, knowing I shouldn't. We don't really get much choice in the matter, though, do we? Who we love? I sure didn't. Now everything I was afraid of is going to come true, and this time it's my own fault. It's all my own fucking fault."

Violet wrapped her arms around herself and began to rock back and forth.

"My fault. My fault."

Streams of magic drew toward her huddled form, circling Violet in a growing vortex of formless power. The magic glowed red, spinning faster and faster around her. She was in pain. The violent maelstrom building around Violet was a physical manifestation of her desire to shield herself from her own breaking heart. She was closing out the world around her, building new tangible walls to replace the emotional ones that had been breached.

Mitch felt betrayed by the lies. He felt stupid for having fallen for an obvious act. Briefly, he wondered if Violet's tantrum was another ploy, but he dismissed the idea immediately. He knew it was not. He had seen how she really felt, and he had also seen the fear and self-loathing that fractured her essence. Her guilt at being unable to save her family and boyfriend from the witches that had come to take her was a permanent part of who she was. So was her desire to cut herself away from the world to protect herself emotionally from anything that might cause her to hurt like that again.

Those emotional walls had cracked, only for an instant, but long enough to let someone else in. Now, she was losing him, too, and it was worse this time because she had done it to herself. She had lied to him at the beginning of their relationship, tricked him and betrayed him. What other outcome could she possibly have expected?

She could not bear it.

Violet's internal storm manifested now in her magic. The woman he loved was being crushed under the weight of her own insecurities and fears, and no matter how he felt about her lies, he could not stand idly by and watch that happen.

Mitch stepped forward, hands outstretched. As soon as he touched it, the swirling power enveloping Violet drove him back, bouncing him away like he had struck a physical barrier. He tried again, but the wall of magic did not relent. He needed to get inside, to reach Violet, but the forces pushing him away were too strong. He did not have the knowledge or experience to defeat whatever spells barred her from him.

Mitch remembered what Violet had told him during their last sparring match. It didn't matter if he understood how a spell worked, the reaction should always be the same: avoid it, deflect it, or disrupt it.

Reaching into the maelstrom, Mitch drew at the power forming the shield. He syphoned the magic from the spell and released it harmlessly behind him. Although he did not have the strength to completely break it apart, he managed to marginally weaken the spell at one narrow, isolated point. Next, he pulled power of his own to form a spike of pure force. He rammed the lance of magic into the weakened spot in Violet's chaotic shell. This created the break he needed. He did not hesitate when he saw the gap forming in front of him.

Mitch pulled at the magic around him and pushed another, larger wedge into the growing opening. He felt the cyclone trying to repair itself, to shut him back out, but Mitch did not relent. He only pushed harder, drawing and channeling more power into his efforts than he had ever previously managed to wield. When the hole he had cut into Violet's defenses was large enough, Mitch stepped through the magical barrier, collapsing by Violet's side and wrapping his arms around her.

110

He felt her shaking in his grasp. She gasped and shuddered against his chest as she tried to cry the pain out of her body. Mitch squeezed tighter. The red vortex surrounding them broke apart, dissipating in the air around and above their kneeling forms.

"I'm here," Mitch told Violet. "I'm not going anywhere."

"I'll go away. You never have to see me again," Violet said, pressing her face into Mitch's uniform shirt.

"No, you won't. I'll just follow you."

"I'll leave the coven."

"No. You won't do that, either."

"What do you want me to do?" she asked.

"Exactly what you've already done. You told me the truth, right?"

Violet sniffled and nodded.

"Is there anything more you left out?"

"No."

"Then all you have to do is keep being my teacher … and my girlfriend."

Violet laughed, but the sound broke into another sob.

"Your girlfriend?" she asked, uncertainly. "Okay. I can do that."

"And no more lies. Ever. We will be absolutely honest with each other from now on."

"Promise," she said.

Mitch kissed Violet's forehead and pressed his cheek against her hair.

"Wow. This soul touching shit is no joke," he said, drained emotionally and physically from his efforts to get through Violet's magical defenses. "What do we do now?"

Violet sniffed again. She pushed away from Mitch and wiped her nose with the sleeve of her dress.

"Now, you go back to work. I'm going to go home, clean up, and try to figure out a way to get back my self-respect after letting you see me cry like a damned baby."

"When can I see you again?" asked Mitch.

"Why don't you come over after you get off work in the morning? We can curl up in bed and I can watch you sleep."

"Just sleep?"

Violet smiled. With her garish red lipstick and the black streaks around her eyes, Mitch thought she looked like a homicidal clown out of his worst nightmare. An adorable homicidal clown, however.

His adorable, homicidal clown.

"Well," she said, "I guess that depends on how tired you are."

CHAPTER

7

Mitch returned to the station to find Jorge in the administrative break room setting up for the first movie of the night. The sergeant stood behind the television set running cables to his portable DVD player when Mitch walked in. Tink and Brad had not yet finished their evening rounds and Mitch assumed they would show up in the next hour or so.

"Hey, Sarge," Mitch called out as he entered the room.

"Mitch," said Jorge, setting the DVD player aside. "That was fast. All done? Everything alright?"

"It will be. It's been kind of a rough night so far, though."

"What was the emergency?"

"There's been some, um … drama, I guess, going on with the coven. Nothing that's going to impact the department, but Violet and I are sort of stuck in the middle of it."

It was not completely a lie. There had been quite a bit of drama in the cemetery tonight, and it had involved some coven business, but Mitch did not think Jorge needed to know any of the specifics.

Jorge's eyebrows pulled together in concern. "Do you need anything from us?"

"No, I don't think so. Thanks, though. I appreciate the offer. Um, Sarge, I'm not feeling very social right now. If you don't mind, I'm going to skip the movies and do a little homework downstairs in the transcription room."

"What's up? What are you working on?"

"The chief gave me permission to reopen Lieutenant Delaney's case. I want to read through all the old documents to see if I can come up with anything new to look into."

Jorge whistled. "Delaney, huh? That one's been a thorn in the County's ass for thirty years. What made you decide to open that can of worms?"

"Something to do." Mitch shrugged. "I don't know. I talked with the lieutenant a while ago and felt sorry for him. He's stuck here, you know. I wanted to see if I could help."

Jorge shook his head in commiseration. "Good luck. And, congratulations, by the way. Simon told me he promoted you to detective. I have to say Delaney is a hell of a first case to take on. Wasn't there something simpler you could do first? You know, before you jump in the deep end like that."

Mitch answered with a rueful laugh and another shrug.

"I'll let Tink and Brad know you're busy and won't be joining us."

"Thanks, Sarge. I'll be downstairs if you need me."

Mitch headed for the stairs and descended to the first floor of the building where the officers' workstations were located. He selected a computer and turned it on. Settling into the desk chair, he typed in his passcode and selected the Sacramento County report software.

Although he had not yet had time to contact the Homicide Detective Bureau to request access to their evidence files, the report writing software allowed him to gather and read the individual reports written over the years by investigators working the old homicide. As he opened each report or addendum, he made copies of the documents and saved them to a personal thumb drive. The digital copies would allow him to review the information at home or on any other computer if he was away from the police department.

Next, he printed a hard copy of everything he had found and placed the pages in a manilla folder. The printed pages were not necessary, but Mitch liked the feel of paper in his hands when reading through old case reports. It allowed him to jot notes to himself and flip through pages faster than if he was forced to open random files whenever he was looking for a specific piece of information.

Mitch started with a glance through the entire stack of printouts to get a feel for how many times the investigation had been opened and stalled out. Glancing at the bottom of the pages for the names of the investigating officers, Mitch discovered his first bit of surprising information. In 2014, the last time Delaney's homicide was actively investigated, the detective on the case was listed as Sergeant Simon Jefferson. Chief Jefferson had worked this case before he became the head of DTPD.

"I wonder why he didn't say anything to me yesterday?" Mitch mused. "He could have made a few suggestions on where I should start."

Then again, Mitch corrected himself, if the chief had any ideas, he would have chased them down when he was the investigating officer. He too had eventually run out of leads and stepped away from the case, so it was likely he would not have any useful suggestions. It was also possible Chief Jefferson was hoping Mitch might see something from a new angle if he was allowed to start from scratch, rather than the chief sharing information that might accidentally lead him down an already fruitless path.

Mitch flipped through the pages in his folder. It was a significant stack, maybe a couple hundred pages. This would take some time.

He would much rather be spending the night with Violet, but she had made it clear she needed a little space after the chaotic events earlier this evening. Mitch understood her feelings and respected them. The pile of reports in front of him were probably a blessing in disguise. Reading through them would keep his mind occupied and help pass the night until he could go visit Violet at the end of his shift.

Mitch turned to the first page of the original responding officer's report of the incident. Because the report had been created thirty years ago, before computers were a regular thing at the Sheriff's Office, the pages were all photocopies of the officer's handwritten documentation. The primary officer responding to the scene of the homicide had scribbled his narrative in sloppy block lettering, and that, coupled with the odd shading left behind by the scanner used to upload the pages into the computer, left Mitch struggling to decipher the nearly illegible scrawl.

With a resigned sigh, he squinted at the blotchy hieroglyphics and started to read.

On August 17, 1994, at approximately five minutes after nine o'clock in the morning, two armed suspects had entered the convenience store at a 76 gas station. They were both armed and wore ski masks covering their faces. They demanded the clerk open a concealed safe hidden behind the register.

Lieutenant Delaney had been in the store at the time of the robbery and confronted the armed suspects. One suspect was shot in the leg by the lieutenant, but Delaney was shot in the neck and died at the scene. The suspects fled the store after the exchange of fire, without taking any money or merchandise.

The attendant at the gas station described the suspects as White or perhaps Hispanic males. One suspect had brown eyes, but the second was too far away for the attendant to see any facial details through the mask.

They left in a vehicle that the clerk heard but did not see. Two surveillance cameras were operating in the store, but all video footage was black and white, grainy, and provided little detail. There were no cameras outside of the gas station convenience store or anywhere nearby.

Mitch nodded to himself, unsurprised by the information. In 1994, cameras were expensive and required constant maintenance. The best equipment available was also extremely poor quality by current standards. The footage would most likely be unhelpful, but he wanted to be thorough. There was no telling where a tiny, previously overlooked piece of evidence might come from. He grabbed a yellow pad of paper and made a note to request copies of all available video Homicide had in their evidence lockers.

He read further into the initial report.

Crime Scene Investigations arrived shortly after the homicide and collected what evidence they could, including shell casings from the lieutenant's Berretta, and blood evidence left behind by the injured suspect. It wasn't much to go on. The casing of the shotgun round fired by one of the suspects had not been ejected. It had been carried off with the shotgun itself, along with any fingerprints it might have had on it. There were also no useful fingerprints found in the store since the suspects were wearing gloves in addition to their masks.

At least there was blood, although in thirty years, it had not led to the identity of the shooter. The initial report showed it had been typed by a lab and determined to be B-negative, but that was the extent of the information obtained. Genetic comparisons were in their infancy at that time, and DNA databases did not become a thing until a few years later.

Mitch made another note reminding himself to ask Homicide what checks had been made with the blood that may not have been detailed in the reports. Later investigators must have availed themselves of newer technologies, assuming of course the blood sample had not been contaminated or discarded.

The first investigator to get the case on his desk was a name Mitch didn't recognize. Detective Ricardo Delgado apparently did nothing with the case for almost three days before finally reaching out and interviewing the cashier. The victimized clerk stated that he thought at least one of the suspects was a former employee of the gas station. The cashier believed this was true because the suspect knew exactly where the safe was hidden and had even attempted to open it using a combination that did not work. The clerk knew all of the current employees and was certain he would have recognized the men in the ski masks if it had been one of them.

Detective Delgado accessed the gas station's employment records and identified six people that had quit or been fired over the past eighteen months. Three of the six were female, so had been ignored. The remaining three provided solid alibis that eliminated them from the suspect pool. Two of the former employees were out of town. Samuel Parish had been in San Francisco tailgating at a baseball game, while Bruce Yost advised he was in a hotel in Reno.

Samuel provided the names of three friends who had been with him at the game. All three had been interviewed and confirmed Samuel was with them. Bruce said he was with his girlfriend, Marlene Tansen, and when questioned, the girlfriend had agreed this was true. A review of lobby footage at the hotel also proved Bruce had been in Reno.

The third employee, Wyatt Munoz, was the only one who admitted to being in Elk Grove at the time of the robbery. He stated he had been alone at a restaurant having breakfast that morning, but no, he did not know anyone that could verify his story. He also had no receipt to support his claim. For a brief time, the investigation focused on Wyatt, but eventually a server at the restaurant came forward to say she had seen him there. Munoz was apparently a regular at the establishment, and the girl told Detective Delgado that she recognized his picture. He had come in to eat at about nine o'clock that morning and left about forty minutes later.

While it was feasible that the waitress serving him could have been wrong about the time, and he had actually come into the restaurant several minutes later, it was unlikely she would have failed to notice a large, bleeding hole in his leg when she sat him at his table. Further, if Wyatt was merely the accomplice and not the shooter, it was equally unlikely while his friend was bleeding to death that he would saunter into a restaurant and spend half an hour enjoying a leisurely breakfast.

These three subjects appeared to be dead ends in the investigation.

Mitch added a few more notes to his growing list of questions. The female employees had not been interviewed because the suspects involved in the robbery were both male. That had been a mistake. Any of the women might have had a grudge against the gas station and used friends to pull off the robbery. Or one of them might have mentioned the safe and the old combination to a third party that decided on their own to plan the theft. It might still prove useful to contact them now and find out if they had any friends or relatives who had been shot in the leg in 1994.

In addition, alibis could be faked. Blood could not. Mitch decided he would research if any of the questioned male employees had the same blood type as the shooter.

After jotting down his thoughts, Mitch went back to reading.

A blood trail, left by the injured suspect, led out the doors of the convenience store and to the curb on the south side of Bond Road. It ended there, suggesting a car had been waiting to take the robbers away. No witnesses were found that could describe the car used, but there should have been significant blood evidence in the vehicle. The shooter was probably badly hurt, both according to the store clerk and based on the amount of blood at the scene.

Despite flipping through the report pages several times, Mitch could not find any reference to whether or not the detective in charge had examined any vehicles belonging to the prior employees. That type of evidence was time sensitive, and if it wasn't checked in 1994, it was lost now. The getaway vehicle would almost certainly be a block of crushed scrap metal today, or a pile of rusting parts in a junkyard somewhere. Assuming there was anything left of it at all.

The end of the report stated that Detective Delgado had contacted every hospital in Sacramento County looking for a gunshot victim, but none were reported. Mitch scoffed as he read the statement. Hospitals were required by law to report gunshot wounds to the police. These phone calls had been redundant and a waste of time. What the detective should have been doing was reaching out to police departments in neighboring jurisdictions to see if any victims had been reported in their areas.

"Was this guy stupid, or just lazy?" he growled. This case could have been solved by a halfway competent detective while the evidence was fresh and the suspects were still scrambling to cover their tracks. Thirty years later and any solid leads were now as cold and dead as the residents of Dasan's Terrace.

Mitch was not ready to give up, but he knew that because so much time had passed since the murder, finding Delaney's killer was going to take more luck than skill this time around.

The next investigator to take a crack at the case was a detective named Barry Rutlidge. Mitch did not know the man personally, but he recognized the name. Lieutenant Rutlidge was currently a shift commander working at the Sacramento County Main Jail.

The lieutenant, then *Detective* Rutlidge, reopened the homicide in 1998. He chased down the same suspects from the original case, but this time he was more thorough. He looked into the backgrounds of the three female employees as well as the males.

Good for him, Mitch thought. Four years too late, but he supposed that was still better than not at all.

Two of the women claimed they never spoke to anyone about the hidden safe or its combination. The third, however, a young woman by the name of Tracy Petevic, provided two names of friends she had talked to, telling them how easy it would be to steal from the store. The friends were investigated, but again, alibis and lack of a blood type match led to another dead end. Mitch jotted the names down on his growing list of eliminated suspects. He might still reach out to talk to them if all other trails proved fruitless.

Reading on, Mitch discovered that Rutlidge also went a step further with the blood evidence than his predecessor. He had compared blood types of the three male ex-employees even though they had already provided clear alibis. None of them matched the evidence left at the scene.

121

Finally, before closing the investigation again, the detective contacted every city and county throughout northern California searching for gunshot victims during the relevant week in 1994. When that provided no additional assistance, he called every veterinary office and medical clinic he could find in the Sacramento directory. Mitch found himself liking Detective Rutlidge much more than Delgado. It was too bad Barry Rutlidge had not had the case when Delaney was first murdered. The homicide might already be solved; the two men responsible rotting in prison right now.

Mitch scratched out the notes he had written to himself regarding the female employees, checking blood types, and following up with hospital reports in other cities and counties. Those boxes had already been ticked by Rutlidge.

There was still no information on possible suspect vehicles. If Detective Rutlidge had done any investigation into potential vehicles, he had not included the information in his report.

Mitch set the second report aside and picked up the third. Another detective Mitch had never heard of had opened the case in February 2005. Detective Lani Goodman's report was thirty-eight pages long and was a complete rehash of everything the prior two investigators had already done. The only new lead was a footnote stating that samples of the blood collected in 1994 were run through the Combined DNA Index System, or CODIS, the FBI's DNA database.

There were no matches.

That did not leave a lot of avenues for Mitch to explore. It was possible his investigation was going to be over before it truly got started. That would be unfortunate, but he had known going in that this case would not be easy. If there was a clear and simple path to solving Delaney's murder, someone most likely would have discovered it over the past 30 years.

He set Goodman's report aside and picked up the last investigation, dated 2014. This was the year Chief Jefferson had taken up the gauntlet. Sergeant Jefferson at the time, Mitch corrected himself.

The chief's report was odd, both in its length and in its content. The full narrative was less than two pages long and it listed an anonymous witness who had come forward. Mitch found no name for the witness mentioned in the report, and the witness' statement had been removed, with the word, "Redacted," written on a large blank space in the middle of the page. In addition, a blood sample from the murder suspect was provided to a company called "13th Circle," where it was used for "study and comparison of potential sources." Other than the outcome of, "Negative results," no additional explanation was provided for the blood testing either.

It was surreal. *Who had signed off on this report?* No self-respecting supervisor would ever let an investigator get away with such vague references. Mitch decided he was going to have to speak with Chief Jefferson directly at some point and try to get clarification on this confusing lack of detail. Maybe it would create a new avenue of exploration that Mitch could exploit.

That was it. There was nothing left in the stack. Turning the last page over and laying it on top of the pile in his folder, Mitch yawned and rubbed at his eyes. He checked his watch and discovered that he had been reading reports and taking notes for the better part of two hours. That was enough for tonight. Tomorrow morning, he would reach out to the detectives in the Homicide Bureau and request all video surveillance and any recordings of suspect or witness interviews. He should also ask for another DNA check through the federal databases. It was unlikely anything had changed since the last check, but it paid to be thorough. New names were being added to the registry every day.

Mitch shut down his computer, pocketed his thumb drive and gathered up the pages in his investigative folder. He took another look at his watch. If he tossed this folder in his locker and headed upstairs right now, he could join the rest of his team and probably catch most of the second movie. Jorge had brought in "The Blackcoat's Daughter" for the second screening of the night, and Mitch had heard good things about that one.

CHAPTER

 8

Mitch woke early the following afternoon. Sunlight peeked through a slender gap in the blackout curtains, creating a streak of light across the foot of the bed that alerted him as to the time of day. The linen sheets and down comforter were warm where they wrapped around him, but not as warm as the softly snoring body pressed against his bare back.

Violet had wrapped herself around him as they slept, her knees resting against the bottom of his thighs, her hips folded around the curve of his buttocks, and one slender arm draped over his waist. Mitch needed to pee, but given his current situation, he decided he did not actually need to go that urgently. The touch of Violet's skin pressed against him comforted him as they lay in her massive bed. It felt nice. It felt right. He did not even mind being the little spoon in this scenario.

Mitch remained where he was, enjoying the sensation of Violet's figure curled tight around his own for a little longer. It had only been a few hours ago that he had almost lost her. Because of that scare, he wanted this moment to last as long as possible. After only a few more minutes, however, Mitch heard Violet's breathing pattern change as she began to wake. She shifted a bit, pulling away as she roused from sleep, but then quickly snuggled closer against him as she realized where she was and who was in the bed with her.

"Good morning," Mitch said softly, when he was certain she was fully awake and not about to drop off to sleep again. "Or maybe I should say, good afternoon."

"Mmm. 'Morning," she muttered back. "Did you sleep okay?"

"I slept great," Mitch told her. "You?"

"I always sleep better with you here."

She ran her hand over his stomach and squeezed him in a one-armed hug.

Mitch flipped the blankets back and slid out of bed. His bladder had finally reached a critical point, and it was time to do something about it. As he walked out of the bedroom through the doorway that led into the master bathroom, Violet called out.

"Wait!"

Mitch turned to face Violet. She was sitting up, braced on her hands to keep herself upright.

"What is it?" he asked, concern creating an edge to his voice.

Violet smiled, mischievously. "Nothing. I wanted to get another look at you. You look pretty good naked."

Mitch barked a happy laugh, then marched into the bathroom to take care of business.

After brushing his teeth with a toothbrush Violet kept by the sink for him, he dressed in the clothes he had worn that morning when he left work. Violet climbed into the shower and turned the hot water level up until it was steaming pleasantly. She beckoned him to join her, but Mitch reluctantly refused, opting to stick his head into the glass enclosed stall only long enough to steal a kiss. Violet frowned, disappointed at his retreat. Mitch smiled back at her, then wandered into the kitchen to make breakfast for the two of them.

He was plating omelets and placing the food on the marble counter of the kitchen island when Violet sauntered out of the bedroom wearing a thick, fluffy pink bathrobe. Her hair was still wet, but she had combed it until it hung straight down, the ends brushing the tops of her shoulders.

Violet pouted dramatically as she settled herself onto a stool at the counter.

"You've never turned me down like that before. You usually like me all wet and soapy. A girl might start to feel a little rejected."

Mitch guided a plate in front of her and handed her a fork. "Sorry. If it helps, I was very tempted, but I have some things I want to get done before I start work tonight."

He set his own plate next to Violet's, then filled two glasses of water to go with the food. Next, he rummaged through Violet's refrigerator until he located a bottle of ketchup. Returning to the counter with his prize, Mitch settled himself on the stool beside hers.

Violet's nose crinkled in distaste as he poured a dollop of ketchup onto his omelet. Mitch only grinned. He knew Violet would sooner "eat eggs off the ground in a cow barn" than ever put ketchup on them, but he had been eating breakfast like this since he was a kid. He wasn't going to change his preferences any time soon. However, they had run through this discussion many times already, and there was no reason to hash it out again. They both let the matter drop without a word.

"You have a lot more ability than I originally thought," said Violet, thoughtfully dragging her fork across her plate as she pushed the eggs from one side to the other. She seemed to have little appetite.

"It's just an omelet," said Mitch. "I've made them for you before.

Violet gave him a small sarcastic smile. "No, wise guy. I'm not talking about the eggs. You're still a terrible cook. I meant last night. You shouldn't have been able to break apart my defenses, but you pushed right through my magic like it wasn't even there."

"I wouldn't say I pushed right through. I chiseled a tiny hole and managed to squeeze into it. And believe me when I say that I knew it was there."

"Maybe, but you shouldn't have been able to get in at all. I'm one of the strongest witches in this state. Alyssandra is the only one in the area that I know who might be stronger. Well, maybe Chang'e, but I've never gone toe to toe with her so I can't be sure."

Mitch turned to face Violet, and his expression grew serious. "I was very motivated to get in," he told her.

"Apparently," she agreed. "Regardless of how you did it, maybe we should keep this between us for a while."

"I'm sorry if I hurt you or embarrassed you…"

"That's not it," Violet hastily assured him. "That's not all of it, anyway. I don't want Alyssandra to hear about it because I don't want her to feel any more frightened of you than she already is. She's already nervous because you're an exorcist. If she finds out your magic might be stronger than hers, she might…," Violet trailed off, trying to figure out how to end her sentence.

"Mitch, she's not a nice person if she feels threatened."

"Okay. Then we don't say anything to her. Problem solved."

"Thank you." Violet took a bite of the omelet and chewed slowly.

"How is it? Good?"

Violet smiled, though the expression did not reach her eyes. "Sure," she said noncommittally.

"Oh, come on. It can't be that bad."

"It's edible. I don't think it's going to kill anyone," Violet admitted, "but I think we should stick to eating out. Neither one of us is going to win any cooking competitions anytime soon."

"I can't argue with that." Mitch looked at the remaining food on his plate, examining the eggs swimming in a flood of red condiment. "Maybe that's why I use so much ketchup. It hides the real flavor."

"Speaking of killing someone," said Violet as Mitch continued to stare at his breakfast.

"Were we?"

"Sort of. Anyway, we're on the topic now. Alyssandra thinks it would be a good idea to introduce you to exorcisms. She wants me to show you how they're done. I know of two haunted objects in the Bay Area, and the owners want my help. Do you feel like taking a road trip?"

Mitch glanced at Violet in surprise. "You think I'm ready?"

"Not really, but that's why I will be doing the exorcisms and you'll be watching from a safe distance away. This is only an introduction. Training comes later."

"Sounds good, but it will probably depend on when we go. There's a lot going on around here at the moment. I don't want to leave the department shorthanded by suddenly disappearing on a personal errand."

"What's going on?" Violet asked. "Why are you so busy?"

"We're still dealing with the ghouls…"

"Ghouls?" Violet interrupted. "I thought it was one ghoul."

"So did we, but when we dug the hole we were ambushed by three of them. One got away, and Jorge thinks there may be more that we didn't see."

"That's bad," said Violet. "Three is bad. More could be really bad. I mean, really, really bad." Her voice was low, and she seemed to Mitch to be talking to herself more than to him.

"I know. In addition to that, I have a new investigation I just started. I wanted to do some follow-up on it this afternoon."

Violet stared into space, still pondering his announcement that the police had found multiple ghouls in the cemetery, but at the mention of a new investigation, she glanced at Mitch with renewed interest.

"You have been in an awful hurry to get out of the house. I was hoping it wasn't because you were trying to avoid me. Is it this new investigation? Tell me, Officer Loman, what are you up to today that is more important than a long, hot shower with a very willing partner?" Violet tapped a slender finger on her chin as she posed the question. "If I might be so bold as to inquire?"

"Not more important," Mitch hastened to clarify. "But important. I re-opened Lieutenant Delaney's murder investigation this week. I need to call and talk to the homicide detectives with the county and get copies of whatever evidence they have. Then, I want to ask them to do some DNA follow up. I'm pretty sure it's already been done a couple times before, and it probably won't do any good, but I figured I should at least give it a shot."

"Delaney has been around DTPD for a long time," Violet commented. "If his murderer was going to be caught, don't you think it would have already happened? Lots of other people have looked into it. Are you sure you want to get involved?"

Mitch picked up his fork, speared a final fragment of cooked egg and mopped it through the remaining spill of ketchup on the plate. He popped the sodden morsel in his mouth as he considered the question. The last bite of omelet went down with the help of a few swallows of water before he responded.

"I'm sure. I know the odds of accomplishing anything aren't great, and I'm not getting my hopes up, but I figure I should try. As the only detective working for Dasan's Terrace, I should at least look through the old case to see if there's anything anyone else missed."

"Oh, that's right," Mitch blurted. "I forgot to tell you. The chief promoted me back to detective Wednesday night."

"Congratulations!" said Violet. She put a hand on his shoulder and squeezed lightly. "You deserve it. They never should have taken away your job in the first place. It was wrong and completely unfair. But as far as this particular investigation goes, Mitch, you aren't the one I'm worried about. I'm glad you're not getting your hopes up, but what about Delaney? He can get rather … intense when discussing his murder."

"I haven't told him what I'm doing yet."

"Good," said Violet. "You should probably keep it that way, at least until you know if you have any new leads to work. Are you doing anything else, today?"

"I also wanted to get to work early so I could talk to the chief before he leaves for the night. I have some questions for him. Did you know he investigated the lieutenant's homicide once? Ten years ago."

"I actually did know that," said Violet.

Mitch stared at her in surprise. "You did?"

"What? I'm allowed to know things," she said cryptically. She took another polite nibble of her omelet. "What were you going to ask him?"

"I ... well, I wanted to know...."

Mitch paused to get his thoughts in order.

"Okay, I don't know if you saw the chief's written report, but it's really weird."

"How so?"

"It's mostly blank," said Mitch. "He mentions a witness to the crime, but I can't get access to a name or what this witness told him. He also ran some blood through a company called Thirteenth Circle, but there's no information on what the company does or where they're located. All I know about them is that they couldn't help his investigation."

Violet began to giggle. She cupped a hand over her mouth so she wouldn't spit out any food, then began coughing as she choked on the small mouthful of egg and cheese. Grabbing her water glass, she took a few sips to help her swallow.

"You okay?" asked Mitch.

Violet nodded, still laughing and coughing lightly.

"What's so funny, then?"

"Not funny, really. A surprising coincidence is a better way of putting it. You know that company? Thirteenth Circle?"

"Yeah?"

Violet held up her hands with a little flourish. "Ta-daa! That's me."

Mitch set his fork down and pushed his empty plate away. "What do you mean, that's you? What's you?"

"Thirteenth Circle. That's me. Actually, it's Alyssandra and the entire coven, but that was the name Chief Jefferson knew us by when he paid us for our help. He was only a sergeant at the time, and we didn't know each other well yet. Instead of trading favors, Alyssandra accepted monetary payment for her help, and Thirteenth Circle is the name of the company she established to account for any income we earn. Even witches have to pay taxes in the real world, and believe me, we pay a lot of it. Thirteenth Circle does very well for itself."

"What did he hire you for?" Mitch asked excitedly. "Can you tell me?"

"Of course. It's supposed to be confidential, but you are the detective working on the case, and I'm sure Simon wouldn't mind you knowing. Besides, I promised I wasn't going to lie to you anymore, about anything. I meant that when I said it."

"So, what did he want?"

"Simon brought us some blood. It was from the man who murdered Lieutenant Delaney. He asked if we could use it to find the killer."

"And…?"

"We tried, but it didn't work. Tracing magic works best when you have a piece of the person you want to find. We found you with a single hair, remember? Normally blood works even better than hair, but with the killer's blood we came up empty. Unfortunately, over time the affinity between a person and an item grows weaker. The longer they are separated, the harder it is to establish a link between them. Twenty years was too much time. The blood led us nowhere."

"I hadn't even considered using magic to find the killer. I guess it doesn't matter though. Even if I had, it wouldn't have helped. Not now."

"No, it wouldn't. Sorry," agreed Violet.

"Chief Jefferson mentioned an anonymous witness in his report. Did he by chance mention the name of that witness to you?"

"No, but I can guess who it was. I think so can you if you give yourself a moment. When your chief came to us with the blood, he told us that he had been talking with the ghost of the man who had been killed. That conversation was the reason he was trying to solve the murder."

"He was talking to Delaney!" exclaimed Mitch. "Damn. That makes sense finally. That's how he managed to find a witness that no one else had spoken with. It also explains why the entire interview was completely redacted from normal reports."

"Yup." Violet grinned. "He had recently met Delaney at that time, so the lieutenant must have been the unnamed witness. Unfortunately, I can't tell you what he found out in the interview. I don't have that information."

"Nothing very useful, I'm guessing. The killer still hasn't been caught."

"Did I help?" asked Violet, pushing her own plate aside, though most of the omelet remained uneaten.

"You did. A lot."

"Do you still have to go to work early and talk to Simon?"

"I ... I guess not. I could talk to Delaney directly and find out what he said, tonight, or any time during my regular shift."

Violet opened her robe and let it fall off her shoulders. It draped onto the stool, leaving her naked from the waist up.

"I think I might go take another shower," she told him. "If I asked you to come scrub my back, would you say no again?"

Mitch shook his head, his gaze drifting downward over the exposed curves of Violet's torso. "If you ask, I definitely will not be saying no a second time."

Sometime later, crossing the front lawn of Violet's front yard toward the sidewalk, Mitch pulled his keys from his front pocket and pushed the unlock button on his car fob. The blue, Ford sedan he left parked at the curb chirped acknowledgement, however he did not hear the familiar "chunk" of the car's door locks disengaging. Mitch paused, examining the car and the fob in his hand.

Had he not heard the locks because he wasn't paying close attention, he wondered, *or had the car been unlocked?* He could not believe he had forgotten to lock the car doors when he arrived at Violet's home this morning, it was such an ingrained part of his routine whenever he left the vehicle unattended. He even locked it when it was parked in his own garage.

He stepped into the street and paced around to the driver's side door.

Mitch rubbed his thumb on the door's keyhole. He did not see any scratches indicating someone had tampered with it, and his thumb came away clean of grease, metal shavings, or other debris. Pulling the door open, he peered into the vehicle's interior, searching for anything amiss. Everything looked exactly as he had left it that morning. To be certain, he even opened the glovebox and the center console and reviewed their contents. Everything was present and seemingly undisturbed.

Maybe he was being paranoid. Nobody had been in the car. He had been tired when he got off work that morning and, in his exhaustion, he had probably slipped up on his routine. It was a simple oversight. Shrugging his misgivings away, Mitch slid into the driver's seat and started the engine.

He put the Ford into drive and pulled away from the curb, leaving the neatly manicured front yard of Violet's suburban home behind. The neighborhood was similar to many others in Rancho Murietta, with larger property lots, and gated communities established outside the crowded limits of nearby Rancho Cordova. Violet had not been exaggerating when she said the coven had significant assets and investments to take care of its members. It made Mitch a little envious as he headed back toward his own cookie-cutter tract home in Elk Grove.

The envy was short lived, however. He was in too good of a mood. He still had a warm glow in his chest, both from the hot shower and from the pleasant workout that had followed. The cloudless blue sky overhead further added to his happy disposition. After the disasters he had endured the last two nights, it was nice to feel that things were shifting in his favor for a change.

Mitch touched the green button on his steering wheel that connected his car's Bluetooth to his cellphone. When he heard the familiar high-pitched tone on the car speakers, he announced, "Call Homicide Bureau."

The car responded to his request with a neutral female voice that told him, "Calling Homicide Bureau. When your call is over, you can hang up by pressing the red disconnect button."

The call was picked up after only one ring. Mitch expected another recorded voice asking him to input the extension number of a particular detective, but he was pleasantly surprised when a man's voice responded.

"Homicide Bureau. This is Detective Minhas. How can I help you?"

"Oh, hey, Ali. My luck just keeps improving. It's me. Mitch, from Dasan's Terrace. It's nice to talk to you again."

"Hi, Mitch. What's up? Did you need something, or is this a social call? Or maybe you have new information on the dead kid's accomplice?"

Detective Ali Minhas had assisted Mitch recently during an investigation into a golem that was committing burglaries in Rancho Cordova. After it killed one of its victim's during a break-in, the Homicide Bureau, and Ali, had gotten involved. Ali had been a tremendous help in the investigation. The man was smart and dedicated, but because of the magical nature of the golem, Mitch had been forced to tell a few lies and keep the detective mostly in the dark regarding the more supernatural elements of the case.

One of those lies was the existence of an accomplice. There was no accomplice, and all involved parties had been accounted for. The story about a second suspect had merely been a necessary ruse to explain the confusing scene left behind after the final confrontation between the golem and DTPD.

Mitch felt bad lying to Ali, but he believed it was better than looking like an absolute lunatic by trying to tell him the full truth about the crimes. Mitch was having enough trouble accepting the reality of magic and artificial constructs himself, and he was right in the middle of it all, living with it every day.

"Nothing new there, sorry. I was calling because I wanted to follow up on a cold case from 1994. I need to see some of your original files and evidence collected at the scene."

"Right. The Delaney murder. My boss got an email from your boss yesterday and he let us know we should give you whatever you want. So, fire away. What can I do for you?"

"I was hoping you could send me copies of all recorded interviews and surveillance videos taken at the scene. I already have the report narratives, but I thought it might help if I could review the videos and recordings myself."

"There isn't much there, but what we have I'll send it your way. Unfortunately, the witness interviews at the scene weren't recorded. Neither were the suspect interviews for that matter. Most of those were documented with hand-written notes that were thrown away or shredded after the reports were written. That's the way they did business back then."

"Crap. There's nothing?"

"Once the detectives established alibis and eliminated any potential suspects, there was no reason to bring them into the station for interrogation. So, no. No recordings."

"What about the surveillance videos?"

Mitch heard the clicking of plastic keys on a keyboard as Ali researched evidence records on the case.

"We have one," Ali said after a moment of hunting. "There was one camera inside the shop pointed at the door. I haven't watched it, so I don't know how helpful it will be. There weren't any other cameras inside or out. That kind of equipment was expensive in the nineties, and it usually wasn't very good, either. I'll email you a file of what we have. What else?"

"The report said there were two cameras. Where's the other footage?"

"Hang on," said Ali. "Let me see. Okay, here we are. The second camera was pointed at a refrigerator holding all the beer. The owner was apparently tired of kids grabbing his stock and running out without paying. Nobody was seen in that video. It's here, though, if you want me to send it."

"Yeah, please. Send me everything you've got. I don't want to miss something because I got lazy."

Mitch sat in his vehicle, stopped at a red light. He stared into space tapping his fingers on the steering wheel as he went through his mental checklist of evidence he wanted to review. The driver behind him tapped his car horn impatiently. Glancing up, Mitch saw the light had turned green and he hurried to accelerate through the intersection.

"Um, hang on," he muttered, as he pulled his thoughts back together. "What about blood work?"

"What about it?" asked Ali.

"What was done with the blood samples, and when was the last time they were compared to the federal DNA database?"

Mitch heard more typing over his car speakers as Ali reviewed the case.

"It looks like the blood was initially typed. The shooter was B negative. Someone did examine a sample of the blood through electrophoresis. They got a basic DNA profile, but with nothing to compare it to, it got shelved until a suspect could be found. The blood was examined again in 1998. They did a more detailed DNA profile, but again there was nothing to compare it to, so it just sat."

"The detectives didn't run the sample through CODIS?"

"It doesn't look like it," admitted Ali. "The federal database had been around for a few years, but it wasn't very big, so it's possible the detective working the case didn't think it would be helpful. It's also possible he didn't know what CODIS was, so didn't know where to send a sample."

"Was it ever checked prior to 2005?" asked Mitch. "Or after?" If it hadn't, that would be a huge oversight in this investigation.

"Um, no. Sorry, it looks like 2005 was the first time it was checked. In 2005, the DNA was run through the feds, but there were no matches. It does look like it was checked again in 2014, but still no hits."

"Damn. Another dead end. Hey, Ali, could you do me a huge favor?"

"What do you need?'

"I just got my detective shield back yesterday and I don't have any of my clearance codes yet to run evidence through the FBI. Would you be willing to put the blood through CODIS one more time? It's been ten years since the last time it was checked and maybe our suspect got arrested and entered into the database since then. I know it's a long shot, but I don't see any other leads to try."

"No problem," Ali assured him. "I'll put in the request later today. Anything else?"

Mitch paused. Was that it? He could not think of anything more to ask. There wasn't much to work with on this case, and once again he was forced to confront the idea that he might be at an ending point before he ever really got started.

"I don't think so, unless you can think of something I'm missing. Thanks for your help."

"Delaney's murder is pretty cold. Any real leads have already been worked and tied up, but if I think of something that might help, I'll give you a call."

"I appreciate it. I'll talk to you later."

Ali hung up on his end, and Mitch disconnected the call.

The conversation had been mostly disappointing. The more Mitch looked, the less promising this case became. He was standing at a blank wall, scratching at a solid surface and searching for the slightest crack where he might get some purchase to move forward. Unfortunately, any cracks had long since been worn smooth by time and the investigators that had gotten there before him.

"Sorry, Tim," Mitch muttered aloud. "I'm trying, but this isn't looking good."

CHAPTER

 9

On Saturday morning, Mitch lay sprawled in his own bed, gazing at the white painted ceiling of his tiny bedroom. He had been like this for almost an hour, ever since he arrived home, stripped off his clothes, and crawled under the covers. Today, unlike Friday, he was alone and completely unable to sleep.

The sun shone brightly outside, but it was not the daylight that kept him awake. The bedroom window faced west, and several mature trees grew along that side of the house keeping the room comfortably shaded from the limited, indirect lighting.

He could hear birds outside in those trees in his postage-stamp-sized back yard, chittering and peeping at one another as they announced their individual territories and their willingness to share a nest with the right partner. Far off in the distance, a dog barked incessantly at a neighbor mowing his lawn, but these noises also were not the cause of his insomnia.

The room was warmer than he liked, but not yet hot enough to trigger the air conditioning. His dark blue, cotton bedsheets were pulled down to his waist, and the comforter – decorated in a green and yellow flower pattern that his ex-wife had bought four years ago then left behind when she moved out – was kicked into a pile at the foot of the bed. He had decided on several occasions that he was going to throw the damned comforter away and replace it with something more closely matching his own personal tastes, but laziness and lack of readily disposable income had so far won out. For now, it remained a reluctant part of his bedroom décor.

Mitch stared at the moving shadows above him, at the flickers of light and dark caused by the blades of his ceiling fan rotating on their slowest setting. The motor of the fan hummed softly to itself as it powered the plastic vanes around in a lazy circle. Usually, the sight was soothing and helped him to drop off to sleep. Today, the spinning rotors offered no relief from his pervasive wakefulness. With an exasperated sigh, he worried that sleep was simply not going to be in his future this morning. His mind would not calm itself. His thoughts repeatedly circled back to Lieutenant Tim Delaney, as determinedly as the fan blades circled overhead.

The night before, work had been uneventful. He had taken the opportunity to review the surveillance video Ali emailed to him. The video was black and white, grainy, and as useless as Detective Minhas had suggested it might be.

The main surveillance camera captured Lieutenant Delaney entering the store. At least, Mitch assumed it was Delaney. The blurry, gray recording made it all but impossible to make out a person's features. The man had been an officer in uniform, of that much Mitch was certain, so it stood to reason he was watching Tim Delaney.

The uniformed subject entered the store, turned right, and disappeared from the fixed sight of the camera. A few minutes later, two men wearing ski masks and dark clothing appeared, passing through the front doors and also quickly disappearing from view. One of the men, the second to enter the store, carried a shotgun. The other, Mitch knew from the report, had been carrying a handgun, but the weapon was almost invisible on film due to the poor resolution. There was no sound to the video, so Mitch watched several silent minutes of a static image of the front doors and a digital clock display running off the seconds in the lower left-hand corner of the screen.

When approximately four minutes had elapsed since the masked subjects' first appearances, they were seen running out of the store. The suspect with the shotgun was still carrying the unwieldy weapon in his right hand. His left arm was slung over the shoulders of the second robber and he was being helped out of the store, limping badly and seemingly unable to put any weight on his right leg. Both men disappeared from view as the automatic doors of the store cycled shut behind them.

In an effort to be thorough, Mitch also reviewed the beer fridge video. There was nothing to see. Mitch searched for anything, including signs of movement in the reflections of the refrigerator's glass door, but despite several viewings he was finally forced to admit the recording was of absolutely no assistance whatsoever.

Groaning, Mitch shifted to his right side, flipping the pillow under his head to find a cooler spot to rest his cheek. He tried again to close his eyes and silence the chaos in his mind.

Still no luck. His eyes popped open once again.

This week was his short work week. Last night was his final shift of three in a row so he did not need to go back in tonight. If sleep wouldn't come, he decided he shouldn't force it. While a couple hours of shuteye would have been nice, he could still muddle through the day and maybe sleep tonight like a normal person.

His thoughts drifted to a list of home and yard chores that needed attending to. He could get them all done if he started right away. Later he could shower and have a peaceful evening to himself. Or he could call Violet and see if she wanted to get an early dinner then come back to his house to settle on the couch and watch some television. They could pretend they were nothing more than a nice normal couple, with none of the supernatural weirdness that seemed to find them lately. They could try to forget about murders, ghosts, and magic for a few hours.

The distinctive crash of breaking glass reached Mitch's ears and he jerked bolt upright in his bed.

The noise came from downstairs, and from the sound, he guessed someone had broken a window in the kitchen or the living room. Whether it was vandalism or someone making their way into his residence, it was impossible to tell. Either way, he needed to deal with it immediately. Fully alert, heart jumping in his chest, he listened for any further disturbance.

An alarm system protected Mitch's house, but he never turned it on when he was home. Too many accidental activations in the mornings, absentmindedly opening a door or window, had broken him from the habit of using it. So, despite the possible break in, the warning sirens remained mute.

With no alarm going out, nobody would be calling to check on him.

He was on his own.

Alone, maybe, but certainly not helpless. His duty weapon was secured in his locker at work, but that was not the only gun he owned. Reaching to his right, Mitch slid open the top drawer of his nightstand and removed the Sig Sauer, 40 caliber handgun he kept at home for self-protection.

His cell phone rested on the nightstand, plugged into its charging cord. He did not pick it up. Mitch felt perfectly capable of dealing with any would-be intruder on his own. He did not need the cavalry rushing to rescue him, especially from what might turn out to be nothing more than a tree branch blowing in the wind and breaking a window.

Mitch slipped out of the bed. Wearing only a pair of loose, gray boxer shorts, he padded out of the room to the top of the stairs. From his vantage, a narrow section of the living room downstairs was visible, but in that space he did not see anything out of place. Slowing his breathing, he strained to hear any sounds coming from the first floor of the residence. All he heard was the rush of blood pulsing in his own ears and the muffled growl of his unknown neighbor's distant lawnmower.

Mitch moved from the landing to the top stair, peering left to right as the downstairs living room came into sight. He briefly wished he had grabbed shoes. There was broken glass somewhere down there and he did not want to step on it while barefoot. He was not going to retreat to the bedroom to find shoes right now, however. Not when someone might be sneaking around the ground floor of his home.

He side shuffled down two more steps. His view of the living room was now mostly unobstructed. Still nothing appeared obviously out of place.

"Anybody down there?" he called out. "I'm a police officer and I'm armed. If someone is there, tell me now or you might get shot. I'm not going to warn you again."

No answer.

Mitch paused and listened. An unfamiliar noise emanating from the kitchen caught his attention. He heard a soft clicking, like the tapping of a stick on stone, or the hesitant tick, tick, tick of an erratic metronome. The sound was subtle, but distinct. He knew he wasn't imagining it, but he also could not identify the source.

He took three more quick steps, descending the stairs. Mitch was a little more than halfway down now, and when he lowered his head and craned his neck, he could see the entrance to the kitchen. The skittering clicking noise continued.

Something low and long appeared, crawling across the linoleum floor like a monstrous insect.

"The fuck?" muttered Mitch, in shock at what he was witnessing.

His intruder appeared to be a knife. A bowie knife to be precise, with an eight-inch blade supported over six spindly, black, spider-like legs. Bare metal gleamed with reflected sunlight as it crossed the kitchen. The handle of the weapon was wrapped in brown leather cords above a shiny, gray steel pommel, while the curved blade protruding beyond the cross guard was honed on both sides to a razor edge, giving it an unpleasantly lethal appearance.

The creature shifted left, then right, as it seemed to search for something it knew must be nearby. The tips of the legs scuttled along the floor, holding the knife aloft and creating the soft ticking noises. The image was surreal, and Mitch wondered for a long moment if he had actually fallen asleep upstairs in bed and was dreaming this entire bizarre situation.

Mitch froze on the stairs, shocked into immobility by the alien intruder that had entered his home. He was growing accustomed to bizarre occurrences at work, the cemetery was a perfect place for strange magical oddities to appear, but he was not prepared for the supernatural to follow him home. The hair along the back of his neck prickled, and he felt a tickle climbing his spine.

This simply was not okay.

"The fuck?" he said again.

The insect-limbed knife paused, then oriented itself toward the sound of his voice. The tip of the blade pointed directly at Mitch. The monstrosity began moving again, shuffling out of the kitchen and into the carpeted living room, making its way to the foot of the stairs.

Mitch shook himself from his shocked paralysis. Whatever was happening was a threat that needed to be dealt with, not goggled at until that spidery knife thing buried itself hilt-deep in his chest. It was clearly seeking something, and the fact that it had broken a window and invaded his house meant it was likely that Mitch was the focus of its hunt.

Mitch leveled his gun at the walking blade, then lowered it. Would shooting the thing stop it? Somehow, he doubted it. If he relied too heavily on the pistol and it failed to protect him, it might be too late for him to try something else. Mitch remembered the ghoul that had shrugged off multiple bullet wounds. This thing could probably do the same. He was bringing a gun to a knife fight, and he was frighteningly certain he was on the losing end of that matchup.

The knife crawled closer to the stairs, moving slowly but deliberately as it homed in on its target. Mitch watched the intruder approach. Under closer scrutiny, he could see the umbra of shifting magic surrounding the blade, animating it. Shooting it would definitely be a bad idea, he concluded. Even if he could hit such a small moving target – and there was no guarantee of that – he might simply break it into several pieces, each fragment still hellbent on impaling him.

He set the gun down on the stairs. He was going to need his hands free to deal with this problem.

Mitch recalled his training with Violet. When facing a magical attack, he could avoid, deflect, or disrupt the threat. But how was he supposed to do that? The magic was so thin in this part of the city that it was practically nonexistent. If he wanted to pull enough force to create a shield, it would take several minutes, if not hours. He was confident he did not have that kind of time.

The knife crossed the living room in a sudden rush, reaching the foot of the stairs in a matter of seconds. At the surprising burst of speed, Mitch jumped up two steps to give himself a little more distance between himself and the crawling weapon.

No, he definitely did not have enough time.

To his surprise, the knife hesitated when it reached the stairs. The point of the blade poked the first step then backed away. It crab walked back to the stairs, approaching sideways, before lifting first one multijointed leg and then another to explore the top of the riser. Before it could gain any purchase, the knife slipped and fell, toppling onto its back. The legs danced angrily in the air for a moment before the gleaming blade managed to right itself.

Mitch felt the first stirrings of hope.

"Can't figure out the stairs?" he asked the creature. "That's too bad."

The knife pivoted, pointing again towards Mitch. The thing had no eyes to speak of, but the eerie posturing left Mitch with the feeling that it was staring directly at him.

"You stay right there," he told it. "I'm going to grab my phone and call someone that will know what to do with you."

The knife, to Mitch's relief, did remain where it was. The blade settled onto the floor and retracted all six of its spindly legs. The limbs seemed to melt into the leather wrapped handle, disappearing completely.

"Good … er, knife. Stay."

The knife shivered on the ground and the handle blurred. The legs did not reappear, but four shimmering dragonfly wings unfurled from the spine of the weapon, stretching outward until they extended half a foot to either side. They fluttered and flapped experimentally, gradually gaining speed until they were moving so fast as to be almost invisible. The knife lifted from its resting place on the living room floor.

"Shit!" cried Mitch. He snatched up his discarded pistol and ran for the bedroom. All pretense of knowing what to do was gone. He only wanted to get something solid between himself and this airborne assassin. He bolted into his room and slammed the door shut behind him.

"Of course, the fucking thing flies. Of course, it does."

Mitch hurried to his bedside table where his cellphone sat, plugged in and charging. He snatched it up. Before he could pull up the phone's number pad, a loud bang made him jump. The knife struck the bedroom door from the other side and the blade pierced through the hollow partition. The tip of the weapon protruded on the interior side of the door where Mitch could see it, the metal end wiggling up and down as the knife tried to free itself. He thought he had more time, but he had not counted on the thing being able to fly so damned fast. It was fortunate he had not dawdled when he decided to head for the bedroom, or that blade might be buried in his back rather than in the bedroom door.

The blade wriggled free, then a moment later it struck again, creating a new hole a few inches to the left of the first.

The cheap interior doors in Mitch's home were not built to provide much protection against intruders. Particularly not intruders made of steel and animated by malevolent magic. Such a flimsy barricade could not withstand this assault much longer. The knife would break through in only a few more attempts.

Maybe when it crashed through the door, the wings would break and the creature would be forced to stay on the ground again, he thought. But that was an incredibly thin line on which to hang one's hopes of survival.

Mitch tapped the button on his phone screen that pulled up his most dialed numbers. He touched Violet's name. She might know how to deal with this type of hostile spell. He certainly wasn't going to dial 9-1-1. Any cops unlucky enough to come out to the house while this flying nightmare was still around would end up dead.

His call went to voicemail. Violet was not picking up, and Mitch's time was running out.

The knife withdrew and struck again, and again. On the fifth attempt, the door fragmented, leaving a hole wider than Mitch's closed fist. It was more than enough room for the attacking blade to pass through, and the pursuing thing was now in the room with him.

Unfortunately, no, the wings were not damaged. The flying blade appeared fully functional and absolutely lethal.

"Something weird is trying to kill me!" he shouted, then tossed the useless cellphone onto his bed.

There wasn't time to try another number, so he left the phone on, figuring Violet would hear his final moments alive, and perhaps be able to piece together what had happened to him.

If she couldn't save him, she could at least avenge him.

The hovering weapon twitched left and right, orienting itself and seeking its prey. Mitch glanced around the room, searching for anything he could find that might help him defend against the intruder. He found nothing promising. The metal assassin's hesitation lasted only a few seconds before it target locked onto Mitch once more. It darted toward him.

Mitch grabbed the first thing that came to hand. It was the pillow on his bed. Not an ideal shield, but it was all he had to work with. He swung the pillow at the oncoming knife, hoping to at least knock it off course. The blade cut into the pillowcase with almost no resistance, punching through the interior cotton batting as if it did not exist. The knife's edge was frighteningly sharp, and it shredded his makeshift bludgeon easily. Fortunately for Mitch, as the flying weapon pierced through the pillow, the cross guard became entangled in the torn material. Mitch completed his defensive swing, and the ensnared knife was carried along with the damaged pillowcase.

Realizing he had the thing captured, if only for a second, he swung the pillow again, slamming it and the knife against one of the bedroom walls. The knife ripped free and tumbled to the ground at Mitch's feet. The wings fluttered experimentally as the magic-driven weapon recovered its equilibrium. It rose from the floor, already back on its mission of murder.

"Shit!" Mitch swore, tossing the ruined pillow aside.

What had made him think slamming the thing into a wall would do any good? It had only moments ago broken through his door. A few bangs and jolts were nothing to the metal monstrosity.

The answer to his question, however, was obvious: he hadn't been thinking at all. He had simply been reacting.

Mitch was fighting a delaying war. He wasn't sure if there was a way to win this confrontation, so he was playing for time. He realized that, but he also was not ready to give up and let the thing have him. He grasped the top drawer of his bedside table and jerked it free. He did not take the time to dump out the few contents inside, the unknown assassin's blade was already reoriented on him. When it raced forward, he swung the drawer like a batter standing over home plate, swinging for the centerfield bleacher seats. He heard the cheap particleboard break apart as he made contact with the flying knife.

The murderous weapon arced through the air, tumbling end over end until it struck the far wall of the bedroom. It fell to the ground with a heavy thump. Mitch did not wait to see if the knife would rise again. He knew it would. The magic animating it was too strong to be deterred by any number of physical assaults. Instead, he grabbed the flowered comforter from his bed and tossed the heavy material over the knife before it could launch itself again.

The comforter shifted and leaped as the weapon underneath attempted to wrest itself free. A gleaming triangle of metal pierced through the flowered bedcoverings; the magic-driven killer was already escaping the obstruction holding it on the ground. Damn, but that blade was sharp. The knife would be loose in only a few more seconds.

Mitch crossed the room and knelt on one corner of the comforter; his right hand poised to grab the handle of the knife the moment it tore free. He did not really want to touch the thing. He had no idea if there were other threats besides the obvious stabby parts of this flying killer. The blade might have poison on it. One tiny scratch might leave Mitch twitching on the floor, praying for the blade to pierce his heart and end his agonized suffering.

Or there could be other magical traps he could not see. The knife was obviously infused with magical energies, why couldn't there be a spell attached to it designed to trigger at his slightest touch? He might grab that handle only to have his brain and entire nervous system fried in an instant of blazing, enchanted fire.

Yet, he did not seem to have any other alternatives right now.

Time was up. The material of the comforter parted with a soft ripping noise, and his relentless pursuer emerged, dragonfly wings fluttering as they came free. Mitch was out of ideas, good or bad. He took the only option he had remaining to him and grabbed the knife, wrapping his right hand around the grip and squeezing desperately to hold the weapon in place.

He immediately regretted it.

CHAPTER

 10

Mitch clutched at the handle of the magically enhanced blade, wrapping the fingers of his right hand firmly around the leather-wrapped grip. The animated knife reacted immediately to his touch. It thrashed and twisted in his grasp, trying to tear free. The thing fought him like a living creature, beating its wings and writhing in his grasp. Mitch felt heat beneath his palm, rising to a level that was uncomfortable but not yet painful. He worried the growing warmth might increase and begin to burn him, but he also knew the inevitable outcome if he released the knife and allowed it to fly free.

He held on desperately, praying the discomfort would not grow any worse.

The knife turned in his hand, bringing its dagger-sharp point in line with Mitch's face and wrenching his wrist to an uncomfortable angle. Mitch wrapped his left hand around his right and forced the blade away from him, aiming the dangerous tip toward the ground where it would be least capable of doing him harm. The knife continued to fight him, but with both hands locked around its handle, Mitch managed to control it.

The knife could not injure him, but Mitch was similarly unable to damage the knife. They had reached a stalemate. Though the moment was far from a victory, at least Mitch had successfully grabbed this tiger by the tail and bought himself time to think. Searching the room around him, he wracked his brain for a way out of this mess. He had no idea how to kill the thing or make it stop, and he knew the moment he grew fatigued enough to allow the tiny assassin to escape, it would come after him again.

Avoid, deflect, or disrupt.

The mantra Violet taught him came to mind. She had explained that it did not matter what kind of attack came at him, his response should always be the same: avoid it, deflect it, or disrupt the source powering the threat.

He had tried avoiding the knife, but that had been a colossally unsuccessful effort. It had followed relentlessly, breaking through a door to get at him. Same with deflecting. Mitch had smacked it around the bedroom several times and it kept coming back. He was uncertain if it was possible to make an inanimate object angry, but if it was, he imagined this flying knife was probably plenty upset with him after being swatted with a pillow and a drawer, then getting pinned to the ground with a bedcover.

The only tactic he had not yet tried was to go after the magic animating the little bastard.

There was no ambient magic to speak of in this part of Elk Grove, or in most of Sacramento County for that matter. It was why Dasan's Terrace was so important to most of the region's magic using population. That lack of power meant whatever spell animated his would-be killer had to be self-contained and powered within the knife itself. It was not pulling power from anywhere outside. Mitch would have seen the trail of magic if it was, and without a source of energy to sustain it, the blade should have fallen inert by now.

Mitch scanned the weapon for hints of internal magic, and although he could see a pale yellow haze around the weapon that indicated magic was being used, he could not "see" the spell itself. Where was the magic coming from?

In a flash of inspiration, Mitch realized the creature must have some kind of magical equivalent to batteries, and with that thought, he knew where that battery might be. He focused his attention on the heat the knife's handle was creating against his palm with a new understanding. He explored the warmth emanating from the leather wrapped grip. The sensation was not a magical trap to burn him if he touched the weapon, and it wasn't some kind of self-defense built into the blade's grip. He was feeling the spell itself, set somewhere in the handle of the bowie knife. The heat was only his mind attempting to interpret the sensations flowing into him from the spell as it continued to operate under his hands.

This was progress. Now that...

"Whoops! Hold still you little fucker."

The knife twisted violently. The movement surprised him, and the weapon succeeded in rotating slightly in his hands. Mitch shifted his grip and steadied the creature. He aimed the point of the blade downward and stabbed it firmly into the floor. Mitch felt the blade bite through the carpet and the underpadding before striking the hardwood base underneath. With both hands locked on the handle, and the tip lodged in the bedroom flooring, holding the knife stationary became much easier.

Mitch released a quick breath and refocused his attention on the magic animating his unwelcome guest. The spell involved was beyond his ability to understand so he did not attempt to disable it, at least not yet. He traced the release of magic from the handle into the wings that allowed the blade to fly and move about. He could not see anything remarkable about the stream of energy, so he attempted to draw on the magic, to pull it away from the knife. The magic refused to be diverted by his efforts. The wings of the knife buzzed angrily at his attempt, fluttering faster until they were a blur of gossamer, almost invisible to his naked eye.

"Don't like that, huh?" Mitch muttered under his breath. "Well, you're really not going to like this next part."

Cautiously, Mitch pushed the point of the knife deeper into the floorboards, then released the handle with his left hand. The weapon twitched, but he was able to maintain control with only one hand. With his free hand, he grasped the delicate wings. He closed his fingers around the translucent membranes and twisted, crushing the wings and tearing them away from the flying knife.

The disconnected pieces fell apart. The particles forming the appendages separated like a collapsing sand sculpture before dissolving and drifting away into nothingness. The heat under Mitch's right hand increased and new wings immediately reformed on the blade.

Before they could expand to full length, Mitch tore them away again. The magic continued to flow from the handle at an increased rate, repairing the damage almost as fast as he could initiate it. With the surge of restorative magic generated from the handle, Mitch realized that a small part of that energy was not as well guarded as the previous, steady current that animated the assassin. He could touch it, pull on it, and draw a tiny bit away from the source reservoir.

Mitch smiled.

"Gotcha!" he exclaimed.

Mitch gathered all the magic he could steal from the knife. It was not much. As the weapon tried to repair itself, he siphoned only a fraction of its output. Hopefully, it was enough.

He compressed the borrowed energy into a red pinpoint of light. When the light touched the tip of the reforming wings, Mitch activated a spell of his own.

"Fire," he said softly, using the word as a mental focus; telling the magic what he wanted from it.

The glint of red acquiesced to his demand, changing to white as it grew hotter. Smoke rose from the ends of the dragonfly wings. Mitch concentrated more intently on his focal point, willing more power into his assault. The creature's wings burned and shriveled under the barrage of heat. The spell animating the knife redoubled its efforts to repair the continuing damage, but the increased outflow of power actually made Mitch's job easier. He stole larger wisps of the new magic, increasing his rate of damage on the wings.

The cycle continued, Mitch destroying the delicate wings of the knife with magical fire while the spell in the blade's handle pumped more and more energy into repairing itself. Several minutes passed with the two combatants locked in this perpetual cycle.

Mitch began to sweat, his body shaking from the effort of maintaining his fire spell. Exhaustion was setting it, and he was not sure how much longer he could continue to mentally hold the magic and simultaneously prevent the knife from escaping his grasp. Twice more already it had wrenched in his hands, trying to pull away from its captor. Mitch had managed each time to maintain control, but how much longer he could successfully hold it in his rapidly fatiguing grasp, he had no idea. He hoped it would be long enough.

At last, the magic began to fail.

Mitch felt the flow of power diminish and, at first, thought it was his own concentration that had slipped. When he attempted to reestablish his draw on the knife's magic source, he realized the trickle of power he was pulling from was what had weakened, not his spell. The heat beneath his right palm also faded. The leather wrapping the knife's handle was still warm, but it was simply the warmth of an object having been clenched so tightly for so long.

As the magic in the handle weakened, Mitch lost his ability to steal energy from the stream. The wings reformed, and the knife began to twitch and turn in a last-ditch effort to free itself and complete its mission.

It took a few moments for Mitch to wrestle the weapon back into submission.

"So much for burning. I guess we go back to the method we started with. Ready for this, old buddy?"

Mitch grabbed the creature's wings and ripped them free. He tossed them to the carpet where they dissolved and dissipated. New wings formed. Mitch tore these away as well, and again new ones grew to replace the damaged ones.

The third time he removed the wings, they did not reappear.

Mitch pulled the knife point from the carpet, cautiously grasping the handle in both hands to be sure it could not suddenly turn and stab him. The knife did not move. He banged the blade against the ground several times in an effort to wake it up or make it angry. There was no reaction to his abuse. Mitch checked but felt no heat from the spell in the handle, and he could not see magic of any kind surrounding or suffusing the blade.

It seemed to be dead.

Or perhaps dead was not the right description. It had simply returned to its initial state as an inanimate object.

Not yet willing to fully trust the thing that had so recently attempted to kill him, Mitch tossed the knife across the room and snatched up the comforter, ready to use it to ensnare the weapon should it rise up and come after him again. The knife remained on the ground where it fell. The attack appeared to be truly over.

Mitch pushed shakily to his feet and walked over to the bed, stepping carefully around the unmoving knife. He set the comforter down at the foot of the mattress, then picked up his phone. It was still connected to Violet's voicemail. He tapped the red button on his screen and hung up the call.

He tried to remember what he had said to Violet when the call first went to her message inbox. It was something dramatic and fatalistic he was sure, even if he could not remember the exact words. If she was anywhere near her phone, she would be noticing that he had left an uncharacteristically long message for her. It would probably make her curious enough to pull up his call and listen to it. The first thing she would hear would be his panicked voice yelling about knives and murder or something like that.

She would not bother to listen to the rest of the message at that point. She would probably...

The phone rang in his hand. Mitch smiled and tapped the cell's screen to answer the call.

"Hi, sweety," he said calmly. "What's up?"

Mitch gave Violet a rough sketch of the ordeal he had survived, sticking to the highlights of his confrontation with the flying knife. She gave him strict – and unnecessary – orders not to touch the weapon again until she got to his house. He wholeheartedly agreed with her assessment. With nothing better to do, Mitch dressed, then went downstairs. To keep himself busy, he cleaned up the shards of glass from his broken window while he waited for her car to pull into the driveway.

Violet wasted no time getting to his house, and Mitch figured she had probably violated a few traffic laws to show up so quickly. When Violet arrived, and after assuring herself that he was alive and unharmed, she demanded that he take her upstairs to see the weapon that had been used in the assassination attempt.

In the bedroom, Violet knelt beside the blade and held her hand over it, searching for something Mitch might have missed or else did not know how to look for. She closed her eyes and cocked her head slightly as if listening to something far off in the distance.

"I don't feel any magic. I think it's completely spent."

Mitch nodded. "I think so, too. It's been on the floor for almost an hour now and hasn't tried to move. Should we do something with it? If it gets a new magical charge, will it come after me again?"

"No," Violet assured him. "Once the magic is used up, the spell breaks apart. You can't simply repower it. You would need to cast a whole new spell."

"That's a little bit of good news at least. This guy isn't a threat anymore. All I need to worry about is another, completely different, homicidal flying knife coming after me." Mitch sighed. "Can you at least tell me who sent this one?"

"Sorry, No. The magic is totally depleted. I don't know what spell was used or how it was cast, so I can't guess who created it. If there was any magic left, I might be able to tell you where it was done, at least. Magic has its own signature based on its primary source. If the spell was cast at Dasan's Terrace, I would recognize it." Violet shrugged helplessly. "But there's nothing left here to examine. It's been completely expended."

161

"Ironic. By trying to deplete the magic and save my life, I wiped out any decent hope of figuring out who wanted me dead."

Violet stood, then settled herself on the edge of Mitch's bed. "Do you have any idea who might want to kill you?"

"None. Not with a spell anyway. I'm sure there are people I've arrested that would love a shot at me, but none of them have access to this kind of magic. I don't think they do, anyway. What about you? Have you heard about anyone that wants me out of the way?"

"No."

"Are you sure? What about...?" Mitch didn't finish the thought, but Violet understood who he was talking about.

"Alyssandra doesn't want you dead. She still wants you trained."

"Maybe. But you did say she could be trouble if she feels threatened by me. She also knows where I live."

"That doesn't matter," Violet told him. "Whoever activated the assassin's spell didn't need to know where you live. A hair, or a small personal item that you've recently been in physical contact with would be enough to target the magic. Anyone with enough power and the knowledge to use it could have been responsible for this."

"You may be right. Maybe. But has she said or done anything that would make you think she wants me dead?"

"Absolutely not. Alyssandra did not send the knife."

"Are you one hundred percent certain of that?" asked Mitch. His voice was soft. He was not directly accusing Alyssandra of anything, but he had to be absolutely sure she wasn't the threat before he began looking elsewhere.

Violet paused, her gaze dropping to her feet. "No. No, I'm not certain, but I'm pretty sure she would have told me about something like this before she sent it. If for no other reason than to be sure I wasn't in the way when it showed up."

"Then we're starting this investigation from scratch. Everybody is a suspect. I'll let Chief Jefferson know what happened and book the knife into our evidence room. I don't want the local PD to get their hands on it, just in case we're wrong and the thing has a little life left in it after all. I'm going to go into work tomorrow and check the blade for fingerprints and a manufacturer. Maybe I can find out who made it and who they sold it to."

"Tomorrow? What are you doing today?" asked Violet.

Mitch gestured in the general direction of the downstairs kitchen. "Today, I've got a window to fix."

"Oh. Right. Okay then, would you mind if I put a few wards on your house while you fix the window?"

"What kind of wards?" asked Mitch, surprised. "Can you stop another attack from getting in?"

"Maybe. I can put protections around the outside of the house that will break apart most spells that pass the outer barrier. It won't do any good against spells that are cast inside your house, but if something like that knife breaks through your window again, my barriers will disperse the magic animating it and cancel the threat."

"That's great," said Mitch with genuine enthusiasm. "How are you going to draw power to do that, though? There is like zero magic around my house."

"I need to run to the cemetery first and charge up."

"Charge up?" Mitch's eyebrows drew together in confusion. "What do you mean by charge up?"

Instead of answering, Violet removed a ring from the index finger of her right hand. It was a gold band with three diamonds set into the top, each a little larger than half a carat. She held it out toward Mitch. "I want you to take this."

"Um, why?" he asked, hesitantly.

Violet frowned. "Don't be a dumbass. I'm not proposing, I'm trying to keep you safe. Gemstones can be used to store magic. Pretty much any type of stone will work. I prefer diamonds, however. Can't blame a girl for liking a little bling. The fewer the flaws in the stone, the more power it can hold. These diamonds are almost perfect. There is enough power in the ring for three small spells, or one big one. You can draw the magic out exactly like you pull it from the space around you at Dasan's Terrace."

Mitch accepted the ring. He tried placing it on his pinky, but the ring stopped at the second knuckle, refusing to go any further.

"It doesn't really fit," he told her.

"Then put it in your pocket, but keep it with you. From now on, you should always have access to magic. I recommend you start investing in some nice jewelry, so you have several sources to draw on. I'll teach you how to recharge the stones later when we're at the cemetery. It's simple, but you need a ready source of magic to do it."

"Thank you." Mitch slipped the ring into the front pocket of his pants.

Violet kissed him then patted his chest possessively. "Stay safe while I'm gone. Whoever wants to kill you, probably isn't going to give up after one failed attempt. They're going to try again. I'll come back as soon as I've collected enough magic to set up the new wards. I also need to speak with Alyssandra and let her know what happened."

"If she doesn't already know."

Violet flinched from the accusation. "Please, Mitch. Alyssandra didn't do this. I'm not saying she isn't capable of it, but she has no reason to want you dead. Particularly since I would leave her if I ever found out she tried to hurt you."

"Maybe that's why she didn't tell you what she was doing."

Violet ignored this last comment. "I'll be back as fast as I can. Then I'm not leaving you again until we know who's behind the attack."

CHAPTER

 11

"Damn it!"

Mitch slapped his pen onto the pad of paper in front of him. Running a hand through his hair in frustration, he reread the information on the computer screen. The bad news remained depressingly unchanged.

As he had advised Violet the day before, Mitch drove into work Sunday morning to access the department computers. He wanted to begin his hunt for potential suspects as soon as possible. The quicker he could figure out who wanted him dead, the more likely would be his chances of avoiding any of their future efforts.

Violet elected not to go with him. She told Mitch as long as he had access to sufficient magic, such as on the cemetery grounds, she felt he was more than capable of looking out for himself. Besides, the other officers working at the police station might not appreciate having a witch hanging around them all day. She decided to stay at his house and attempt to add some additional protections to the wards she had erected around his property. Better safe than sorry, she had admonished him before he left.

"I know, right? Damn them. Damn them all!"

Mitch jumped at the sound of the unexpected voice nearby. He thought he was alone in the officers' computer room. Turning to the door, he saw a uniformed man wandering in from the hallway holding a motorcycle helmet under his left arm. The officer was older, maybe somewhere in his fifties, with a ruddy windburned complexion that suggested he saw quite a bit of sunshine but had never quite managed to develop a tan. Watery blue eyes peered merrily at Mitch from over a burly white mustache trimmed into an upside down "U" shape. The facial hair completely covered the man's upper lip before drooping downward all the way to his jaw line. The mustache clearly did not meet regulation grooming standards for the Sheriff's Office, but then, few things about the DTPD technically met regulation standards.

A brass nametag on the officer's uniform shirt read, "S. Papadados."

"What, or who, were we damning, by the way?" asked Officer Papadados. His mustache stretched outward, outlining a mischievous grin. He approached Mitch, extending his right hand in greetings. "I've seen you in passing in the locker room from time to time, but I don't think we've been properly introduced. I'm Stu Papadados. Day Shift. You are?"

Mitch twisted in his chair to grasp the man's hand. "Mitch," he told the older officer. "Mitch Loman. B-Nights."

"Mitch. Oh, *Mitch!* You're the guy that got his bell rung by that golem a couple months ago. I heard you put up a hell of a fight." Stu pumped Mitch's fist with more exuberance. "Pleasure to finally meet you. I don't often get to run into the guys that work the opposite end of the week."

Stu pulled out a chair and settled in at the computer station next to Mitch. He dropped his helmet onto the desk beside him.

"What are you working on? What's so important that it's got you here on your day off?"

"Somebody tried to kill me yesterday. They sent a…,"

He paused, hesitant to start talking about magic and spells to a stranger. Then he remembered, Stu was a Dasan's Terrace cop, too. If he couldn't discuss the supernaturally weird stuff that was happening to him with another DTPD officer, who could he talk to?

"They sent an enchanted, flying knife to my house to kill me." Mitch pointed at the bowie knife resting on the table next to his computer keyboard.

Stu whistled, impressed. "Whoa. A golem *and* a magical assassin. You graveyard boys have all the fun. And what had you all twisted up when I walked in? What are you working on?"

"I'm trying to get a lead on where the knife came from. I found a manufacturer name on the blade, but it's a company out of Texas that sells knives all over the world through all kinds of distributors. Between sporting goods stores, cutlery sellers, malls, gun shops, outdoor markets, and gas stations, there are hundreds of places the knife might have been purchased from all over Sacramento County. By the time I track down every potential point of origin, I could die of old age. Or the killer might get me first."

Stu gestured toward the knife. "Do you mind if I look at it?"

Mitch picked up the weapon and extended the handle toward the uniformed officer. Stu reached to take it but hesitated.

"You already dusted it?" he asked, making sure the knife had already been checked for fingerprints before he handled it.

Mitch nodded at him. "Unfortunately, the only prints I found on it were mine. I still put them through the computer to check in case I'm wrong, but I'm pretty sure there won't be any leads there."

Stu accepted the weapon. He held it in both hands and examined it from all angles, checking the blade, handle, and even the metal pommel.

"You said it flew when it attacked you?"

"Yeah. It grew some kind of weird insect wings and flew after me."

"Do you know if the spell was active or a one-time trigger?"

Mitch paused before answering. "I'm not sure. I'm not positive what you're asking."

Stu lowered the knife and met Mitch's eyes as if surprised by the response.

"A one-time trigger is like a booby trap," he explained. "It's completely inactive until something sets it off. Imagine a hand grenade with a trip wire tied to the pin. You kick the wire, the pin jerks out and bang! It all goes off at once. An active spell, though, is always running. It pulls magic constantly to keep going, and the only time it stops is if it runs out of magic or it finishes the job it was sent to do."

"I didn't stumble over it. The knife came after me from somewhere, so I guess that means it was an active spell."

"Do you have a lot of ambient magic where you live?" asked Stu.

"Practically zero."

Stu nodded and examined the knife again. His tongue poked out of one corner of his mouth, and he absently licked at the edge of his mustache while he pondered. The gesture reminded Mitch of Lieutenant Delaney, who he had often seen doing the same thing.

"No magic in the air," he said at last. "This little guy needed its own power supply then."

"The handle felt hot when I grabbed it. I think it was carrying its own magic."

"Probably," Stu agreed. He tapped the leather wrapping on the handle. "How would you feel about cutting the leather off? Unfortunately, there's no way to unwrap it and put the cover back on later. The knots are probably glued, so you have to cut them to get the braiding off."

"Why? Why do you want to take the wrap off?"

"Because I think you're right about it carrying its own magic. Metal is a lousy storage material, so I'm betting there's a gemstone in there somewhere. You see that bulge in the middle?"

Mitch looked to where Stu was pointing. The wrapped handle thickened noticeably in the center. Mitch had initially assumed that the widening was done intentionally to make the grip feel more secure in the palm of the hand. Now that Stu was bringing it to his attention however, he was no longer so sure it was a standard design feature.

"I see it," Mitch said.

"I think we need a closer look at what's causing it."

Mitch considered Stu's suggestion. On the one hand, cutting the leather wrapping might be considered tampering with evidence. On the other, it could be argued it was part of a continuing investigation. If Stu thought it might tell them something important, then maybe it was the correct next step.

"Okay. Cut it off."

Stu went to work. He removed a folding knife clipped to his duty belt and snapped it open, revealing a three-inch blade with a serrated edge along its entire length. The motor officer raked the saw-toothed blade back and forth along the base of the leather braids covering the handle of the bowie knife. One of the braids separated, then another. When three of the leather cords were severed from the securing knot, the entire handle wrapping loosened and unraveled with no further resistance.

Stu unwound the leather cords until he had revealed the metal tang of the bowie knife underneath. He grinned in triumph as he held it out for Mitch to see.

"Ta-daa!" he exclaimed.

A hole had been bored through the exposed tang, and inset into the opening was a multifaceted purple gem the size of a robin's egg.

"What is that? A sapphire?"

"Amethyst," said Stu. "Capable of holding a lot of power, but still relatively cheap to purchase."

"How do you know so much about magic and gemstones?" asked Mitch. "Are you a witch, too?"

Stu's shaggy white eyebrows went up at the question, and Mitch kicked himself mentally for adding the "too" to his query. He had given away a little more about himself than he had intended.

"No," Stu said. "I'm only a motor guy. DTPD recruited me because I know how to ride a motorcycle and they needed people to do escorts for funeral processions. I don't even see ghosts, to tell you the truth. I've been working for Dead Town for ten years, though, so although we day folk don't see as much voodoo crap as you night owls, I've still run into my fair share. It pays to know the clientele around here. Don't you think?"

"Definitely," Mitch agreed.

"And now you have a new lead to chase."

"I do?" asked Mitch, tentatively.

"Look at the setting on that stone," Stu told him. "The leather wrap on the handle might be amateur hour, but a pro set

171

that gem in there. I'm betting whoever tried to kill you didn't put the amethyst in there by themselves."

Mitch accepted the blade back from Stu.

"You're right," he said, taking a closer look at the amethyst and the shaped prongs that held it in place. "Someone knew what they were doing, and I don't imagine many jewelers are going to forget making a custom job like this for a client."

"Nope. Now you don't need to chase down the store that sold the knife. You only have to find the guy that set that stone."

"There are dozens of jewelry stores in this county," Mitch pointed out.

"Yeah, but dozens is better than hundreds." Stu pushed to his feet. "You've got some phone calls to make, so I'll leave you to it. It was nice meeting you Mitch. Don't be a stranger."

With that, Stu Papadados snatched his helmet off the desk and strolled out of the room.

Just like a day shifter, thought Mitch. As soon as there's work to do, he disappears.

Simon Jefferson double-checked the number on the side of the small, Victorian-style home. He wanted to be sure he had located the correct address before knocking. The numbers on the porch post matched the hastily scribbled note in his hand, so he stuffed the scrap of paper back into his pocket.

Traffic whizzed along the street only a few feet away from where he stood on the elevated concrete porch, so close he thought he could almost feel the rush of disturbed air as they passed. The front yard consisted of no more than a narrow strip of dying lawn and a pedestrian sidewalk before it gave way to two lanes of busy, downtown roadway.

This area of Sacramento had at one time been a thriving residential community, but as the city expanded, family residences had quickly been swallowed by the sprawling businesses and larger buildings of a growing metropolis. While the owners and the original houses themselves had been allowed to stay, any property once surrounding them had suffered from attrition and eminent domain until the private homes remaining were completely surrounded by asphalt streets, liquor stores, nightclubs, and the buzz of big city activity.

Even at this time of day on a Sunday, the cars moving through the city created a constant stream of noise and exhaust in this nominally residential neighborhood. Simon glanced back and forth along the rows of homes interspersed with office buildings and shops. It was an odd dichotomy of new and old. Many of the business fronts gleamed with fresh paint, new brick, and burnished steel, while the majority of the hundred-year-old houses appeared in desperate need of structural repair and yard maintenance.

Simon rapped on the wooden door with four quick taps. Chips of green paint flaked away from the sun damaged surface and fluttered to his feet. The house seemed to be relatively sound, especially in comparison to its neighbors, but it could certainly use some cosmetic help.

The door opened. An elderly black woman poked her head through the gap, blinking suspiciously into the bright sunlight. She was thin, emaciated almost to the point that she appeared to be ill. The white linen dress draping her from neck to toe did nothing to alleviate the image of a walking skeleton. The flowing garment hung shapelessly over her shoulders, looking like a sheet tossed over a wooden post. A red bandana was pulled over the top of her head, snugged tight to her skull and knotted into a neat bow in the back.

The curious expression on the woman's face melted into a scowl as she identified her visitor.

"Lost Child," she grumbled. "How very unfortunate to find you at my doorstep."

"Hello, Alyssandra," said Chief Jefferson politely. "You told me how upset you were last time because you did not like being summoned to my office. I thought this time it might be better if I came to you."

"Frankly, I do not find an unannounced appearance at my home to be much better. I would prefer a simple message requesting a meeting. We can then decide on the appropriate time and place. That would be most to my liking."

"Yes," agreed the chief of police. "That would probably be the best way to handle these things. Today, however, I have issues of some urgency that I did not think should wait for more normal channels of ... discourse."

Alyssandra stood silently, glaring at Simon.

"May I come in?" he asked. "We have important things to talk about."

"No," the witch said curtly. "State your piece and be quick about it."

Simon cleared his throat. Alyssandra was always irritating, but she seemed in rare form this morning.

"Very well. Dasan's Terrace is under attack, and I am strongly considering locking you out. Was that quick enough?"

Alyssandra's frown grew deeper. She took a step back from the door and waved Simon inside. "You damn fool," she muttered. "You come to my house and then challenge me like that? Well, come inside, then. I don't need the neighbors watching when I flay the skin from your living body."

Simon ignored the threat and entered the house.

Alyssandra closed the door behind them, then led her unwelcome guest through the foyer and into a parlor immediately to their left. To the right of the front door, Simon observed a hallway leading into a kitchen and to a flight of stairs that went upward to the second floor. Simon did not ask for a tour of the home, nor was it offered.

The parlor was a small sitting room with two, padded wooden chairs placed along one side of a low coffee table. On the opposite side was a two-person loveseat with plush, bright red cushions. China cups and saucers were set on lace place settings in front of each chair and within reach of anyone reclining on the small couch. The floor in this room was hardwood, overlayed by a green, oval carpet that reminded Simon of homes decorated back in the 1970's.

Pictures of women Simon did not know hung on the walls surrounding them, and though none of the faces bore any resemblance to one another, being of various ages, shapes, and races, they all shared one common characteristic. Each of the women appeared to be glaring at the camera with a cold condescending gaze. Simon decided he would not particularly enjoy running into any one of them in a dark alley.

One side of the room was dominated by a bay window that afforded a view of the street in front of the house. Billowy white curtains draped along either side of the window where it projected outward toward the front yard. Simon saw several cars drive by, but the sitting room remained peacefully quiet and undisturbed by any traffic noise. The quiet was more than could be accounted for by normal construction techniques, and he wondered what spell Alyssandra had used to create the clever sound barrier.

Alyssandra settled herself on the loveseat where she could face the street and gestured for Simon to take one of the seats across from her. He obligingly accepted the offered chair.

"Under attack. How?" Alyssandra began without preamble.

"Someone tried to kill Officer Loman yesterday. A knife was spelled to hunt him down and kill him. Fortunately, he escaped. He's trying to track down where the knife came from as we speak."

"I am aware of the attempt," Alyssandra replied. "Violet informed me of the incident soon after it happened."

"And...?" asked Simon.

"And ... what?"

"What do you plan to do about it?"

Alyssandra cocked her head quizzically. Her eyebrows lifted in bland inquiry at the question, and then she shrugged.

"Nothing, I suppose. Our agreement was that I would see to the officer's training. Beyond that, I have no responsibilities regarding his wellbeing. I am not his protector, nor am I particularly concerned with whether he lives or dies. In short, his safety is not my problem."

"That sounds like something the person that tried to kill him might say."

The unruffled calmness Alyssandra had been attempting to project suddenly crumbled. Heat flashed in her eyes.

"Are you accusing me of something, Lost Child? I warn you to tread lightly."

"We both know there aren't many around here with the strength and ability to create a spell like this one. Witches that powerful are on a very short list. You and your coven are on that list."

"Why would I want him dead?"

Simon threw the question back at her. "I don't know Alyssandra. Why would you want him dead?"

The witch growled, clenching her teeth to control her emotions before responding. After a few calming breaths, she forced herself to relax and resumed her air of unconcern.

"I did not send the knife. For the moment, I have no reason to consider your officer a threat or an enemy. Are we finished?"

Simon settled back into his seat and crossed his right leg over his left, emphasizing that he had no present plans of leaving. "Not really. I also wanted to let you know that when we attempted to remove the ghoul from the cemetery, we found others. We encountered three in fact, and there may be more."

"Violet has informed me of this as well. Again, I do not see how this directly concerns me or my coven. I did as you asked and located the ghoul's lair. Numbers were not discussed, nor was any further assistance beyond finding the beast."

Simon sighed. He was growing tired of Alyssandra and her games.

"Whatever is happening at Dasan's Terrace is far beyond our ability to deal with alone," he said to her, deciding the direct approach was his best tactic. "I need your help to find out who is creating or calling the ghouls to the cemetery, as well as who attacked Mitch Loman. I believe the two things are linked. Both require skill levels most witches or supernatural creatures lack, so it seems unlikely they both happened coincidentally. I need to meet that strength with strength."

"Your problems are not my problems," Alyssandra told him. "Of course, if you are in need of assistance, I'm sure arrangements can be made. We can find an agreement that is amenable to both..."

"No! No agreements. No contracts, and no deals." Agitated, Simon rose to his feet. "You have a vested interest in both Dasan's Terrace and in Officer Loman. I am asking you to help me and I am giving you the opportunity to protect both of those interests at the same time. If you refuse to assist me then I have to consider you a potential threat. If that is the case, I will be forced to try to find help elsewhere. I have considered speaking with Chang'e and finding out if she would be willing to look into the matter."

At the mention of the rival coven leader, Alyssandra leaped up from her seat as well, locking eyes with Simon. All pretense of cool detachment fled her expression. She leveled a bony finger toward Chief Jefferson.

"You are forging a dangerous path, Lost Child. Chang'e is a hazard to all of us due to her truck with demons. You know that."

"I also know she has the power to help, and I'll do what I must to protect my people. By the way, before I leave, I want to remind you that next week is a full moon. Until this issue with the ghouls and Officer Loman is resolved, I don't want you in the cemetery. If you show up next week, I will instruct my officers to arrest you for trespassing."

"We have never been friends, you and I," Alyssandra said, her voice grating as if she spoke through shards of broken glass. "However, we have never been enemies, either. You would not enjoy me as an enemy."

Simon stood up straighter in the small sitting room, his gaze locked in challenge with Alyssandra's. He felt for the warm pocket of power he always carried with him low in his belly. Stoking the flames of his magic, he let a glint of green light flash in his eyes. Alyssandra flinched when she saw the display.

"If you come for me, coven priestess, you will not find helpless prey. I advise you to be certain of what you want before you make threats like that or attempt to act on them. War will be costly, and if you succeed in taking me down, I have taken measures to guarantee that when I am gone, you will never be permitted inside the cemetery gates again. Even if you win, you lose."

Simon let the magic go. His eyes returned to their normal smokey gray.

"I'm going to ask one more time," he said, softening his voice. "I need your help. Will you work with me, or leave me to take more desperate steps than I already have?"

Alyssandra, unable to fully hide the rage still inside of her, chuffed out a frustrated breath. She dropped back on her couch in a billow of white linen, then waved brusquely for Simon to sit as well.

"For the moment, I will allow that our goals are aligned," she said. "Don't think I will ever forget how you have spoken to me today, however."

Simon sat down. "I don't. And I promise you, the dislike is mutual."

The witch's eyes narrowed. "What do you need?"

Simon sighed quietly. The first step, the hardest step, was done. Alyssandra was willing to work with him, albeit reluctantly.

"Until we know who is trying to kill Mitch, I want to get him out of town for a little while. If he isn't home, he will be a more difficult target for our enemy to find."

"I can help with that," Alyssandra said. "Violet has been asking for permission to take him away and begin his training as an exorcist. I will tell her to leave on Monday."

"Next, we need a way to identify who is both behind the attack and creating the ghouls. Do you have any ideas how we can accomplish that?"

Alyssandra nodded. A grim smile crossed her lips. "I think I know where to begin with that as well."

At the same time that Chief Jefferson was confronting Alyssandra, and Mitch was having his epiphany with the amethyst in the knife handle, Violet set out on a mission of her own. After bolstering the magical wards around Mitch's home, she decided to run an errand for the coven. Alyssandra had asked her several days ago to follow-up on her meeting with Tanya Kushing, the young witch that recently joined Missy Eaton's coven, and today seemed like an ideal time to do just that.

After a brief phone call, Tanya agreed to meet Violet for a cup of coffee and a chat at a small cafe near Tanya's house. The business the girl chose was a hole in the wall coffee shop with only a few tables available for customers to sit. The limited seating ensured most of the shop's clientele chose to get their beverages to go, entering and leaving with their drinks of choice after a brief wait in line. The lack of lingering guests would let the two women discuss sensitive coven matters without much fear of being overheard.

Violet ordered and picked up her coffee from the barista. She grabbed two paper packets of sugar from the rack beside the register along with a tiny disposable cup of cream and a plastic stirring stick. She carried her drink and accessories to the last table at the far corner of the shop.

Tanya, having arrived several minutes earlier, was already seated and sipping from her own steaming paper cup.

"Hey, Tanya," Violet said, smiling warmly as she set her drink down and plopped into a chair opposite the girl's. She reached across the square plastic tabletop and gave Tanya a friendly handshake. "Thank you for agreeing to meet with me."

Violet removed the cover from her coffee and dumped in the sugar and cream she had carried over. She stirred the mixture until it turned a light caramel color. The plastic cup lid she left sitting on the table, allowing her beverage to cool.

"No problem. You're not going to change my mind, but I don't mind talking. You seem like a really nice person."

Tanya was in her early twenties, with red hair, a pale complexion, and a dusting of freckles over her nose and cheeks. The girl was short, only an inch or so over five feet tall, with a wide face that positively glowed when she smiled. She had a look about her that was hard not to like, with open, honest hazel eyes that focused so intently on Violet that it made her feel like the most important person in the room.

Alyssandra wanted Tanya for the coven, and so did Violet. She had serious potential as a magic user. In addition to her power, though, Violet simply enjoyed the girl's company. She was pleasant, bubbly, and fun to talk with.

"Thank you. I like to think I'm a nice a person." Violet took a careful sip of her coffee, trying not to burn her tongue in the process. "Anyway, I promised Alyssandra that I would try to get you to join us, but it was really just an excuse to hang out with you again."

"You don't need an excuse," Tanya told her. "Call me anytime. I'm usually free if I don't have classes, or I'm not helping my parents with the restaurant."

"Your parents have a restaurant? That's cool. Why didn't you want to meet there? I bet the coffee would have been free." Violet laughed to show the comment was only a joke.

"It would be, but I spend enough time at that place already. I don't want to waste my free time there, too."

"Fair enough. Okay, sorry, but I have to do this. Let me get the boring parts of this meeting out of the way, then we can chat. Alyssandra really wants you. I think we have a lot that we can teach you, too. You sure you don't want to give us a shot? Maybe come visit at the cemetery one night to see what we can do?"

"I'm good," said Tanya, with a chuckle. "Thanks, though. I'll stick with Missy."

Violet sighed. She had already known the answer, but she would need to be able to honestly tell Alyssandra that she had tried. "Missy is sweet. I understand why you feel loyal to her, but you know she doesn't have any real power of her own. You must have figured that out by now. She has taught herself a few tricks, but if you're going to really learn how to use your gifts, you need someone that shares them."

Tanya sipped from her cup, taking a moment before responding. Looking pensive, she swallowed and put the cup on the table, holding it between both of her hands.

"I know. Missy isn't a real witch, but she knows enough to help me get started. Maybe someday, if I get to a point where I'm ready to learn more, I'll let you know. For now, I'll tell you the same thing I told the other woman when she asked me to join her. It's not about the power. Missy is a friend. I won't do anything to hurt her, so I'm going to stay with her coven."

Violet froze, trying to keep the concern off her face. She took another sip of coffee to cover any tells Tanya might otherwise see.

"What other woman? Who else talked to you?" Violet spoke slowly, keeping the tone of her voice casual. She thought she already knew who the other woman was, but she needed to be sure.

"Oh, I can't really pronounce her name. She said she ran another coven in Sacramento, and she wanted me to join her, too. She was about your age. She was Chinese, I think. Chang? Or maybe Chun? Does that sound right?"

"Chang'e?" suggested Violet. She pronounced the name as, "Chung-uh."

"Yeah! That's right. You know her?"

Violet nodded. "I know her. Not well, though. We've met a few times." Violet did not think detailing her personal feelings about Chang'e would be helpful. It might simply make her sound petty to Tanya, so she did not elaborate on their relationship.

Instead, to change the topic of the conversation, Violet reached into the front pocket of her jeans and removed a slip of paper. The paper was a folded, three-inch square, white sheet. Violet opened it and showed Tanya that it was blank. Setting the paper on the table in front of her, Violet placed her coffee cup on top of it, then glanced around the shop to be sure they were not currently being observed.

"Combustum," she whispered.

The trigger word activated a spell bound to the paper. A flash of light and heat burst between the two women causing Tanya to startle backward in her chair. The pyrotechnics quickly burned out and disappeared, as did the paper and the mostly full cup of coffee.

"We have things we can teach you that Missy does not know how to do. I wanted to be sure you understood that, so I figured a little demonstration might not hurt."

"Wow," Tanya breathed. "That was really cool. How did you do that?"

"Someday, maybe I'll have the chance to teach you. That's enough business talk today, though. I respect your decision to stay with Missy and I'm not going to push anymore."

Tanya continued to stare at the empty space where Violet's coffee had been. Violet saw the curiosity in her gaze and mentally patted herself on the back for having made a positive impression on the young girl.

"Tell me, Tanya," Violet said brightly. "What is your parents' restaurant like? I might have to check it out."

CHAPTER

 12

Mitch and Violet sat in the front seats of Mitch's car, cruising eastbound on Interstate 80. The yellow, lane divider lines flashed past as they moved along at a steady 70 miles per hour. His speed was a little above the existing speed limit for that stretch of highway, but not so much that any nearby Highway Patrol officers would take much notice of them.

Mitch spotted the offramp that would take them from I-80 west onto Interstate 680 southbound. He turned on his blinker and moved into the right lane to exit.

"I don't like this," he said.

Violet reached across the space between them and stroked her fingers through his hair. "So you've told me. A few times. Stop treating it like a punishment."

"How am I supposed to see it as anything else? It's like the chief doesn't trust me to take care of myself. He runs me out of town rather than let me try to find whoever sent the knife. To make it worse, he doesn't even trust me when I'm gone. He sends a babysitter along with me."

Violet laughed. "I'm not babysitting, pal. Remember, I sort of got kicked out of Sacramento, too. Anyway, this is a good thing. I wanted to show you an exorcism, and this is the perfect opportunity to do it."

"It still feels like running away," he growled.

"We're only going to be gone a week. Lighten up. We'll get to our hotel and relax a little bit. I'll call the family and set a time to meet with them tonight. The whole deal should only take a few minutes, then bang, zam, we get out of there and have a nice romantic dinner. Afterwards, we get back to our hotel and we have all night to … spend some uninterrupted time together."

"Bang, zam?" asked Mitch. "Did you really just say, bang, zam?"

"Hey," Violet cautioned. "Don't piss me off or you aren't getting any bang or zam tonight."

Mitch patted Violet's knee. "Okay. I'll think of this as a vacation," he promised. "A working vacation, though. As soon as we get to the hotel, I'm going to call a few more jewelry stores. It took me most of the day yesterday to make a comprehensive list of places that might have worked on that knife, and I need to call every one of them until I find the one that did it."

They drove in silence for a while, lost in their individual thoughts.

"How did they find you?" Violet asked, finally breaking the lull in the conversation.

"I'm not hard to find. My address can be found in a dozen places online."

"Yeah, but it's more than simply knowing where you live. You might have been gone when the assassin arrived. You could have been shopping, at a restaurant, or maybe even at work. The knife found you. It had to be attuned to you specifically somehow,

186

or whoever sent it wouldn't have done it remotely. They had to be certain it was going to locate its target before they let it go."

"What are you saying?"

"I don't know. I guess I'm wondering if the person who sent it knows you personally. How else would they have access to you to attune the assassin spell?"

Mitch pondered the question. He did not know anyone that was close to him that also had the ability to create such a powerful spell. No one except Violet and Alyssandra. Violet would not have sent it. Mitch was certain of that. Alyssandra? Well, Violet assured him she was not the threat, and while he did not believe the coven leader always had his best interests at heart, he did trust Violet's word.

"I have no idea. If you don't think Alyssandra did it, who else could?"

"Have you had anyone over to your house recently?" Violet asked. "Not necessarily a friend, but anyone. A contractor? Or a plumber? Has anyone been inside your house in the last week?"

No one had been in Mitch's home other than Violet in several weeks. He told her as much.

"What about at work? Anyone new working there? Maybe someone has been lurking around the locker room or the bathrooms? All they need is a hair, or maybe a thread off your uniform."

"No. Nobody. I don't know anyone who could do this that would have access to me."

Violet stared between her feet at the floorboards of the car, wracking her brain for ideas. "What about strangers in the cemetery? Anybody touch you? Has anybody been in your car or handled any of your clothing?"

"No. I keep telling you, I haven't…. Wait." Mitch paused. His skin prickled uncomfortably as a memory crawled its way forward in his mind. "My car. When I left your house on Friday, my car was unlocked. I thought it was a mistake and I'd forgotten to lock it that morning. Nothing was missing or moved around, so I figured no one had been inside. What if someone had gotten in, but they weren't looking for money or a car stereo."

Violet stared at Mitch, her eyes widening with sudden excitement.

"That could be it. They could have taken something you didn't notice," she said. "A hair off your car seat. Or something else with a connection to you. A used tissue, or an empty plastic water bottle you drank from."

"Yeah," he admitted. "I might not have realized something like that was gone."

"This helps," she told him.

"How does it help? It doesn't give us any leads."

"No," Violet agreed. "But it means that someone you have never met could be responsible. Anyone might have been your car burglar. It doesn't have to be someone close to you."

"And that's helpful, how?"

"It means you weren't necessarily betrayed. *I* wasn't betrayed."

Mitch realized she was referring to Alyssandra. Despite all of her previous reassurances, Violet had not been completely convinced Alyssandra was not involved in the attempt. Now, knowing that the suspect pool had significantly widened, she could more easily believe her coven priestess was innocent of the attack against Mitch. An outside force with a grudge against him, personal or otherwise, was more likely.

Oddly, it made Mitch feel slightly better as well.

"The attacker could be anyone," he said. "I might have stood right next to him at a store or coffee shop and never even realized the threat. Maybe getting out of town wasn't such a terrible idea."

"Maybe not. We'll do a little sightseeing in San Jose for a couple days, then drive to Carmel for the exorcism at the bookstore. A couple more days of fun there and hopefully, by the time we get home Sunday, Alyssandra will have found our suspect and this whole thing will be over."

"Hopefully," Mitch echoed. "I still feel like I'm running away, but for now, one step at a time. I have phone calls to make, and you have ghosts to catch." He reached toward the radio knob on the dashboard.

"Music?" he asked.

Mitch pulled his Ford to the curb at Violet's urging. With a flick of the key, the engine grumbled to a halt and both occupants were left in sudden silence.

After checking into their hotel that afternoon, Violet had called the family in question and arranged a meeting. The desperate woman on the other end of the line had begged her to come over as soon as possible since the haunting was due to reoccur at any moment. Violet and Mitch did not take time to unpack or change out of their travel clothes. They dropped their luggage in their room and climbed back into Mitch's car.

A few minutes later, here they sat outside the house in question.

The residential street to which Violet had guided Mitch was a winding, narrow strip of asphalt through cookie-cutter tract homes in the heart of Willow Glen. It was an older, established neighborhood in the suburbs of San Jose with well-tended lawns and fully mature trees along the front edge of each property. The mature oaks and birch trees provided a welcome shade and protection from the warm, June afternoon sun. A handful of kids played in a front yard a few houses away, but most of the homes were quiet, their residents either at work or choosing to while away the summer hours indoors.

Violet checked the address on the house and opened her door.

"This is it," she said.

Mitch climbed out of the car on his side and walked around the front of the vehicle to stand beside her on the sidewalk. He glanced at the watch on his wrist. It was twenty minutes before four o'clock.

"We made good time. Didn't the wife say the echo turns up at four every day?"

Violet nodded. "Do you still have that ring I gave you?" she asked.

"Um, yeah. I do. It's in my pocket." He reached into the pocket of the tan cargo pants he had selected to wear that morning and pulled out the diamond ring to show her.

Violet reached into the front pocket of her jeans and removed another ring. It was a heavy gold band with a wide, square setting on top. In the setting, affixed at the center of the square was a brilliant cut, red stone, at least three carats in weight.

"Ruby?" Mitch asked, indicating the blood-red stone.

Violet nodded again. "Here. I'll trade you. This might be more to your taste than the diamonds."

Mitch handed the diamond ring to her, and she slipped it onto her right hand. When she gave Mitch the ruby ring, he found it fit neatly onto the middle finger of his left hand.

"It looks good on you," Violet told him. "It's fully charged if you need to draw magic from it. I'm not anticipating anything difficult in the house, but there isn't much magic around us in this neighborhood, and it never hurts to be careful."

"It's nice," Mitch told her, admiring the ring on his hand. "Where did you get it?"

Violet glanced up and down the street, examining the surrounding homes in the neighborhood. For a moment, Mitch thought she hadn't heard his question, or had decided not to answer it.

"It was my father's," she said at last. She turned to the client's house and began walking toward the front door.

Mitch followed. He did not say anything further about the ring. He knew the circumstances of her father's murder and he also knew she did not like to talk about the incident. The very fact that she had given him this ring was testament to how she felt about him. Nothing more needed to be said.

A couple in their late fifties, or perhaps early sixties, answered Violet's knock on the door. The wife was pretty, in a motherly fashion, with a face tanned to a glowing olive tone, suggesting she spent a great deal of time in the sun. She had deeply worn smile lines along her cheeks and around her eyes. The woman wore a shapeless, flower print dress, which gave no hint as to her size or figure beneath.

The husband, however, appeared less pleasant. He had a pinched, narrow face that Mitch immediately disliked. He reminded Mitch of a rat, sniffing at the air in search of danger while it foraged through garbage. Thick-lensed glasses perched on the husband's long, pointed nose, sliding precariously down toward the tip as the man peered suspiciously at his visitors.

His complexion was also in direct contrast to his spouse's, with an almost sickly pale cast, as though he much preferred the shadowy recesses of indoors to any exposure to daylight. He wore a polo shirt that squeezed him around his paunch of a belly, and an old pair of slacks that hung on his waist as shapelessly as his wife's dress did on her.

They both smiled politely as Violet introduced herself, but Mitch could see the man was less than thrilled by their visit. The smile on his lips was tight, and the expression of friendly greeting never reached his cold, brown eyes.

Violet had been invited to their home most likely over the husband's objections, Mitch guessed. Which seemed a bit odd. Didn't they both want the ghost gone? Or did the husband think Violet was a charlatan taking advantage of their bizarre situation? Either way, it didn't matter. They had a ghost to remove, and Violet was more than capable of handling the job.

"And who is this?" asked the wife, indicating Mitch.

"Elizabeth, this is Mitch Loman. He is observing me today. He is … I guess you would call him a trainee. I'm teaching him how to do what I do."

"Hello, Mitch," the woman, Elizabeth, said to him. She extended a hand. He accepted it and returned the greeting.

"David," said Elizabeth, prodding her husband's arm with two fingertips, "step out of the way and let our guests inside. They can't help us if we keep them standing on the porch."

David reluctantly moved, allowing the unwanted strangers into his home.

The house was not large, but it was comfortable and tastefully decorated. The furniture and drapes had all been selected in warm tones of brown, burgundy, and cream, which gave the rooms a welcoming feel. To the left of the entryway was a carpeted living room, with a long, L-shaped couch and a lounger situated around a coffee table. The furniture in the room faced a wooden console built into the wall from floor to ceiling. The console held books, pictures, and knickknacks, all swirling in the orbit of a large television screen which dominated the largest space in the middle.

To the right was a kitchen and dining area separated by a marble covered island perfect for laying out food and drinks when entertaining guests. The marble counter was currently bare, with not so much as a pitcher of water on display. Further testament that Violet and Mitch were not wholly welcome in the eyes of the suspicious husband.

Beyond the dining space, there was a single step leading down into a formal family room. This room was immaculate and clearly meant to be a showpiece in the home rather than a space where people actually congregated. Two loveseats and two large reclining chairs were arranged in a horseshoe pattern to allow any occupants to face one another, while still drawing everyone's focus to the large brick fireplace at the far end of the room.

The family room reminded Mitch of old-style library parlors, where the lord of the manor would rest in his leather, high-armed chair, smoking a pipe and reading the paper in front of a roaring fire. Only this room was much smaller, and there were no bookshelves in sight. A few paintings of city streets and buildings decorated the surrounding walls, but that was the extent of the décor.

"This is where he shows up," said Elizabeth, pointing toward the empty family room. "My father comes in every day and sits down in that recliner." She indicated the chair furthest to the left and closest to the fireplace.

"Apparently, he shows up every morning about eleven, and every evening at four," said David. "Elizabeth has also come out in the middle of the night and found him in the chair, but she doesn't know if he appears every night or only once in a while."

"Apparently?" echoed Violet. "David, have you ever seen this ghost?"

David glanced toward his wife. The look was furtive and guilty. When he turned back toward Violet, he shrugged unhappily. "No. I've never seen him. But I trust Elizabeth. If she insists that the ghost of her father is haunting this room, then I believe her. That's the only reason I let her reach out to you people. If you can ... help her with this problem, I would appreciate it."

Mitch realized that David did not believe there was any ghost in the house. He thought his wife was suffering from grief at the loss of her father, and that grief was causing her to see the man in her house every day. Perhaps David was hoping that by allowing Violet to perform an exorcism, it would give Elizabeth some peace, and she would be able to move on with her life and set her sorrow aside. Along with the spirit of her dead father.

Was the ghost merely wishful thinking? A reflection of Elizabeth's loss? Mitch supposed they would all know the answer to that question at four o'clock.

"When did your father die?" Violet asked.

Elizabeth paused to do the calculations in her head. "About three months ago. On March eleventh."

"When did his ghost first start showing up?"

"A week or so later. David and I picked up a few boxes full of his things from the assisted living facility where he stayed before he died, and the night we brought them home, he started to appear. I'm sure he came here with his things, but I don't have the heart to throw all of his stuff away just to get rid of the ghost. We haven't even gone through the boxes to see what's in there, yet."

"You're probably right," said Violet. "The ghost is most likely attached to something you brought into the house."

Elizabeth led them into the living room, admonishing Violet not to trip on the step down. When they had all gathered into a huddle once more, Elizabeth rested a hand fondly on the leather recliner before speaking again.

"The people that work there said he liked to wander into the main room in the late afternoon and sit in front of the fireplace. He would stay there for hours, until the staff served dinner, then he would go back to his apartment to eat. I guess that's why he picked this room to haunt."

Mitch caught the pained expression that twisted David's features as his wife talked about her father. The poor guy probably thought his wife was having some sort of mental breakdown. It was possible she was, but they would not know for certain for a few more minutes. A glance at his watch showed him four o'clock was less than five minutes away.

"He would dress up for dinner," Elizabeth continued. "He would put on his suit pants, a tie and a vest, then he'd sit in front of that fireplace...." She trailed off.

"It's okay," said Violet. "I understand this is difficult."

"I've tried talking to him," Elizabeth told her. "He never answers. He doesn't even seem to notice I'm there."

"That's normal. It isn't your father, so it can't respond to you. It's just an echo, a ... well, I guess the best way to put it is that it's an image of who your father used to be. It does not need to be here, and I can make sure it doesn't bother you anymore."

Suddenly, Elizabeth's eyes went wide. "You're not going to hurt him, are you?" she asked, panic lacing her words. "I don't want you to hurt him."

Violet placed a calming hand on the woman's shoulder and stroked it gently. Mitch was impressed at how easily Violet dealt with distraught people. She would have made a great cop, he thought.

"I won't hurt him. Your father is already gone. Like I said, this ghost is only an echo. It can't feel pain. Think of the ghost as a movie of your father. You can watch the movie over and over again, or you can ask me to turn it off for you. Does turning off a movie change who your father was, or harm him in any way?"

"N-no," Elizabeth said hesitantly.

"No," agreed Violet. "It doesn't. I am here to turn off the movie that you don't want to watch any longer. That's all."

Movement at the corner of his eye drew Mitch's attention. He turned to see a stooped, elderly man wearing a vest and tie, walking through the dining room toward them. The man was bald, with only a fringe of downy white hair at his temples and running around the back of his shiny pate. As he walked, his neck bent forward and his head remained down, ignoring the people around him. His attention seemed focused solely on the ground in front of him, choosing his path carefully as he shuffled his feet forward one slow step at a time along the tiled floor.

At first Mitch thought the man might be real, but the hazy insubstantial edges of his clothing told him he was seeing something less than completely solid. When the corner of the dining room table passed through the man's hip, it confirmed to Mitch that this was the spirit of Elizabeth's dead father.

Elizabeth and Violet ended their conversation when they too caught sight of the apparition. David could tell something was happening when everyone turned toward the dining room, but his glance darted aimlessly back and forth, unable to find what had grabbed everyone else's attention.

He really can't see it, Mitch thought, watching David's confusion.

The spirit of the elderly man moved from the dining room into the family room. Rather than stepping down into the recessed level, the ghost continued to shuffle forward at its prior pace as it gradually drifted to the lower elevation of the next room. Violet and Elizabeth parted to give the old ghost room to pass between them.

The spirit collapsed into the waiting recliner.

Patting at its chest, the ghost searched for something in its clothing. Whatever it wanted did not appear to be where it belonged. Slipping one finger into the pocket of its vest, the ghost of Elizabeth's father prodded ineffectually in the empty recess a few times, then seemed to give up its quest. The echo settled back into the chair and sat quietly, staring forward into the cold fireplace.

"You see him, too?" David asked Mitch. He had watched everyone in the room apparently tracking the movement of something that he himself could not see.

"Yeah," Mitch told him. "You don't?"

"Describe him," David said brusquely. "Beth, don't say anything. I want to know what this guy sees."

Mitch took a closer look at the old man in the recliner. "He's an old White guy. Bald. His eyes look … brown. Maybe a little hazel. He's wearing suit pants, a vest and a tie, but not dress shoes. He has slippers on."

Elizabeth smiled. "Yeah. That's right. Dad always hated the way dress shoes felt on his feet."

"What color is the tie?" asked David.

"Red," said Mitch. "With a black crosshatch pattern. The knot isn't tight, and the top button of his shirt is undone."

David took a step backward and dropped down to sit on the riser leading into the dining room. He placed his hands over his face, but Mitch could not tell if he was relieved that his wife wasn't completely crazy, or if he was distraught that for some reason he seemed to be the only person in the room that could not see the ghost.

"Unbelievable," he muttered through his hands.

"Dad?" asked Elizabeth. "Dad, can you hear me? It's me, Beth."

"This isn't your dad," Violet said, gently. "It's only a movie, remember? Here, look."

Violet reached out a hand and passed it through the ghost in the chair. "He isn't really here."

Elizabeth stepped forward cautiously. She paused next to Violet, holding out a hand but not yet reaching for her father.

"Is he safe to touch?"

"Of course. This echo can't hurt you. It has no physical form."

Elizabeth extended her hand until the fingers would have been pressed against her father's chest. They passed through the material of his vest. She snatched the hand back, examining her fingertips as if checking for burns.

"See. He isn't really here. This is a memory. A pleasant memory it seems, of sitting in front of a fireplace and waiting for dinner, but still only a memory."

"What would happen if you left it alone?" asked Elizabeth. "Would it sit in the chair every day forever?"

"No. It would eventually fade on its own, but it could take a few years. This echo appears to be a strong one, and it could be around a long time. Do you want me to leave it alone?"

Elizabeth shook her head emphatically. "No. Please make it go. It isn't my dad," she said, sounding like she was attempting to convince herself more than Violet of that truth.

Mitch opened his vision to examine the echo's substance more closely. He noticed a pale, gray, ethereal strand trailing away from the ghost's form. The strand passed through the back of the chair where the old man sat, trailing through the living room until it disappeared through the wall to their left. The trail was only about the thickness of a string of yarn. It reminded him of the streaming tendrils he had seen flowing away from Delaney in his office, except this was much thinner, and there was only a single tether.

Mitch gestured toward the wall.

"What's next to this room?" he asked.

"That's the old back patio. We took down the screens and put up metal walls to make it into a storage shed. The only way into it is from a door that faces the back yard. We walled up the inside door when we converted it into a shed."

"Are any of your father's things in the shed?"

"All of them," Elizabeth said. "We put everything we got from dad's apartment in there. Like I said, we haven't had time to go through it all, yet."

"Can we see his things?"

"Of course."

Elizabeth waved at David until he stood up, and together they led Violet and Mitch out of the house to the back yard.

As they followed, Violet patted Mitch surreptitiously on the butt and whispered in his ear.

"You saw his tether, you clever duck. I didn't teach you that trick. How did you know about it?"

Also keeping his voice low, Mitch told her about what he had seen when he had examined Delaney's ghost a couple weeks earlier.

"I'm impressed how quickly you're figuring this stuff out."

Elizabeth and David paused at the entrance of the converted backyard patio. David fished a ring of keys from his pocket and unlocked the door to the shed, pulling it wide. Reaching an arm through the opening, he flicked a switch on a side wall, and the dark interior was instantly illuminated by several overhead lights.

He indicated Violet and Mitch should enter first.

"Okay, smart guy," Violet said to Mitch. "You saw the tether first. Show me where it goes."

Mitch entered the shed and moved to the back where it shared a wall with the main residence. He searched the smooth, solid surface, looking for the spot where the thread trailing from the echo came through. It took him only a moment to find it. With his eyes he traced the tether through the shed. It passed completely through a stack of three cardboard boxes balanced one on top of the other before penetrating into a second, identical stack. The thread entered the middle box in the second stack but did not reappear on the other side.

"This one," Mitch said, approaching the second pile of boxes and tapping the one sandwiched in the middle. "Whatever the ghost is linked to is in this box."

"I agree," said Violet, turning to face Elizabeth. "May we open it?"

Elizabeth entered the shed to see which box they had located. "Yes. Go ahead. That's one of the boxes we got from Dad's place.

Mitch removed the top box in the stack and set it aside. He grabbed the middle container and placed it on the floor in the center of the shed to give himself and Violet room to search its contents. Elizabeth moved to one side to give herself a better view of the proceedings, while David elected to stay outside. He might currently be more inclined to believe what was happening, but he still appeared to want no part of it.

The box in question was taped shut. On the top and on all sides, the name Alexander Gareux, presumably the name of Elizabeth's father, had been written on the cardboard with a black marker. Removing the folding knife he always carried with him, Mitch split the tape along the seams of the box and pulled the top flaps up. Layered across the top of the now open box, he found a heavy, woolen blanket, folded neatly within. He removed the blanket and handed it to Violet. She, in turn, set it carefully atop the first stack of three boxes they had not disturbed.

The remaining items inside looked like someone had swept the contents off a dresser and dumped them into a loose heap before placing the blanket on top to hold them in place. He found a couple of tattered paperback books, a deck of cards still in the cellophane wrapping, notepads, pens, plastic lighters, and a sleeve of three golf balls. It was the collected junk of years of emptying one's pockets and dropping the contents onto the nearest convenient horizontal space. Mitch reached in and stirred his hand through loose change, business cards, and other detritus.

It was garbage, he thought. Nothing of any importance. Then he noticed a small wooden jewelry box in the tumble of items.

The jewelry box looked hand carved. It was the width of a man's wallet and about four inches tall. Made from a rich brown wood Mitch could not identify, the box appeared expensive and

201

well cared for, at least in comparison to everything else in the carboard container.

The wood box stood out among the rest of the contents, but it wasn't merely its appearance that made Mitch pick it up. The slender gray tether they had traced out to the shed terminated where it touched the jewelry box. This, or something inside, was the source of the ghostly echo.

Mitch held up the item for Violet to see.

"Ah," she said, taking the box from his hands. She turned toward Elizabeth. "Whatever is keeping your father's ghost here, it's connected to this box."

A small silver clasp held the box closed, and Violet flipped up the top tab to free the catch. The jewelry box opened easily, revealing its contents.

Violet removed a pocket watch from the interior.

The back of the watch was gold, or gold plated, and the casing had several dents and scratches attesting to many years of use. The front crystal was similarly scratched and marked with fine lines, but still intact. Bold, black, Roman numerals circled the white face of the timepiece, and two slender arms sat motionless, proclaiming that the watch had stopped working at 3:27. A long, delicate gold chain trailed from the bow around the winding crown.

"It's the watch," Violet announced. "He's connected to this watch. Was it important to him in some way?"

"He loved that watch," said Elizabeth. "He always had it with him."

Violet offered the watch to Elizabeth, but she retreated a step, waving it away with a hurried gesture.

"No, thank you. Can you … un-connect him from it? Or if you take it with you, will he go away?"

"Both," said Violet to Elizabeth's questions. "I can take it or sever him from it. Both will make the echo stop appearing."

"Do it then. Whichever is easier." Elizabeth retreated into the backyard to join her husband.

Violet turned toward Mitch and whispered. "Watch me closely. Pay attention to how I extend my spirit."

In response to her directions, Mitch gazed into Violet, finding the hazy, silver-gray that formed her essence. The spirit swirling throughout her torso sent a questing branch of light trailing along her right arm until it filled her hand. The formless branch of soul light passed through her extended index finger, protruding an inch or so from the end of her fingernail.

Violet waved the exposed piece of her soul through the slender tether linking Elizabeth's father to his pocket watch. The tether broke as easily as a string touched by the blade of a scalpel. As Mitch watched, Violet's soul retreated back into the depths of her body.

"That's it?" asked Mitch.

"That's it," Violet agreed. "Echoes are really easy. They don't fight back. Not like a real ghost, or some of the nastier poltergeists. Come on, let's go outside and tell Elizabeth."

Elizabeth and her husband, David, locked up the storage room when Mitch and Violet exited, then led them back into the house. Mitch was surprised to see Elizabeth's father still seated in the lounge chair when they returned to the family room. By the expression on her face, so was Elizabeth.

"He's still here," Elizabeth said, pointing at the ghostly image of her father.

"Yes. I cut his ties to the watch, but the echo is strong enough that it may hang around for a few more days. It will eventually disappear completely. I can make that happen faster, but it may be a bit disturbing for you to watch."

"Do it," said David. "Finish the job. Get rid of whatever is in this room so we can get on with our lives."

Violet smiled at the husband and nodded her understanding. She extended a hand toward the old ghost in the chair. Mitch saw her spirit stretch out from her fingertips once again. She waved her hand through the echo. The ghost of Alexander Gareux startled at the touch, his face twisting in fear and shock. Mitch remembered a similar reaction from Harold, the ghost in Dasan's Terrace, when Mitch had touched him. The figure attempted to rise from the chair, but it was too late to attempt an escape. The image of Elizabeth's father popped and collapsed like a pricked balloon, leaving a drift of ethereal mist that drifted in the wake of Violet's hand. The remaining essence of Alexander's echo drifted through the family room a moment longer before fading from existence.

"He's gone," Violet said. "He won't be back."

Violet held the pocket watch out for Elizabeth a second time, but the woman again refused to touch it.

"Keep it," she said. "I don't think I want it in the house anymore."

Violet shrugged and handed the watch to Mitch. Unsure what he was supposed to do with it, he slipped the item into his pants pocket.

"Is he really gone?" David asked his wife, not trusting Violet's word alone.

When Elizabeth nodded confirmation, David reached into the back pocket of his slacks and removed his wallet. He unfolded it, removed a check from the billfold, then thrust the slip of paper at Violet.

"Here," he said, tersely. "As agreed. Two thousand. If we're finished here, I think it's time that you two left."

"Of course," agreed Violet graciously. She accepted the check, folded it and slipped it into her own back pocket.

Violet headed for the front door without another word, and Mitch hurried to follow her. As they stepped out onto the front porch, Elizabeth smiled and waved at them.

"Thank you so much…,"

Whatever else the woman had meant to say was cut short as her husband closed the door with a loud bang.

"I don't think he likes us much," Violet mused with a grin tugging at the corner of her lips.

"Two thousand?" asked Mitch. "Two thousand *dollars?* Did you charge them two thousand dollars to get rid of their ghost? That seems excessive."

"Hey. Thirteenth Circle is still a business, and we don't do charity work. We offer a very specialized service and people are expected to pay for it. Customers know what we cost up front. They don't have to hire us if they think we're too expensive."

"Maybe, but shouldn't you be doing this stuff for free? Who else is going to help people like this if you don't?"

Violet turned toward Mitch and placed a hand on his chest, forestalling any further complaint. Her expression turned serious.

"Mitch. You're thinking like a cop. You help people and you don't ask for anything in return because that's the way your job works. But this is how *my* job works. Exorcisms can be tricky, sometimes even crazy dangerous. I don't agree to do them often, and when I do I expect compensation for the risks I take. Honestly, I only agreed to do this one and the one in Carmel because you need the experience, so you don't one day end up in a padded room with a shredded soul and a broken mind."

Having said her piece, Violet stepped off the porch and headed across the front lawn of the couple's home toward Mitch's car. She glanced over her shoulder to make sure Mitch was following.

"I'm hungry. Get in the car and take me somewhere nice for dinner. Thirteenth Circle is buying."

In Sacramento, in the main room of the Drop-In Diner, Tanya Kushing busily bused tables, tossing dirty plates and glasses into the gray plastic bin she carried under one arm, and doing a quick wipe down of each table before new customers were seated. She hummed to herself as she labored.

She was not humming because she enjoyed the work. She didn't. The job was exhausting and always left her sweaty and dirty by the end of her shift. She was humming because she was happy. For perhaps the first time in her life, people were fighting over her.

Boys had never shown much interest in her, she never got picked for sports teams in school, and other than her parents, no one had ever offered her a job. For the most part she went through her day-to-day existence being ignored by the world around her. But not now. Suddenly, everyone wanted her to join their covens. Missy had found her first so, of course, her loyalties would always remain with her new best friend. Still, it was nice to hear the others tell her how wonderful she was and how much they would like her to come study witchcraft with them.

Chang'e had been intense, and a little bit scary, but she also seemed really eager to have Tanya join her coven. The tall Chinese woman had complimented her and praised her potential power. The pretty lady from Alyssandra's coven, Violet, had also told her how much potential she had and how much they wanted her to join them. Tanya had to admit, Violet's little demonstration with the disappearing coffee cup had been impressive. She would not mind learning how to do things like that.

Missy could not do the same kinds of things that Violet showed her. In fact, as Violet had mentioned, Missy seemed a bit limited in her actual understanding of magic. Maybe, if Tanya sat down with her and had a friendly discussion about the benefits of learning more powerful magics, Missy might see the wisdom in letting her go study with Violet. Not permanently, certainly. Maybe only a few days each month. Missy would always be her coven leader. She would not abandon her. A lifetime of having very few friends made Tanya fiercely loyal to those she had.

Tanya's mom, standing at the greeter podium at the front of the restaurant, waved a hand to get her attention. When Tanya waved back, her mother held up three fingers. Tanya's smile faded a bit, and she gave a quick nod in return.

Table three needed to be cleared.

Tanya hurried over, gathered all the dirty dishes left behind, then wiped down the table and booth benches. The customers had left a ten-dollar tip behind when they left, and Tanya slid the cash to the corner of the table where their server would see it and be able to scoop it up on her next pass by the booth.

With her dish bin full, Tanya headed into the kitchen. There, she would give the plates and silverware a quick spray down and load them into the dishwasher. The bin would also get a rinse out before she came back into the restaurant's main room to start the collection process over again.

As she passed through the swinging doors into the kitchen and preparation area, she saw her dad working at the grill. He was checking order tags on the wall then making sure the food he had sizzling on the cooktop matched the customer requests. Too busy to turn around, he did not notice her entrance.

Tanya set the gray bin on the stainless-steel counter next to the rinsing sink. The space should have been cleared from the last time she unloaded dishes, but someone had left a large knife on the counter. Other staff leaving dishes or silverware by the sink for her to clean was not unusual. What caught Tanya's attention was the knife itself. It did not belong to the restaurant.

The knife was long, with a curved blade, like a hunting knife rather than anything a restaurant kitchen would have. Including the handle, the entire thing was over a foot long. The handle had been carefully wrapped with leather cords, forming a soft, slip-free grip. The cord-wrapped surface might be perfect for a day hiking in the woods, but leather was difficult to properly clean, making it much too unsanitary to give to customers or use to prepare food.

Confused, Tanya pushed the knife out of her way and began emptying her bin into the sink. She glanced around to see if the person who had left the blade behind might be coming back to claim it. There was no one nearby.

When her bin was empty and the dishes inside had all been rinsed and stacked into the washer, Tanya picked up the plastic container and prepared for another sweep through the restaurant. She glanced at the sink once more, looking for the knife, but discovered the counter was bare.

The knife was gone.

She had not seen anyone walk by. Had she accidentally grabbed it and washed it with the other dishes? No. She was certain she would have noticed the leather wrapped handle immediately if she picked it up. The odd occurrence bothered her a bit, but not so much that she stuck around to ponder it at any length. She was too busy at the moment. The mystery of disappearing knives would have to wait to be solved later.

Tanya tucked the dish basin under one arm and turned to leave. As she spun toward the kitchen doors, she startled, muttering a soft, "Oh!" of surprise.

The knife was back.

This time, however, it did not sit idly on the counter. The knife hovered in the air only two feet from her face. Four glimmering, translucent wings extended from the base of the curved blade, buzzing menacingly as they fluttered to keep the weapon aloft. The point of the gleaming metal dagger aimed directly at her.

Tanya tried to back away, but the counter behind her prevented any escape.

The wings beat faster. The humming noise they made rose in pitch as the flying assassin prepared to engage its target.

Tanya dropped the basin and screamed.

CHAPTER

 13

Mitch sat on the haphazardly made bed of a downtown San Jose hotel room talking into his cell phone. After waking and dressing, he had pulled the rumpled bed sheets mostly flat and arranged the pillows to give himself a comfortable nest to work while Violet showered and got ready to go out to breakfast and do some sightseeing.

Determined to find the jewelry store that had modified the knife that tried to kill him, Mitch took every free moment available to work his way through the list of numbers he had compiled before leaving Sacramento. So far, those free moments had been limited, with Violet insisting on monopolizing his time. Not that Mitch minded in the least if he was being honest with himself. Regardless, in the past two days he had managed to contact only a dozen stores, and each time he had received the same answer. The employees could find no records of their store setting a large gemstone in a knife handle.

The list of uncalled numbers on his notepad remained depressingly long, but he resolved to call every last one of them if necessary.

Violet stepped out of the bathroom running a brush through hair that was still damp from her shower, pausing a moment to waggle her fingers coyly in Mitch's direction. She looked well rested and refreshed from their impromptu vacation, and seemingly eager to begin their day out. Anticipating another warm day, Violet opted for a pastel blue T-shirt and a pair of white shorts cut high enough to reveal most of her slim, muscular legs. Mitch took a moment to admire how good she looked even as he said goodbye on the phone and disconnected his latest call.

"Another no," he commented, picking up the pen sitting on the bed next to him. He scratched a blue line through yet another phone number on his list.

Mitch pulled up the dial screen on his phone and prepared to type in the next number.

"Wait, wait," Violet said. "No more phone calls. You can do that later. You promised to take me to get pancakes, then go on a tour of the Winchester Mystery House. I've been dying to see the place since Alyssandra moved us here to California. I can't wait to find out if there are any real ghosts in the building or if Old Lady Winchester was just totally nuts."

"You will. *We* will. I want to make one more call first. If I don't keep working on this list, I'll never get through it." Mitch saw the unhappy look on her face and hastened to add. "I promise we will have plenty of time for breakfast and the Mystery House."

Violet harrumphed, dropping onto the corner of the bed with enough force to jostle Mitch and cause him to drop his notepad. She flopped onto her back and sighed dramatically.

"Make it quick," she told him. "We've got shit to do today, Officer Loman."

"Yes, ma'am."

He tapped the call button and lifted the phone to his ear. On the second ring, a male voice answered.

"Kristin Lee Jewelers," said the man on the other end of the line. "This is Max. May I help you?"

"I hope so, yes," Mitch said. "My name is Detective Mitch Loman with the Dasan's Terrace Police Department. I am currently investigating an attempted homicide that occurred in Elk Grove on Saturday. I called to find out if you might have any information about a knife that was used in the crime."

"A knife? I'm very sorry Detective ... um... what was it?"

"Loman," Mitch repeated.

"Detective Loman. I'm sorry, but we don't sell knives here. We never have. I don't think I can help much in your investigation."

"No, sir. I know you didn't sell the knife. You see, the knife was specially modified. A large amethyst was placed into the tang ... the handle part. I'm trying to locate the jeweler that did the setting on the gemstone."

There was a long pause. After several seconds of silence, Mitch wondered if he had lost his connection with the store.

"Hello? Max? Are you still there?"

"I ... I'm here. Did you say that the knife was used in a murder?"

"It was an attempted homicide. No one was actually killed. But, yes, the knife was used in a crime."

"Detective, can I ask you a question?"

"Of course."

There was another long pause before Max went on. "Let's say, um, hypothetically, you find the person that modified the knife. Would that person be, uh, liable, I guess, in any way for the crime that occurred?"

Mitch understood immediately what Max was asking, and he hastened to reassure him.

"Absolutely not. You, or whoever may have placed the amethyst in the knife, did nothing wrong. You were only doing your job and giving a customer what they wanted. You hold no responsibility for what the customer did with the knife after you modified it. The only reason I'm checking jewelry stores is because I'm trying to figure out who the knife belonged to."

"Ah, that is very good to know. In that case, yes, we did in fact handle that order."

Mitch's heart rate increased with the unexpected response. He felt his face flush with excitement. This was the store! He was making progress.

"Just to be certain we are talking about the same thing," he said, keeping his voice neutral despite wanting to yelp with joy, "the weapon was a bowie knife, and the handle held a circular amethyst about an inch wide."

"We are definitely talking about the same thing," Max assured him. "It's difficult to forget a custom order like that one. Three, brilliant cut amethysts, four carats each, inset into the metal handles of three hunting knives."

It was Mitch's turn to be stunned into silence.

"There were three of them?!" he blurted when he could speak again.

"Y-yes," said Max. "You didn't know?"

"We knew about one. Not the other two. Max, do you have the name and information for the person that brought you the knives?"

"I have the purchase orders for the work, but…,"

"Yes?"

"Look, Detective Loman, I don't want to be rude or say something that will get me in trouble with the police, but I don't really know who I'm talking to right now. I'm happy to share any information you need, but I think I would have to do it in person. I would need to see some I.D, or a badge, or something."

"I completely understand your feelings. You're right, you only have my word on the phone that I am who I say I am. Do I need to request a warrant for your records?"

"That's not necessary. I'm completely willing to assist your investigation once I'm sure I'm actually talking to the cops. I mean, um, the police."

"Great! Thank you, Max. I can be at your store this afternoon. Will you still be working?"

"I'll be here."

"Then I'll see you in a few hours. Thank you, again."

Mitch hung up his phone. He turned to Violet, who was now sitting up and glaring in his direction.

"This afternoon?" she asked. "Are you serious?"

"We have to go back to Sacramento," Mitch told her. "Today. Right now. Pack up and I'll let the front desk know that we're checking out."

"Can't you call someone else on your team to go talk to the guy? It doesn't have to be you, does it?"

"I need to get back to Elk Grove as soon as possible."

When Violet did not immediately begin to move, Mitch said, "There were three knives, not just one. I'm not the only target. It's one thing to run away when my life is the only one being threatened, but there are others in danger. I can't stay here and do nothing."

Violet pressed her lips together, grimly. She clearly was not pleased by this turn of events, but she nodded her understanding. "Okay. I'll get us packed. I'll call Alyssandra from the car and let her know we're on our way back."

As Mitch guided his car onto the freeway, heading back towards Sacramento, Violet synched her cellphone to the vehicle's Bluetooth feature. The moment the synthetic voice announced her phone was connected, she dialed Alyssandra's number.

"Yes?" Alyssandra asked curtly. She sounded distracted and irritated. To be fair though, thought Mitch, she always sounded irritated.

"Alyssandra. It's Violet," Violet announced, although the old witch must already know who was calling. "We're on our way home. We just got onto the freeway and should be back in a couple hours."

"So, you already heard, then?" the coven leader responded. She did not seem at all surprised by Violet's announcement.

"Heard what?" Violet asked, confused.

"About the girl. Ah ... Tanya, was it? Yes, I think that's right. She was murdered last night."

"Another knife," said Violet. It was not a question.

"Another knife," agreed Alyssandra. "She was killed in her parents' restaurant with plenty of customers and staff in the business, yet no one got a good look at her attacker."

"Damn. That poor girl. I talked with her on Sunday, and she was really sweet. She wasn't a threat to anyone. But listen to me, she won't be the last one," Violet warned. "Mitch says there are three knives that were modified to hold a jewel in the handle."

"Yes. Three sounds about right," Alyssandra said. She again did not sound surprised by the news.

Violet glanced toward Mitch. He only shrugged and continued driving. He had no idea where Alyssandra was getting her information, but it seemed she was better informed than they were.

"Chang'e spoke with Tanya before I did," Violet continued. "The girl turned her down. With the attack on Mitch and now Tanya's murder, I think Chang'e is eliminating people she believes may become a threat to her in the future. If she couldn't get Tanya to join her, she wanted to make sure such a powerful new witch never joined our coven either. She doesn't know anything about Mitch, but she knows I'm training him, and maybe that was enough to put him on her hit list."

"I thought Chang'e might be involved as well. However, this morning I am no longer so certain."

"What changed?" asked Violet.

"Chang'e called me. A new member of her coven was also killed a few hours ago. Chang'e called to accuse me of the murders. She believed that because Mitch survived his attack that it was all a careful setup to make us look like victims as well."

"The third knife?" Violet asked.

"Yes. Her girl died the same way Tanya did: a knife in the heart from an unseen attacker."

"Someone is killing witches," mused Violet, "but they are targeting new witches who haven't learned how to properly protect themselves from spells yet. Are all three victims simply targets of convenience, or is there something tying them together that we haven't figured out?"

"A very good question," Alyssandra told her. "I do not have an answer for you."

Violet sighed. "Okay. Mitch has a possible lead on the person that owned the knives. He's going to follow it when we get back to Sacramento. I'll let you know if we learn anything."

Alyssandra did not respond. The call simply disconnected. Violet was accustomed to the older woman's abrupt dismissals and questionable phone etiquette so was not bothered by the lack of response. She slipped her cellphone into her pocket without commenting on the discourtesy.

Mitch similarly kept his opinions about Alyssandra's behavior to himself. Instead, he said, "I should call Chief Jefferson and let him know what's going on, too."

Before Mitch could make the call, his phone began to ring. The name on the display screen said "Det Ali Minhas." Curious as to why the homicide detective might be calling him, he pressed the connect call button on his steering wheel.

"Hey, Ali. Please tell me you've got some good news."

The sound of Ali's rueful laugh came through the car speakers. "Sorry, man. I don't have anything good for you. I got an email from CODIS this morning. They found zero matches on our DNA sample."

"Shit," Mitch muttered. He hadn't really expected anything different, but it was disappointing to hear, nonetheless. "Okay. Thanks for checking. I appreciate the help."

"Anything else I can do for you?"

"No. This investigation just went on the back burner. I've got something else that needs my full attention right now."

"Sounds serious. You need any help with it?"

"Not right now. I got it. If something comes up later, though, I may hit you up."

"Any time, man. Sorry the DNA didn't pan out."

"Me, too," said Mitch. "I'll talk to you later."

When Mitch disconnected the call, Violet asked, "What's codis?"

"CODIS is an FBI acronym. Combined DNA Index System. It's a database of DNA profiles. Anyone arrested for a felony or sex crime gets put into the database. Missing persons end up in there, too, if they've been missing for a long time. Whoever shot Delaney, hasn't been arrested for anything serious in the last thirty years."

"Is that the end of the investigation? Are you going to close it again?"

"It was my last real chance of finding the shooter. I'll still reach out and interview the cashier at the market, the owner, and anyone on the suspect list. I don't expect I'll get anywhere with those interviews, but they're the only options I have left. After that, yeah, I guess I'll have to give up. Right now, though, those interviews are going to have to wait. We've got an active killer we need to find, first."

When Mitch and Violet arrived in Elk Grove, the first stop Mitch made was at his home. He changed out of his vacation clothes and into a pair of slacks, a cream, button-up shirt with a tie, and sport coat. Although he was in a hurry to get to the jewelry store, Max, the salesman, was expecting a police detective, not some sweaty guy in a T-shirt, rumpled from a two-hour drive. For the finishing touch, Mitch ran a comb through his hair and pronounced himself ready to go.

Violet also changed, rummaging through her luggage until she found a sundress that looked less casual than her shorts and shirt. The dress was light and flowy on her, and it looked expensive enough to put a high-end jewelry store salesman at ease.

Forty minutes after that pitstop, they walked through the double front doors of Kirstin Lee Jewelers.

The clear doors and windows of the shopfront let the afternoon daylight in, giving the store a bright welcoming feel, and air conditioning hummed in the background, keeping the interior temperature cool and pleasant. Glass topped display cases formed two concentric squares, one in the center of the room, and one adjacent to the outer walls. The entrance guided customers along a predetermined path through the aisle between the two rings. Two sales employees, one man and one woman, wandered the space between the wall and the outside square, while a third was inside the inner box.

The two outer employees were currently helping customers, so Mitch approached the man at the center of the store.

"Excuse me," he said. "I was wondering if you could point me to Max?"

The salesman, a short, pleasant-looking man in his fifties, smiled and held out a hand. "I'm Max. Can I help you?"

Max wore a perfectly tailored, gray suit, that added illusory shape to his blocky frame. The made-to-order, and obviously expensive, suit included a vest and a red bow tie. The salesman's face was wide and round, with narrow eyes and a broad nose under a thatch of jet-black hair that he greased and combed straight back over his scalp. His flat, shiny hair looked almost painted on, except for one stubborn cowlick that poked out defiantly at the back of his head.

Mitch took the proffered hand and shook it.

"Hi, Max. Nice to meet you in person. I'm Detective Loman. We spoke on the phone."

"Oh, yes, Detective. I remember."

Mitch removed his wallet and showed Max his identification card and badge. The salesman grinned and nodded his approval. His eyes then flicked toward Violet.

"Can I see hers as well?"

"She isn't a police officer," Mitch told him. "No badge. She's a consultant hired to assist on this case."

To Mitch's surprise, Violet reached into her purse and produced a business card. The image on the front was a large black ring, and Mitch had time to read "Thirteenth Circle" beneath the symbol before Max took the card from her hand.

"Private investigator," Violet told Max. "I was hired by the victim and the police have graciously allowed me to participate in this portion of the investigation."

Mitch forced himself not to smile. Violet was smooth, but then, he already knew that. Besides, her cover story technically was not even a lie. Mitch was a victim in this investigation, and he had asked Violet for her help.

"Thank you," said Max, pocketing the card. He turned back toward Mitch. "After our phone call, I researched the customer through our sales records."

He removed a folded square of paper from his vest pocket. "Her name is Mary Johnson. Her phone number and address are written there, too."

Max handed Mitch the paper. "Mary Johnson," Mitch read aloud. "Maybe. Did she show a driver's license."

"No," Max said. "She paid in cash, so we didn't ask for proof of identity. I know. I think the name sounds fake, too."

Mitch looked around the shop. He checked the doors, the locations of the other salespeople, and lastly, he searched for cameras mounted in the ceiling or along the walls. He counted eight security cameras throughout the store.

"When did Mary Johnson pick up the knives?"

Max paused to think. "Um, the date on the receipt was for last Wednesday. So, about a week ago. Two forty-eight in the afternoon. I think that was the time. I can double check."

"Do your security cameras work?" Mitch asked, pointing at the nearest smokey glass dome protruding from the ceiling.

"Absolutely. State of the art equipment."

"Can you show me the video for last Wednesday, when Mary came in?"

"No," said Max.

"No? Is there a problem."

"No, no, no, there's no problem," Max assured him hurriedly. "I would be happy to show you, but our system doesn't have a local recorder. Our monitor shows real-time images but doesn't save them. It's one of the safety features that prevents thieves from stealing or deleting the video. All video feeds are uploaded and recorded at the main offices of our security company in Baltimore."

"Balti...?" Mitch stopped and took a breath to calm himself. This conversation was not going quite as smoothly as he had hoped. "Okay. Baltimore. Can you request a copy of the video feeds for the time Mary came into the shop?"

"Of course. I can get you copies of the video from every camera. I only need to fill out a request and explain why it's needed."

"How long would it take to get the video?"

Max grimaced, looking uncomfortable. "Well, they're a big company. I have to put the request in remotely since there isn't anyone there that answers the phone. It would take them about a week to get the request, make copies, and send them to our store."

"A week? All right, let's try this instead. What if I went to a judge and got a subpoena for the video? How long do you think it would take then?"

"About a month," said Max. He shrugged apologetically. "With a subpoena, the company would have to run the request through their legal department first, and that is not a quick process.

I think it would be best if I put in the request without the subpoena."

Mitch had to agree. He did not like the delay, but a week was still better than a month.

"Okay, Max. Let's do it that way. Thank you." Mitch took one of his own business cards from his wallet, borrowed a pen from Max and wrote his personal cellphone number on the back.

"Please call me the second you get that video. It could be a matter of life or death."

CHAPTER

14

Mitch returned to the police department the following evening for his regular Wednesday shift. Based on the new murders and the knowledge that only three knives had been commissioned, he no longer seemed to be in danger of imminent attack. Whoever sent the knife after him had moved on to other targets and was continuing with whatever plans they already had in motion.

After briefing Chief Jefferson on everything he had learned and the leads he was still pursuing, the chief agreed the immediate threat to Mitch's life had most likely passed and allowed him back to work.

Alyssandra had reluctantly agreed to assist DTPD with clearing the ghouls out of the cemetery after Chief Jefferson's unwelcome visit, and the removal of the creatures was supposed to begin that same week. Due to the two additional deaths of unprotected witches, she changed her plans. She delayed the sweep of the cemetery until Friday the following week, which not coincidentally would be a full moon. In the meantime, Alyssandra and every member of her coven were taking the time they needed to bolster their magical defenses on both themselves and their homes.

It was unknown if, or when, future attacks might occur, and the women did not wish to be caught unprepared like their unfortunate sisters.

The chief did not question the coven leader's decision to wait. In fact, he agreed with it. He was also taking a few precautions of his own, including closing the cemetery for the next two weeks and ordering all foot patrols to be conducted by at least two officers remaining in constant visual contact with each other.

The name, address, and phone number provided to Mitch by Max at the jewelry store had all proved to be fake. The address did not exist, and the phone number belonged to a burner phone that had since been turned off or destroyed. Mitch considered requesting a warrant for the phone records, but it would probably give him no more than he already had through the jewelry store: an item purchased with cash and another security camera picture of his suspect. Not much help there, and certainly not worth the effort of requesting the warrant. If the jewelry store footage proved to be a complete bust, he might reconsider, but for now, he put the idea on hold.

With both of his investigations currently stalled, Mitch was aching for something to do. Sitting and waiting for a killer to come to him was contrary to his nature. On his first night back at work, to keep himself busy, he reviewed the reports on the murders of Tanya Kushing and the girl from Chang'e's coven.

Tanya had been killed in Rancho Cordova, so obtaining those files had not been difficult. Rancho was a contract city patrolled by sheriff's deputies, and they shared their reporting database with the Sacramento County Sheriff's Office, just like Dasan's Terrace. The second girl died in the city of Sacramento, and their police department was a completely separate entity. Obtaining those records had required more effort.

Initially when Mitch reached out to Sac PD, the detectives investigating the death did not want an outside agency reviewing their cases. They were reluctant to even discuss information that had been publicly released. When Mitch advised them that Sacramento County had another murder that was undeniably connected to theirs, and he was willing to share with them any known leads so long as they agreed to the same, they suddenly saw the wisdom of comparing notes.

Mitch provided copies of Tanya's report, and in return he was emailed the Sacramento case file.

The girl murdered in Sacramento was named Zinea Ayad. She was nineteen years old; barely out of high school. *Only a kid*, thought Mitch as he read through the report SPD had forwarded to him. Her picture on the front page of the investigation file only reinforced his opinion of her youth. Zinea had dark eyes and black hair. She looked like she was of Middle Eastern descent, with deep brown skin, high cheekbones, and a shallow cleft at the point of her chin. Her nose was slightly crooked which, rather than detracting from her looks, only gave her cherubic face character. The wide-eyed, innocent smile she displayed in the photograph made her appear even younger than her actual age.

The pictures of both girls side by side on his desk made Mitch angry. Somebody was murdering children. Coming after him was bad enough, but these girls had no way to defend themselves from these cowardly ambush attacks.

Neither investigation had any witnesses to the actual murders, and there was no suspect information of any kind. Mitch, having been one of the targets of the unidentified magic user, knew more about what was going on in the homicides than any of the investigating detectives. Unfortunately, he could not share what he knew. At best, no one would believe him. At worst, he would be labeled as crazy and nobody would want him anywhere near their cases.

He was standing at the precipice of another dead end. Frustrated, but with no idea how to move forward, he gathered up the files and secured the papers in his locker.

The rest of that week, Mitch went through the motions at work, but he remained distracted. He could not move either of his investigations any further forward, but he also could not simply push them out of his mind. The murder of the two girls in particular weighed heavily on him.

As the long, painfully uneventful days passed, Violet did her best to occupy his time. She taught him how to build defensive wards and showed him how he could draw and store power in gemstones.

In addition to his magical training, she also forced him to practice his exorcist skills, retracting and expanding his spirit outside the confines of his own body. It was during one of these lessons that Violet made another discovery regarding Mitch's abilities.

Mitch was staring at his hand, admiring the arching tendrils of spirit extending from the tips of each of his fingers. The glowing grey wisps of soul he manifested were not the same neat scalpel-like blade Violet used but instead appeared like the pointed and curved claws of a large cat.

"You're doing very well," Violet complimented him. "You're picking this up much faster than I did. Not being able to see the manifestation of your own soul can make it difficult to focus on a tiny part of it, but it doesn't seem to slow you down."

"Huh?" Mitch asked, dumbly.

He could see his soul clearly and was surprised by the comment.

"I see it just fine," he told her. "Am I not supposed to?"

Violet cocked her head in puzzlement. "You can see it? Really? What does it look like to you?"

"Um, like silver claws coming out of the tops of my fingers. It isn't as clean as the way you do it, but it looks like it would get the job done."

Violet nodded. "You really do see it. Don't you?"

"Yes," Mitch assured her. "Is that a problem?"

"No, I.... No, I guess not. Other than you and me, I've only met two exorcists. None of us were able to see our own souls, so I just assumed that was always true. You know, like aura readers can't see their own auras, that kind of thing. I guess I was wrong."

Violet shrugged off the seemingly minor revelation, and the two went back to practicing; extending his spirit, holding it for several minutes, then retracting it into the safety of his physical body.

When Mitch grew too agitated to focus on this training any longer, Violet sparred with him in the graveyard, showing him new ways to defend himself from various magical attacks. The distraction was helpful, but despite Violet's best efforts, Mitch's thoughts always traced back to the two dead girls.

Dasan's Terrace remained tensely quiet that week. No more witches were attacked, which was good news, however with the killer lying low, there were also no new clues as to their enemy's identity.

Alyssandra, Missy, and Chang'e were not speaking to each other. Each one of them suspected the other two might be behind the killings, either individually or working together. Mitch was uncertain if this unwillingness to talk was for the best, or if it was only making things harder for everyone. The coven leaders had bad blood between them, and when they interacted the outcome was never peaceful, but they also might have independent information that, if pieced together, could lead him toward a suspect and a solution to their problems.

Mitch had no intention of opening that particular can of worms, however. It was not healthy to situate oneself in the middle of those three witches.

The workweek finally ended, and Mitch left for his days off. He soon discovered that being stuck at home was worse than going to work. During the weekend, he did not have the other members of his team to help him pass the empty hours. Violet was also suddenly unavailable. Alyssandra had ordered Violet to meet with her Sunday morning, and the two had been almost inseparable over the next two days, leaving Mitch to kill the tedious, empty hours on his own.

To keep himself from climbing the walls, Mitch practiced the skills Violet had showed him, but with the limited magic around his home, he quickly grew bored. It was like dry firing his pistol at paper targets; the repetition might be useful but there was no satisfying bang to keep him interested.

Next, he watched movies on television, but again his attention wandered. Five minutes after a program ended, he could not remember what it was he had watched.

Finally, in desperation, he even ran out to buy a cookbook and do some grocery shopping. He decided to experiment with a few recipes with which to surprise Violet the next time she came over.

The meals he attempted all turned out unsurprisingly awful.

He could not stop thinking about the two murdered kids. The nervous expectation he had felt on Wednesday night while reading the homicide reports had, by Monday, condensed into a tense ball of frustration that felt like a physical presence inside his chest. If he did not find an outlet for that frustration soon, he would...

What? What would he do?

Probably something reckless and stupid, he supposed. Confront the coven leaders directly?

Yeah, that would be pretty stupid.

On Tuesday morning, the day before he was scheduled to return to work, Mitch's luck finally changed. His break came from an unexpected source and involved a matter that he thought had already been closed unsuccessfully.

"Hey, Ali. What's up?" asked Mitch, answering an 8:00 AM phone call.

"Hey, Mitch. I didn't wake you, did I?"

"No. I'm on my weekend, so I actually get to sleep in the dark and wake when the sun comes up like a normal person. What's going on? You got a case you need help with?"

"No, my brother. I am calling to help *you* out. I think I may have blown your case wide open."

Mitch stroked a hand over light stubble on his cheeks as he thought about Ali's words. Which case was he talking about? He had not talked to Ali about the witch killings. Had he? Mitch did not think his memory was so bad that he had called the detective and then forgotten about it. Maybe Ali had gotten the case on his own. He did work for the Homicide Bureau after all.

But if he was working the killings, how had a complete normie like Ali gotten a lead on the murders that Mitch himself had not found?

"Okay. I'm listening," he said.

"I got DNA results back this morning. We got a hit."

A bell went off in Mitch's brain as he suddenly realized what Ali was talking about. This was not about the two dead girls. He was still following up on Delaney's murder. The fog in Mitch's head cleared and the impact of what the detective was saying landed.

"What?! You got something? How? I thought you said CODIS came back empty."

"CODIS did," Ali agreed. "But I didn't put all my eggs in the federal basket. I also sent the sample to several of the private ancestry tracking companies. Sac County has a membership that lets us run comparisons to their databases as well."

"I don't get it. I thought those were private. Did you have to pull a warrant?"

"Like I said, the county bought a membership. Lots of police departments do it. You know how when you sign up for one of these places, they make you sign a waiver that says they can use outside resources for the purpose of identifying and locating DNA relatives?"

"I guess." Mitch had no idea what the waiver might or might not say as he had never personally used one of the genetic background services.

"Well, we are one of those outside resources," Ali continued. "All I did was submit the sample and ask if this person had any known relatives in their records. No fuss, no muss, and no warrant needed."

"And you found a relative?" Mitch asked. His voice rose in pitch as his excitement grew. "Who? Where?"

"Not just a relative. I found our shooter's kid," Ali announced. "Christopher Yost. He lives a rock's throw outside of Phoenix, Arizona."

"Yost? Why does that name sound familiar?"

"Because Yost is the name of one of the suspects that was interviewed thirty years ago. He was a fired employee with an axe to grind against the owner."

"That's right. I remember now. Bruce Yost. But I also remember he had an airtight alibi. He was in Reno at a casino hotel. His girlfriend was with him and there was even video proof from the hotel lobby and casino cameras."

"Ah, yes. The video," said Ali, slyly. "Do you remember the time stamps for those videos? We have irrefutable evidence that he was in the casino the night before the robbery and the night following the robbery. During the morning of the actual shooting, Yost's girlfriend is the only thing corroborating his alibi. If we can show she was in on it, his whole defense completely drops into the shitter."

Mitch did a victory fist pump in the air. "Ali, I could kiss you right on the mouth. Do you have a lead on where Yost is now?"

"I do," said Ali. "His last known address is the same as his kid's. They live together in Phoenix, but that's not even the best part. When I tried to locate Marlene Tansen, you know, the girlfriend who gave Yost his alibi, I couldn't find anything on her. She's disappeared."

"How is that the best part?" asked Mitch, skeptically.

"Get this, man. She's the kid's mother."

Mitch swore. "You did it. You found them all. And they all live at the same address?"

"No. It looks like the mom divorced dad and split years ago. I did a quick search on her as Marlene Yost, but that name came up empty, too. I'm hoping that the kid or our suspect will know where she is, though."

"Text me the address and any contact information you have. I need to call my chief and get permission to fly down there, then I've got some travel arrangements to make. I owe you big time, my friend."

"Yes, you do," Ali agreed. "Again. I'm telling you, buddy, your tab keeps getting bigger. When you get back from Phoenix, let me know what you find out."

"Absolutely."

Mitch disconnected the call and immediately dialed the employee phone number for Dasan's Terrace. Dot answered after one ring. Her voice was pleasant and professional when she spoke.

"Dasan's Terrace administrative desk. This is Dot. May I help you?"

"Hi, Dot. It's Mitch ... Loman. How is everything going?"

"Hi, Mitchell. It's nice to hear from you. Everything is going fine, I think. Nothing new has gone wrong, anyway, so I suppose that's something."

"Good. I'm glad. Is the chief in yet? I need to talk to him. I have a lead on Delaney's shooting, but I need his permission to go after it."

"That's wonderful news, Mitchell. Yes, he got in a few minutes ago. I'll send your call to his office phone."

There was a click on the line, a moment of silence, then the phone began to ring again. Mitch could imagine Dot shouting into Chief Jefferson's office to let him know who was calling. After several rings, the chief picked up.

"Mitch. Dot said you have good news about Tim. What's going on?"

Mitch repeated everything that Ali had told him moments before. He explained the DNA match and the address that father and son shared in Arizona. When he asked for permission to fly to Phoenix and confront their suspect, the chief was hesitant.

"Why don't you call him first and get a statement?" he asked. "Maybe set up an appointment for him to come to us so we can do a proper interview?"

232

"I thought about that," Mitch admitted, "but then I thought about the fact this guy has gotten away with murder for thirty years. If he sees that we're suddenly closing in on him, he might be in the wind. I don't want to give him the chance to disappear on us. When I see him, I plan on placing him under arrest."

"You don't have any jurisdiction down there," Simon warned. "Don't do anything that jeopardizes the case, or your career."

"No, sir. I plan on contacting the Maricopa County Sheriff's Office and handing him over. I want him in custody so he can't go anywhere while we start extradition to bring him home."

There was a pause as Chief Jefferson considered Mitch's plan.

"Okay," he said at last. "Good work, Mitch. If this pans out, you've done something no one else has managed in thirty years. How quickly can you get down there?"

"There's a flight leaving Sacramento early this afternoon. I can be talking with our suspect by tonight. If everything goes smoothly, I'll be home tomorrow morning and Bruce Yost will be in jail."

"Wonderful. When you book the flight, make sure to get two seats. Dot is going with you."

It was Mitch's turn to pause. Dot? Why was the chief's administrative assistant going with him on a murder investigation?

"Um, Chief? No offense toward Dot, but…"

"She's better than any lie detector I've ever seen. If your suspect is lying to you, she'll know it. If he's telling the truth, she can tell you that, too. Trust me, son. You want her with you for this."

"Okay. Two tickets then. Let her know our flight leaves Sacramento at 1:35. Pack light but bring pajamas because our return flight isn't until tomorrow morning. We'll have to find a hotel once we're in Phoenix."

The flight to Arizona lasted almost two hours, depositing them at Phoenix airport in the late afternoon. Once the plane landed, Dot and Mitch rented a car and drove directly to the address provided by Ali. Fortunately, the car had decent air conditioning since they were driving through mostly desert to get to the house. The outside temperature was in the triple digits, and the car's AC battled valiantly to keep the vehicle's interior comfortable for its two passengers. Mitch looked forward to heading home in the morning and returning to Sacramento's slightly more temperate weather.

When they arrived at their suspect's home, Mitch asked Dot to remain with the vehicle until he made the initial contact at the front door. She agreed. As he climbed out of the car, he touched a hand to his hip, where his duty weapon was currently holstered.

Chief Jefferson had provided Mitch with a letter on Department Stationary giving him permission to fly with his pistol in his carryon bag. The chief figured he should have the gun with him in the event their murder suspect did not wish to be arrested quietly.

Airport security had called Dasan's Terrace to verify the letter was legitimate but had otherwise not delayed his trip more than necessary. Mitch was happy now for the chief's forethought as he did not relish the idea of being unarmed while confronting a suspect that may have already killed one police officer in his lifetime.

With his heart pounding in his chest, both because of the potential threat that Bruce Yost posed, and his excitement at being so close to closing a case he wanted desperately to solve, Mitch knocked on the door.

He heard movement in the home. Floorboards inside the house creaked as someone walked through the residence, approaching the front. Mitch stepped to the side of the doorway, making himself a more difficult target for anyone inside that might decide to shoot a few holes through the front door at whatever unseen company waited on the other side. He did not anticipate that sort of trouble, but it was a habit he had learned in his first few weeks of field training, and it was an automatic precaution now.

The doorknob rattled and the door swung open.

A man in a tank top and tan cargo shorts greeted him from the shadowy entryway. The man had tousled brown hair and several days growth of beard. Surrounded by all the dark hair, his eyes were strikingly blue. Like freezing, storm-tossed seawater, they were so pale as to almost be gray. He held a soda can in his right hand, and he swirled the liquid contents impatiently when he realized he did not recognize his visitors.

His pale blue gaze locked suspiciously on Mitch as if uninvited guests in his life always arrived bringing bad news.

The man was young, no older than thirty, so Mitch assumed that this must be Bruce Yost's son.

"Yes?" he asked, clearly not pleased to find a stranger standing on his front porch.

"Hello. Are you Mr. Christopher Yost?"

"Why? I'm not buying anything today if that's what this is."

"No, sir. I'm not selling anything." Mitch removed his wallet and opened it to show his identification. "I'm Detective Mitch Loman. I was hoping to speak with you and your father. I have a few questions I would like to ask you. Bruce Yost is your father, right? Is he here now?"

"Yes, he's my father. No, he's not here," said Christopher. "What's the problem?"

"There's no problem. Do you know when he might be coming back?"

"Never."

"Oh, sorry. He doesn't live here anymore? Do you know where I could get in touch with him?"

Christopher Yost barked a laugh, but there was no humor in it. He took a sip from his soda, eyeing Mitch over the rim of the can.

"I could tell you where he is, but I don't think he's going to talk to you. He's been dead for three years."

"Shit," Mitch whispered under his breath.

Dead. I'm an idiot. Mitch mentally kicked himself. He should have checked before they got on the plane. Ali had given him this address, and he had been so eager to make an arrest, he had not even bothered to do the basic research to make sure his suspect was still alive. That had been stupid.

Mitch sighed, accepting the situation for what it was. He was here, and the son was home. Maybe he could still learn a few things about Bruce Yost before he left. There would be no arrest today, but perhaps this case could still be solved.

"I'm sorry to hear about your father, Mr. Yost. Would it be possible to ask you a few questions before we go? I'm hoping you can tell me a little bit about him."

Mitch waved toward Dot who was still standing beside the rental car. She approached the house. At the gesture,

236

Christopher noticed her for the first time. His eyes tracked his new guest as she moved up the paved walkway toward him, smiling pleasantly as she drew nearer. When Dot reached the porch, Christopher stepped back a pace, pulling the door wider to allow room for the two of them to enter.

Mitch's lip wanted to twitch into a smirk, but he forced his expression back to something more neutral. It appeared that bringing along a pretty, young girl was providing benefits other than her ability to identify lies. Mitch was fairly certain Christopher Yost would never have let him past the porch if not for his lovely travelling companion.

"It's hot out here," said Yost. "Come inside."

Christopher closed the door behind them, then led his guests into the living room. He pointed, indicating they should seat themselves on a battered, green cloth couch. He settled himself into a recliner that faced a television set mounted on the far wall. The tv was on, but currently muted. Yost took another sip from his soda but did not offer anything to Mitch or Dot.

"What do you want to know?" Yost asked.

"First, may I ask how your father died?"

"Cancer," said Christopher. He scratched at the dark stubble on his face. "In his pancreas. He came to live with me when he got sick. I took care of him for a while, then he had to go to a care home. About three years ago it got him. After he died, we buried him in a cemetery about two miles away from here."

"We?" said Mitch. "Who is we?"

"Me and Uncle Kenny. He isn't really my uncle. Not by blood anyway, but he's been my dad's best friend since before I was born."

"Where is your mom? Did she come back for the funeral?"

Christopher shook his head. "Nah. I haven't seen her since I was little. She bounced when I was three, or something like that. Haven't heard from her and, honestly, don't really care to. I don't even know if she realizes dad is dead."

"So, you have no idea where your mother is?"

"Nope. Like I said, don't care."

Mitch glanced toward Dot. She gave him a slight nod. She was watching Christopher's aura carefully, and so far it showed her no signs of deception. Christopher was telling them the truth. Bruce Yost was dead, and Marlene Yost was nowhere to be found.

This was not the outcome Mitch had hoped for. He had imagined arriving in Sacramento as a conquering hero, closing a case nobody else had managed to crack in thirty years. Instead, he would be returning home empty handed.

There was still a chance he could track down Marlene. She might be willing to talk about her ex-husband now that he was dead. That is, of course, if she didn't mind incriminating herself in the murder at the same time. The blood evidence was compelling, but it would be so much better if they could find someone with personal knowledge of what happened. So many questions remained in Mitch's mind. How had they gotten away? Who treated the gunshot injury to Bruce's leg? What happened to the getaway car?

The trip had thus far proved useless. He could have learned this much by taking Chief Jefferson's suggestion and making a phone call. Mitch decided it was time to be more direct with his interview. If Christopher lost patience and threw them out now, he would be no worse off than he already was.

"Christopher, the reason I'm here is to investigate a homicide that happened about three decades ago. Did your father ever talk to you about a robbery of a gas station in 1994? Or did he talk to someone else about it and you overheard part of that conversation?"

"No. Never." Christopher sat up straighter in the chair. He did not appear pleased by the new line of questioning. "My dad was a shitty dad, but he wasn't a criminal. He never took anything that wasn't his, and he never hurt anyone, even if they really deserved it."

Dot gave Mitch another short nod.

"Did he ever talk about your mom? Did he tell you stories about her looking out for him, or lying to protect him?"

"No. Look, I don't like what you're implying about my dad. Do you have any proof he did anything wrong?"

Mitch was losing him. He knew it was only a matter of minutes, maybe seconds, before they were kicked out of the house.

"We're almost done," he told Christopher. "One more question. He left blood at the scene. What did your dad tell you about the scar on his leg?"

"What scar? Dad didn't have any scar."

That was impossible, Mitch thought. He almost said it aloud but stopped himself. The video evidence and witness testimony showed that Bruce Yost had been shot in the right leg. He was hurt and bleeding badly when he left the convenience store.

"He had a bullet wound in his right thigh. I don't know if the bullet was ever removed, or if it was left in the leg, but there must have been a scar. You never saw it?"

"Dad never had any scars on his legs. It sounds like you're talking about Uncle Kenny. He has a scar on his right thigh where dad shot him. When they were kids, they were drinking and target shooting, and dad accidentally shot Uncle Kenny in the leg."

Mitch turned to Dot, eyebrows raised in surprise.

"He's telling the truth," she said.

"I'm...? Of course, I'm telling the truth. Why would I lie to you about something like that?"

"Christopher," said Mitch, shifting forward on the couch. "Tell me about Uncle Kenny. What's his last name, and how did he meet your dad?"

Christopher stared at Mitch, a dubious expression on his face. He was clearly debating how much more he should say. Mitch stayed quiet, waiting to see if the man would answer the question, or decide it was time to show his guests the door.

After a long moment, Christopher's expression relaxed and he said, "Kenny Dalton. Kenneth Dalton, I guess. He and my dad, and my mom, too, from what I've been told, were all really close as kids. They grew up together. They were almost inseparable, except of course, until my mom took off. Neither one of them ever saw her again."

"Can you tell me, where does your Uncle Kenny live?"

"Sure. He still lives in California where they grew up. In a city called Elk Grove."

Mitch looked at Dot, who nodded again. She gave him a chagrinned expression that seemed to say, "Who could have seen that coming?"

They had flown six hundred and fifty miles to find out their murder suspect was living in Mitch's own backyard.

CHAPTER

15

Mitch and Dot returned to Sacramento the following morning, tired but in good spirits. Mitch wanted to run home, change, then immediately begin pursuing his new lead in Delaney's murder. He was eager to finish this investigation as soon as possible. The trail that led him to Phoenix had taken an unexpected turn, but he felt he was still headed for an arrest and, hopefully, closure for Tim and his family.

His plans did not survive the walk to his car. More pressing matters got in the way.

As Mitch strolled out of the airport terminal, following Dot to find their cars in the overnight parking structure, he took his phone off airplane mode to check his messages. He discovered a missed call from Max and a recording in his voicemail. Opening the messages screen, he tapped on the new recording and brought the phone to his ear.

"Detective Loman, this is Max at Kristin Lee Jewelers. I wanted to let you know that I finally received the copies of the interior camera video from our security office. I know you said that I could email the videos to you when I got them, but the files are too big to send through email. They bounced back to me. Anyway, I have them here at the store if you would like to come by and get them in person. I will be working today until three thirty this afternoon. If you come after that, ask for Lisa and I'll make sure she knows where the thumb drive is. Call me if you need to make other arrangements. Thank you."

The message ended and Mitch glanced at his watch. It was currently fifteen minutes until eleven o'clock, which gave him almost five hours to get to the jewelry store to pick up the video. Identifying whoever was hunting and killing new witches needed to be his priority. Further lives were at risk as long as this suspect remained free and anonymous, meaning Mitch needed to put all of his focus on that killer first. Delaney's murder was thirty years old; it could wait one more day.

Mitch escorted Dot to her car, updating her on his plans so she could fill in the chief when she returned to the office. He told her goodbye as she dropped her luggage into the trunk of her vehicle and then hurried off to find his own car.

Mitch drove himself directly home, wanting to clean up and change before heading to the jewelry store. After dropping his luggage, he showered, dressed, and headed back out, hoping he would soon have a picture of the killer in his hands. He pulled into the parking lot of Kristin Lee's at a few minutes past two o'clock.

As he stepped through the front doors, a man he did not recognize greeted Mitch in the store entryway. The salesman smiled politely and asked if there was anything in the showroom Mitch was looking for. Before Mitch could answer, Max walked up and tapped the other man on the shoulder.

"I've got this, Darrin. Thank you. This is the detective I mentioned."

Darrin nodded and went back to his post beside the central ring of counters.

Max slipped a hand into his suitcoat and removed a blue, plastic thumb drive. He held it out toward Mitch.

"There are four good camera views on here. We have six cameras monitoring the floor, and all six recordings are on the drive, but two of them didn't show anything when she came in. I already watched the videos." Max looked sheepish as he admitted viewing the recordings. "I wanted to make sure you didn't waste your time with empty footage. You can skip files 2A1 and 3A1. I left them on there, of course. It's all on the drive, and you can watch them if you think you need to. I'm not a detective. I don't know how you do these things."

"Thank you," Mitch told Max, pocketing the thumb drive. "I really appreciate your help. What kind of files are they? Do I need a special program to view them?"

"They're all WMV files. They play on Windows. If you have an Apple, you'll have to download the Windows Media Player for Apple. It's easy, though. I asked for everything between 2:40 PM and 3:05 PM. The woman comes into the store at 2:48, in case you want to fast forward to that point."

Mitch thanked Max again, and two minutes later, he was back in his car headed for home. He debated going to the police department to view the videos, but his house was closer, and he desperately wanted to see what his attacker looked like. He did not want to wait the extra forty-five minutes it would take to access a work computer.

Mitch's stomach growled. He hadn't eaten since last night, and his body was complaining about the neglect. He thought about stopping to pick up some fast food, but again, his desire to start watching the security video trumped any detours. There were crackers and some cheese in the fridge at home to keep him from starving. He could have a real meal later.

After he knew who had tried to kill him.

He might have broken a few traffic rules in his haste, but he made it home safely, and Mitch was finally able to sit down at his desk computer and plug in the thumb drive with the jewelry store security footage. With a glass of water and a box of Wheat Thins next to him, he clicked on the only folder that appeared on the drive. When it opened, as Max had promised, there were six files available for viewing.

The files were numbered WMV1A1 through WMV6A1.

Mitch clicked on the first file. When the video started, it was in color and showed an interior view of the store's front doors. It was a high angle, as the camera was mounted on the ceiling, but it was set far enough back from the door that it provided some facial features of customers entering the store rather than simply recording the tops of people's heads. At 14:48 on the camera digital clock, a young woman with dark hair entered the shop.

The resolution of the video was good, better than most security cameras Mitch had seen. The woman had dark brown skin, suggesting she could be Hispanic, or possibly Middle Eastern, but Mitch could not tell anything more about her as she had her head bowed and her phone to the side of her face when she walked in. Her features were obstructed by her hair and phone during the three seconds it took for her to walk forward and out of the camera's range of view.

"That was a bust," he muttered, but he continued watching the video until the same woman exited the store several minutes later. This time he could only see the back of her head, but he recognized the clothing she was wearing when she entered: a white button-up blouse, a narrow gray skirt, and a white purse slung by a strap over her shoulder. On her way out, she carried a black paper bag she had not had with her when she entered. The hair on the back of Mitch's neck prickled as he imagined the items in that bag.

Mitch closed the file. He skipped the next two files as Max had suggested. He could always come back to them later if he felt it was necessary. Placing the mouse arrow over file WMV4A1, he clicked it open.

This camera view was from behind the main counter at the back of the store. The camera was placed on the far wall high enough to see over an employee's shoulder and capture the face of anyone standing at the register. It was a perfect view to see the entire shop, but also ideal for capturing images of those making purchases, collecting items, or perhaps robbing the store.

The digital clock at the bottom corner of the screen counted to 14:48, and the woman appeared again at the front of the store. From a distance, he recognized the clothing: the gray skirt and white blouse. She walked directly to the back counter and waited for someone to assist her. Mitch clicked pause. The girl – and she was a girl, much younger than Mitch had initially expected – glanced toward the back wall precisely at the moment he stopped the action. He had a perfect frontal view of her face.

"Gotcha," he said.

Mitch did a screen grab of the image and set it aside. Then he took a long moment to examine the frozen video frame. Something seemed familiar about this girl, but he could not quite place where they had met. Dark eyes seemed to look directly at him from the paused image, daring him to remember her. Or perhaps daring him not to.

"Shit."

He knew who she was.

They had never met. He had only seen a photograph one time before, but it had been recent, and it had been memorable. The high cheekbones and the long, slightly crooked nose were distinctive.

This was Zinea Ayad. The dead girl from Chang'e's coven.

"How...?"

It made no sense. Did it? The girl that had ordered the modified knives so they could be used to assassinate witches, was also a witch. That much was not a surprise. Witches frequently fought one another for power or prestige. But one of the knives she herself had created had been turned against her. That was harder to understand. She would not have commanded one of the knives to take her own life, which meant someone else must have done it. But what would be the motivation for that? If there was someone else involved, wouldn't they be working together, as a team?

She must be merely a go between, Mitch reasoned. She had arranged to have the knives modified, but she was not part of the decision making as to who they would be sent to remove.

Whoever had hired her, must have gotten rid of her to cover their own tracks, to keep her quiet so she could not point the finger at them later. They were making sure the weapons could never be traced back to them.

Zinea was a new witch in Chang'e's coven. Could she have been a plant from some other player in this game that Mitch did not know? Except, if she was a mole, what was her goal in joining the coven? Who had sent her? Most importantly, why infiltrate a group only to kill your insider once they got in?

No. Mitch was missing something. Zinea was not a mole. She was a victim.

The targets of all three knives pointed to only one possible person. Mitch was a strong unknown that might one day become a threat if he allied himself to Alyssandra. Tanya, the girl who joined Missy's coven had turned down opportunities to join

Alyssandra and Chang'e, which also made her a potential threat to both covens.

Finally, Zinea herself. She was the only link between the murder weapons and the mastermind guiding them, therefore she was a liability to whoever had used her. Plus, there was the added bonus that when she died, Chang'e could also claim to be a victim of the unidentified killer.

Chang'e was the threat. She had orchestrated all three attacks. It had been well planned, but she had been colossally unlucky in the execution. By failing to kill Mitch, then subsequently murdering Zinea, she put the girl's name and photograph right into Mitch's hands. Alyssandra and Missy probably had no idea who Zinea was or what she looked like. They might have even succeeded in gaining a copy of this security footage but still been left completely in the dark as to who this mystery girl was, and who might be manipulating her from the shadows. There was nothing to connect this girl in the jewelry store to Chang'e.

By surviving the assassination attempt against him, Mitch became the only person in exactly the right position to put the pieces together.

Soon, however, everyone was going to know. Mitch was not certain he could do anything to bring her to the justice of a human criminal court, but he was quite confident that once Alyssandra and Chief Jefferson were aware of what Chang'e had done, the wily, murdering witch would have bigger problems to worry about than merely getting arrested.

CHAPTER

 16

Mitch called Simon and Violet, filling them both in on what he had discovered. He explained in detail his reasoning for why Chang'e must be the orchestrator of the murders, and they both seemed to agree with his assessment, although Chief Jefferson counseled caution on any actions until they had more definitive proof of Chang'e's direct involvement.

With that chore done, there was not much more he could do to help with the investigation. He opted to crawl into bed and try to get a couple hours of sleep before he needed to be at work that night. The chief had offered him the night off since he had been in Phoenix only that morning and must be exhausted, but Mitch had refused.

"Remember, I can't pay you overtime for your detective duties," the chief told him. "However, I can let you flex your hours a bit."

"I appreciate that, but I remember you also told me you expected me to meet my night shift patrol responsibilities."

"I think they'll survive without you for one night."

"I'm good, Chief. But thanks."

"All right, Mitch. Do what you think best, but please don't make a martyr out of yourself."

As Mitch curled into a ball beneath the sheets of his bed, he wondered briefly if he would be able to sleep with so many things he still needed to do swirling in his brain. He had to follow up on Delaney's murder suspect, book the video evidence he had obtained from the jewelry store, and update the Sacramento detectives on how to get copies of the video for their own records. He also had reports to write and file, documenting his activities over the past few days.

Despite the flurry of thoughts all vying for his attention, Mitch surprised himself by dropping into a deep slumber almost as soon as his head hit the pillow.

A few hours later, more rested and refreshed, he took his second shower of the day, then went to work.

At the police department, and following briefing, Mitch went to the transcription room to write two separate reports. The first was to document his discovery of the video showing Zinea at the jewelry store. This report would be forwarded to the investigators working Zinea's and Tanya's homicides. Mitch was fairly certain the detectives would be unable to do anything with the information, but since they had graciously, if somewhat reluctantly, allowed him access to their files, he figured he should at least let them know what he had found.

The second report was for the Dead Town Police Department files only. In this report, he documented the connection between Zinea and Chang'e's coven, as well as his belief that the murder weapons were directed by Chang'e herself. This report would never be seen outside of DTPD, so he included details on how the amethysts were used to power the murder weapons and provide the knives with the ability to crawl and fly.

When he was finished with both report narratives, he boxed up the spelled knife he still had in his locker, labeled it with a DTPD evidence number, and turned it over to Sergeant Smythe. The supervisors on each shift were the only people who had keys to the evidence room, and despite Mitch's inquiries, he had never been allowed inside this mysterious storage area. It made him insanely curious to know what other kinds of magical items or cursed objects might be in there besides the few things he himself had turned over to Jorge in the past few months.

After booking the knife, Mitch had nothing pressing that needed his attention for the remainder of the shift. The following day, he had big plans to confront the man he believed to be Lieutenant Delaney's murderer, but for now, in the middle of the night, there wasn't much to keep him occupied.

To fight the boredom, he decided to wander the cemetery grounds. Per Chief Jefferson's orders, he called Tink on the radio and asked him to partner with him on his patrol.

At the same time that Mitch prowled through the dark corners of Dead Town with Tink, several miles away, in the unincorporated countryside of Sacramento County known as Wilton, Alyssandra stood in front of the open trunk of her car. Unlike Mitch, she had plenty to do to keep herself occupied this evening. She and three of the stronger members of her coven gathered in the gloom of early morning in the front yard of a small farm-style home located in the middle of a five-acre plot of land. The house was not large, perhaps 1800 square feet, and it was in need of some repair, but the acreage around the building was neat and well-tended.

The home belonged to Chang'e, and like Alyssandra's own residence in midtown Sacramento, the condition and size of the structure was not the reason it had been purchased. Chang'e had located a small pocket of latent magic in this neighborhood, and her choice of residence was based on having ready access to this rare source of power, rather than on any monetary or comfort factors.

Chang'e's coven was banned from the cemetery, and because they were not allowed inside the gates of Dead Town, she needed resources from which to draw magic and power for her spells. This house in the middle of nowhere had turned out to be perfect for that purpose.

Alyssandra dropped the second of two empty, plastic gas tanks into the trunk of her car. She retrieved a walking staff and a road flare from the same space, then closed the trunk lid carefully, pressing downward until she heard the soft click of the latch engaging. In a few more minutes, silence would no longer be so important, but for now, Alyssandra tried to minimize any unnecessary loud noises.

She hefted her staff, gazing fondly at the softball-sized gemstone affixed at the top. Alyssandra did not generally enjoy carrying the bulky rod, it was cumbersome as well as a bit trite for a witch of her stature, but there was no arguing that the stone it carried was an effective way to keep large amounts of raw power readily available. Power that could prove useful when about to enter a fight where magic might otherwise be difficult to find.

Alyssandra waved at the women around her, indicating they should similarly check the power reserves of their own staffs. When all nodded their readiness, she gestured for them to follow her toward the house.

Willa, Audie, and Gabby, the witches with Alyssandra, were a few of the more powerful members of her coven. All three were fiercely loyal to her and willing to follow any order, no matter how dangerous or morally distasteful it might be. Alyssandra had wanted Violet here with her tonight, as Violet was stronger than any of these three, but she was unsure how the girl might react to tonight's stealth mission.

Violet was loyal, Alyssandra knew, but she had a soft heart, as well as an exceptionally irksome moral compass that frequently got in the way at the worst possible times. Alyssandra had hoped that when Violet's parents were killed, the girl would develop more of a killer's instincts, that she would thirst for any opportunities for revenge, as well as seek out ways of sharing the hurt and pain she herself had suffered. Unfortunately, the reverse had been true. Violet had grown a conscience. She felt empathy for others in pain.

It was damned inconvenient at times.

There was still plenty of pain and anger that Alyssandra could use and manipulate, but she had to be careful never to push too hard or force Violet past her righteous lines in the sand. When tonight's work was done, Alyssandra was certain her second in command would see and understand the necessity of what her coven leader had done. What she did not know was how Violet would react to being invited to participate. So, to be safe, Alyssandra had simply not asked.

"Touch my hand," Alyssandra directed the women with her.

Each in turn approached their coven priestess and tapped one finger into her outstretched palm. A delicate tracery of white magic extended from Alyssandra's hand to the witches as they stepped away.

"Do you hear me?" she asked softly.

The three women nodded in response. Satisfied, Alyssandra bid them to take their positions, one witch at each corner of the single-story home. Alyssandra placed herself at the northwest corner, closest to the residence's front door. As long as the white lines of power connected the four of them, Alyssandra could communicate with her coven mates without needing to shout or rely on mechanical assistance.

Of course, modern technology still had its uses, she mused, removing her cellphone from a pocket in her skirt.

Alyssandra dropped the unlit flare she had been holding, letting it fall next to her feet. She then tapped a few icons on her phone screen, opening the call function and scrolling through her lists of recently called numbers.

"Are we ready," she asked.

Gabby announced she was, followed by Willa and Audie immediately after.

"Good. Stand silent and listen carefully."

Alyssandra tapped the name "Chang'e" on her phone screen. She held the phone by her hip, but she could still hear the soft intermittent purr of the phone's internal ring. She strained her ears, listening for any sounds inside the house. She was rewarded with the soft sound of music playing somewhere deep in the interior.

It took her a moment to recognize the song, but when she did, she frowned. It was the energetic voice of Elton John, singing one of his hits from the 1970's. Alyssandra listened a moment longer as the singer crooned, "the bitch is back."

"Indeed, my dear Chang'e," she whispered. "The bitch *is* back, and she's coming for you."

Alyssandra dropped the phone back into her pocket. She did not disconnect the line. When the ringing, and the song inside the house, ceased she heard a muffled voice on her phone growl, "What the fuck do you want, Alyssandra?"

"Begin," she told the witches.

Together, all four women raised their staffs and directed bolts of pure force at the house. Streams of yellow lightning struck the structure, meeting a barrier of red and blue wards. The attacks caused the protective wards to flare bright in the surrounding darkness, but they did not cause any damage. The lightning was ultimately turned away.

Alyssandra's squinted against the glare as her night vision burned away. When the assault ended, she blinked several times until she could see the home clearly once more.

"Again," she said.

Four more streaks of yellow lightning met the house's magical shielding. Another flare of red and blue protective force lit the night air. The wards flickered slightly under the second assault but continued to hold. The lightning died away and the defensive shield dimmed back to invisibility.

Chang'e's wards held firm under their attack. Alyssandra had not anticipated anything less. The goal was not to break the lone witch's defenses, merely to weaken them.

Alyssandra raised her staff, but before she could announce a third strike, the front door of the house swung inward. A tall, willowy, female figure appeared in the doorway. The woman's face was angular and severe, with narrow, triangular eyes, a long jawline and a pointed chin. Waist-length, black hair fell in a loose ponytail down her back. She wore only a blue T-shirt that hung to her thighs, her legs and feet bare beneath it.

Good, thought Alyssandra. *We caught her in bed and unprepared. This will make things much easier.*

Chang'e stepped out onto the porch, her dark eyes blazing with anger and hatred as she spied Alyssandra on her front lawn.

"What are you doing?" she screamed. "How dare you come here and attack me like this."

"Save your false outrage for someone who might believe it. This isn't an attack, it's retaliation for the murders you have already committed. When you come for me, this is what you can expect in return."

"When did I attack you?" Chang'e demanded.

"Mitchell Loman stopped the assassin spell you sent at him, but others were not so fortunate."

Chang'e paused, glancing around in confusion as if something peculiar had caught her attention. She sniffed the air, and her face twisted in disgust and disbelief. "You are out of your mind, Alyssandra! I lost a witch to those attacks, too. Have you forgotten?"

"Oh yes, "Alyssandra drawled, her voice dripping with sarcasm. "The girl you lost, her name was Zinea Ayad, was it not?"

When Chang'e did not respond, she continued.

"Did you think we wouldn't figure it out? Did you think we were so stupid? She purchased those knives, had them modified to hold the assassin's spell. The spell you wove."

Chang'e stood on her porch, stunned to speechlessness.

"You killed one of your own. You cannot be trusted. That alone is enough reason to destroy you."

"I never attacked you. I have not killed anyone. I certainly would never kill one of my coven."

Alyssandra laughed, a high, unpleasant cackle. "Do you expect me to believe the women in your coven are anything more than a series of batteries to you? I know you better than that."

Chang'e threw her hands out in front of her, her clawed fingers aimed toward Alyssandra. Magic poured from her fingertips. Alyssandra expected the attack and wove a shield of blue light with her staff. She placed the shield between herself and the approaching spell.

Chang'e's attack touched Alyssandra's magical defenses, creating a flash of harmless pyrotechnics. The conjuration dissipated before it could do any harm.

Alyssandra noticed a strange reaction from her shield after it had fended off the approaching magic. The disk of protection glittered with red sparks that danced across the defensive lines of blue force. Where the sparks traveled, the shield flickered and guttered away. Alyssandra grimaced, then dismissed the barrier spell with a shake of her hand. She glared at the witch on the porch.

Chang'e was fighting with demon magic.

Yet another reason she needed to be destroyed.

"Again," Alyssandra announced through her link to the circle of witches.

She raised her staff, and four simultaneous bursts of lightning struck the house once more. As the wards flared to stave off the assault, Chang'e fled. She ran back into the recesses of her home, slamming the door behind her. The wards flickered under the strength of the assault, but they held yet again, turning away the attacking magics as they had before.

When the third bombardment ended, Alyssandra retrieved the road flare from the ground. She removed the cap and raked it against the treated top of the flare. The striker instantly brought a hissing red flame to life. Triumphantly, she held the flare above her head like an Olympic torch bearer.

"Step back," she ordered her group. "But remain close enough to watch all windows and doors. I don't want her to escape."

Alyssandra lowered the flare and tossed it underhanded onto the porch. The gasoline she and her coven sisters had poured onto the porch and around the base of the house earlier that morning burst into roaring flames. With a loud whump of displaced air, the fire raced around the structure's perimeter, licking at the wooden structure from all sides. The heat of the sudden conflagration forced Alyssandra two paces back, but the light from the fire danced in her excited eyes and glinted from her bared teeth.

The defensive wards around the house came to life once more as the fire gained purchase along the walls and wooden framework of the porch. The magic pushed the inferno back for only an instant before they failed completely, winking out of existence. The wards had been erected to turn away hostile magic, not physical assaults like natural fire. That design flaw, along with the previous magical attacks, left the defenses too weak to protect the doomed house. The fire licked at the front door, continuing to burn and grow.

Alyssandra watched the flames climb higher along the walls, seeming to dance in glee as they reached the eaves of the roof. The light cast by the fire was much more intense than the relatively weak glow of the earlier magical assault. It was only a matter of time before one or more of the neighbors noticed something terribly amiss. Chang'e might also have called for help when she saw the fire outside her home working its way in. Alyssandra and the others would need to leave soon, before the fire department or police could arrive and detain them. She did not, however, want to go before she was certain Chang'e was trapped inside with no way out.

It certainly would not do to let the woman escape.

The fire formed a complete circle, covering every inch of the building's perimeter. All the doors and windows, having been thoroughly soaked with gasoline, burned merrily, completely engulfed in flame. Glass heated and cracked, and the fire caught drapes and curtains inside the window frames. Alyssandra heard a scream from somewhere inside the house.

She smiled.

"This was too long in coming," she said. "I should have eliminated you a long time ago."

She watched for several minutes more. The fire raged through the interior, and the walls outside were completely swallowed by tongues of red and yellow flames. Black smoke swirled in a vortex of heat and ash from the roof and up into the early morning sky.

In the distance, Alyssandra heard the first faint sound of sirens. Time had run out.

"Did anyone see her come outside?" Alyssandra asked.

All three witches responded that they had not.

"Do you see any movement in the house?"

Another negative response.

"Excellent. I think we can leave now."

CHAPTER

17

When his shift ended Thursday morning, Mitch returned home and forced himself to sleep for a few hours. He awoke before noon, still tired, but too excited to remain in bed any longer. It was time to go meet the man he believed had shot and killed Lieutenant Tim Delaney.

His excitement was a bit dampened by his trip to Arizona. He thought he had found the lieutenant's killer once before and flown hundreds of miles to find the person responsible. He had been mistaken. Not completely, but enough that the flight home had been a quiet somber affair. In light of that mistake, he tried to keep his expectations under control. He did not think he was going to confront the wrong suspect twice in a row. The trail he followed felt right this time.

Although, to be fair, less than six months ago, he didn't think he was a warlock, and he had been pretty certain there was no such thing as magic in the world. It seemed he had been wrong about a lot of things lately.

Christopher Yost had provided Mitch with an address for Kenneth Dalton, but to double check – and to make sure Dalton had not also died recently – he had researched the man through the federal and state databases. Kenneth Dalton was presumably alive and well, and his last known address was exactly where Yost had said he could be found.

The address was the same location where Dalton had lived thirty years ago when the murder happened. He had not run, choosing instead to hide in plain sight the entire time. Mitch figured the killer was either very confident he would never be found, or else was too afraid to change anything about his lifestyle that might draw police attention towards him. Either way, it did not really matter. His time as a free man was now measured in minutes.

Before leaving the house, Mitch made a phone call to the police department. He hoped Dot was available to play human lie detector one more time. What had worked so well once was worth trying again.

Dot agreed to meet Mitch at Kenneth Dalton's home and help as she had done with Christopher Yost in Arizona. In his car, with the engine running but before he pulled out of the driveway, Mitch sent her a final text stating he was headed for Dalton's neighborhood and would wait for her arrival before he contacted their suspect. Dot responded immediately that she was on her way.

Mitch arrived at Dalton's home fifteen minutes later. He parked half a block away and turned the car engine off. He did not want to attract any attention to himself prematurely, so he had opted for a shirt and tie today rather than his officer's uniform. While he waited for Dot, he ran scenarios through his mind of what might happen when he knocked on the door. Dalton might run through the house, out into the backyard, and start hopping over fences to escape. In which case, Mitch probably should have arranged for backup to be available the next block over.

He picked up his phone, then set it back down.

No. He was not going to run. If Dalton had been the kind of person to run from police, he would not still be living in Elk Grove. He probably also would have been arrested a couple times for panicking and bolting from officers over the years. His criminal record was absolutely spotless. Mitch had checked it last night, and Dalton did not have so much as a speeding ticket to his name. The man was good at remaining unnoticed by law enforcement. He was not a runner.

A spotless record also indicated Dalton did not have a temper or a problem with drugs or alcohol. Either one of those things would have guaranteed at least the occasional run in with law enforcement. That was a good sign.

Dalton would not run, and he probably would not fight.

It was still important for Mitch to stay alert. This man had shot and killed a police officer at least once in his life. This was not the time to get overly complacent.

Dot arrived a few minutes later, locating Mitch's vehicle and pulling up behind it. Mitch started his car, pulled forward until he was two houses away from Dalton's, then killed the engine again. Dot followed his example. As he had done in Arizona, Mitch asked Dot to wait by her car while he knocked on the door.

"Let me know when it's safe to walk up," she said.

Mitch crossed the street and approached the driveway of Dalton's home. Before going to the front door, he rested a hand against the butt of his gun where it rested under his suitcoat, reassuring himself the weapon was where it was supposed to be. As ready as he could be, he stepped up to the door and knocked.

No one answered.

After a moment, he rang the doorbell, keeping his finger pressed to the button a few seconds longer than absolutely necessary.

This time, he heard movement from the rear of the house. Mitch took a step back and moved to one side of the door, using the same precautions he had taken in Phoenix. He did not expect gunfire, but it was always better to play it safe.

The door opened, revealing a slightly stooped man in his late forties, wearing jeans and a gaudy, yellow and green Hawaiian shirt. He was a few inches shorter than Mitch's own six-foot stature, with gray stubble covering his face and darker brown hair receding far back on his forehead. The man gazed at him with eerily familiar blue-gray eyes.

"Yes?" the man asked.

"Are you Mr. Kenneth Dalton?"

"I am. And it's Kenny, please. Can I help you?"

Mitch removed his wallet and held out his identification.

"My name is Detective Mitch Loman. I'm here investigating a homicide that occurred about thirty years ago. The victim's name was…"

"Lieutenant Timothy Delaney," Kenny Dalton finished Mitch's sentence. He did not seem startled or nervous. He said the name without any inflection whatsoever, as if he were stating his own name in answer to a question.

Alarm bells went off in Mitch's head. Uncertain what he was facing, he opened his soul sight and peered deeply into the man. He needed to know what kind of person he was dealing with. Was the calm pronouncement of Delaney's name the cold, emotionless response of a sociopath? Had he made an enormous error and walked into an ambush?

Mitch found Dalton's spirit and extended a small portion of himself to touch it. He wanted to know this man to the core of his being, to understand his essence and to know what sort of threat he might be facing.

His soul touched Kenny's, and his concerns evaporated.

Kenny Dalton was not a sociopath. He was barely more than a frightened child. At forty-eight years old, his soul was frozen in time, trapped by the events that had shaped it thirty years ago. Mitch found no anger or violence as he had initially expected from a cop killer. This soul was passive, empathetic, even loving, though it was also quite damaged. In Dalton, Mitch felt grief, regret, and a deep longing to correct the wrongs he had done in his past. The only thing in Kenny's soul stronger than the longing for his nightmare to end was a deep-seated belief that he could never be forgiven for his sins. Not in this life. And not in the next.

No fear resided in this man. He was not going to run. He understood he had been caught, but the only reaction to that certainty was … relief. Kenny Dalton did not have the strength to turn himself in for his crimes, but he also secretly longed for the day that he would no longer have to hide what he had done.

There was also no deceit that Mitch could detect. Dalton would not lie to protect himself. Not now. He was certain of that.

Mitch withdrew from Kenny's soul, extricating himself easily. He did not flounder as he had the first time soul touching with Violet. Their practice was paying off. When he was free and fully back in his own body, he turned and waved toward Dot. As she approached, he stepped onto the lawn and met her.

"You can go," Mitch said. "I'm sorry you drove all the way out here for nothing. I can handle this from here."

Dot gazed at him intently. "You're sure?" she asked. "I don't mind staying."

"I got it."

"Okay," she responded, resting an affectionate hand on his arm. Dot smiled and stroked his sleeve like a mother sending her child off to school on his own for the first time. "Good luck, Mitchell."

Without further argument or question, Dot walked to her car and climbed inside. Mitch returned to the door where Kenny still waited patiently.

"I think you know why I'm here," he said.

The man nodded. The expression on his face was not one of concern or disappointment. He appeared relieved that the decades long ordeal had reached its end. A weight was coming off of his shoulders; a weight he had carried with him for more than thirty long years.

"Can I ask, how did you finally find me?"

"We matched your blood. It took a while, but we got there. Can we go inside? Talk for a bit?"

Surprise registered on Kenny's face for the first time. "Um, sure. You aren't going to arrest me?"

"Yes," Mitch told him honestly. "But I wanted to hear the whole story first. I want your side of what happened. There are things I don't understand yet, and you are the only person that can fill in any of the holes."

Kenny ushered Mitch inside and closed the door. The interior of the house was dark and cool, almost cold. The thermostat must have been set at 74 degrees or lower. There was very little furniture; the décor minimalist to the point of being austere. Kenneth clearly did not seek the creature comforts of modern living. Mitch did not even see a television set in the house.

Kenny led him to the kitchen and invited him to sit at a small wooden table pushed into the angled nook of a bay window.

"Can I get you anything? Something to drink?"

Mitch declined and asked Kenny to sit with him. He pulled out a digital recorder from his coat pocket and set it on the table between them. Pressing the button on the side of the recorder, Mitch watched until he was certain the counter on the display screen activated. When he was confident the machine was on, he settled back in his chair.

"I want to record our conversation. Is that alright with you?"

"Sure," said Kenny. "Why not?"

"Can you tell me what happened back in 1994? What happened between you and Lieutenant Delaney at the 76 gas station?"

Kenny paused. He did not hesitate out of fear of incriminating himself but instead seemed to be trying to decide where to start. This would be the first time he had ever had the opportunity to tell this story, and Mitch could tell Kenny wanted it to come out right.

"What happened was entirely my fault. I take all the responsibility for shooting that officer. I don't want to get anyone else in trouble for something I did."

"I understand how you feel. You don't want your friends to get in trouble. I respect that. I even admire it a little bit. Loyalty is important. But Bruce is dead, Kenny. He can't get into any trouble if you talk about him. He was your partner, right? Bruce Yost?"

Kenny nodded and said softly, "Yeah."

"In fact, I think it was probably his idea. He used to work for the gas station, and he wanted to pay them back for firing him, but he needed you to help him do it. Right? Is that about what happened?"

"No, it wasn't like that. He wasn't mad at the owner. He didn't care that he got fired. He just needed money, quick, and he thought he could get it from the safe. He knew the combination and thought he could get in and out without any problems. It didn't work. The combination to the safe, I mean. They changed it after they fired him."

Mitch leaned forward in his seat, moving physically closer to Kenny and trying to build a bond between them as they spoke. He lowered his voice to keep the conversation more intimate and asked, "What did Bruce need the money for?"

"His girlfriend was pregnant. Bruce didn't have a job, and he was flat broke. They were living in his dad's garage at the time. He needed money so he could get his own place and take care of her."

"Was that Marlene? His girlfriend? Marlene Tansen?"

"Uh, yeah. Marlene. Bruce was crazy about her. He would have done absolutely anything for her and the baby."

"You cared about her, too. Didn't you Kenny?" Mitch asked. He nodded to demonstrate his understanding of the man's situation. "So, when Bruce asked for your help, you wanted to do what you could."

"Bruce was my best friend. Of course, I was going to help him. And Marlene, well, she was great. Everybody liked her."

Mitch let that statement pass. He knew there was more, but it was not relative to the information he wanted.

"Did Marlene know what Bruce was doing? What both of you were planning? She was his alibi at the casino, so I'm guessing she had some idea that you guys were up to something."

Kenny went quiet for a moment, sitting stiffly in his chair. He glanced around the room as if searching for a safe answer, or maybe a change of topic.

"I don't want to talk about her," he said, finally meeting Mitch's gaze. The intensity and honesty in the look surprised Mitch. "I said I don't want to get anybody else in trouble for something that is completely my fault. I meant that. Marlene doesn't need to be part of this."

Afraid that he might lose Kenny's cooperation if he pushed this issue too hard, Mitch relented. "You're right. You told me. You know what? It doesn't even matter. I have no idea where she is, and I have no interest in searching for her. I don't care about her at all. Let's pretend I never brought her up. Deal?"

The relief on Kenny's face was clear. He sat a little straighter in his chair, and even smiled a bit.

"Deal," he said.

"What I would like to know, more than anything, is how you guys got away after you got shot. Can you tell me about that? Wait, back up. How did the shooting happen in the first place? Do you mind telling me that story?"

"Yeah, I can tell you that. Where do you want me to start?"

Mitch thought a bit, then said, "Tell me who's car you used, and who drove to the gas station. Start there."

"Sure. Well, it was my car, but Bruce drove because he was a better driver..."

...We didn't know what was going to happen after we emptied the safe, but we figured if we had to run from the police, Bruce had a better chance of getting away than I did. It was sort of stupid reasoning, but we were both eighteen at the time, and most of the things going on in our heads were probably pretty stupid.

The night before we robbed the gas station, Bruce drove with Marlene to Reno. They checked into a hotel and Bruce made sure to be seen by as many people and cameras as he could. A little after midnight, he left Marlene at the hotel and drove back to my house. He left his car at my place. To be honest, I guess I should say it was my parents' place since I was still living with them at the time.

Before we went to the gas station, I got some blue tape and changed my license plate number in case someone saw us and reported it. Just a couple simple things, you know. I made the F into an E, and the P into an R. Again, it was pretty stupid, but we weren't exactly hardened criminals, you know? I thought I was being so clever.

When we got to the station, we didn't go into the parking lot. We parked on Bond Road so we could jump in the car and get out of there as fast as possible. We also didn't want any cameras to see us. Bruce said there weren't any cameras around the gas pumps, but there were a couple inside the store. I don't know if the store cameras could see the cars outside or not, but we didn't want to take the chance.

Before we got out of the car, we put on ski masks and gloves. No faces and no fingerprints was the idea. We figured if we didn't leave anything behind that could be traced to us, there was no way we could get caught.

Bruce took a revolver out of the glovebox and checked that there were bullets in it. I grabbed the shotgun from the floorboards in the backseat. The guns belonged to Bruce's dad. His dad was a hunter, so he kept all sorts of rifles and stuff in a garage cabinet that wasn't locked. They were easy to find, and easy to get to. Bruce told me no one would miss them as long as we got them back before Bruce's dad went on his next hunting trip.

I didn't like having guns with us when we went into the gas station, but Bruce said we needed them to make the workers inside take us seriously. I wish we had left them behind. I wish we had at least brought them in unloaded. There wasn't any reason they had to be loaded. We never planned to hurt anyone.

There are so many things I'd like to change about that day, but like most things in my life, it's way too late for that.

We got out of the car and ran to the store. I'm sure we looked ridiculous, but we didn't want to be out in the open carrying guns and wearing masks for any longer than we had to. Anybody outside walking by, or people at the gas pumps filling up their cars might have seen us and gotten suspicious that something really bad was happening. We didn't want anyone to call the police before we had a chance to get out of there.

The front doors opened, and we ran in and let the doors close behind us. Bruce told me as soon as we were inside and the doors were shut that I should rack a round into the shotgun. The noise was supposed to make everyone notice us, so that's exactly what I did. It worked better than we thought. The lieutenant, Lieutenant Delaney, was in the back of the store and must have heard the sound immediately. I don't know what he was thinking when he realized what we were doing, but he didn't come out right away. He stayed hidden in one of the aisles.

Bruce went right to the worker at the counter. He was the only employee in the store that day, so we focused on him. I didn't know him. I'm not sure if Bruce did or not. Bruce ordered the guy to empty the safe, but the kid pretended he didn't know anything about a safe.

Bruce went behind the counter and pulled away the cover on a hidden cabinet. First, he dialed in the combination he had been given when he worked there. It didn't work. The owner must have changed it after Bruce got fired, or maybe after another employee left later. Anyway, it didn't work.

When he couldn't get it open, Bruce ordered the kid at the counter to open it. He threatened to shoot him. He wasn't really going to hurt the guy. I know Bruce would never shoot anyone, but it was the fastest way to get him to open the safe so we could leave. The kid was going to open it, too. There was no reason for him to risk his life to protect someone else's money. I think Bruce even told him that to make him hurry up.

I thought we were home free. We would be in the car and getting the hell out of there in a few more seconds.

That's when I heard a hiss and some static, like one of those really old, boxy television sets when you turn them on. Then a really scratchy voice said something about chasing a truck and pulling it over. When the voice started talking, I realized it was some kind of radio and that there was someone else in the store with us.

I looked around to find where the sounds were coming from, and I saw this head pop up from behind one of the shelves in the store. The guy had on a big hat with a wide brim, like one of those Smokey the Bear, forest ranger hats. It was Lieutenant Delaney, although I only learned his name a week or so later.

He shouted something at me, but I didn't really hear what he said. It was probably something about not moving, or maybe lying down on the ground. I was so shocked to see him there, I turned to face him, the shotgun I was holding pointed at him when I moved. I swear I wasn't aiming at him or trying to hurt him.

He started shooting. Something hit my leg, and it felt like somebody was pushing a burning metal rod through my thigh. I screamed. I remember that. My finger was on the trigger of the shotgun and I must have squeezed it. The gun exploded in my hands, and the kick of it in my ribs, along with the pain in my leg, knocked me to the ground.

I looked up and saw Lieutenant Delaney pointing his gun at Bruce. He didn't say anything, though. He just pointed the gun. He looked confused and a little bit panicked. The officer stepped out from behind the shelves and pointed his gun at me and I immediately dropped the shotgun and put my hands up. I didn't want to get shot again. I was ready to give up. I figured jail was better than dying.

The officer still didn't say anything, which I thought was weird. Bruce grabbed the store clerk and ducked behind the counter. Then the strangest thing happened. The officer dropped his gun on the floor and grabbed at his throat. That was when I saw all the blood. It covered his hand and ran down the front of his shirt.

I remember how much that bullet in my thigh hurt. When I think about it today, I can still feel that piece of metal burning in there. But the pain in my leg was nothing compared to the sick feeling I got when I realized what had happened. When my shotgun went off, I hit the officer. He was dying.

I wanted to get up and run to him, to try to help him. I really did. I even tried to stand, but I couldn't move. When I tried getting my feet under me, that horrible pain in my leg dropped me back to the ground.

The officer fell, rolling onto his back and still grabbing at his throat.

I have nightmares about that moment. Even today, I have them all the time. I see that poor man on his back, his hand squeezing his neck where the bullet hit him while coughing up blood. His hat fell off, and it was just sitting on the floor next to him. There were tiny dark spots on the brim and on the badge on the front. Each time he coughed, I saw a few more spots show up. It was his blood spattering the hat and ground around him.

It was horrific. That image is fully burned into my brain. Even when I'm awake, it never completely goes away.

Bruce came out from behind the counter and checked on him. I asked him if the officer was okay. I think I was crying when I asked it. Bruce told me, no.

He said, "You killed him."

Those were his exact words. "You killed him."

That was the moment I became a murderer.

Bruce asked if I could walk. He said that we needed to go, but I told him I couldn't. I needed help because of my leg. I think I even told him to leave me behind. I was in shock, both because of the wound in my leg, and because of what happened to the officer.

Bruce grabbed my arm and told me to pick up the shotgun. This part is kind of hazy, but I must have grabbed the gun while Bruce pulled me to my feet. We hurried out of the store and ran for the car. I don't know how much blood I lost, but it felt like a lot. I do remember seeing blood all over the floor of the store, and a trail of it following us into the parking lot and all the way to my car.

Bruce pushed me into the passenger side, and we tossed our guns into the back seat. As soon as he got the car started, we raced away from the store. At least that's what he told me later. Like I said, I think I was going into shock.

Bruce wasn't completely stupid. As he drove us away from there, he didn't go above the speed limit, and he took off going east on Bond Road. We wanted to get to the freeway, but anyone who might have seen us leave the gas station would tell police we were headed away from the freeway toward Grantline Road. Hopefully, that would send the cops looking in the wrong direction.

Bruce turned at the next street, and a few minutes later we were headed toward highway 99, which had been the original plan. We were supposed to go back to Reno to meet with Marlene and hide for a couple of days.

After getting shot, I figured the plan had changed.

We drove for a while, I remember that. I was kind of in and out of consciousness at that point. When Bruce got onto

Highway 80 and started driving east, I woke up enough to realize where we were. I got worried.

"I need to get to a hospital," I told him.

"I know. I'll get you there, but we can't do it here. We need to get to Reno."

I thought I might be dying. I had heard about people bleeding to death from leg injuries. There are a lot of major arteries that run through the leg, and if one of them is damaged, it could be fatal within a few minutes. I think I said something to him about that.

"It isn't that bad," he told me, trying to calm me down. "Put pressure on it and I'll take you to a hospital as soon as we get into Nevada. If we go to a hospital here, we're going to get caught."

"I don't really care about getting caught," I told him, and it was the truth.

I was hurt, scared, and I had just killed a police officer. I felt like I deserved to get caught. I deserved to be punished. Bruce had no intention of letting that happen. I suppose I should have been angry at him for that, for putting his freedom ahead of my life. I could have died during the hours it took to drive from Sacramento to Reno.

I probably should have hated him for it, but I didn't. I couldn't hate him. I loved him too much. He was like a brother to me.

I sat in the car, bleeding, and Bruce drove. To keep my mind occupied, Bruce made me memorize our cover story for how I got hurt. I don't know where he came up with the idea, but his story was detailed and sounded plausible, at least to the stupid, eighteen-year-old me. After I repeated the story back to him a hundred times and Bruce was satisfied I wouldn't forget it, he left me alone.

I passed out again. Or maybe I only fell asleep, but either way I don't remember anything more about that drive until he woke me up in the parking lot of a hospital.

I felt Bruce shaking my shoulder. I looked around and the car was stopped in front of a great big, red and white sign that said, "Emergency Room Entrance." There was a huge red arrow on the sign, too, with the name of the hospital underneath. I think it was called Renown Regional, or something like that. It's been a while, so I can't be certain.

When Bruce saw that I was awake, he drove the car to the curb at the emergency room front doors and ran inside for help. I panicked for a second when I thought about the guns, and I checked the back seat. At some point he must have stopped and put them in the trunk of the car. I don't know when that happened, but the guns were gone. It was about that time that a couple people came out of the hospital with Bruce. They had a wheelchair with them. With the help of two guys in white scrubs, I got out of the car and into the chair. They brought me into the emergency room and took me to the back for an exam.

Someone hooked me to an IV because I had lost so much blood. I was dehydrated, but apparently the bullet hadn't hit anything critical, and I wasn't in immediate danger of bleeding to death. I think I kind of already figured that out by the fact I had survived the drive there. But still, it was nice to hear the doctor say he didn't think I was going to die.

While they examined me, one of the doctors asked me how I got hurt. I remembered what Bruce had told me to say.

"Me and a couple friends were target shooting in the woods. We started screwing around and taking stupid chances. I was holding a bottle for Bruce to shoot at, and he hit me in the leg."

"What kind of gun was it?" the doctor asked.

"I don't know, actually," I told him. "It belongs to the other friend we were with. I don't know a lot about guns." That last part at least was the honest truth.

"Who is the other friend?" he asked. "Not the boy who brought you in?"

"No. Bruce brought me in. He's the one who shot me. I'd rather not say who the other guy is. He didn't do anything, and I don't want to get him in any trouble."

The doctor didn't press any further on who our imaginary friend might be.

"Okay," he said. "I still have to report this to the police, though. They are probably going to have some questions for you when you get out of surgery."

"Surgery?" I asked, surprised. Although, I guess I should have realized they needed to get the bullet out of my leg.

The nurses prepped me for surgery and knocked me out. The doctor was right. When I came to, there was an officer from the Reno Police Department in my room. I was groggy and barely awake, but I guess he thought that was the best time to question me about what happened. If I was still under the influence of the meds, I wouldn't be able to make up a lie very easily. Fortunately, Bruce and I had rehearsed our alibi so many times in the car, I didn't have to think too hard to remember it. I told him the same story I told the doctor.

The officer also didn't push very hard to get information on our made-up, third friend who owned the gun. He believed us when we said the whole thing had been a stupid accident. Since he had the shooter and the victim together at the hospital, he didn't think it was important to identify any potential witnesses. Bruce and I were telling the same story, and we both appeared upfront about how dumb and careless we had been. He must have figured there weren't any visible loose ends, so why pull at threads that didn't need to be pulled.

He told me he was going to file an incident report to document the shooting, but that would probably be the end of it. He warned me that charges might be filed later against Bruce for reckless endangerment and discharging a firearm in a manner likely to cause an injury, but since I insisted I didn't want to press charges, he thought the odds of an arrest were pretty low.

Turns out the officer was telling us the truth. We never heard anything more from Reno PD. Which was a good thing, because we used our real names at the hospital. That might have been our biggest mistake, other than committing the robbery itself of course. We didn't have much choice, though. We didn't have fake identities to hide behind. Any lies we told the police about who we were would have been caught immediately, making the rest of our story suspect.

Bruce came into my room after the officer left. He was grinning. I don't know what he thought was so funny. We were still murderers. And we were still broke.

I checked out of the hospital later that day. Bruce took me to his hotel room and the three of us stayed there two more days. I needed a little time to heal before I went home, and Bruce wanted to firm up his alibi. While I was stuck in the room, he got the car washed and detailed, cleaning up the blood in the front seat.

When we went home, Bruce picked up his car and he and Marlene went back to his dad's house. He replaced his dad's guns, and nobody but us knew they had ever been gone. I told my parents the same story we told the police when they asked about my leg. Other than warning me I shouldn't hang out with Bruce any longer, they let the matter drop.

The police contacted Bruce about a week later and asked him a bunch of questions about the robbery at the gas station. He had a solid alibi, and he didn't have any injuries from being shot. The detectives moved on to check out other possible suspects. There was nothing connecting me to Bruce that the police knew about, so no one ever came looking for me. My leg healed, and Bruce and I put this whole thing behind us.

No one was after us, but about a month after the police interviewed Bruce about the robbery, he and Marlene decided to move to Arizona. They still didn't have any money, but they wanted to get away from Elk Grove as fast as possible...

"...They borrowed some cash from Marlene's parents to pay for some of the expenses and to put a deposit down on an apartment. I stayed in Elk Grove. When my parents decided to move to Idaho a few years later, I bought their house. I've never left."

Kenny paused. He took a deep breath and released it as if breathing easily for the first time in thirty years. He looked at Mitch and waited for the detective's reaction to his story.

"When Bruce and Marlene moved to Arizona, why didn't you follow them? He was your best friend, right?"

Kenny shook his head. "They were having some problems at the time. Marlene was pregnant, and they were fighting a lot. When they moved, they got married and tried to put their issues aside for the baby. I knew if I went with them, any chance they had of making the relationship work would be gone. I would just get in the way."

"You loved Marlene, didn't you?" asked Mitch.

"Marlene was great," Kenny said, dodging the question. "Everyone loved her."

"*You* loved Marlene, didn't you?" Mitch repeated. "And she loved you."

Kenny went rigid. He closed his mouth and glanced at the recorder on the table. Mitch touched a button, turning the machine off. He picked up the digital recorder and slipped it into the pocket of his jacket.

"This has nothing to do with the investigation. No one needs to hear this part," Mitch assured him. "You didn't go to Arizona because you and Marlene were in love, but you didn't want to get between your best friend and his girlfriend. Am I right?"

Kenny nodded. "Marlene loved both of us, but she chose Bruce. I had to respect that. I needed to stay away so she wouldn't be tempted to leave him and her family. I didn't want to, but it was the right thing to do."

Mitch sighed. He had what he needed to arrest Kenny. Any additional information he wanted would merely be prying into the man's personal life. He debated butting out at this point, but some part of him deep down kept pressuring him to continue meddling in affairs that did not concern him.

"Kenny. When are you going to tell him?" he asked.

"Tell who what? Bruce is dead. What do you think I should have told him? That I loved Marlene? He knew that already. I told you, the three of us grew up together."

"No, not Bruce. Christopher. When are you going to tell him that you're his father?"

Kenny stared at the table between them. He said nothing. He did not argue or deny Mitch's accusation.

"Don't you think he has the right to know? Did Bruce know?"

"No," said Kenny. "I don't think he did."

"But Marlene knew, didn't she? That was probably the reason she divorced Bruce and left. Christopher has your eyes, Kenny. I noticed it the second I saw you at the front door. I imagine after three years, Marlene couldn't stand looking at your son and seeing the evidence of her betrayal any longer. Is that why she ran? Maybe she needed to start a new life where she didn't have to think about the husband she cheated on, and raising a child that wasn't his."

"I think so. Yes," Kenny whispered.

"Shouldn't you tell him the truth?"

"How am I supposed to do that? Especially now. How do I tell Chris I'm his dad when I'm about to go prison for the rest of my life for murder? A murder I committed, by the way, with the help of the man he until recently thought was his real father. And then what? Should I also tell him, 'Gee, Chris, your mother ran away because she couldn't stand to look at you any longer.' Do you think he deserves to know *that* truth?"

Mitch made an empathetic grunt. "I understand how you feel, but he's going to find out eventually. I think he should hear it from you first. When you're arrested, it's going to make national news."

"He'll know that his Uncle Kenny got arrested. He will have no idea about the rest of it."

"I went to see him the other day. I told him that I was looking for his dad because he might have killed someone in a robbery. I didn't know about you and his mother when I said that. I'm sorry. When this story appears in the news, he'll hear that the blood evidence I was following came from you. He's going to put the pieces together at some point. Assuming he hasn't already."

Kenny crossed his arms on the table and dropped his head onto them, hiding his face.

"Oh, shit. Oh, my God. How am I going to face that poor kid?"

"He's a grown man, not a kid. He'll deal with it. I still think it will go better though, if he hears it from you directly."

Kenny sat up.

"When am I supposed to do that? I'm going to jail, aren't I?"

"Yes," Mitch said. "Eventually. But maybe not right this minute. I'm going to leave now. When I go, I'm going to call another detective to come arrest you and take you to jail. It could be an hour before he gets here. Would that give you enough time?"

"Maybe. I mean, it will have to be enough, won't it?"

"And you promise you will be here when the detective arrives?"

"I'll be here. I promise. I haven't gone anywhere in thirty years. I'm not going to change that now."

Mitch trusted Kenny's promise. He had seen the depths of the man's soul and knew the type of person he truly was. He would not run.

Mitch rose from his chair and walked to the front door. Kenny remained at the kitchen table, staring open mouthed at his retreating back. Despite Mitch's words, he had not truly believed that a police officer would simply walk away and leave him alone after the confession he had made. Mitch, on the other hand, felt comfortable leaving him on his own precisely *because* of the confession he had made. Kenneth had clearly demonstrated he was not only willing, but eager to pay his debt for the crime he committed.

Mitch let himself out, closing the door behind him. He glanced up and down the street and saw that, as she had promised, Dot was gone. He had wondered briefly if she would stick around to make sure he was alright while he interviewed Kenny. Mitch thought it was nice to see that she had faith in his ability to take care of himself.

After climbing into his car, starting the engine, and turning on the air conditioning to cool down the interior, he tapped the button on his steering wheel that connected to his cellphone.

"Call Detective Ali Minhas."

The car responded, "Calling Detective Ali Minhas."

"Come on, man, pick up the phone. This is important."

It took three rings, but Ali did pick up.

"Hey, Mitch. How's it going? Did you get your guy in Phoenix?"

"No, that trail ran cold. The suspect died about three years ago."

"Ah, crap. Sorry about that. Are you going to close the case?"

"No. But you are."

"What?"

"Do you remember when I told you that I owed you a big favor?"

"I recall that you owe me *several* favors," replied Ali.

Mitch laughed. "Well, I'm about to even the score with this one, my friend. I want to hand you the biggest arrest Sac County has seen in decades."

"Bigger than the Golden State Killer?"

Mitch paused, taken aback. Then said, "No. Okay, second biggest arrest. Look, man, just take the win, okay? Bruce Yost wasn't our shooter. He also wasn't Christopher Yost's dad. The real dad lives right here in Elk Grove, and I got a full confession recorded. The guy's name is Kenneth Dalton and he's ready to turn himself in. I'll email you a copy of his confession, but you should get him mirandized and do it again anyway."

"Wait a minute, Mitch. You caught the shooter, but you want me to arrest him? This is your case. You should get the collar."

"I want you to have this one," Mitch told Ali. "I only found him because you made the DNA connection. You solved this case and I really think you should get the credit. Besides, there's still some details to nail down, and I don't have the time to do it. I'm giving you the bust, but I'm also handing over the paperwork. Fair?"

"Fair," Ali agreed.

"Okay. Do you have a pen? You need to do a few things."

"Shoot."

"After he was shot, Kenneth Dalton went to Reno to get treated. That's why we never found hospital records of a gunshot victim. Agencies in different states barely talk to each other today, and it was a whole lot worse back then. Nobody even thought to look further than their own backyards. Kenny landed at Renown Regional. That's where they took out the bullet. Reno PD also came and took an incident report. You're going to need to contact both of them and get copies of their records. Got that so far?"

"Got it," Ali told him. "Anything else?"

"Yeah. The murder weapon was a shotgun that belonged to Bruce Yost's father. Bruce wasn't our shooter, but he was still involved. He was the second gunman. Run down the father and see if he still owns that gun."

"Damn, Mitch. You really sank your teeth into this one. Nice job. You sure you don't want the arrest?"

"No. I have another case I'm neck deep in and I can't afford the time or the publicity to finish this up right."

"This case could get you sergeant stripes, man," Ali suggested.

"Sergeant stripes will look good on you," Mitch replied. "After I hang up, I'll text you his address so you can pick him up. He's waiting for you."

"Wait! You left him alone? What if he bails?"

"He isn't going anywhere. Trust me. You should still come get him as quickly as possible. We don't want him changing his mind about the confession."

"Renown Regional. Reno PD. Run down the father for a possible murder weapon. Okay. Find out anything about the car they used?"

"Nope. I actually forgot to ask what he did with it. Ah, well. I'm sure Kenny will tell you what happened to it if you ask him. So, what do you say? Are we square?"

"We are way more than square after this, man. This is huge. I take back every nasty thing I ever said about you."

"Um, when were you saying nasty things about me?" Mitch asked.

"Later," Ali said, then disconnected.

Mitch laughed again and texted Kenny's address to Ali. He would need to send the homicide detective the audio file of Kenny's confession, but he could do that when he got back home. He also needed to call Chief Jefferson and give him a heads up on the case before the whole story broke and went public.

After that, there was nothing to do before work tonight besides watch the arrest report on the evening news. Ali was a good man, and a good detective. He deserved the attention he was about to receive, and hopefully it would end up with him getting a nice little promotion for his accomplishment.

Mitch wondered if Ali would mention his name at the press conference.

CHAPTER

 18

Briefing that night was a bit more contentious than most Mitch had attended, either in Dasan's Terrace or at any of his other assignments within Sacramento County. Tomorrow, Alyssandra's coven would return to the cemetery to conduct the delayed ghoul hunt. Because they did not know if they would find one ghoul or a hundred, the entire coven would be present. In addition, Chief Jefferson had arranged for Day Shift and Grave Shift to overlap for several hours, putting nine officers on the grounds to assist the witches in their search.

The relationship between witches and the Dead Town PD was difficult at best, and volatile at its worst. The tentative truce that Chief Jefferson and Alyssandra had negotiated over the past few years was about to be sorely tested.

"It's a bad idea," said Tink, repeating himself for the tenth time. "I know they've helped us out before, but that was only one or two of them at a time, and usually the chief had us stay as far away as possible while they were here. This many witches around nine cops is going to blow up in our faces."

"It's my job to make sure it doesn't," Jorge told him. "I intend to do my job. All I need is for you and Mitch and Brad to follow the plan. Do exactly what you're told, when you're told, and don't engage with the witches beyond what you absolutely have to."

"I can do that," Tink promised, though the angry flush to his face suggested otherwise. "What about Day Shift? They haven't worked around Alyssandra as much as we have. They might get jumpy and do something stupid."

"Sergeant Ricci is responsible for his people, and I trust he will have them properly under control. He is going to be having this same discussion with his team in the morning. I'm meeting with him at two o'clock tomorrow afternoon, so when you guys show up at three, we can be sure we're all working on the same game plan."

"I'm surprised you're so calm about all of this, Sarge," said Brad. For once, he seemed completely serious. There was no sign of amusement or humor in his expression. "Especially since one of those witches tried to kill you last year."

"What?" asked Mitch, shifting his gaze back and forth between Jorge and Brad. "Who tried to kill you?"

"Nobody tried to kill me," said the sergeant, glaring at Brad. "The girl, Gabby I think is what they call her, was in the cemetery on a day she wasn't supposed to be. She was new and didn't know the rules yet, and I didn't recognize her as one of Alyssandra's people. I found her wandering the grounds and told her to leave. She ignored me and kept walking, so I grabbed her by the arm."

Mitch winced, guessing what came next.

"She's young and was still figuring out how to control her magic," Jorge explained. "She punched me in the chest and must have added a little something to the hit, because she tossed me ten feet through the air."

"If you hadn't been wearing your vest, she could have killed you," added Brad.

"Well, I was, and she didn't," Jorge insisted, slashing a hand through the air to dismiss the accusation. "Yes, the witches are dangerous. I have my concerns, just like the rest of you, but I also have my orders. Besides, we have something now that we didn't have back then." His gaze swept the table and landed on Mitch. "We have you. As long as Mitch is working with the coven, it should be smooth sailing."

Mitch was not so certain of that last statement. Alyssandra was a snake, and everything the woman did was for the sole benefit of one person: Alyssandra. If she decided murdering the entire Dead Town Police Department could help her in the long run, Mitch had no doubt she would do it.

Or at least, she would try.

He did not share his thoughts with the rest of the team. They were worried enough about partnering with the witches without him adding to their misgivings.

Instead, he told them, "I'm not worried. Violet has our backs."

"I like Violet," said Tink. "She seems nice, and I'm really happy for you two. But let's face it, Violet isn't in charge. Alyssandra calls the shots, and I don't trust a word out of her mouth. If she offered me an umbrella in a rainstorm, I think I'd rather get wet."

"You're not wrong," said Brad. He leaned across the table and extended a fist. Tink bumped it with his own.

"Okay," said Jorge. "Fair enough. Don't trust Alyssandra, but do trust me. And trust Simon. He's going to be out there with us tomorrow making sure Alyssandra keeps to her part of the agreement. He's also going to make sure we keep ours."

Tink put his arms up in surrender. "I'll do my job. I never said I wouldn't. I just wanted to say, I think it's a bad idea."

"Noted," said Jorge. "It's a bad idea, and we're doing it anyway."

The sergeant picked up the clipboard that held his briefing notes. He flipped through the first couple pages.

"Logistics for tomorrow, gentlemen," he continued. "Edged weapons are the word of the day. Ghouls only stop when you burn them or cut them into pieces so small that they aren't a threat anymore."

Brad tapped the handle of his katana. "Never leave home without it," he said.

"Everyone else follow Brad's lead and make sure you're carrying something long and sharp. We are not using the crossbows this time. Too many people, and not enough room to properly triangulate without risking hitting one of our own. It's going to be close quarters and hand to hand."

Mitch remembered the last time he got close to a ghoul. The stitches were gone, but the wound in his arm was still healing. He was not looking forward to a repeat of that incident.

"Alyssandra and her coven will be searching for tunnels and ghouls. Their job, when they find one of the nasty buggers, is to flush it to the surface. We then cut it down, burn it, and move on. All thirteen witches will be there, but only six will be actively searching. The other seven will partner with the first six to provide skill support."

"What's skill support," asked Tink. "Making sure the magic doesn't get out of control and kill all of us?"

"No, I don't think so," said Jorge. "At least I hope not. I don't really know what they're doing. Mitch? Any ideas?"

Mitch had been training with Violet for months now, and he had seen several of the witches in her coven working magic in pairs or groups. He had witnessed the weaker witches adding guidance and direction to spell workings done by the more powerful members of the group.

"Not all of the witches are that strong," he said. "In fact, most of them, the seven that will be assisting, don't have the ability to hold and work magic on their own. They can, however, help shape spells that another witch is crafting. I'm not sure of the best way to explain it, but Violet said it's like golfing. Imagine you have a partner with you who doesn't know how to golf, but he wants to help, so he stands next to the hole while you're putting. If you miss the putt, your partner can give the ball a little kick and nudge it into the hole."

"That's cheating," said Brad.

"Yeah, but it still works. The first witch, the one with real power, is going to pull magic, create a spell and direct it into the ground at the ghoul. The second witch, providing skill support, gives the spell that little kick to make it more accurate and, hopefully, more effective."

"Alright. Now we know," said Jorge. "Moving on. After we eliminate the ghoul, the witches will collapse the tunnel beneath us so no other ghouls can move in after we pass through the area. We will start in North-West while it's still daylight, since there isn't any lighting in that part of the cemetery. We'll make passes east to west then back, working our way forward through Back Half and then Front Half until we reach the parking lot."

Jorge paused for questions. When no one commented, he continued. "Each of the six lead witches will be walking side by side about thirty feet apart from each other. I was told they can't be any further than that or there's a risk something could slip between them unnoticed. That means that each pass will be covering a path almost two hundred feet wide."

"Two hundred feet?" asked Brad. "Sarge, you realize Dead Town is almost 600 acres, right?"

"I know."

"This is going to take forever. We could be out there for days."

"Not days, Brad. Don't be so dramatic. Simon and Dot calculated if we don't find any ghouls, we could cover the entire cemetery in nine or ten hours. Chances are, however, we will find a couple of them out there, so add whatever time it takes to deal with them. Plus meals, and whatever breaks we take."

"Days," Brad whined again.

"Stop being such a baby," Jorge told him. "The witches are going to be doing the hard work. They have to march the entire grounds in formation. All we have to do is be nearby so we can help when they find something."

"Let's hope they don't find anything," suggested Tink. "That way, they can do all the work, and we can sit back and watch."

"That's a nice thought," agreed the sergeant, "but we already know there's still at least one ghoul out there. I'm guessing we're going to find more than that."

Tink moaned dramatically.

The briefing continued for another twenty minutes as Sergeant Smythe discussed the tactics he wanted the team to follow when taking down a ghoul, and the officers continued to complain about the amount of time it would take to cover the entire expanse of Dead Town. The discussion finally ended with Jorge listing the movies he had brought in for Movie Thursday.

Friday was going to be a long and potentially dangerous hunt. For that reason, Jorge advised the officers to skip their normal evening patrols and stay together in the police department building for the entire shift. There was no point in risking a surprise run in with a stray ghoul the night before they planned to eradicate the threat completely.

"Hey, Jorge," Mitch said as the briefing broke up. "Can you give me a few minutes before you come upstairs and start the movies? I want to go up to Delaney's office and see if he's there. I wanted to let him know what happened today, and I'd appreciate a little time to talk to him without a crowd."

"Of course," Jorge agreed. "Take all the time you want. Come down and get me when you're done."

"What happened today?" asked Tink.

"Don't you ever watch the news?" asked Brad. "They caught Delaney's killer this afternoon. They arrested the guy in Elk Grove. Can you believe it? He was right here the whole time. He never left the county."

"Holy shit! That's great," said Tink.

Brad turned to Mitch. "Weren't you working that case for a while? That must really suck that someone else figured it out first. Especially after all these years. Too bad you couldn't be a little quicker, then you could be the golden boy of the hour instead of some jerk from County Homicide."

"I don't mind," said Mitch with a private grin. "As long as the guy is caught. That's what matters."

With that, Mitch headed upstairs to the administrative offices. He hoped Lieutenant Delaney was there. He wanted the chance to talk to him, but part of Mitch wondered if the ghost had already disappeared. Maybe he instinctually knew the moment the killer was found, and he had moved on to whatever existence, or non-existence came next.

He didn't think that was how it worked, but there was still so much about the supernatural world Mitch did not understand. Anything seemed possible.

When Mitch called Chief Jefferson that afternoon, the chief had suggested that Mitch should be the one to deliver the news to Delaney. He had promised not to say anything until Mitch could get to work and talk with the ghost himself. The chief felt Mitch's work deserved some reward, and being able to tell Delaney his killer was in jail was a nice start.

Despite his concerns that the lieutenant might already be gone, when he knocked on the door of the Assistant Chief's office, he heard an immediate reply.

"Go away."

Mitch chuckled, then pushed open the door.

"I said... Oh. It's you again."

Delaney was seated at his desk staring at the same open folders of notes and photos that had been there for as long as Mitch had been at DTPD.

"You've never listened to me before," the ghost moaned, "I don't know why you would start today. Come in, then. I don't suppose I can stop you."

"Hello, Sir," Mitch said. He stepped inside the office and closed the door behind himself. "I have some good news I wanted to deliver in person."

"You're quitting?" asked the ghost. "You're leaving and I never have to be bothered by you again?"

Mitch smiled, unbothered by Delaney's frustrated comments.

"You are partly right," he said. "You never have to be bothered by me again, but no, I'm not leaving."

The spirit that had once been Lieutenant Timothy Delaney rose from its chair. "You're being particularly confusing today.

More so than usual. Fine. I'll bite. What do I need to do to get rid of you?"

"Leave," Mitch told him. "Leave Dasan's Terrace and go wherever it is you need to go next."

Delaney's face screwed up in an angry scowl. "I can't do that! I've already told you I'm not going anywhere, not until I find the man who…"

"I found him," interrupted Mitch.

"You found who?"

"I found the man who shot you. I found your killer. Sir, your family has already been notified, and the murderer, a man named Kenneth Dalton, is in jail. Right now. It's over."

Lieutenant Delaney stood quietly for several long seconds, digesting the news he had waited thirty years to hear.

"You are sure it's him?" he asked at last. "No mistakes? You have the right person."

"No mistakes. He made a full confession when I found him. His partner, the other man in the store, died a few years ago, but we know who he is, too. Bruce Yost. I don't know if you care about him or not, but I thought I'd tell you."

"You solved it," Delaney said, softly, surprise and relief clear in his voice. "It's really over."

"It really is."

Delaney stepped closer to Mitch, though he remained far enough away that he could not be touched should Mitch suddenly reach out. "Chief Jefferson told me you would figure out who shot me. I didn't believe him. I'm sorry I doubted you, Officer Loman."

"He … he told you I reopened your case? I didn't think he wanted you to know."

"Chief Jefferson has a great deal of faith in you and what you can accomplish. Now, I understand why."

Mitch had no idea what to say following Delaney's pronouncement. He was flattered and embarrassed all at the same time. Clearing his throat, he tried to change the subject.

"Do you want me to tell your family anything? Is there a message you'd like to pass along?"

"Yes, I...," Delaney paused. "On second thought, no. I don't think there is. I don't want them to know I've been stuck here, waiting. Knowing my killer has been caught will be a relief for them. I don't want to taint that happiness with the thought that I've been trapped here this whole time."

"That sounds like a good idea."

"I do have a message for you, however. Or rather, a message I'd like you to pass along to Simon. You tell that man that he owes you another favor on my behalf. He may have discharged one debt by letting you start this investigation, but the way it turned out, he and I both owe you another big one. Be sure to tell him that."

"I will," Mitch assured the ghost.

Delaney glanced at his desk, his eyes scanning the files strewn over its surface.

"Will you clean this up for me?" he asked, facing Mitch again. "And turn out the lights when you go?"

"I will."

The lieutenant looked around at the walls and ceiling of his office as though searching for something. Perhaps he was simply trying to burn the images of the space into his memory.

"I think this is it," he said. "I feel ... something pulling at me. There is somewhere I need to be."

"Good luck, Sir," said Mitch. "I hope you find happiness wherever you go next. Or I hope you at least find some peace."

Tim Delaney grinned, baring shiny white teeth under his bushy mustache. "I wish the same for you, Detective Loman," he said.

Mitch watched as the heavy tethers that trailed from Delaney and flowed toward the graveyard thinned and faded. They broke apart, dissipating like a trickle of ink diluted by flowing water, leaving Delaney's spirit free to wander. The ghost turned in the opposite direction of his decades-long anchor and began to walk, disappearing through the south wall of the office.

Mitch waited, wondering if the lieutenant might return one last time, but knowing in his heart that he would not. He was gone, forever and for good.

As he had promised, Mitch tidied the lieutenant's desk. He gathered all the loose pages and photographs and replaced them into their respective folders. When the entire pile was gathered together, he tucked the stack into a side drawer of the desk.

Mitch exited the now silent and empty office, turning off the lights as he left.

CHAPTER

19

Mitch arrived at the gate that linked North-West to the rest of the cemetery at ten minutes before three o'clock on Friday afternoon. He thought he was arriving early, but he saw Alyssandra and her entire coven already on the grounds. The Day Shift officers had also congregated, of course. They had been on duty since seven o'clock that morning. Their sergeant, Alonzo Ricci, was standing beside Jorge, and the two supervisors had their heads bowed in deep conversation, most likely comparing final notes about the upcoming hunt.

Chief Jefferson and Dot stood a few feet inside the gate and off to one side. They were having their own animated discussion with Alyssandra and Violet. The chief was dressed in his usual gray suit, while Dot had chosen a more appropriate blouse and a pair of shorts for this outing. Alyssandra wore a loose fitting, flower-patterned dress that hung unflatteringly on her thin figure. Mitch was not surprised at the wardrobe choice. He could not remember a single time he had seen Alyssandra in anything that did not simply hang like a wet sheet on her skeletal frame.

Violet was in what she called her "uniform," a black dress, long black wig, and goth makeup. She had made one concession to the daytime sun and donned a wide-brimmed gardening hat that looked humorously incongruous to the rest of her outfit.

Almost everyone assigned to this taskforce seemed to already be here. The only people missing were Tink, who Mitch had left in the locker room and knew would be here soon, and Brad. That meant everyone was accounted for. Brad would show, Mitch knew, but he would not arrive until three o'clock exactly. Not a moment early, and not a second late. It was his nature to arrive last, and that was not going to change because of something so trivial as a ghoul hunt that might go badly awry and get everyone killed. The man had a reputation to maintain after all.

Today, Mitch had opted for his short-sleeved uniform. He was not accustomed to day shift hours, and with the temperature today being an unseasonable 92 degrees Fahrenheit, he was already sweating, even though all he had done so far was walk from the police department building to the meeting location. This was going to be an unpleasant afternoon, he guessed. Mitch hoped they would be lucky enough to get an early evening breeze to cool things down, but even that theoretical relief would not occur for several hours.

The search was starting in the North-West. That was at least a minor break. The oldest part of the cemetery was mostly untended. It was a partially wooded sprawl of plant life, including several ancient trees that would provide patches of intermittent shade the overheated searchers could use for shelter when needed. The grounds were left wild because they were protected under federal and state law. The trees, shrubbery and uneven terrain that dominated the area had to remain untouched due to the fact anyone with a shovel or backhoe might accidentally turn up one of the hundreds, perhaps thousands, of unmarked graves left behind by the long-gone natives of this area.

Mitch glanced around, looking again for Tink, but there was no sign of him yet. He didn't want to interrupt the sergeants as they discussed whatever strategy they were working on, and he definitely did not want to get between Alyssandra and the chief. Whatever was going on there was none of his business. He decided to wander over to the B-Days team. He did not know them well, but maybe this was an opportunity to correct that oversight.

He glanced once more toward Chief Jefferson and noticed Violet looking back at him. She smiled and waved him over. Mitch declined, gesturing with a tilt of his head toward the other members in her group. Violet's smile turned to a frown, and she gesticulated more emphatically. The rest of the group noticed her distraction and turned to see what had her attention.

"Mitchell, please join us," called Dot pleasantly, as Chief Jefferson and Alyssandra returned to their conversation.

Mitch swore under his breath, pasted on a smile, and walked over to the gathering. He had taken only two steps when he paused again. Something was not right. A soft green haze surrounded Chief Jefferson. Inside that haze, Mitch suddenly saw a boy of about sixteen years of age standing where the chief had been a moment before. The boy was slender, with dark skin, and black hair cut close to his scalp.

At first, Mitch thought he was witnessing a spell that Alyssandra or one of her coven had cast, but the haze quickly faded and Chief Jefferson returned to his former appearance, apparently unharmed by whatever had occurred.

When the scene returned to normal, Mitch realized what he glimpsed had nothing to do with the witches. He had seen it before, a couple of times, and it seemed whatever was happening with the chief, only Mitch was aware of it. No one else showed any reaction to the temporary change in Simon's appearance.

Mitch forced himself to resume walking. Everyone else was behaving normally, and he did his best not to show the confusion he was feeling. As he moved closer, he heard Chief Jefferson speaking with Alyssandra.

"...in the open, stay back. Let the officers deal with the ghouls. Many of them don't trust magic, and for good reason. Casting spells while they're fighting will only distract them. I don't want their attention divided at a crucial moment."

"Are you asking me to remain defenseless when the ghouls are out of the ground?" Alyssandra asked.

"No. Of course, not. Defend yourselves if necessary and protect the weaker members of the coven. I'm simply asking that you refrain from getting involved in the fighting if there is no good reason to interfere."

"Interfere?" the coven leader asked. She almost spat the word back at Simon. "May I remind you, Lost Child, you are the one who demanded I be here."

"Sorry. Interfere was a poor choice of words. Intervene may be a better way to say it. Once you drive the ghouls above ground, move a safe distance away. We will take care of dispatching them."

"It would be faster if you allowed us to help," she said.

"I'm not worried about fast. I am worried about safe. It will be safer if we have a clear delineation of responsibilities that keeps our two groups apart as much as possible."

"Very well. I must say, however, I do not look forward to marching back and forth across the cemetery all day and all night. I have much better things I could be doing with my time. Particularly tonight during the full moon."

Chief Jefferson sighed. "You picked the day. Remember? Do not try to lay the timing at my feet."

The chief raised an eyebrow at Alyssandra as a new thought occurred to him. "Speaking of better things to do. Did you know that Chang'e's home burned down Wednesday night?"

"Did it?" asked Alyssandra, her voice softening almost to a purr.

"It did. The fire department says an accelerant was used around the base of the house. They think the fire was set deliberately."

"What a shame," Alyssandra told Simon. "Is there a reason you're telling me this?"

"I'm still an officer of the law, Alyssandra. If I find out you had anything to do with the fire, I *will* arrest you. You don't get a free pass to commit arson because you're helping me today."

"Are you accusing me of something? If so, I hope you have proof of any wrongdoing. Besides, if I did have anything to do with the fire, you should be thanking me. Chang'e tried to kill one of your officers." She pointed directly at Mitch. "Him. She killed two other people, and there is no doubt in my mind she would have killed more. You should be grateful she is gone and can no longer harm anyone."

"She's gone," agreed Chief Jefferson. "I would not be so certain, however, that she can't harm anyone. The fire department said the house was completely empty. They did not find any survivors or bodies when they went inside. All you did was put her on the run. She's more dangerous to us now than ever. She knows we figured out who killed the witches, and she has nothing left to lose."

Alyssandra did not respond, but the look on her face made it clear to Mitch that she had not known that Chang'e escaped the fire. She appeared pensive, and maybe even a little afraid.

"We don't have a means of figuring out where she went because everything that might potentially be used to track her burned up in the fire. You not only sent her running, but you made it impossible for us to find her."

Alyssandra remained quiet.

"All of this is assuming that you set the fire," continued the chief. "Which, as you pointed out, I can't prove. I guess we will simply have to let this matter drop for the moment. We have ghouls to remove from the cemetery. It's three o'clock. Organize your people, and I'll brief mine. We should get started as soon as possible. It's going to be a long night."

Chief Jefferson turned his back to Alyssandra and marched away. He headed towards Sergeants Ricci and Smythe to give them the order to organize their teams. Dot followed, but not before giving Mitch a brief apologetic wave.

Alyssandra also spun on her heel and strode away. Violet moved to follow.

"Wait," said Mitch, placing a hand on her arm. "Did you know about the fire? Were you ... there?"

"No," she told him. "I didn't know anything about it. Alyssandra didn't say anything to me about going after Chang'e."

"Good," Mitch said, relieved. "I'm glad."

Violet paused, then turned to face Mitch. "Just so we're clear, I did not burn down Chang'e's house, but only because Alyssandra didn't tell me what she was doing. That woman tried to kill you. Although she failed, she did succeed in killing two innocent girls that did not deserve to die. If Alyssandra had asked me to go with her, I can't promise that I would have said no."

"I know," Mitch told her.

It was the truth. He knew what was in Violet's heart, and while she did not like the idea of killing someone in cold blood, she was also fiercely protective of the people she loved.

300

"I'm still glad you weren't there."

"Me, too," said Violet grimly.

"Oh, one more thing."

"Yes?"

"Nice hat," he told her.

Caught off guard by the comment, Violet laughed, a genuine, open laugh. She kissed him lightly on the cheek, then hurried to catch up with Alyssandra.

Mitch joined the other officers. Tink and Brad had finally showed up and were chatting with the four members of the B-Days team. With his focus on Chief Jefferson and Alyssandra, he had not seen them arrive.

He said hello to everyone, shaking hands with a few of the day shift officers. Before he could say anything more, Jorge and Sergeant Ricci called for their attention and announced it was time to begin. They had all been thoroughly briefed the night before, so there was no delay as the officers took their assigned positions.

Alyssandra's coven already stood in place, aligned in a double row of six and seven, with Alyssandra to the far right. Violet stood on her left followed by four others. The seven women behind them would be providing support for their more powerful coven mates. Mitch and the others formed a third line, several yards back from the witches but spread out to the same width across the cemetery.

The two sergeants stood behind the officers, overseeing the execution of the hunt. Chief Jefferson and Dot had moved to a location close enough that they could see what was happening, but far enough away that they would not be an obstruction.

Alyssandra called out, "Find your focus. Tell me when you are ready."

The women in the front line to her left responded one at a time, starting with Violet.

"Ready."

When the sixth and final witch in line announced her status, Alyssandra growled, "Stay at my pace. Begin."

The front line moved forward as one. The coven members in the second line stayed close behind, matching the progress of those in front.

"Follow," said Sergeant Ricci, sending the line of officers after the coven.

The entire group moved forward at the speed of a casual afternoon stroll. It was slower than Mitch would have preferred, but surprisingly, faster than he had expected. The women were using their magic to feel the ground beneath their feet, searching for tunnels in the earth, or signs of movement. Despite having to feel their way through the dirt several feet straight down, they covered the distance almost as easily as if they were merely observing the open spaces in front of them for interesting wildlife.

Mitch's respect for their abilities to sense the surroundings solely through their connection to the magic grew as he watched them progress through the cemetery. He told himself that the next opportunity he got, he was going to have Violet teach him this trick. She had used it effectively on him during their sparring matches. He could not wait to add this weapon to his slowly growing arsenal. Mitch could already think of several ways the ability might come in handy in the future.

The coven covered the entire North-West efficiently, marching eastward to the property walls, turning, and returning to the west. On the western boundary, they turned again and repeated the process. The only thing slowing the progression was the uneven terrain of the ancient cemetery grounds. Rocky patches and roots tried to trip the hunters, while trees forced them to make constant small detours around the immovable impediments.

When they reached the gate separating the wilds of North-West from the main cemetery, the witches – and a few of the officers as well – breathed a small sigh of relief. The remaining area was larger by multiple magnitudes, but at least it was mostly level and landscaped with grass. It would be much easier walking.

"I'm surprised we didn't find anything in North-West," Mitch told Tink while Sergeant Ricci secured the gate lock behind them.

"Why is that?"

"It's the oldest part of the cemetery. It's also the creepiest. I thought if we were going to run into a ghoul, that would be the place it would happen."

"Nah," said Tink. "It's the oldest part of the cemetery, sure, but that just means there aren't any fresh corpses buried in there. No corpses means no food. I figure we might not see anything until we get to Front Half. That's where the cemetery sees the most new burials."

Mitch shuddered. Tink was right. It was morbid logic, but it made sense. Ghouls had to eat, and that meant they would tend to congregate where food was most plentiful.

"Maybe we'll get lucky and there aren't any more ghouls to find," Tink said. Then he corrected himself. "No, that's wishful thinking. At least one got away from us a couple weeks ago and I don't think it went anywhere. It's still lurking around here somewhere."

"Probably," Mitch agreed. "So, let's go find it."

When the gate was secured, the hunters all reformed their lines and started again at the far north end of Back Half. Back and forth they marched, covering swath after swath of grass, dirt, headstones, and the occasional above ground tomb. After dozens of the half-mile treks from one walled side of the cemetery to the other, one of the witches paused and raised a hand. The witch, a woman with wide, dark eyes, and dark hair woven into tight cornrows, cocked her head as if trying to hear a distant noise more clearly. She stood fourth in line from Alyssandra, and she waved her hand in front of her to catch the coven leader's attention.

"I have something in front of me," she called out. Her voice was high pitched and unsteady with poorly concealed excitement.

Alyssandra shouted for everyone to stop. "Hold your positions. No one move. Willa, what do you have? An animal?"

"No," the woman identified as Willa replied. "Too big for an animal. It's one of … them. It's not moving. It's curled up in a tunnel."

"I see it, too," said the woman on Willa's right. "Definitely a ghoul."

"Willa and Isadora, you ladies found it, you may drive it out. Everyone else hold your place in line and don't let anything else slip past you while we deal with this ghoul. Sergeant Smythe," Alyssandra shouted over her shoulder. "I suggest you move your people into position."

Jorge directed Mitch, Brad, and Tink to a location in front of the line of witches. Before beginning the hunt, the sergeants had agreed the B-Nights team would face the first ghoul. They had some experience fighting the creatures, and it would give the day shift team the opportunity to see what the ghouls were capable of and how they reacted when forced to the surface before the officers had to actually confront one. When a second ghoul was discovered – if a second ghoul was discovered – it would be B-Days' turn to subdue it.

Mitch drew his machete and stood between Tink and Brad. The others also held edged weapons ready, Brad with his katana, and Tink holding another department-issued blade identical to Mitch's own.

Mitch watched as Willa and Isadora closed their eyes to focus more carefully on the ghoul beneath their feet. The two women standing behind them also closed their eyes, lending what limited talent they possessed to their stronger coven mates. Although Mitch could not see what was happening, Violet had explained what the witches would be doing. They were attempting to generate a small fire underneath the creature they had found.

It was extremely difficult to keep a flame burning underground with so little oxygen available, so they could not simply burn the ghoul to ash. Which was a shame since that would have made this hunt much faster and easier. They were instead attempting to generate enough heat to panic the monster and force it to dig upward to escape the unexpected attack.

If the ploy was successful, the officers would have only a few seconds warning as to the ghoul's location before it appeared on the surface.

"It's moving," announced Willa, her eyes still closed. A slow smile spread across her face. "It's working. The ghoul is digging its way up."

"Where is it?" Mitch asked.

Willa maintained her internal concentration, but raised her right hand, pointing a finger roughly at Tink's feet. Tink backed away two steps, machete raised and ready.

Mitch heard the creature before he saw it. A rough scraping and shuffling sound emanated from the ground in front of Tink. He and Brad shifted to form a circle around the source of the noise.

"Brad," said Mitch, pointing at the officer's katana. "Then Tink, then me."

Tink and Brad nodded their understanding.

The ghoul breached the surface, claws tearing at the dirt to make room for the rest of its body. When its pale, hairless scalp appeared, Brad stepped forward. He waited another second until he could see the ghoul's entire head, then swung his katana in a short vicious arc. The monster's head tumbled and rolled away from its body.

The decapitated body continued to thrash and dig, pulling itself free of the hole it had created. It tumbled directionless in the grass, attempting to climb to its feet. Without its head to guide and orient it, the body stumbled and fell.

As Brad stepped back, Tink moved in. His machete flashed in the late evening sunlight as he hacked down once, twice, three times.

Tink's cuts removed the creature's right arm and left a large open gash in the hamstring of its right leg. The officer then leapt back as the ghoul slashed in his direction with its remaining arm. The monster's claws were sharp, but they missed Tink by a wide margin.

This was Mitch's cue to take his turn. He stepped behind the flailing ghoul and with a hard, two-handed swing, he severed the left arm from the body a few inches above the elbow. Mitch reoriented and cut at the leg Tink had damaged, finishing the job the other man had started.

Missing three limbs and its head, the ghoul was rendered effectively helpless. Still, it continued to fight. Brad and Tink kicked the head and severed extremities into a pile with the rest of the body.

"Any others?" Mitch asked Willa.

"No," the witch replied. "Only one."

Mitch sheathed his machete and held out an empty hand. He pulled magic to his palm and focused it as he had during their first ghoul hunt. Concentrating and compressing the magic to a pinpoint, he directed the tiny ball of power to the ghoul.

"Fire," he breathed, giving his thoughts direction.

The ghoul smoldered for a moment, then burst into flames. Mitch directed more magic at the creature until he was certain the flames would continue to burn on their own. When he released the spell, the fire remained bright and active.

A sickly-sweet odor drifted from the blaze to tickle Mitch's nose. The smell itself was not terribly unpleasant, but the thought of inhaling the drifting particles of burning ghoul caused him to shuffle a few paces further away.

The writhing body parts within the conflagration slowed in their movements. They blackened and charred, finally collapsing into harmless ashes.

A few minutes later, the flame died. Brad knelt to poke his katana into the smoking pile and stirred the ash, making sure nothing large enough to constitute a threat remained. When he was satisfied, he stood and sheathed the sword.

"Willa, please collapse the tunnel," said Alyssandra.

Willa nodded and Mitch felt a rumble beneath him, like a small, localized earthquake.

"Closed," Willa announced.

The hole remained where the ghoul had dug itself free, but that could be filled in later by the cemetery grounds crew. What was important was that the tunnel the ghoul had used to travel was now closed to further traffic. Another ghoul could always dig it free, but hopefully, after tonight, there would be no more ghouls available for the job.

Mitch and the rest of his team resumed their positions behind the coven. At a word from Alyssandra, the hunt resumed.

Several hours passed uneventfully after dispatching the first ghoul. The sun was still in the sky, but close enough to the horizon that the temperature had finally begun to drop. A small breeze blew through the cemetery adding to the relief from the stifling heat of the day.

The group was most of the way through Back Half, and Alyssandra and her coven had recently started a westward pass through the tended cemetery property when Violet raised a hand.

"I have one," she said. She cocked her head, then amended, "No. I have two."

Alyssandra commanded the line to stop and hold their positions. She stared at the ground, scanning to her left, then said, "I see them. They're moving away from us. We need to be quick."

Alyssandra and Violet took two more steps forward while the remainder of the line remained in place.

"Stop them before they go any further," Alyssandra directed Violet. "I will take the one in front. You take the creature following."

Violet nodded.

Violet and Alyssandra closed their eyes to focus on their task. The cemetery went silent as the gathered group waited for something to happen.

"Send them up," Alyssandra said, indicating Violet should begin driving her ghoul toward the surface. "Sergeant Ricci and Sergeant Smythe, I suggest you get your officers ready. There are two ghouls this time. Enough for everyone to participate."

B-Nights and B-Days rushed to position themselves in front of Violet and Alyssandra. The seven officers remained split into their respective teams, planning to each face one ghoul as it reached the surface.

"Brad, then Tink, then me," Mitch said again, establishing their order.

B-Days similarly organized their order of attack. Ready for what came next, the officers watched the witches and waited.

Alyssandra raised a finger and pointed. "There," she said.

The B-Days officers surrounded the indicated location. With edged weapons raised and ready, they prepared to descend on the ghoul the moment it appeared.

"There," said Violet, indicating where her ghoul would reach the surface.

Mitch and his team oriented themselves around the second location. He and Tink remained one step back, while Brad prepared to make the first cut.

Mitch heard shouts and saw motion out of the corner of his eye as the first ghoul appeared at B-Days' location. He did not spare the time to glance their way. He and his team had their own responsibilities, and he needed to trust that the other team could handle their end of this plan.

A hole appeared. Frantic pale hands poked upward and clawed at the earth, widening the opening until the waxy gray skull of the creature popped out into open air. Brad stepped in with his katana. As they had with the first ghoul, Mitch, Tink, and Brad efficiently dismembered the creature. Rather than stopping after one round of attacks, Brad stepped in a second time and removed the ghoul's remaining leg, leaving a writhing, delimbed torso twisting on the ground.

Mitch heard shouting from nearby and turned to see one of the B-Days officers standing over a pile of ghoul pieces, slamming a short sword into the heap again and again. A second officer, not wanting to risk getting cut by his out-of-control partner, stood a few paces back trying calm the man down.

"Loni! Loni, that's enough! It's over. You killed it."

His comments remained largely ignored.

"It's still moving," said Loni, striking another blow at the pile.

"They told us it would," reassured his partner.

Mitch recognized the second man as one of the day shift motor officers. He thought he remembered his name was Dave, or Doug, or … Dale! That was it. Dale Triple.

"It will keep moving until we burn it," said Dale. Loni appeared to run out of steam, and Dale risked moving closer. "That's it. It's over."

Loni turned wide haunted eyes toward Dale. He held out his left hand to show something to his partner.

"It bit me," said Loni.

In the dying light of the day, Mitch could see blood on Loni's hand. The day shift team must not have managed to get the ghoul's head off at first and the beast had succeeded in getting its teeth into Loni.

Brad took a step forward, hefting his katana as a mischievous grin crossed his features. Mitch put a hand on his shoulder and jerked him back.

"No," he told Brad. "It wasn't funny the first time."

Brad smiled wider, but stopped. "Fine. Killjoy."

When he was certain Brad would stay put, Mitch approached Loni. He held out his right arm so the other officer could see the healing bite on his own forearm. The stitches had been removed, but there was still raw, pink skin where the ghoul had torn into him.

"Stings a bit when they bite you, huh? Yeah. One got me a couple weeks ago."

Loni turned to Mitch. "You got bit by one of those? What's going to happen to me?"

"Nothing. You're going to be fine. When we finish tonight, you're going to go to the hospital to get a tetanus shot and maybe a couple stitches. Maybe some antibiotics. You'll be back at work tomorrow morning."

"I'm not...?"

"Nah," Mitch said. He leaned closer to Loni conspiratorially. "I was afraid I was going to turn into one of them when I got bit, too. I found out ghoul bites hurt, but they're not dangerous like that. You're fine."

Loni seemed to breath a bit easier at Mitch's explanation.

"Thanks," he said.

"No problem. Go let your sergeant know what happened. Their supposed to have a first aid kit with them and he can bandage you up for now."

Loni nodded his appreciation and headed toward the back of the lines where Sergeant Ricci and Sergeant Smythe were stationed.

"Hey, Mitch," called Tink. "You should see this."

Mitch returned to his team to find Tink squatting next to the ghoul they had cut apart. The creature's torso still twisted and flexed in the grass. Tink pointed toward the side of the limbless trunk.

"There's a wound in its side. I think this might be the ghoul that bit you. Your machete fell out somewhere underground, but it left a hole in this guy."

"Maybe," agreed Mitch. "Could be the same one that bit me, and this could mean we got them all, now. It would be nice if we don't find any more tonight."

He turned toward the day shift team. "Put both ghouls into one big pile. We need to burn it. Make sure you don't miss any pieces."

The officers went to work, collecting all the hacked pieces of the ghouls and dropping them into one large mound. When all of the body parts had been collected, Mitch stood over the pile and held out a hand. He began pulling magic from his surroundings to create a fire.

"Ignis," said a voice beside him, and the wriggling pile of ghoul bits burst into flame.

Mitch found Violet standing next to him. She glared at him with a look of disgust he did not understand. When he tried to ask what was wrong, she shook her head to quiet him but said nothing. Without a backward glance, Violet returned to her place in line with the rest of her coven. Confused by her behavior, Mitch also returned to his position behind the line.

The hunt continued.

Several more hours passed as the group made their way from one side of the cemetery to the other, back and forth, again and again, without any further confrontations. Darkness claimed the world, but between the full moon overhead and the frequent pathway lights illuminating the more landscaped areas of Dasan's Terrace, no one had much difficulty navigating the grounds. The officers carried flashlights with them, just in case, but no one was currently using them.

As the search party worked their way through Front Half, the southern portion of the cemetery property, Mitch began to wonder if they had already seen their last ghoul. Maybe the three they had found were the last of them. Originally, the chief believed they were dealing with a single ghoul. The fact they had now eradicated five of the disgusting scavengers could mean there weren't any more of the beasts to find.

He allowed himself to relax a little, figuring that with two more hours of marching they would be done. Day shift could go home to get some sleep, and he could spend the last minutes of his shift hanging out with his team until it was time to leave for their long weekend.

He needed to talk to Violet tomorrow, he decided. She seemed to be mad at him for some reason he could not figure out. Had he said or done something? Not said or not done something? It was frustrating, but he was certain, whatever it was, they could work out a solution.

It was while Mitch walked, lost in his own thoughts about the future, that everything went to hell.

The witch at the far end of the line raised her hand. She was a petite, Hispanic woman who barely looked old enough to be out of High School, much less be one of the strongest witches in a coven as powerful as Alyssandra's.

"I see one," she announced.

Alyssandra called another halt as the young witch focused on the ghoul below her feet.

"Arrgh," the girl growled. "It's running. It's trying to get away."

"Gabriela, stay in line. Gabby!"

The young witch, Gabby, either did not hear Alyssandra's command, or else chose to ignore it. She darted forward in pursuit of the fleeing ghoul.

"I can get it," she shouted over her shoulder. "Don't worry, I'll bring it back."

Mitch heard Alyssandra muttering under her breath, but the coven leader did not follow. She remained in line with the rest of her coven, waiting for Gabby to return.

The headstrong witch ran another few paces, then jerked to a halt in front of one of Dead Town's mausoleums. There were several of the above ground tombs throughout the cemetery, built by people that wished to inter their deceased family members together in one location. This structure was a concrete edifice towering ten feet high. Built to mimic a white marble structure from the Roman era, it had four steps leading up to a wooden door, and a porch bracketed by four fluted columns.

Gabby paused by the bottom step of the mausoleum, looking confused.

"Where did...?" She turned back toward Alyssandra, uncertainty in her expression.

The door of the crypt burst open. Five ghouls rushed out, tumbling down the stairs in a cascade of entwined bodies in their haste to exit the building.

"Gabby!" cried Violet, but the warning came too late to help the girl.

The mass of swarming ghouls crashed into Gabby where she stood at the bottom of the steps, engulfing her in a tangle of pale gray limbs. The witch girl screamed as she was buried beneath the hungry creatures.

All semblance of order or structure collapsed as witches and police officers broke ranks and rushed toward Gabby. The witches arrived first but hesitated when they reached their coven mate. They did not have physical weapons with them, so could not go hand to hand with the ghouls, and they were afraid to launch lethal magic into the group of creatures for fear of injuring Gabby. The girl continued to scream as the ghouls bit and tore into her.

Several officers, including Mitch, reached the ghouls next. They cut into the pile with machetes and swords, careful to attack only the ghouls at the outer edge of the swarm. They also did not want to risk causing injury to the young witch trapped under the writhing mass. The ghouls, realizing they were under assault, turned from their intended victim and charged their attackers.

A female officer from the day shift tripped and fell as she attempted to backpedal away from one of the retaliating ghouls. The creature dropped on top of her, pinning her to the ground. It raked a hand with long, jagged nails across her chest. Her uniform shirt tore, but fortunately for the officer, the ghoul's claws did not penetrate her ballistic vest underneath.

Loni, who had already been bitten by one of these raving monsters, and most likely was looking to get some payback, leapt to her assistance. He kicked the creature in the shoulder with his boot, knocking it to the grass beside his partner. The female officer, now able to move, rolled aside and pushed to her knees. With a two-handed grip, she swung her machete with every bit of strength she could muster. The blade whispered through the air in a downward arc, removing the ghoul's head from its shoulders before the weapon's edge buried itself in the soft earth beneath the creature.

"Thanks, Loni," she said, then went to work cutting the ghoul into more manageable pieces.

Mitch and Tink squared off with another one of the pale monsters and were taking turns hacking at it. Each time the creature turned to face one of them, the other would step forward and attempt to remove an arm or a leg. So far, they had been unsuccessful at getting a clear enough swing to remove its head.

It was Mitch's turn to make a cut, and he swung his machete with all his strength. The blade cut through the ghoul's right arm and sunk several inches into its side. The weapon wedged between two ribs, so when the creature spun in reaction to the attack, its movement ripped the machete out of Mitch's hand.

Fortunately, Tink was ready to step in and bury his own blade in the monster's skull. The ghoul's head split, half of it breaking away and falling to the grass. The other half remained attached, perched precariously on top of the creature's slender neck, but the ghoul's coordination was impacted. It stumbled right then left as it attempted to remain upright and continue its fight with the two men.

Mitch drew magic into his hands. All of the recent practice with Violet had improved his skill, and he was much faster now at collecting and using the ambient power around him. He continued to gather magic even as he thrust his palms forward, releasing it all at the last second when he touched the ghoul's chest. The percussive force blasted through the monster's body like a small bomb, bursting the rib cage and fragmenting the torso. The only parts of the creature left intact were the legs from the waist down.

Tink let out a single whoop of celebration, then rushed away to try to help someone else. Mitch recovered his machete from where it had fallen a few feet away, then went after any remaining ghouls.

He found Alyssandra standing over one of the creatures. She had it pinned to the ground with a shield of blue and green force. Where the shield touched the ghoul, sparks of red light ate into Alyssandra's magic like tiny embers of fire eating through paper. The shield began to flicker as the sparks continued to break down the magic trapping the ghoul.

"Do you see that?" Alyssandra said, indicating her failing magic.

"Yeah. What's happening?"

"That's demon magic," the coven leader told him. "Demonic magic interferes with earth magic and burns it away."

"The ghoul is a demon?" asked Mitch, shocked.

Alyssandra cackled, amused. "No. It is not a demon, but it was created using demon magic. That magic is part of its life force now, so it affects my spell."

Mitch held his machete over his head and nodded toward Alyssandra. She released her spell completely, freeing the ghoul.

316

Before it could rise, Mitch swung his blade through its neck, cleaving the head from the body. He circled the decapitated creature carefully, avoiding the flailing claws as he hacked and cut, removing pieces of flesh and bone until the ghoul was rendered mostly immobile.

Mitch started to move away in search of anyone else who needed assistance, but Alyssandra grasped his arm.

"Chang'e," she growled, her breath hot in Mitch's face. "This is her work. She is the only one I know for a fact to partner with demons and who also has the strength to raise ghouls."

Alyssandra released him and stormed away.

The fighting calmed as the last of the ghouls were cut to pieces under the blades of the police officers, and the two sergeants began shouting directions to bring order to the remaining chaos. Mitch surveyed his surroundings and found several witches and officers with bloody scratches and cuts, but none of them appeared badly hurt. It seemed as if they had weathered this fight rather well, considering how it started.

Mitch whirled to face the mausoleum as he remembered what had triggered this mele.

Three witches, including Violet, knelt in a small circle at the base of the mausoleum steps, their heads bowed. He hurried over to the group, his gut tightening in anticipation of what he would find when he arrived. The look on the faces of the three women was enough to tell him something very bad had happened.

Mitch stopped a few paces away from Violet, though close enough to see the still form of the young witch sprawled in the grass in front of her.

Gabby lay on the ground between the kneeling women. Her clothing was little more than bloody shreds, and the skin beneath it had not fared any better. The girl had dozens of bites, cuts, and wounds covering her tiny body, but the real damage, the injury that drew the eye immediately, was a deep gash across her throat. One of the ghouls had buried its teeth in the tender tissues beneath her chin and torn away enough flesh to expose the bones of her spine. The damage to the arteries and veins in her neck had been almost instantly fatal. Gabby had bled to death in seconds.

Mitch retreated, unable to help, and knowing there was nothing he could say to make the situation better. Another girl had died senselessly this night. No words or offers of sympathy would fix that.

If Alyssandra was right about the demonic magic that created the ghouls, then Chang'e had just claimed another victim.

CHAPTER

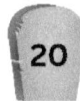 20

Mitch sat at the edge of the couch in the living room of his home. A mug in his right hand rested on his knee as he stared into empty space, listening to the cacophony of unorganized noise in his head. He did not focus on anything in particular, instead letting the chaos drown out any individual thoughts.

He had been this way for a while. The coffee in his cup had long ago gone cold.

He didn't care.

Gabriela Rubio. That was the name of the young girl who had died early that morning. Another child victim of some crazy person's campaign to … to do what? What was Chang'e trying to accomplish?

After Gabby died fighting the ghouls, Chief Jefferson suggested stopping the hunt. Alyssandra had been the one to insist they continue. She argued if they stopped before finishing the job, they would have to start all over from the beginning at a later time. She was not wrong, but Mitch wondered at how cold and unfeeling she had appeared when she said it. The coven's leader did not seem terribly concerned over Gabby's death.

Alyssandra was angry, that was obvious, but Mitch could not tell if the anger was for the loss of a talented magic user in her coven, or grief from personal loss. He strongly suspected it was the former. Alyssandra had never come across to Mitch as an overly sentimental individual.

Violet, on the other hand, had been devastated. She agreed with the chief that they should stop to attend to Gabby before coming back and trying again. She was loyal to Alyssandra, however, so at the high priestess' orders she got back into line with the remaining members of the coven to complete their task. They all had. The officers and sergeants, and even Chief Jefferson had fallen back into position, leaving Gabby's body to lie, cooling in the grass, until they could finish clearing the cemetery and go back for her.

They left a dead child alone on the ground, for two hours.

The image of her bloody, torn body lying at the bottom steps of the mausoleum would not leave Mitch's mind.

There were a hundred justifications for what they did, but that's all they were: justifications.

It felt wrong. Like her death didn't matter. What made Mitch feel even worse was that the cemetery was already clear. They did not find any more ghouls on the property. The five creatures hiding in the mausoleum had been the last of them. Of course, he could not have known that at the time, but that thought did not help ease his guilt.

The doorbell rang, jolting Mitch out of the mental pit he had fallen into. He set his mug on the coffee table in front of him and answered the bell. He found Violet standing on his front porch and hurried to invite her in.

He guided her into the living room, and they both settled onto the couch.

"How are you doing?" he asked Violet. "Can I get you something?"

Mitch indicated his mug, but Violet shook her head.

"No thanks. I really came to check on you."

"I'm a mess," he said with a smile. "But what else is new? What is Alyssandra doing with Gabby?"

"Her family has her body. They're going to bury her next week. Chief Jefferson was kind enough to volunteer Dead Town to handle all the arrangements for free. Alyssandra will make sure that any other financial needs the family might have are taken care of as well."

"What did she tell them happened to their daughter?"

"The truth," Violet said.

Mitch's eyebrows rose in disbelief.

"Her parents knew what Gabby was," Violet explained. "They knew what she could do. She died a hero, and Alyssandra told them exactly that."

"I guess that's for the best," he said. "It's nice when we can tell someone the truth about what we deal with. Easier than making up lies."

Violet let herself sink backwards, resting her head on the back edge of the couch. She closed her eyes and appeared to fall asleep. It had been a long night for both of them, Mitch realized.

"Can I ask you a question?" Mitch asked softly, not wanting to wake her if she had indeed managed to find some relief in slumber.

"Of course," Violet responded without opening her eyes.

"Are you mad at me?"

Violet sat up, suddenly fully alert.

"Am I...? No. I'm not mad at you. What in the world gave you that idea?"

"Last night, you kind of gave me a dirty look," Mitch said sheepishly. "When you burned the two ghouls, you glared at me like I did something. Maybe I was imagining it?"

Violet sighed, then tsked softly. "You didn't imagine it," she said. "But I wasn't mad at you. I was surprised and a little concerned that you were using magic in front of so many people. I thought you were trying to keep it secret about what you could do."

"The exorcism stuff, sure. But I wasn't trying to keep the magic secret. Besides, everyone there was either a witch or works for Dead Town. They all know what's going on."

"You should still be careful," Violet warned. "Alyssandra doesn't need to know how strong you're getting. For that matter, maybe you should be careful about how much Chief Jefferson knows, too."

"Chief...?" Mitch paused, surprised that there might be anything he should be hiding from his boss. He trusted the man implicitly. Although now that he thought about the chief, there was one thing still bothering him.

Mitch met Violet's eyes, and he debated whether or not he should ask his next question. If it had been anyone other than Violet, he might have kept quiet, but he felt he could trust her with anything. Even the possibility that he might be losing his mind.

"I saw something weird yesterday," he said, trying to sound casual.

"Hmm?"

When I got to North-West, right before we started the search, I saw Chief Jefferson talking to Alyssandra."

"Okay. So?"

Mitch took a short breath and forced himself to go on.

"The chief looked like a sixteen-year-old boy. It isn't the first time, either. In the hospital after the golem gave me a concussion, I saw the same thing. Maybe it was the head injury that time, but I don't think so. Why would I see it again last night? There's something strange going on there."

"There is," Violet agreed. "I'm surprised you could see through the glamour, but then, you are constantly surprising me. That only proves how strong you are and reinforces my feeling that you shouldn't let anyone know."

"Why?"

"Because anyone that feels threatened by you might try to hurt you."

"No, not that," said Mitch. "I mean, why does the chief look like a sixteen-year-old boy?"

It was Violet's turn to pause.

"I'm ... not sure I should say anything. I promised I would never lie to you again, and I intend to keep that promise, but this isn't really my story to tell. You should go talk to the chief about it."

A thought occurred to Mitch. "Is that why Alyssandra always calls him 'Lost Child?' Does it have something to do with what I'm seeing?"

"Talk to your chief," Violet repeated.

"You and Alyssandra know something about him, don't you? Why won't you tell me?"

"Talk ... to ... your ... chief."

Mitch gave up. Violet was not about to share anything she knew about Simon Jefferson's mysterious transformations, so there was no sense pushing any further. When she made up her mind not to talk about a subject, she was immovable.

"So, what do we do now?" he asked.

"About what?"

"About everything. Do you think Chang'e is coming back? Alyssandra burned her house down. Maybe she ran off and we'll never see her again. This whole thing, the murders, the ghouls, it all might be over."

Violet's shoulders slumped slightly. She looked mildly defeated. "I don't think so," she told Mitch. "Chang'e murdered two witches. She tried to kill you. She also filled the cemetery with ghouls. Those are all overt acts of a person trying to accomplish some greater goal. I think she was building an army."

"An army? For what?"

"I don't know. I wish I did. She put a lot of time, magic, and effort into whatever plans she had, and I don't believe she would simply run away and abandon all of that. She wants something, and she isn't afraid of killing to get it. She's coming back, Mitch. I'm sure of it."

"What do we do?"

"We keep doing what we were already doing," she told him. "You go to work, keep spending time with me, and keep training. You get better, you get faster and stronger, and when the time comes, we pray that we're ready."

"Ready for what?"

Violet leaned against him, laying a hand across his arm and resting her head on his shoulder.

"Ready for war."

About the Author

G. Allen Wilbanks, an internationally best-selling author, was born and raised in northern California. For twenty-five years he worked in law enforcement to pay the bills while writing horror and fantasy fiction during his free time to keep himself sane. In 2016 he decided to retire from real life and live in a fantasy world of his own making full time. For additional information about G. Allen, including where you can find more of his writing, please visit his website at www.gallenwilbanks.com.